Fortune's Lot

A Retelling of
Francis Lathom's
Live and Learn

By Wayne Goodman

First paperback printing, March 2018

Version 1.1

13 May 2018

ISBN: 978-0-9989007-1-1

Library of Congress Control Number: 2018902417

wayne goodman books

waynegoodmanbooks@gmail.com
Twitter: @Wgoodmanbooks

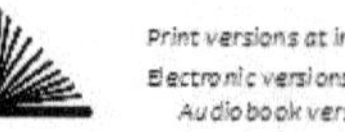

TABLE OF CONTENTS

Acknowledgments iii

Francis Lathom v

Homosexuality in Great Britain vii

Chapter One: *A Turn of Fortune* 1

Chapter Two: *A New Lot* 20

Chapter Three: *The White Man Appears* 33

Chapter Four: *The First Volleys* 42

Chapter Five: *The King of Rags and Patches* 54

Chapter Six: *Our Maladies Unseen* 69

Chapter Seven: *An Actor's Tale* 80

Chapter Eight: *A Ghost Reappears* 96

Chapter Nine: *Furthering My Education* 109

Chapter Ten: *Love in a Blaze* 122

Chapter Eleven: *Sir Julius Maberly's Tutelage* 136

Chapter Twelve: *Angels' Flight* 149

Chapter Thirteen: *A Scoundrel in the Suds* 160

Chapter Fourteen: *An Evening in Heaven, an Evening in Hell* 171

Chapter Fifteen: *Mysterious Business* 185

Chapter Sixteen: *The Rascals Carry On* 198

Chapter Seventeen: *Many, Many Masks* 211

Chapter Eighteen: *A Time of Treachery* 225

Chapter Nineteen: *At the Mercy of Foreigners* 237

Chapter Twenty: *A Glimmer in the Dark and a Shock of Despair* 250

Chapter Twenty-One: *Escape!* 264

Chapter Twenty-Two: *Revelations and Retributions* 276

Chapter Twenty-Three: *Further Explanations* 290

Chapter Twenty-Four: *Good News* 304

Chapter Twenty-Five: *Bad News* 316

Chapter Twenty-Six: *A Matter of Trust* 329

Chapter Twenty-Seven: *Packets from Glasgow* 340

Chapter Twenty-Eight: *The Court at Lincoln's Inn* 347

Chapter Twenty-Nine: *Happy Ends* 360

Acknowledgments

THE FIRST PERSON I should acknowledge is the original author of the work *Live and Learn*, Francis Lathom. Without his dedication to the craft, and his willingness to challenge social norms of the time, we would not have his works to examine two centuries hence.

There are very few copies of *Live and Learn* available, and obtaining a digital version proved quite challenging. It took a month to accomplish the task, and I wish to publicly thank the person who assisted me in obtaining the files from a university library, but for fear of retaliation by a secret society of librarians, I will maintain the anonymity of both the school and my source.

Of course, none of my works could ever see the light of day if it were not for the dedication and support of my partner in life, Richard May. Without him, I would not enjoy the wonderful life I have.

Francis Lathom

FRANCIS LATHOM (14 July 1774 to 19 May 1832) was born in Rotterdam during the time his father Henry conducted business for the East India Company in South Holland. His family settled to Norwich in 1777, where Francis grew up. Or, according to ribald speculation, he could have been born in Norwich as the illegitimate son of an English peer.

He began writing plays before attaining the age of 18. His first, *All in a Bustle*, opened at Theatre Royal Norwich, which went on to produce all his later dramatic works.

Beginning in 1795, Lathom turned to writing Gothic novels. *The Castle of Ollada* followed in the literary footsteps of Ann Radcliffe (and other Gothic writers), who used fear of the supernatural to titillate readers with blood and horror. Radcliffe had helped to make Gothic fiction more respectable in the 1790s.

With the success of *Ollada*, Lathom went on to pen *The Midnight Bell*, which many consider to be his best work. However, it is also his most famous (or infamous), as Jane Austen included it in her list of "horrid novels" presented within *Northanger Abbey*.

Lathom went on to craft a total of 21 Gothic novels, the last published in 1830. His plots generally involved subterfuge, jealousy, greed, kidnapping, ransoms, disguises, and unknown identities wrapped in tales of slowly unfolding secrets. He felt it was his duty to comply with the public's taste for such stories. His success as a writer suggests he gave his audience what they wanted.

Little is known about his personal life, but some consider him to be the first among modern gay writers. A few of his works contain love between two men, while other subvert the theme, such as a heroine who behaves rather man-like.

He married Diana Ganning, the daughter of a wealthy Norwich lawyer, in 1797, and they produced three children. In 1810, Lathom left Norwich suddenly for reasons unknown. Some suspect he had been caught with his lover, another man. He travelled extensively, but settled in Fyvie, Aberdeenshire, Scotland, where he constantly feared the threat of being kidnapped and held for ransom due to his amassing fortunes. His grave marker incorrectly lists him as "Mr. James Francis."

The book on which this retelling is based, *Live and Learn, or The First John Brown, his friends, enemies, and acquaintance in town and country*, was published in four volumes by A. K. Newman and Co. in 1823. It has been touted as the First English-language Gay Novel. The homosexual themes were there for astute readers to discover, but I retell the tale from the point of view of the main character, allowing for the description of his inner feelings and motivations. I also changed the sex of his love interest from female to male, as this character in the original seems more of an effeminate man than a young woman, thus fulfilling Lathom's desire to portray same-sex couples openly in literature. Also, I have revised or eliminated many of the superfluous constructions used by early 19th Century Gothic authors that I felt distracted from the advancement of the story. One addition I felt appropriate was frequent reference to the works of William Shakespeare, which helps to act as a unifying thread throughout this long, meandering tale.

Homosexuality in Great Britain

FROM THE TIME of the Roman invasion of Britain in 43 A.D., acts of homosexuality were frowned upon, illegal, or led to a death sentence. The *Julian Laws* criminalized adultery among males. However, Emperor Hadrian (the one who built the famous wall) openly engaged in sexual relationships with young men, including his beloved Antinous, whom he had deified following an untimely (and suspicious) death.

King Edward II (1307-1327) favoured Piers Gaveston, a courtier. This love affair has been well-documented and represented in literary and theatrical works.

In 1533, King Henry VIII passed the Buggery Act, which made all male-male sex acts punishable by death. "Attempted buggery" resulted in only a two-year jail sentence and time on the pillory.

Upon the death of Queen Elizabeth in 1603, King James VI of Scotland assumed the throne of his English cousin. Throughout his life he maintained same-sex relationships with noblemen, the most famous being George Villiers, whom James bestowed royal titles upon. At one point, Villiers was the most powerful man in Britain outside the royal family.

Two women attempted to marry in 1680, with one of them assuming a man's name. After the discovery of the fraud, the court annulled the marriage.

King William III (1650-1702) maintained close relationships with men, some of whom he granted titles. William and his queen, Mary II, never had children, and her sister Anne succeeded them.

During the 18th Century, a society of homosexual men known as "Mollies" flourished in London. Congregating at public houses and coffee houses (referred to as "Molly Houses"), they created an environment to support their extraordinary lifestyle. Frequently use of the Female Dialect in referring to themselves or other men, as well as adopting women's names, and cross-dressing were part of the culture. Ritualised same-sex marriage ceremonies and mock-births took place on "Festival Nights."

In 1724, Margaret Clap, also known as "Mother Clap," opened a coffee house in Holborn. It became popular with this underground homosexual community, and she catered to and cared for her Molly clientele. Authorities closed the coffee house in 1726 after some of her clients turned informants.

Despite the looming threat of legal consequences, same-sex couples persisted, usually in private and mostly consisted of the well-to-do. The government generally pursued action only when a spurned lover or distraught turncoat alerted officials to the situation.

The Buggery Act was replaced by the Offences Against the Person Act in 1828, and the death penalty for buggery was finally abolished by 1861. In 1895, the trial against Oscar Wilde for "gross indecency" with Lord Alfred Douglas (and Wilde's subsequent imprisonment in Reading Gaol) captured the nation's attention.

It was 1967 when homosexual acts in private finally became decriminalised, but it wasn't until 2001 that all laws punishing same-sex acts were removed from the books. Same-sex marriage gained approval in 2014.

Chapter One:

A Turn of Fortune

T HE QUEST FOR LOVE—while already complicated enough—turned out to be even more difficult when a man preferred the company of other men in Regency Britain. From an early age, I had realised my predilection separated me from other lads, and I figured it best to keep my particular interest to myself.

My parents had given me up at birth to a military serjeant and his wife. The unfortunate soldier died of a fever in Ireland (his regiment had been temporarily deployed to Cork, on their way to the Americas), and my adopted mother moved to Oldham to live with her brother, Peter Chapman, the town barber. She died soon after that from a lingering decline, and my uncle raised me in his shop. He taught me his skills, the plan being for me to take over his business when he grew too old.

Unfortunately, a few months before the commencement of this tale, an epidemic disease took Mr. Chapman's life, and I had to assume responsibility for his shop earlier than we had anticipated. As the townsmen knew me to be the barber's nephew, they had no difficulty entrusting me with their coiffures. What they most likely did not know was the longings I concealed for many of these men whose aromas and countenances I had been in so close a proximity.

This story begins one unusually cold Wednesday afternoon in September 1821, my twentieth year. The Prince Regent had his coronation in late July, and most Britons appreciated having a true king, rather than a stand-in, ruling them once again.

A knock at the barber shop door preceded the entrance of a well-dressed fellow wearing a richly appointed suit. His head searched the small room until he spotted me sitting toward the rear.

"You, sir. Are you the barber?" His voice suggested middle-age, but his vigorous appearance stirred my interest in the male sex. Slender and slightly tall, with piercing light-blue eyes, almost the opposite of my shorter, more sinewy stature. What my uncle called wavy auburn hair framed my ruddy, roundish face. I stared at him for a few seconds too many. "I said, 'Are you the barber?'" he repeated.

"Yes, sir!" I leapt out of the chair and approached him hastily. "How can I be of service, sir?" He wore a well-kept periwig, and my first assumption was that he was not about to be my newest client.

The fellow looked down at me in amusement, a sly smile betrayed his lips. "My name is Radford, and I serve Mr. Clarington of Ashbank Hall. Are you available to travel to Mr. Clarington's home to perform your tonsorial work?"

Up until that moment, I had only accomplished barbering in the shop. However, the business had declined slightly, and I did not wish to turn away good money. "It depends on the price, I suppose."

Mr. Radford examined my face, and it appeared that he wanted to smile, but his status would not allow for such frivolity. "One guinea, sir, and not one ha'penny more." He continued to stare at my eyes.

A guinea would be more than I could usually earn in a month. "Yes, sir! A guinea sounds quite reasonable, indeed!" My uncle had left a small satchel for carrying the tools of the trade for such occasions, should they arise, and fortune had supplied the opportunity. I quickly gathered the razor, strop, soap, and bowl. "Will your gentleman require a trim of the hair as well, sir?"

The manservant tilted his head and blinked a few times. "Yes, I believe it might be best to have his locks shorn." He returned his piercing gaze to me. "It is to be his last barbering, you see." He looked down.

I grabbed the comb and shears, throwing them into the bag as well as a few small towels. From their peg, I retrieved my cap and coat against the chill September air. "Let us go then, Mr. Radford." As we left the shop together, I locked the door securely behind us.

We walked out the main road and onto a broad lane leading to a grand manor house. I had never been to this part of Oldham before, neither had I ever seen a home so majestic. It had three levels and five chimneys, a double front door and a carriage house beside. A sturdy-looking postchaise, polished to a gleaming, stood near the entrance. We walked around to the side door and entered through a narrow hall.

Mr. Radford led me to a great library, with bookshelves from marbled floor to coved ceiling, overflowing with gold-embossed, leather-bound volumes. Seated at one of the tables sat a grey-haired elderly man in conversation with a younger, but serious and officious, fellow. As I looked upon the older man's face, it seemed vaguely familiar yet age-worn and weathered.

"Have you any relatives, Mr. Clarington?" the serious one inquired.

The older man coughed and wiped his mouth with a cloth. "I had a sister and a nephew, but a great lapse of time has intervened since I had heard from either of them. They could still be in existence, or they might have died and left issue." He dabbed the cloth upon his forehead. "From what little I can recall, she had married sir Robert Brockelsbie, a Scotch baronet from Dumfriesshire."

"I suppose we can attempt communication; however, it would be an almost unparalleled instance for a Scotch nobleman to exchange his parental estate for any other residence." The serious chap began scrawling notes onto a small writing tablet.

Mr. Radford coughed twice into his balled fist.

The older gentleman turned to us. "Yes, Radford. What is it?" He caught my eyes, and a momentary flash of recognition seemed to flicker upon them and fade. "Who is that ragamuffin, and why is he here?" He attempted to point at me, his arm moving ever so slowly.

"Mr. Clarington, this is the barber. He is here to shave you." Radford pushed me forward, almost as if it were a dare.

"Yes, yes. Come forward, my young fellow." The pointing finger transformed into a motion to approach.

With much apprehension, I moved, inch-by-inch, toward the old and wrinkly man. His nearly-white hair pointed in all directions. I bowed once I got near enough.

A tight smile spread across Mr. Clarington's face, and he uttered a sharp, "Ha!" at my performance. "Do what you can with this unsightly muddle, as it is to be my farewell style." He slowly ran a hand over the remains of his hair. "And do be careful with the straight razor, my boy, I bleed easily and have very little blood left due to this damned gout!" He smiled, leaving me to believe he had attempted some sort of humour.

As I looked about for a small table to place my satchel upon, Mr. Radford wheeled a teacart toward me, and I set my instruments out and prepared to work.

"Pray continue your attorney duties, Mr. Fortescue," Mr. Clarington ordered.

"Yes. What information have you regarding your nephew?"

"Hmmm." The older fellow stroked his chin in thought, and I could hear the rasping of whiskers. "Not much at all, I fear. The last thing I remember was that he had eloped with a young lady whose friends had been averse to their union, but I had not been told her name."

"The only chance, then, of discovering them must be to advertise for him in the public prints," the attorney responded.

"No, no," Mr. Clarington objected. "That is a method to which I shall not resort. It might only excite in him false hopes of my intentions toward him or his." He turned his eyes to me. "Oh, I suppose I should hold my head still for you or you should never complete your task."

"Thank you, sir," I said, holding up the comb and shears.

"If any branch of the Brockelsbie family be found, I consider it more than probable that they can furnish some intelligence concerning him," Mr. Clarington continued, attempting to keep his head still while I began attempting to comb his unruly, wiry hair. "If not, my researches after him will terminate, but I wish you to lose no time in endeavouring to summon either my sister, or her representative in law, to visit me before my death, or, at all events, to attend my funeral."

How eerie to listen to a man planning for his imminent death. And I had been summoned to perform his last barbering. If I did a good enough job, perhaps that might encourage more business at the shop.

As the two older men discussed their business, I chopped and trimmed Mr. Clarington's hair, keeping foremost in my mind that it would be the way people remembered him.

After a while, Mr. Fortescue collected his belongings, and Mr. Radford showed him out. I mixed the soap and began to lather my charge's face. As he relaxed, I applied the foam, and I said a silent prayer that he might survive my attentions.

Fifteen minutes later, Mr. Radford appeared, just as I wiped Mr. Clarington's freshly-shaved face. I began polishing the tools and returning them to the satchel. We both looked at my handiwork and nodded together. My client now appeared as dashing and youthful as possible.

"This way," the servant commanded, and he led me back out the hall. He opened the servants' door, picked a guinea from a waist-coat pocket and placed it in my palm. With his other hand, he squeezed mine gently. It felt warm and slightly moist, and I grinned without thinking.

On my walk back to the barbershop, I rubbed the gold coin be-tween my fingers so much that I probably wore it down slightly. This guinea would keep me fed for months, and I smiled my big-gest smile ever.

That evening, to celebrate my newfound capital, I went to the local public house, the Black Bull, for a pint. The shilling whist-club fellows sat around various tables, shuffling and slapping cards.

A few minutes later, Mr. Graveton, one of the town's physicians entered. The roundness of his belly fairly matched the roundness of his balding pate, which only added to his regular gravity. Some of the men asked after the health of his most eminent pa-tient, Mr. Clarington. Graveton waved them off, procured a drink, and sat himself in the chimney-corner.

Once situated, he began to speak, "Why, gentleman, it pains me severely to be obliged to confess that I consider our respected friend and neighbour no longer of this earth." He took a sip at his glass.

Cries of, "Poor man!" "He was most agreeable." "Well-disposed, indeed!" hailed from around the room.

The doctor opened his snuff-box, an accessory he always carried, almost like an extra appendage, and took a deliberate pinch.

"His will is made! I am one of the witnesses." He titillated his nose with the powder.

"The deuce it is!" exclaimed Mr. Slapp, a local lawyer, placing his cards on the table. "What I have heard hinted is true then, it seems. A professional man has been sent for from London. Well, in Heaven's name, let every man please himself, if he knows how, say I, but I thought Mr. Clarington and I were very good friends–intimate ones, I considered, and I certainly had my ideas–you understand me."

"Five hundred or a thousand, no doubt, attached to that compliment," remarked Mr. Clack, a curate. "And, pray, sir, who is the other witness?"

"His steward, Mr. Radford," answered Mr. Graveton.

"So, so, so!" proclaimed Mr. Clack. "Well, in Heaven's name, let every man please himself, if he can, as my friend Mr. Slapp says, but in my opinion, Mr. Clarington had friends about him quite as well-adapted to the trust, the office, the–what shall I call it?– the compliment, I'll say, as his steward."

Mr. Slapp picked up his cards again. "Wherever the bulk of the fortune goes, I would wager any gentleman present a five-pound note the steward comes in for a neat legacy." He smiled primly. "I never knew a steward yet that could not take care of himself." After glancing at his cards, he laid one down.

"What, are they so like the lawyers as that comes to, eh, neighbour Slapp?" inquired Mr. Tomkins, a plain, old farmer who sat smoking a pipe on the other side of the fire.

While continuing to study his whist hand, Mr. Slapp mumbled, mostly to himself, "I will thank you not to direct your remarks to me, sir, as I did not address my observations to you."

The curate approached Mr. Graveton. "Have you any notion how he will cut up?"

"Sir!" Graveton spat. "I am a physician, not a slapdash surgeon!"

"Come, thank you for that, doctor. That is a very good one, indeed." Mr. Tomkins stood and approached a priggish little man, foppishly dressed, who had sat quietly at a table by himself. "Why, master Dickens"–he pointed with the pipe stem–"you should know best about that, should you not? It is your trade to handle the knife, I believe. Was not it you who cut off the carter's leg the other day?"

The previously insignificant Mr. Dickens drew himself up to reply, his little grey eyes flashing fire. Before he could speak, a voice from across the room called out, "What could be the reason that he had not himself been called in to Mr. Clarington?"

Following an audible sigh, Dickens spoke. "It is not the first time, sir, that prejudice and misrepresentation have delivered to me a disadvantage." He cast a sarcastic glance at Mr. Graveton, which seemed to operate as a balm for the cut he had just suffered at the hands of the farmer.

Another voice rang out, "Does anybody know whether Mr. Clarington has any relations?"

"None, sir, none," Mr. Clack answered. "Not an individual. I believe that if he had possessed an heir, he would have dropped a hint of it to me in one of the many interesting conversations we have had together."

"I think I knew him quite as well as you, sir," challenged Mr. Slapp, "and I could perhaps mention, but I am dumb"—he paused in thought—"it might possibly be said that I was piqued at not being employed—you understand me."

Mr. Tomkins turned to Mr. Graveton. "Doctor, can't you let any light upon this subject? Witnesses generally have a pretty good guess what they put their hands to."

"I believe, sir, I was never yet reckoned guilty of disclosing the secrets of my friends," Graveton responded, taking another deliberate pinch from his snuff-box. After returning the case to its pocket, he pulled his watch from another, tapped the face twice, and put it back. "Gentlemen." He stood, downed the remains of his glass, then took up his hat and cane.

As he strode toward the door, Mr. Clack called out, "What, doctor, don't you play a rubber to-night! Where are you going so soon?"

"I am going to my own house sir," Graveton replied with increased gravity. "I think it not unlikely that I may be called again to Ashbank Hall this evening, and I regard it unpardonable for a medical man to be from home when he considers it

probable that a patient may require his services." He cast a dis-
approving look at Mr. Dickens. "Isn't your Mrs. Barnes of
Oakham Farm confined at this very moment and not long to
birthing?" he asked then hurried out into the cold night.

The moment the door closed behind Mr. Graveton, clucks of con-
demnation broke out from the assembled. As I saw it, he had
most likely been wheedling himself into Mr. Clarington's good
graces, hoping to procure a fat legacy, backbiting all his friends
and neighbours for his own private advantage. He must have already had a handsome fortune from his medical practice, and not
a child to bequeath it to.

Mr. Dickens stated, "It is not becoming for a physician to display
such avarice."

"He has been rather charitable with our church in the past," Mr.
Clack mentioned, "although I do believe it may have proceeded
from ostentation, rather than feeling."

"If the good doctor were considered more favourable in friend
Clarington's will than any of us," the farmer opined, "he must be
a deceitful friend and a bad Christian."

All heads nodded at that disparagement. I emptied my pint and
hurried home.

A few days later, Mr. Radford once again graced the barber shop
with his handsome form. This time, his expression suggested a
more serious mood.

"Good day, Mr. Radford," I greeted him with a smile.

"Not for me, I'm afraid," his face appeared grave and drawn.
"You see, Mr. Clarington passed away last evening, but that was
to have been expected." I could see small drops of moisture forming in the corners of his eyes.

"My condolences, sir," I replied, attempting to be as sombre as
possible. "Is there some way that I can be of service, sir?"

Radford nodded, the curls of his freshly-powdered periwig bounc-
ing slightly. "Yes. That is why I have come to see you this day."
He reached inside a coat pocket and produced a sheet of paper.
"Are you able to read?"

"Yes, sir! I have schooling in literature, as well as in the mathematics." I examined his expression for a hint of understanding or acceptance but found none.

He handed me the notice. It described the late Mr. Clarington's desires to be interred in the Oldham churchyard with no stone or monumental slab erected. Rather than a hearse, he was to be conveyed to his grave borne by twenty-four of the poorest men in the parish on a grand bier. Each pall-bearer would be furnished with a mourning-suit and receive five pounds a-piece for their remuneration. *Five pounds!* That could feed a person for months.

"Are you, yourself, a member of the parish?" he inquired.

While Mr. Clack might not see me as a regular attendee at his services, my mother and uncle participated in the religious rituals with some regularity.

"You might say so, sir." I did not wish to let another stroke of well-paying good fortune pass me over.

Mr. Radford nodded. "Might I implore you to assemble such a coterie of able-bodied men who might be willing and able to perform the duties therein described?"

"Would such services garner me any additional funding, sir?" I knew it might be risky to ask for further coins, but you could not blame a poor fellow for trying.

The steward smiled politely. "I appreciate your keen business sense, young man. What the notice does not mention is that there will be a breakfast at Ashbank Hall in the morning before the proceedings. At that time, the pall-bearers will receive silk hatbands, scarfs, and gloves." He studied my expression, which I held steadfast. "Yes, I can see my way to increase your reward by a quid for services rendered."

I hopped over to the gentleman and shook his hand energetically. "Thank you, Mr. Radford. Thank you most –"

Our eyes met while still holding each other's hand. I could not speak for the other fellow, but I know that my well-honed sense of attraction aroused in my trousers.

"Kindly." I completed the sentence before withdrawing my hand.

Mr. Radford clasped his joined hands in front of his waist, suggesting he might have experienced a similar awakening. "I shall leave the notice with you." He turned back to the door. "Until the morrow, then." With a pert grin, he nodded his head to me and ducked out, closing the door behind.

The remainder of the day filled with interrogatories and discussions. Most of the other young men had no idea who Mr. Clarington was or where he lived, but five pounds is five pounds. By sunset, I had subscribed twenty-three other lads to assist with the task of bearing the late Mr. Clarington's bier from his home to the churchyard.

With such a turn of good luck latterly, I finished the evening at the Black Bull with a pint. The men of the village took turns singing the praises of our late neighbour, in turn relating or enumerating the times they had helped Mr. Clarington over the many, many years. It was as if each of them pleaded their case to the deceased as to why they deserved a slice of the dead man's estate, as if any of them were so worthy. I kept my laughter to myself and toddled off at the bottom of the glass.

I travelled back to Ashbank Hall the next morning, arriving shortly before nine o'clock, the hour fixed for the breakfast. This time, we entered through the large double-doors at the front, like proper guests. The generously large entry hall had been set with tables of toast and tea, dried fish and little sausages. I recognized the attorney, Mr. Fortescue standing off to the side with a cup and saucer in his hands.

Mr. Radford, dressed all in black for the occasion, announced to the growing crowd, "Mr. Graveton!"

The doctor shuffled into the room with a new black suit. His hair had been neatly curled and powdered, while his features maintained an air of the deepest solemnity. "I know that I am early," he proclaimed to anyone who might happen to be listening, "but I am always more particular in paying a tribute of respect to a deceased friend than a living one." He glanced at the few other people in the room, but no one responded.

Mr. Fortescue set down the cup and exited the room. I stepped up to the tables with an empty plate and an empty stomach.

"Well, Mr. Radford," continued the doctor, "I think I may already venture to give you joy, for I have not the slightest doubt that you will find yourself a much more affluent man in the course of a few hours than you are now." He approached the steward with an outstretched hand.

Radford glanced down at the empty hand but did not take it. "I entertain neither hopes nor expectations of the kind, sir." He looked back at the entrance. "I have saved a small independence in the service of my late, kind master, with which I am amply satisfied. All the wealth in all of England could not compensate me for the loss of his society."

Something about the steward's depiction of his late, kind master suggested more than just an operational relationship. The barely-noticeable redness of his eyes gave him away.

"Nobly and generously spoken!" the doctor exclaimed. He took a pinch of snuff and applied it. "It is not the value of the money which a man receives as a legatee that affects the heart of sensibility, Mr. Radford, it is the esteem in which it proves him to have been held by a departed friend that produces the satisfaction which results from being remembered in a will."

It seemed to me that Mr. Graveton could be much more charitable with his words than his own money. My uncle would have said of him: He is the type of person that if you asked, "What's o'clock?" he would explain, in exacting detail, how to construct a pocket watch.

The doctor took another step closer to Mr. Radford, whose expression communicated the proximity uncomfortable. "Between you and me, sir, I believe Mr. Clarington esteemed us two above all his friends and acquaintances. Is not that your opinion, Mr. Radford?"

"I believe, sir"–the steward took a step away–"he held us both in very good esteem, but I never heard him particularise any one of his acquaintances as possessing a greater share of his partiality than another." He snuck a glance at another pall-bearer entering. "He was a man who considered it illiberal to draw any preference from comparison, and, therefore, forbore to weigh the merits of his friends against each other."

Mr. Graveton nodded. "Very true, sir, very true indeed. He was a man of equal goodness and judgment, but sometimes trifles disclose the bent of the inclinations as eloquently as diffuse declarations could do." He winked. "I have often heard him speak with pleasure of the many evenings which he had passed in social conversation with you, and I assure you, Mr. Radford, he has often told me that he considered me a better judge of those books than any man he knew." He pointed at the open door of the library. "Ah! I know not any treasure upon earth I should value equal to the possession of a few of those volumes of my old friend's."

Just as he concluded his remark, Mr. Fortescue returned. "It is a very moderate wish and deserves gratifying."

The doctor turned to face the attorney. "It is more than I dare hope, sir. Don't you consider it too sanguine a hope for me to entertain, Mr. Fortescue?"

"A very short time will now reduce all hopes to a certainty, Mr. Graveton," the attorney rejoined with a smile.

The doctor's eyes sparkled, and he beamed satisfaction. After two short knuckle raps on the lid of his snuff-box, he took a long pinch, and then walked deliberately to the tables with the breakfast laid out. From time to time I noticed his head turning in the direction of the library.

"Mr. Clack and Mr. Slapp!" Radford announced. The curate wore his canonicals, and Mr. Slapp had donned a rusty suit of sable.

"Notwithstanding your ideas to the contrary"– Mr. Clack seemed to continue an ongoing conversation–"you perceive no relation has appeared. Consequently, there is no legal heir."

"By no means granted," argued Mr. Slapp. "There may be legal heirs, though not acknowledged by the deceased."

"Somebody must have his money!" the curate proclaimed. "He cannot take it with him."

"Mrs. Slapp procured him a couple of ortolan hens only a few days before he died, and I sent him a half-a-dozen of Madeira, that had crossed the sea three times, about a week after."

"I have not much in my power," Mr. Clack argued, "but I can truly say that I was unremitting in my attentions, offering to pray with him, or sit up with him, if he thought proper to accept of my services. I could do no more, you know." He raised his eyes heavenward.

The two strode to the food tables, continuing their protestations of worthiness. Waiters began to pour glasses of ale to those who so wished.

Mr. Tomkins, the old farmer, arrived and I had just begun my second sausage when the clatter of a large carriage approaching grabbed my attention.

Mr. Fortescue strode to the open doors and peered outside. I stood directly behind him. Sitting in front of the avenue of elms sat an elegant post-chariot-and-four with two outriders. One of the servants alighted and proclaimed in a voice of thunder, "Announce Sir Malcolm Brockelsbie, nephew of the late Mr. Clarington!"

Another servant opened the chariot door, and a wispy thin man, a few years older than me, stepped out. His face gleamed white with powder, and his hair even whiter. The clothes he wore looked very expensive, with ribbons and bows, ruffled cuffs, silks and satins everywhere. His rouged lips puckered slightly, and his eyes squinted in the morning sunlight. Even so, I could sense him to be most attractive.

Mr. Radford proclaimed, "Gentlemen, sir Malcolm Brockelsbie, nephew of the late Mr. Clarington!"

Mr. Fortescue gave a slight bow.

"Oh! I conclude you are Mr.–um…"–the stranger paused with an amused expression. "Upon my honour! In the hurry of the business, I have forgot your name, from whom I received those letters respecting Mr. Clarington?"

"Yes, pray enter," the attorney invited sir Malcom into the great hall. "We are to convey your uncle to his final resting place shortly."

"All right, all good!" exclaimed the baronet. "I am here just in the nick of time, I find, and that is quite as well as if I had been here a month ago. But if I had not come at all, as I am his heir-at-law, you know, I must have come in for the stuff." He glanced about the room. "This estate, in addition to his personal property, seems a tolerably-good concern. What do you rate his income at, sir?" Two piercing blue eyes stared intently at Mr. Fortescue.

The attorney balked slightly at the mention of his client's worth in open society—and so recently after the man died—but then responded, "The late Mr. Clarington's income was about three thousand a-year."

"The devil it was!" sir Malcolm exploded with a genuine smile. "Excellent! Better than I expected. Very fair, upon my honour!"

"The coffin is not yet screwed down if you would wish to take a view of —"

"Oh, no, no!" sir Malcolm interrupted. "I never saw him in my life, and, therefore, I don't perceive the least occasion for an introduction now." He looked about at the other attendees and then down at his bright-blue vestments. "I suppose I had better pop on a suit of black. I ordered my valet to put up one in case of necessity." He stepped to a rope hanging near the side of the entrance. "This bell, I presume, will bring me a servant who will shew me to a chamber and send my own man to me?" He pulled the rope with a violence that snatched it from the pulley.

Mr. Radford stepped up and took the loose cord from him. "I shall see to your room, sir. Give me one moment." He walked off.

"Permit me to ask you one question, sir," Mr. Fortescue implored, "can you give me any information of a nephew of your late mother's and of Mr. Clarington's?"

"Positively not!" came the terse reply. "I believe there was such a person when I was in arms, but I have not heard of him these hundred years."

"Did he not marry?"

"He might," replied sir Malcolm laughingly, "but I was too young then to go to weddings, and I never remember any transaction that I have had no share in." He glanced out one of the front windows. "Lots of game in this country, gentlemen, I should imagine. I will have a glorious pop at the hares and pheasants tomorrow." He turned left and right with arched eyes, apparently searching for like-minded fellows.

Drawn-down lips and half-averted countenances responded with brief phases, such as "I believe so," "I really can't say," "I fancy there may be," and the like.

Mr. Tomkins pushed his way forward. "Yes, sir, plenty. A very great plenty, indeed. If you want a guide in your sport, I shall be happy to attend you. I earnt the independence I now enjoy in a farm of your uncle's, sir, and shall always be proud to do anything in my power to oblige any of his family."

"Thank you, I will trouble you," sir Malcolm returned, looking down his slender nose at the farmer in the overly-mended suit. "You seem a fine old fellow, and I dare say I shall find you very useful." His head turned to the library door. "What legions of books!" He took a step toward the shelves. "There are sufficient to furnish a bookseller's shop. Are they valuable, I wonder?"

"I am very well acquainted with them all, sir," boasted Mr. Graveton as he approached the baronet. "I can assure you that they are extremely so." He smiled and nodded with satisfaction.

Sir Malcolm returned the smile and stated, "I am very glad to hear it, for I shall certainly bring them to the hammer."

The doctor's expression shifted to one of scorn. His face seemed to be saying, "I trust it will not be in your power to do so."

"The most of them seem devilishly old," sir Malcolm continued, "and there are only two old things in the world I set any value upon: old plate and old wine." He chuckled and glanced about. "No scarcity of them in this old mansion, I imagine, but I shall take an early opportunity of rummaging. Old books I class with old women. Neither of them possess any charms for me, and, therefore, I always make a point of removing them both out of my sight as fast as possible." A gay cackle erupted from his pointed mouth. He looked about as if expecting the others assembled to join in his joke, but no one else laughed or smiled.

Mr. Radford returned and addressed the disruptive guest. "This way, sir." He led Malcolm up the grand staircase. The foppish fellow's head turned this way and that, as if cataloguing each nook and cranny, all the appointments of this grand manor, soon to be at his disposal for fast money.

Once the acquisitive baronet moved out of earshot, the hubbub began in the hall. I could hear whispers of, "Who does he think he is?" "Where did he come from?" "The nerve!" and some other phrases I should not print for public reading.

In a room full of black and grey mourners, sir Malcolm had cut an azure swatch. Showing up at the very last moment to claim the estate of a relative he had never even met, nor cared to honour by looking upon his body, set the cauldron of the crowd a-bubble.

Mr. Radford descended the stairs with cloaks, hat-bands, and gloves for the twenty-four of us who would bear the bier. He handed some to me to distribute. After a few minutes, we all had donned our mourning-gear.

We stationed ourselves around the cloth-covered wooden convey-ance and lifted as one. Mr. Radford and Mr. Graveton took their place at the head of the corpse, and we began to move at a solemn pace. Sir Malcolm soon followed behind, now in his dark suit. Mr. Clack passed us and walked briskly ahead, presumably to meet us at the churchyard.

The protracted journey took us nearly an hour due to our unhur-ried velocity. As we passed through Oldham, people stood by the side of the road or hung out their windows, gawking at our pro-cession. Mr. Clack waited at the churchyard gate and led us to the open grave. Other townspeople had gathered, most likely de-sirous to listen to the reading of the will.

With much strain, we lowered the bier to the ground and depos-ited the coffin into Mr. Clarington's final abode. Mr. Graveton dropped the first handful of kindred dust, followed by Mr. Radford and sir Malcolm, who quickly and briskly slapped his palms together to rid himself of the unwelcome dirt.

Those who knew Mr. Clarington, and those of us who had carried him, took turns covering the box of the departed. Mr. Radford circulated among the pall-bearers, distributing five-pound notes. Smiles erupted everywhere, soon to be squelched due to the gravity of the situation.

He came to me last with empty hands. "I am so sorry. Perhaps you could accompany me back to the hall after the ceremony. I have a small cache of funds there from which I could pay you."

I could not discern whether this occurrence of insufficiency hap-pened naturally or by artifice, but, none-the-less, spending more time with the handsome steward did not offend me at all. I merely nodded and smiled.

Mr. Fortescue moved to the front of the crowd and removed a parchment from his coat. As he unfolded it, sir Malcolm moved ever closer while adjusting his cravat, playing with his embossed seals, and settling a ring upon his finger. The expression on his face suggested a man perfectly satisfied to be fortune's chosen favourite of the hour.

Mr. Graveton pulled his cambric pocket-handkerchief and applied it to his face. Perhaps he did not wish any of the surrounding spectators to detect any change in his features due to the reading of the will. Mr. Radford stood dutifully contemplating the grave of his late lamented master, occasionally wiping a tear from his eye. Farmer Tomkins stared directly at Mr. Fortescue as if the words to follow were for him alone.

The remainder of the group engaged in directing to each other winks, smiles, and sneers. The beadle called for silence three times before the throng settled.

Mr. Fortescue began reading words I could barely understand. They sounded dusty and unfamiliar, perhaps some Latin, legal jargon necessary for funerals and wills. But then he spoke plainly, thus.

"To each of my old faithful servants I bequeath one hundred pounds sterling, and a year's wages."

A rumble sifted through the crowd. Mr. Clarington seemed quite charitable after all.

"To my steward, Joseph Radford, I bequeath the sum of two thousand pounds."

Radford began sobbing. I could not tell if the tears came from joy or melancholy.

"To each of my friends, who shall have attended my body to the grave, in the quality of a mourner for my decease, I give ten pounds to buy a ring."

I began adding in my head. Five pounds, plus a quid, and now another ten for a ring. That sum should keep me sorted for the remainder of the year and then some.

"To the poor of the parish of Oldham I bequeath one hundred pounds."

Mr. Clack grinned. I imagined he could put the money to good use. However, sir Malcolm began to display symptoms of impatience. He looked about and fidgeted with his fingers.

"To my respected friend, William Graveton"–a loud sigh could be heard through the doctor's head covering, and he applied a hasty pinch of snuff–"twenty volumes from my library, to be selected by himself." Mr. Fortescue paused, presumably to indicate the sentence concluded. Mr. Graveton groaned and grabbed at the cambric.

"To such of my relatives as may attend my funeral, I individually bequeath the sum of five hundred pounds, to indemnify them for the expense which they may have incurred in travelling to the spot of my interment, and farther, to convince them that they have not been forgotten by me, but have no farther claim whatever upon my property, and also desiring it to be understood that I cut off all individuals, whomsoever or whatsoever, except those specified by name in this, my testament, from any pretensions to a share of my worldly goods or estates."

Sir Malcolm paled even more than the white powder already applied to his face. His eyes beamed flames, his lips quivered with stifled curses, his cheeks blanched and then blazed crimson with fury. His heightened disappointment appeared obvious to all present. Following a sarcastic laugh, he drew his watch from a pocket and fixed his eye upon it. Perhaps he wished to know the time, or, perhaps, he used the diversion to hide his confusion or, more likely, his impatience to depart from this spot where common decency no longer required his presence.

Mr. Fortescue continued in a softened voice, "I appoint Henry Fortescue the sole executor and administrator of this my last will and testament. In requital for his acceptance of which trust, I bequeath to him the sum of one thousand pounds sterling."

Mr. Clarington must have been very wealthy to have been able to gift so much money to his friends and associates. I thought back on the few minutes I had spent with him and felt happy to have made his acquaintance.

"And finally"–the attorney started up again–"when all the bequests above-mentioned shall have been justly and lawfully executed, I declare, as my residuary legatee, and the sole heir of all my estates, real and personal, the first John Brown who shall claim them."

People began to murmur. Surprised looks and slack jaws abounded. Heads began to turn in my direction.

I stepped forward and raised my hand. "My name is John Brown, sir, and I claim them."

Chapter Two:
A New Lot

A BRIEF SILENCE AND DRAWING IN OF AIR preceded a cacophony of responses to the turn of events. The following catalogues some of the things I remembered hearing: "Well, to be sure, his name *is* John Brown," "Of all I ever saw or heard," "And *he*, nothing but the nephew of a poor penny barber," "I'll not believe it can be, till I hear more about it," "Nothing is impossible," "Better to be lucky than wise."

I had never feared for my life before, but at that point, it felt as if the entire town stood ready to cut me to pieces for my unexpected stroke of luck. The lottery had been drawn, and none of the lot held the winning ticket.

Mr. Fortescue pushed through the throng and approached. "What is your name, young man?"

"John Brown, sir."

He looked about. "Is there anyone here who can vouch for this?"

Mr. Radford stepped up. "I have made the acquaintance of this fellow, and I can say with all certainty that his name is, in fact, John Brown." Mr. Fortescue nodded. "He is a very well-behaved, and, I believe, a very honest young man, sir. He assumed his late uncle's barbering business, and it was young Mr. Brown here who provided the final shave and trim for Mr. Clarington."

"Indeed!" the attorney barked. "And a very fine job of it too, I must say."

Mr. Slapp approached with a bit of a sneer on his face. "His uncle has shaved me a thousand times."

"That does not by any means disqualify him from reaping the advantages to which he is become entitled by the will of the late Mr. Clarington, sir," responded Mr. Fortescue. "Nor–if his conduct corresponds with the station and character which he is in future called upon to sustain–can it deprive him of the respect of the unprejudiced part of society."

Mr. Graveton strode up, giving a sagacious nod of approbation. "Mr. Brown, I give you joy." An obviously-false and obsequious smile blossomed across his toady face. "Can I do anything to serve you, sir?" The vultures began to loom, searching for any bit of stray meat.

"I thank you, sir," I answered, "but I have already had so much done for me that I appear to have nothing left to ask."

Sir Malcolm announced as he drew on his gloves, "Well, gentlemen, I have enjoyed a much greater treat than I expected. I conceived myself invited only to a tragedy, but the tragedy, if not converted into a farce, has at least been followed by one. I never saw 'Fortune's Frolic, or the Ploughman Turned Lord' better exhibited in my life. I have the honour to bid you all good-morning." He turned to me. "My lord, Robin, I wish you the most transcendent delight in kicking about dumplings and feasting on beef-steaks and barley-sugar." With a quick about-face and an irritated stride, he sprang into to his waiting carriage. A bothersome feeling snipping at my innards told me it would not be the last time I would encounter this Sir Malcolm Brockelsbie.

Mr. Fortescue inquired, "Mr. Brown, who might your relatives be?"

I explained to the gentleman what I knew of my adopted family, the Browns, and that Mrs. Brown had decided to return to her native Oldham following the death of the serjeant. As far as I knew, not being able to identify my true parents, I had not a single relation in the world.

"Although you have heard the will of your benefactor," Mr. Fortescue continued, "and are consequently acquainted with the most material point concerning yourself, I am still in possession of many injunctions from the deceased, not contained in his will, which I am, by his command, peremptorily to deliver to his heir. We will, therefore, if you please, proceed to the Hall, where we shall have leisure for conversation."

Mr. Radford gazed at me, instantly grasping the confused state of my feelings. Unable to congratulate me in front of the others, nor respond to the sarcasms of the villagers, he merely took my hand and led me along a private path out of the churchyard. It felt good to have him taking a somewhat fatherly role, as I had never known a father, and I had good feelings about the steward. Also, the comfort of his warm hand caused stirrings elsewhere.

Once we reached the main road, I shuddered and said, "I can scarcely persuade myself to believe what I have just heard." I looked at Mr. Radford beside me. "I can at present consider it only as a dream. But I hope, Mr. Radford, if it is indeed a truth, that I shall be honoured with your friendship. For although I trust I am not very idly or viciously inclined, the possession of such unexpected wealth is enough to bewilder the senses of any man, let alone someone of my years. With no older relations to guide me, I have no one to give me advice or caution."

Radford smiled. "Your words, young man, do your heart great credit." He nodded. "And depend upon it, that, as far as my knowledge of life extends, my counsel shall ever be at your service."

I squeezed his hand, both as an acknowledgment and as a symbol of my affections for this man. The sight of the house caught my eye. "What, sir, could be Mr. Clarington's motive for making a will of so uncommon a nature as that which constitutes me his heir?"

"From hints which he has at times dropped to me," Mr. Radford said more softly, "I have reason to believe that he had an insuperable dislike to his relatives collectively and was careless who possessed his property after his decease, so long as he cut *them* off from inheritance."

Mr. Fortescue had reached us just as the steward expressed his opinion. "That Mr. Clarington, at the time of my delivering to him his instructions for the drawing up of his will, had made an open declaration to me to that effect, but had forborne to give the slightest explanation from what cause his enmity to his relations had sprung."

Upon entering the Hall, Mr. Radford walked me about the ground floor, showing me the rooms I would take on. I had never entered another manor house, and could not determine it the most lavish, as its appointments proved sparse but adequate. My mind whirled with visions of parties and public events. The steward left me in the grand library with Mr. Fortescue and withdrew.

The attorney stared directly at me for a few moments, and I could not discern the reason for his intense scrutiny. Then he spoke, "Mr. Brown, please let me begin by expressing my gratitude that you are not one of those puffed-up, idle, vain, young men filled with boyish pride. I appreciate your unlooked-for happiness of unexpected possession of affluence and independence. I do truly believe you shall make the late Mr. Clarington proud." He reached into an inside-pocket and produced a paper.

"Thank you, sir. I am not sure as to how to respond to such plentiful compliments."

He glanced up from the paper at me and said, "Here are the conditions of your inheritance." From the document in his hands he read:

"To my unknown heir I direct Henry Fortescue to communicate the subsequent injunctions, and in quality of the executor and administrator of my last will and testament, I authorize and command the said Henry Fortescue to enforce a due obedience to them, or to be rigorous in exacting the penalty which I have adjudged to their neglect.

"I enact, first, that if the individual, named John Brown, whom fate may select to become my heir, be not arrived at his twenty-fifth year at the period of his advancing his claim to that effect, he shall not come into possession of his wealth till he has attained that age, but be provided till the completion of that time, with an annuity of one thousand pounds, and be permitted to make Ashbank Hall his residence."

He looked up at me. "And what is your current age, Mr. Brown?"

"I am but twenty years of age, Mr. Fortescue."

"I see. It seems the additional provisions of Mr. Clarington's declarations shall be in force until such time as you reach your twenty-fifth year."

"There is no need for hurry on my part, sir." A thousand pounds might have been more than I earned in my entire life as a barber, and I shall receive such moneys once a year. What good fortune!

"Pray, let me continue, sir." The attorney read from the paper again:

"Secondly, that the said John Brown, if he is not already romantically-entangled or a husband, shall be constrained not to engage in such affairs of the heart till he has attained the before-mentioned age of twenty-five."

It brought some relief to me that I would not be seeking a marriage, as I had no interest in women as spouses or otherwise.

"And, thirdly, that if before the attainment of that age, he shall contract a debt of more than one hundred pounds, he shall forfeit every claim to the inheritance of my property, and it shall be transferred to the first of my relatives who shall appear to demand it."

With an income of one thousand pounds a year, there could be no foreseeable debts in my future, whether for one pound or a thousand.

"These conditions I have annexed, because, as I do not consider any young man competent to govern his passions, and exercise his judgment, till he has reached the age of twenty-five, I do not wish it to be alleged, that in excluding my family from their inheritance, I have wantonly substituted a fool or a rascal in their place. The terms, therefore, which I have proposed, are intended to preserve my heir, whoever he may be, from becoming a spendthrift, the dupe of a designing woman, or a gamester. If he is not proof against temptation, he must abide by the event of his intemperance. If he has fortitude to shun those three rocks of temptation which I have named, my blessing accompanies my bequest. Signed, Oliver Clarington."

Given my humble nature, not given to gambling, not given to women, and not given to excessive spending, it seemed as though the next few years should pass rather uneventfully.

"Are you up to the task, my young master?"

I nodded my head deliberately. "Yes, sir. I believe I can remain true to the gentleman's ideals as stated."

A grim smile grew across Mr. Fortescue's lips. "Let us hope so, Mr. Brown. Let us hope so." He grabbed my hand and shook it vigorously. "I shall provide you with a copy of this annex, as well as the testament itself, before publishing them, as required by law, in the local newspaper of record."

Following Mr. Fortescue's departure, Radford resumed the tour of the great house. So many rooms, but not much furniture. A side table here or there. A chair beneath a window, a painting every so often.

My head filled with questions. "Where do I sleep?" As soon as I had reached the end of the interrogatory, I realised, and sputtered, "And where do *you* sleep, Mr. Radford?" We had just begun to ascend the grand staircase, and I stopped mid-stride.

He had taken an extra step and turned back to face me. His face seemed flushed, whether from the exercise or embarrassment, I could not say. "When Mr. Clarington first acquired this estate–I had, a short time before, been employed with the former family, the Ashbanks–he asked me to stay on. There is a Steward's House behind this building, but after a time, I moved–at Mr. Clarington's request, you understand–into the main house here." He waved a hand, gesturing toward the upper floors. "However, with the recent turn of events, I shall return to the Steward's House and take up residence there once again."

We started up the stairs once more.

Again, I paused. "But wait a bit," I implored, "there is no reason for you to remove yourself unless –" It took me just a second too long to grasp the prior arrangement between master and steward. "I should not wish to put you out, sir, and if there is a room somewhat adjacent to my chamber, I would appreciate your proximity immensely." I smiled with my eyes in hopes of warming the old fellow up.

He began ascending the stairs again. "I shall consider your kind offer, young master."

At the end of a hall on the first floor, Mr. Radford opened a set of narrow double doors to the master bedroom, an apartment of great size and rich appointments. The bed seemed large enough for a whole family, and faded tapestries hung from each panelled wall. I should never wish to leave this chamber.

"Your room, sir," Radford announced unnecessarily. He strode to a rope hanging near the side of the bed. "Pull this when you require my services. Along with my responsibility of managing the estate, I am here to assist you with bathing, dressing, correspondence, and arranging your meals. Should there be any other duties required, we can then determine whether they fall into my prescribed jobs." A weak smile led me to think there might be some other functions a steward might perform.

"Thank you, Radford," I mumbled as I gawked at all the rich trappings. Yards of gauzy, sepia-coloured fabric covered the bedposts, plump embroidered pillows covered the mattress. I imagined this similar to what the Kings would have in their palaces royal.

As he drew back the dark-plum velvet draperies, he continued, "If I might suggest, sir, you should not leave the Hall, nor receive the visits of any of your acquaintances, till you appear in mourning at the village church Sunday next, when the funeral services shall be preached."

"Yes, yes. Good idea." I must admit I wasn't entirely sure what I had agreed to, but I trusted Mr. Radford implicitly, and whatever he suggested became gospel to me. I feared he must have gotten some amusement out of watching me, awestruck, wide-eyed, full of wonder.

"This way, sir." He led me out into the hall and continued the tour. The remainder of the floor contained guest rooms, a sitting room, a small music room and a sun room. The second floor housed the staff. While there were accommodations for a dozen servants, only three remained: the cook, the maid, and the stable hand.

Radford led me back to the bedchamber. "I shall send for the tailor to measure you for a suit of sables that you shall wear to the funeral services." He measured me with his own eyes, and I enjoyed the attention. No one had ever looked at me that way before, and it excited me wholly.

"Mr. Radford, may I ask a question of a very personal nature?" I wished to know if he had been one of the previous occupants of that large bed.

His head turned to the side slightly. "I would prefer it, sir, if we could keep my personal business out of our current conversation. If that meets with your approval, that is."

"Yes. Of course. How silly of me." I did not intend to embarrass him, but it appeared I had succeeded nonetheless.

"I shall leave you now to acquaint yourself with your new surroundings. In a while I shall return with your luncheon." He bowed and exited, closing the door behind him.

It still had not fully occurred to me that this was all to be mine. John Brown, the orphaned nephew of a penny barber in Oldham,

Lincolnshire. It would take some time to accept the uncommon luck that came with the rather common name.

First off, I examined the wash stand, with its ornate, gold-rimmed mirror and beautifully-painted porcelain bowl. The matching pitcher sat below, filled with water. Plush hand-towels hung at either side of the stand. The razor set did not match the quality of the tools at my shop, and I would have to send for them, as I was not allowed to leave for a few days.

Next, I went to the giant armoire and opened one of the heavy, carved oak doors. Inside hung shirts and jackets, with trousers folded and stacked neatly below. Given that Mr. Clarington had been taller and stouter than me, I doubted that any of these fine clothes would fit me, unless tailored first.

Behind the other door I found shoes and boots arranged on shelves. Perhaps our feet were of similar size. I bent down and grabbed a slipper and placed it over one of my feet. It proved to be a few sizes too large. It would seem that some of my first annuity would be going to a new wardrobe.

After closing the tall cabinet, I looked around the room again and stopped facing the sprawling bed. Like an unrestrained child, I took a running jump and leapt upon it, hoping in mid-air that my falling weight would not cause its destruction or demise. The down-filled mattress and coverlets easily absorbed the onslaught, and I giggled outrageously. I had to wonder what the malicious sir Malcolm would have been doing had he assumed the properties instead. I imagined him skulking about, listing each trinket and bauble, calculating their value at sale. That made me giggle even louder.

A loud knock stifled my gaiety. "Yes?" I managed to say without laughter.

The door opened, and Mr. Radford followed with a silver-plate tray. "Your repast, sir." He laid it upon the desk by the window overlooking the grounds. Then he shot me a side-glance, suggesting he had heard my boyish frivolity. "I trust everything is to your liking, sir?"

I nodded vigorously, afraid to speak for fear that I would burst out again in giggles.

He bowed and left, but not before glancing back one more time with a warm smile and gleam in his eye.

In the afternoon, I went down the stairs to the great library. The number of volumes intimidated me. From the floor almost all the way to the cove of the ceiling, shelves held innumerable books—the gateways to knowledge, they say.

A slender ray of sunlight caught the gold imprint of one, and I stepped to it. *Twelfth Night or What You Will*, proclaimed the title, and I recognised it as one of the plays of our beloved Bard, William Shakespeare. With gentle hands, I slowly slid the book toward me. As I pulled it free, a very old-looking and fragile paper-bound pamphlet fell to the floor. I put the book on the nearest table and retrieved the pamphlet. *Gl'ingannati* appeared to be its title. Inside, it contained dialogue of a play; however, the language looked like Italian, which I had never learned. I placed it carefully back in the space left by the Shakespeare work.

Seeing as I could not leave, nor could I entertain anyone else, I spent the rest of the afternoon reading and reciting out loud the comic play. What a confusion! A girl dressed as a man and pretended to woo another woman. And to make things even more confusing, their names were Viola and Olivia. Surely our Mr. Shakespeare intended a tremendous puzzlement of the audience. Although, when Viola appeared in men's clothing, she used the name "Cesario." Later, her long-lost twin brother Sebastian showed up and people confused the two of them. Thank Heaven our real lives are not such a preposterous farce.

The idea of dressing as a member of the opposite sex had no appeal for me. While I have professed to enjoy the intimate company of other men, I would not have wanted to pass myself off as a woman to achieve such a goal. Although, I felt forced to admit, it would be easier to proceed in normal society if one of us assumed the costume of the opposite sex.

Our teacher at school told us that before the reign of Charles II, women were not allowed on the stage, and young, beardless men played the roles of women. The convolutions of being a man who played the heroine Viola, who then played the role of a man.

Fortunately, everything was sorted in the end, and all the players found love, except for poor Malvolio the steward, who pined for his mistress Olivia. It made me wonder if there might not be some Malvolio in Mr. Radford.

As the sunlight faded, the steward, now my steward, appeared to announce dinner. We walked to the dining hall together, and when I saw the large table set with only one platter, I turned to Mr. Radford, "Will you not dine with me this evening? I know it is most likely against some protocol, but could we not dispense with such rules for tonight? It would be my honour to have you join me."

Radford's facial expression changed from bland to questioning to frowning, pouting, back to bland once more, and then a hint of a smile. He walked off and returned with his own plate and placed it next to mine on the table. With a bit of a flourish, he held the chair for me and slid it under once I had begun to sit. No one had ever performed that ritual before for me, and it unnerved me a bit. Up until that day, it was me who served others.

Over our dinners, I asked Mr. Radford after the history of the manor and he described the Ashbank family and its slow demise during the preceding century. When the last Ashbank passed on thirty years prior, the house went up for auction, and Mr. Clarington purchased it for a bargain price because manors such as this were built during a time when servants were plentiful and economical. With him being the only resident, there proved no need for a full staff, and he got on with a minimum of expenditure.

Following that, Mr. Radford inquired into my own history, and I repeated what I had heard about my adopted father being a military serjeant who died when I was an infant. Mother brought us here to Oldham to live with her brother, and then she passed on as well. With no knowledge of my true parents, that left me an orphan, but fortunately for me, my uncle took me in and trained me well.

"An evening such as this deserves a bit of a celebration, don't you think?" I asked. "As I am not able to leave the Hall to go to the Black Bull this night, might there be some potent drink available for us to make our toast?"

Mr. Radford stood, walked to a nook and returned with a silver tray containing an engraved crystal decanter and two short-stemmed glasses. "Have you ever had Madeira wine before?"

I had never even heard the word "Madeira" until that morning when Mr. Slapp bragged of gifting some to Mr. Clarington. Perhaps this bottle contained some of that beverage. I shook my head in answer to the question.

He set the tray on the table and poured a small amount into each of the short glasses. After handing me one of them, he raised the other and toasted, "To Mr. Clarington!"

"To Mr. Clarington!" I echoed. It seemed fitting to honour the man whose home I had claimed. Before tasting, I observed the nearly-opaque liquid and sniffed at its aroma. For some reason, it reminded me vaguely of coffee, but with some sweetness. I let it rest on my tongue for a second or two before swallowing. In my mouth it tasted more like a caramel sweet. The strength of the liqueur nearly choked me! I coughed a few times, and Mr. Radford seemed amused by my reaction.

When my powers of speech returned a minute later, I asked, "Is this by any chance, the gift of Mr. Slapp? I heard him mention this morning that he had given Mr. Clarington half-a-dozen bottles."

"As a matter of fact," the steward said as he refilled our glasses, "I do believe it is. How observant you are, young master."

"He also made a point of saying they had crossed the sea three times. Why would anyone send barrels of wine back and forth across the sea?" I picked up the little glass and sniffed at it again cautiously.

A smile crossed Radford's face. "That does sound a bit confusing, I say. I believe that I heard Mr. Slapp tell my master—my old master, that is—the proper way to age Madeira wine is over a long period of time in a hot climate. Ships would haul it through the tropics a few times to produce the correct conditions necessary."

After the third glass, I began to feel quite warm and friendly. I turned to my drinking companion, "I like you Mr. Radford. I like you very... very... much!" The final word might have sounded more like "mush!" due to my incipient inebriation. With a wide sweep, I reached over and placed my hand on his.

Radford tensed and pulled his hand away with a quick jerk. "Mr. Brown, I do not believe it proper for us to conduct ourshelves in thish manner!" The Madeira had a similar effect on the steward.

"My apologies, sir." I rose from the table. "Perhaps I misunderstood, but I believed you had taken a liking to me as well. From what I can see, you and the late Mr. Clarington were closer than master and steward... If I may say so, sir."

He closed his eyes, and I could see the tears beginning again. "Mr. Clarington and I had a special kind of relationship, you might say, but that is none of your business at present." His head turned away.

I hoped that I had not insulted my only connection to this new world. He had treated me with such kindness and understanding. Also, the way in which he looked at me suggested a similar inclination.

"Please understand"–he turned back to face me–"how difficult this situation... the difficulty I face..." He had not previously had difficulty with completing his sentences. "It might take some time for me... Mr. Clarington... so many years... The truth of it is... I find you quite compelling, a comely youth of above-average intelligence. If some sort of intimacy developed between us, such tidings would spread quickly. Can you see how my reputation as a revered steward would swiftly degrade to that of a common fortune-seeker?" More tears began to flow, and he wiped at his eyes with a sleeve.

"I am most sorry, my good man. You have caught me up short. It was not my intention to embarrass you but to demonstrate my fondness."

He reached over and patted the back of my hand gently. "Young master, I cannot express the joy you bring to these old ears to hear those words from the lips of one such as you." He smiled, and some of the tears dropped off the side of his face. "Perhaps in time–once the chitter-chatter of the townspeople dies down– we can revisit this matter anew, but for now, know that my affection for you is true, even though I cannot act upon it."

What restraint! He could have easily played upon my youth and inexperience, making an attempt to re-capture the home that once fell under his auspices, the prime property that most others seemed to prize rather highly.

"I appreciate your candour, Mr. Radford. My hat to you."

He glanced at the Robert Bryson longcase clock. "It is getting late. I shall turn down the bed for you."

It had been a very long time since anyone turned a bed down for me. This life of luxury seemed more like a dream, and when I climbed onto the giant four-post bed, I prayed it would be a dream from which I never awoke.

Chapter Three:

The White Man Appears

THE NEXT FEW DAYS PASSED SWIFTLY. Mr. Radford carried on my education upon the innumerable ways of the Hall. We began with the accounts, continued with the stockrooms, and finished with the stables. I had not realised how much work went into maintaining a great house like Ashbank Hall. It impressed me how Radford had been able to keep the old place going, not only serving Mr. Clarington but supervising the servants and overseeing the tenants of the land.

The village tailor came one morning to measure me for the funeral suit. He appeared to be someone with many years of experience, demonstrated by his long side-whiskers and severely-receded hair. With a cloth tape, he began criss-crossing my body as if preparing me for a battle. I had never been assessed like that before, and some of the measurements tickled a bit. It surprised me at first when the fellow went to take the inside leg, but his hand and tool in such proximity to my own tool became less unnerving as time went on.

When not studying with Mr. Radford, I confined myself to the great library. Most of the books had been written in languages I could not read, but, perhaps, in time, I could acquire such skills and take full advantage of their knowledge. At least the Shakespeare volumes contained English, although dated and opaque at times. Mr. Clarington had acquired translations for some of the scientific treatises, and I continued my schooling thusly.

Saturday morning, Mr. Radford displayed the mourning rings, which had arrived from Lincoln. He placed the case upon the desk and opened it for me to see. One stood out particularly, as it seemed double in size than all the rest. He plucked it from the velvet-lined case and presented it to me.

"This ring had been intended for myself," Radford began, "You will perceive that it is of far greater value than those which are to be distributed to the mourners at the late funeral." He paused and wiped at a tear. "Prompted by the respect which I bear, and the gratitude which I feel for the memory of him who is now no more, I gave private directions for this ring—at double the price

of those for which, in compliance with the will of my poor master—an order was issued by Mr. Fortescue." After another short
pause—concluded by a glance at the large, empty bed—he continued, "Place it on your finger. It is of infinitely more consequence
that you should to-morrow be seen to pay every respect and ven-
eration to the memory of your benefactor than anyone else.
Therefore, let not even this particular—as the omission can be
avoided—be neglected. I shall pass unnoticed. In you, every trifle
will be a matter of observation and comment. In the course of a
few days, a similar one can be procured for me." He looked into
my artless eyes while dropping the ring into my palm. "Place it
on your finger."

I could hear a bit of anguish as the steward endured in this matter. One special ring had been cast especially for him, but he felt
it better for me to be seen wearing it. Once again, he displayed
such desirable qualities, and it made me happy to have his
companionship.

"In consideration of the motive from which you desire me to do
so, sir," I replied, "I will gratefully comply with your request.
Truly are you proving yourself the friend which, on the most
memorable day of my existence. I petitioned you to become to
me, and it is now the most fervent prayer of my heart, that I may
live to merit your esteem."

Once I had slipped the large ring onto my finger, Radford clasped
my hand to get a better look. In doing so, he also pressed it in a
cordial and quite agreeable manner.

The morning of the funeral, Mr. Radford assisted me in habiting
the sable suit. The waistcoat felt a bit tight around the chest, but
otherwise it seemed very impressive, with its long tails that
draped nearly to my knees. I had never worn anything so rich
and smart before. In the mirror, I could hardly recognise the man
I had known just one week prior. I held up the hand with the
mourning ring, and its reflection caused me to smile.

We descended to breakfast, and just as Mr. Radford had seated
me at the table, a loud knock sounded upon the front door. We
looked at each other with raised eyebrows regarding the unanticipated caller. The steward turned and walked off. I heard the
door open and heavy steps upon the entryway stones.

"Mr. Graveton for Mr. Brown," Radford announced. Moments later, both men entered the dining hall. "Does the doctor desire some breakfast? I was just preparing to serve the young master."

Comporting himself with an expressive countenance, as if he were the bearer of some extraordinary or unexpected intelligence, Mr. Graveton intoned, "A sombre good-morning to you, Mr. Brown. It is no matter of trifling import that brings me so early to Ashbank Hall on such a prominent morning. Given the events of the day to come, I do not wish to be overburdened with the exertion of unnecessary digestion, and perhaps a small, light meal might best serve my particular situation." He glanced at me with a stern expression that transmuted into one of his obsequious smiles. "If you have ample supplies, that is." He turned to Mr. Radford. "A rasher or two, sausage–if you have them–a couple of eggs–whichever style is easiest for you–with toast and jam, and some morning coffee if it is available, thank you, my good man."

The doctor seated himself across the broad table and took stock of my new suit. His gaze quickly dropped to the large ring on my hand, and one of his eyebrows arched curiously. His expression changed to one of concern, and I began to wonder the true reason for this unexpected and rather abrupt call.

Mr. Graveton then addressed me, "I considered that you might feel interest in being informed, that I yesterday evening saw a person who was very particular in his inquiries relative to your deceased mother and yourself."

A few moments passed as I awaited him to continue. Once it appeared that he had paused to determine my interest, I replied, "Indeed, sir. Pray who might this person be?"

He summoned his snuff-box. "Why, sir, I have seen a considerable deal of the world. My observations on mankind have not passed without reflection, and I regard myself no mean judge of character." A pinch went to his nose, and the box returned to its pocket. "However, I confess that it would puzzle me to guess either the rank or disposition of the being whom I have just mentioned to you." With a measured eye, he once again observed me briefly. "Give me your patience, sir, for a few moments, and I will acquaint you in what manner we met, and what passed between us."

Mr. Radford appeared with a large tray. From it, he placed on the table in front of us plates with eggs, bacon and toast. He then poured steaming coffee from a small carafe. After he placed the jam pot between us, he withdrew.

"Last evening, Mr. Brown"—the doctor resumed as he began to spread jam on toast—"I was engaged to meet two or three friends at the Black Bull, and as I was passing the kitchen-door, in my way to the parlour, I saw several persons collected around it, whose countenances, and broken expressions of surprise, informed me that they were contemplating some object which excited their wonder." He paused to take a few crunchy bites. "As I was on the point of inquiring the cause of their admiration, I heard a mild but manly voice within the kitchen pronounce, 'Is there anyone here who can inform me whether the widow of a serjeant Brown, who, I have understood, had relations in this village, and her son John, are in existence?'"

Upon hearing this information, I almost choked on the bit of coffee I had begun to take. When I stopped coughing, Mr. Graveton continued.

"The farmer Tomkins answered, 'The widow Brown has been long dead, but her son John is alive, and the richest man in the parish. He has just fallen into a great fortune and estate.' My curiosity was raised. I stepped forward, and standing in the middle of the kitchen, I beheld one of the most extraordinary figures that ever —"

His face went pale and his eyes fixed. I followed his gaze over my shoulder and out the window to the lawn.

"Why there!" He stood and pointed outside. "There, I declare, is the very being of whom I have been speaking!" Mr. Graveton turned to me. "He said he should request to see you to-day."

I rose and walked to the window to behold a figure calculated to inspire us with the sensations of surprise. The mysterious stranger appeared to be remarkably tall. His silvery-white hair fell upon his shoulders, and his beard—of a corresponding hue—descended to the midway of his breast. A white hat with a short, flat crown and remarkably deep verge shaded his countenance from the rays of the morning sun. A loose white habit confined by a belt of russet leather rippled slightly in the faint morning breeze. Upon his feet I could see shoes made from a material similar to that of the leather belt. In one hand he carried a peeled staff, upon which he leaned. The other hand held one end of a cord that fastened to the collar encircling the neck of a white goat. Much like a loyal dog, the goat demonstrated fondness by gambolling and licking its master's hand.

The white-robed man advanced with a slow and majestic step. As he drew nearer the Hall, toward which his eyes pointed, it became possible to observe his expression. While given to age, one could detect the remains of masculine beauty in the face, furrowed by many a line of sorrow and dejection. I could, at once, grasp that he appeared venerable, commanding, and interesting. The intelligence of his features seemed to apologize for the eccentricity of his garb and deportment.

I walked out to meet the gentleman alone. Mr. Graveton and Radford remained inside. As I approached the stranger, I began, "Understanding you to be a friend of my late parents, I beg that you will enter the abode of their son without ceremony and join us for a morning meal."

He merely glowered at me, and his expression hinted that he searched the very depth of his very soul for a response. His lip quivered, suggesting he checked a painful emotion.

After a minute, I repeated my invitation, "Please come inside and join us for breakfast."

"Young man," he answered at last in a mild but decisive tone, "these gaudy mansions are not for me. I have long since abjured them." A moment of reflection passed. "I shall not detain you long. The communication I would have with you is short, and I beg that it may be held on this spot."

I turned behind to see Mr. Graveton and Radford standing in the open door observing the passing scene. When I returned to the stranger once again, I could see that he also took note of the steward and doctor, and he had receded a few paces from the steps, the goat in close proximity. The mystifying fellow beckoned me to follow. I waved at the men behind me to assure them of my safety, and they withdrew. Once the door had closed, I complied with the request and approached my curious visitor again.

"Your parents are both dead?" he inquired.

"Yes."

"And you are suddenly become the possessor of unexpected wealth?"

"I am."

"Beware then, young man, how you use it. Riches are only given to man in trust for the dispensation of good to his fellow-beings." He raised the hand holding the staff and pointed a finger toward me. "An account of your stewardship will not fail to be required of you in a world to come. *Remember* that it *may* be demanded of you in this. Therefore, sleep not over your charge, I enjoin, I *command* you. And so, farewell!" He turned to depart.

His authoritative oration raised so many questions within me. "Quit me not in this mystery. If you are the friend of my deceased father, accept from his son some offering, as a proof that he knows how to value those who respected his parent."

The stranger halted and turned with a softened expression. "What could I accept at your hands from which I should derive benefit? Society I have long since relinquished." The colour began to rise in his face, a sharp contrast to its pale surroundings. "It is intercourse with mankind which breeds superfluous wants, and from these I am exempt in the solitude which marks my days. Once more farewell, and forget not my instructions!" He began away but suddenly stopped. "There is one thing I will accept of you." He glanced down at my hand. "Give me the ring which I see worn upon your finger in respect to the memory of your benefactor. You cannot, young man, respect him more than I do."

I could see the barest of tears start in his eye. With little thought, I drew the ring from my finger and presented it. The mysterious man received it, and as he took it, he pressed my hand firmly in his. "Now farewell, *perhaps for ever!* Attempt not to follow me. The shade of your father commands you to obey me!"

As he and his attendant goat walked quickly away, I stood watching his progress until he passed out the gate from the lawn onto the high road. He never glanced back, and I remained in place, filled with wonder and almost with dread.

Some minutes passed before I felt able to return to the Hall. I found myself no longer hungry, and I heard voices coming from the library, where Radford stood next to Mr. Graveton, who examined various volumes.

"Ah, Mr. Brown. Tell us of your visit with the White Man," Mr. Graveton prompted.

"The White Man?"

"Yes. That is what the others have named him, and it seems highly appropriate, given his dress and his choice of comrade."

"I see. Well, he claimed to have shared society with my adopted parents, the Browns, as well as the late Mr. Clarington."

Mr. Radford glanced down at my naked ring finger, and I followed his gaze.

"Ah, yes, the ring." I took a moment's pause to determine an adequate method for explaining my actions. "I had offered to give the gentleman a token of respect for having known my parents; however, he chose to have the mourning ring, as he claimed he had more respect for the deceased than I did." Radford squinted at me, suggesting some anger and resentment at my action. "Given his speech, I felt I had no other recourse."

Mr. Graveton cleared his voice with a couple of sharp hems. "Mr. Brown, may I call upon you to confer upon me a most inconceivable happiness? If you would permit me to avail myself, in part, of my lamented friend's bequest before we quit the Hall."

After a quick glance at Radford, I responded, "Please explain yourself, without reserve."

"Allow me, sir." The doctor picked up from the library table a quarto prayerbook. "This volume always accompanied Mr. Clarington to church. Please allow me to claim this as a portion of my legacy, and to enjoy the unspeakable satisfaction of making it my companion in my attendance on public worship this morning." He patted the cover reverentially.

"You must be aware, sir," I replied, "that I have no authority, and let me assure you, I have no inclination to impose any restraint upon your choice." Mr. Graveton smiled. "I beg that on this point you will consult only your own feelings."

The doctor bowed and placed the coveted volume under his arm. The three of us walked to the church together in silence. Mr.

Radford held the box of mourning rings, and Mr. Graveton carried his prized book and a proud smile.

As Mr. Clack delivered a fairly humble sermon, I glanced about for any sign of the so-called White Man. Given Mr. Radford's disdain for my action, I had hoped to repossess the mourning ring, should the fellow be amenable. The steward had predicted that all eyes would turn to me, and he had been quite correct in that. Each person, in turn, smiled at me whenever my face pointed in their direction.

Following the sermon, I quit the pew and moved toward the church-door. Many of my former acquaintances thronged round, presumably in hope of being honoured by my notice. Others hung back in silent observation of the passing scene. Any of the villagers who greeted me received a smile, a nod, or a shake by the hand. All together, this proved my first public appearance as the new lord of the manor.

When farmer Tomkins approached, I implored of him, "Could you please make inquiries regarding this stranger, the White Man as they are calling him, as to whether he had left the village, and what conduct had been observed whilst he remained in it?"

"Oh, master Brown," Tomkins answered, "I believe no one has seen the White Man since last evening. After having advanced several questions relative to Mrs. Brown and her son at the public-house in the village, he departed without refreshing himself, and he had not returned again. From what I heard, he did not lodge in any house in Oldham. I only wish I could tell you more."

Mr. Clack had heard this interview and approached. "You are discussing the appearance of the strange White Man, are you not?" He looked at me and I nodded. "Well, let me tell you that early this morning I caught him—and his scrawny goat—wandering the churchyard. He asked after the grave of Mr. Clarington, and I pointed it out to him, as it has no marker by request of the deceased. I stood watching in awe as he fell on his knees by its side and bowed his head upon the green turf covering the grave. He remained on the spot, in silent prayer, I would imagine, until he quit the grounds a few hours back."

He had visited Mr. Clarington's grave before approaching the Hall, the sentimental, old character. Perhaps this White Man knew more of my past—and my future—than I did. At that moment, I said my own silent prayer that we should meet again, if only to assuage my fascination.

Chapter Four:
The First Volleys

ONDAY BEGAN THE BUSINESS of commanding Ashbank Hall. Based on my previously-held discussions with Mr. Radford, I called upon each of the land's tenants to assure them I would renew their leases upon the same advantageous terms on which they held them during the lifetime of Mr. Clarington. Each, in turn, thankfully accepted and provided me with samples of their wares.

Following my excursion throughout the property, I met with the remainder of the domestic staff to announce there would be no change in employment. The maid and cook, who both seemed older than Radford and bordering on the ancient, gleefully accepted the news. However, the stable boy decided to leave his position immediately, stating he did not wish to serve one younger than himself. This turn caused me no anguish, as I found him rather haughty and generally unattractive. I instructed Mr. Radford to employ a more agreeable and comely fellow.

Throughout the rest of the day, callers arrived hourly to compliment and congratulate me. Some issued invitations to exchange visits, as had been the practice under Mr. Clarington.

While the steward and I dined together that evening, I examined the stack of cards left behind. "Radford, have you any recommendations on the propriety of accepting all of these invitations?"

"By all means," he responded quickly, "I recommend you to do so without hesitation. You are destined to live with them on friendly terms. Should you decline their society, they will perhaps judge your conduct to proceed rather from pride than a contrary feeling." He glanced both ways before grasping my hand gently. "If you entertain any scruples respecting the station of life in which you have hitherto moved rendering you, in the first instance, as you may imagine, inadequate to your appearing to advantage in superior society, let me assure you, that with the exception of the doctor, Graveton, there is not an individual in this place whose education has been superior, or whose manners are more refined, than your own. The only difference is that fortune has hitherto placed them as far above you in the scale of affluence as you now exceed them in wealth and expectation. Besides, you will never be without me at your elbow, for I am in the habit of visiting all these people, and they will, no doubt, invite me when they do you."

I shuffled through the veritable pack of cards, not knowing which were trumps and which were merely ordinary. "Have you any suggestions as to where to begin?"

"If I might recommend, young master, the physician, Mr. Dickens. I plainly perceive why he is thus early in his invitation. He has long endured great mortification at Mr. Graveton having been the medical adviser of the late Mr. Clarington. By shewing you the first attention in his power, he no doubt wishes to secure you his patient." He smiled weakly. "You will clearly discover—when you have paid one or two of the visits in agitation—that it is with truth they express themselves on their cards when they request the honour or favour of your company."

"Indeed." How fortuitous for me that Radford held my best interests in his considerable and warm heart. "I hardly know the man outside of the Black Bull. Do you maintain any history of the fellow you might be able to impart to me?"

Mr. Radford smiled pertly. "It would be my honour, sir, to enlighten you upon Mr. Dickens's story."

As we continued to dine, the steward informed me of the physician's charmed life. Born to poor farmers, upon his father's death, he was bound apprentice to a surgeon and apothecary in Stamford, Lincolnshire. Following his termination of articles, he opened a shop in the small town of Louth. Fortune supported him with one hand while she deserted him with the other. His concern eventually failed, and as he stood locking the door to his practice for what he thought might be the final time, a blind votary approached seeking the attentions of a medical man to attend a patron. The forty-three-year-old widow Belton, née Molly Burkitt, had sprained her ankle and sent the monk for assistance. At that time, Mr. Dickens was merely twenty-three with seventeen shillings and sixpence in his pocket. The widow's jointure provided two hundred fifty pounds a-year. Mr. Dickens worked his way from the woman's ankle to her heart, and the young man's kindnesses soon set her upon her legs. The widow then set the physician on his legs by proposing a marriage.

Molly Burkitt Belton, now Dickens, had herself fallen into fortune when, in her twenty-second year, she caught the eye of an old farmer. After twelve years of marriage, she became widowed with a handsome independence for life. While Mrs. Dickens possessed one of the best temperaments and best hearts, her language tended to the coarse and vulgar.

The pair removed themselves to Oldham a few years later when an advertisement in the newspapers sought the successor for a retiring physic. The situation required one hundred pounds for the goodwill. Mrs. Dickens immediately paid, settling in a trice, and they left sleepy Louth behind.

The following evening, Mr. Radford and I walked to the Dickens home. He sounded the knocker, and the door opened in a second by a footboy enveloped in a blue woollen apron that descended all the way to his toes.

From another part of the home rang a shrill, female voice, "Bob, you dog! How durst you go to the door wi' that dirty apron *afore* you?"

The footboy turned away, "*Whoy, Missus*, I were helping our Bridget to make the *to-ast*, and so for 'fraid I should grease my breeches!"

"*Breeches*? Indeed! Hold your tongue, you Cheshire cat!" came the snarling reply. "Speak another word if you dare." Mrs. Dickens appeared and conducted us into the parlour. "I sure hope you allow me to apologise for the vulgarity of the *sarvants*."

As described by Mr. Radford, Mrs. Dickens seemed rather a distance from demure. Her wardrobe defined a woman of comfortable means, a modest, floor-length grey pelisse. The home also indicated comfort, with padded chairs and divans.

In one of the Hepplewhites sat an elderly female, tawdrily dressed in gewgaws that appeared to have metamorphosed from one fashion into another. In compliance with the giddy freaks of the Goddess of *ton*, her costume defied rank. She rose as we entered, a self-conceited and smirking countenance occupied her face.

"That is my cousin from Lincoln, Miss Niobe Nettle." Mrs. Dickens indicated.

I watched as Radford took her hand and kissed it lightly. Miss Nettle's eyes lit at the affection. After I had duplicated the steward's actions, our hostess indicated seats for us.

"I am sure, M*u*ster Brown, I am monstrous obliged to you for the favour of this visit," Mrs. Dickens drawled. "I am quite ashamed M*u*ster Dickens is not here to receive you, but people in the doctor line has so m*o*ny calls abroad that I hope you'll excuse him, but he *moight* have been here by this time too." She rang a bell and Bob appeared. "Go and tell your master that M*u*ster Brown has been here this half-hour, and see for what he do'ant come down stairs."

The footboy made a minimal bow. "He'll be here *inter*mediately, *missus*, for I were up *steers* just now wi' his *shoen*, and he'd got on his breeches, and –"

"*Breeches* again, you varlet!" roared Mrs. Dickens, snatching up the hearth-brush. "Let me hear that word once more and I'll let you know where yours hang, I promise you!"

Bob instantly flew behind the door and retreated from the apartment. I had the feeling that he and the hearth-brush were no strangers to each other.

Mr. Dickens appeared a few minutes later. At the same moment, a knock sounded at the front door. Mr. Tomkins, his wife and daughter appeared, and the apartment began to get rather small.

I had only seen Mrs. Tomkins the few times she came to the Black Bull to retrieve her husband. Although her stature lacked in height, her chatter made up for it.

Their daughter Jane I had never met before. An every-day kind of girl, her nature and appearance seemed tolerable.

Everyone else had previously made the acquaintance of Miss Niobe Nettle, and no further introduction proved necessary. Everyone took a seat, and only a few remained.

Mrs. Tomkins, who had removed and carefully folded up her black satin cloak trimmed with catskin, spoke, "I beg your pardon, Mrs. Dickens, for being so late, but I have had the *chimbley*-sweeps this morning, and you know what a house is when they have been in it." She began to unpin her worked muslin apron. "And you know I always have an eye to everything that is going on myself. I never trust servants any farther than I can see them." A side-glance at Bob caused him to exit quickly. "No, no, I have cut my eye-teeth, and been long enough in the world to know their pranks."

"One would think you had been in the oven yourself, dear," remarked her husband, "as the old woman said when she looked for her daughter."

She shook an admonitory finger. "None of your slapping and jeering at me, Dick Tomkins. I am sure you are indebted to me for the best part of what you have got. Late and early I have been out of my bed, to make you what you are." She nodded curtly. "There is more got by saving than toiling—I know that—though there is toil enough in saving. I know nothing more laborious, for my part. My poor mother used to say that there was nothing could be done without trouble, except it was sitting by the fire till you let it go out. And I remember I made answer and said to her, 'There is the trouble of lighting it again then, mother,' and heartily did she laugh at my remark, you may depend upon it. She was the cleverest woman I ever knew, I will say that of her, though she was my mother, and taught me all I know." A tight smile appeared.

"Like mother, like daughter," Mr. Tomkins said with a wink at Mr. Radford.

His wife did not reply. Her look became one of the greatest concern as she rummaged in her pockets. "Why, Jane, if I don't think I have come away without the key of the pantry!" she addressed her daughter. "If I have, I shall go back for it to a certainty. I am robbed enough with my eyes open without leaving my doors unlocked."

"Mother, you gave me charge of it before we left." She held up the missing key for all to see.

"Oh, I remember—I remember now!" Her mood began to subside. "But I am so flurried, what with one thing, and what with another, that I sometimes think I shall lose my senses." She turned to our hostess. "If you'll believe me, Mrs. Dickens, ma'am, I have not been myself since it rained all last week at our *great wash*. I was almost *muddled* to death, as well as grieved to the heart, for the coals it consumes to dry within doors is unaccountable, as every considerate housekeeper knows."

Mrs. Dickens nodded in agreement. "We must take the good with the bad. Neither wind nor weather puts me out. I always think grumbling over sores only makes 'em sorer." She smiled, then frowned. "I wish the Clacks would come, for it is almost seven o'clock, and I want my tea. I generally *sups* mine about six, and I am like the man's tabby cat, I look for it when the time comes."

As if Heaven answered her prayer, a loud knock at the front door preceded the arrival of the Clack family. The curate, his wife and daughter entered. Mrs. Clack blended quickly into the wallpaper pattern. Their daughter, Jemima, seemed to have inherited all the fire her mother lacked. Radford had informed me she had only recently returned from a Lincoln seminary of the first eminence. Aside from being more than an ordinarily-handsome girl, I heard she had knowledge in all fashionable accomplishments, such as French, drawing, music, dancing, fancy-work, embroidery, and a few other trivial acquirements.

"Come now, who'll come and help me to make tea, whilst I pour out the coffee?" Mrs. Dickens questioned. "Will you, Miss Clack?"

Miss Jemima stood and replied, "I am shocked to death to be so *uncommon* rude, as to find myself under the necessity of refusing your request, but I have been so *uncommon* nervous all day. If I were to lean my head over the teapot for five minutes, the effluvia would shatter me to pieces." She sat.

Silence prevailed. Mr. Radford and I exchanged bemused little smiles at the girl's impertinence.

Mr. Tomkins picked up the dropped gauntlet. "Well, I am sure it would be a great pity to see you tumble to bits, Miss. I dare say my Jane can take the task off your hands without any injury to her nerves—or her noodle either." He turned to his daughter. "Come, Jane, go and lend Mrs. Dickens a hand with the tea."

Jane stood and took her place in silence at the tea-table.

Mr. Clack cleared his throat audibly. "My daughter studies herself to death. In spite of all the cautions I give her respecting her health, I do believe she was full two hours at her drawing and music this morning." He smiled at Jemima with parental pride.

"And *my* girl," interjected Mrs. Tomkins, "was five hours and a half at the ironing-board this morning, and yet she is able to pour out a dozen pots of tea, you see, Mr. Clack."

The curate smiled upon his favoured child. "Health is an enviable blessing. My poor Jemima has been in a very delicate state of health ever since she returned from Lincoln."

"Have not I, pa?" Miss Clack drawled out. "*Uncommon* so?"

"Yes, my dear," answered her pa, with an assenting nod.

Suppressed smiles appeared round the room.

"Miss Nettle," Mr. Dickens quickly changed the conversation, "what can you share with us regarding the appearance of the country you might have observed on your journey?"

"Oh! Beautiful! Exquisite for the time of year!" answered the elderly lady. "I think I never remember such an autumn as this." A wrinkled smile possessed her face. "The weather was so fine, and the prospects so delightful, that for miles together I was tempted to travel on the box. A friend of mine, who drives four-in-hand, himself brought me to Grimsby just this morning."

"I know him very well, ma'am," Mr. Tomkins acknowledged. "And a very fine-hearted fellow he is, as any man on the road. I was in Grimsby myself this morning, and saw you come in. Yes, there is not a man in his line bears a better name than Joe Snap that drives the Lincoln Telegraph."

Miss Niobe's face coloured and she fidgeted on her seat. She bit her lip, but answer made she none. Once again, suppressed smiles made the round of the room.

The first cup of tea went round as well, silence prevailed, *à-la-mode Anglaise*, with the commencement of the meal.

At the resignation of her last empty cup, Miss Jemima Clack dropped her fan and directed her eyes at me, as she had done frequently throughout the evening. Not wishing to seem the lout, I rose, with an expression of extreme complacency, lifted the errant fan from the ground and presented it to her.

"Oh, dear, Mr. Brown!" she exclaimed. "You are so *uncommon* polite. I have given you such an immense deal of trouble. *Je vouz demandez mille pardon*, but perhaps you don't talk French, Mr. Brown?

"I am sorry to say I have not that advantage, ma'am," I replied.

"Dear, what a pity!" she batted her pale eyes. "For I have some such *uncommon* beautiful French charades on my fan–you might try for a week, and could not guess them." She smiled at me with a whiff of superiority. "I'll endeavour to explain some of them to you, if you please—you can't think how entertaining they are. Pray, Mr. Radford, have the politeness to change places with Mr. Brown for a few minutes, that I may shew him these riddles."

"Some riddles are easily guessed," whispered farmer Tomkins to Mr. Dickens but loud enough for all to hear.

My steward stood, with one admonitory, squinting eye, and I sat next to Miss Jemima, as requested. She raised her fan and motioned for me to hold it conjointly. None of the indecipherable characters inserted into the design of her fan made any sense no matter how many times she attempted to describe them to me.

Bob rolled the tea table away, then he and Mr. Dickens produced the card table. Mrs. Dickens proposed, "How about a round game, such as the *animating* game of Commerce?" The others assented, and the table shifted to the space directly in front of me and Miss Jemima.

People called out their desires: "Trade two!" "Trade three!" "Trade two!" "Corner!"

"'Nation!" cried Mr. Tomkins, "I needed but one for Butter."

"Language, Mr. Tomkins," warned Mrs. Tomkins. "Besides, how can you lack but one when we trade in twos and threes?" She shot him a stern glance.

Mr. Dickens confessed, "My luck appears worse than yours, Tomkins. None of my cards even match!" Everyone else laughed.

"Perhaps you could make yourself more useful, Mr. Dickens, if you would fetch some cream-a-tartar from your shop so I can finish up brewing this punch," his missus requested, and the physician stood up and ran out at a sprightly pace. "That he should be a fool to buy lemons when cream-a-tartar was just as good, and in their line they could get plenty of it for almost nothing!"

Following the final hand of Commerce, Mrs. Dickens rang the bell, and Bob appeared. "Tell Bridget to start frying up the fish and to serve up supper as soon as it is ready." The footboy dashed off. "Well, M*u*ster Brown," she proclaimed after gazing at the game scores, "it appears that you are the conqueror this evening."

"This is what I little expected," I responded, attempting to sound as sincere as possible. I had been genuinely not attempting to corner at all, but the others kept trading me matching same suits.

"Here's your pool winnings, M*u*ster Brown." Mrs. Dickens placed a bowl full of coins in front of me. Feeling a bit like the famished King Midas, I hoped for a meal soon to be served not made from metal.

"Ah, Mr. Brown! You know you are Fortune's favourite," simpered out Miss Jemima.

"I wish I may never prove Fortune's fool," came my reply.

"La! Mr. Brown!" returned Miss Jemima, "I am sure there is not anybody else in the world that would ever have thought –"

Bob burst in, mouth wide open and his eyes almost starting from their sockets. "Oh, Lud-a-mercy, *Missus*, there's such an *accidency*! Help, master, help! Our Bridget will be burnt alive as sure as death! She's flaming like a torch! Help! Help!"

Mrs. Dickens ran toward the kitchen followed by all the males of the party. In the middle of the room stood poor Bridget, screaming, arms raised above her head, surrounded from her waist upwards by a blue, sepulchral flame.

While everyone just stood gawking and gaping at the fiery spectacle, I seized the blanket hanging on the back of a nearby chair and threw it over the shrieking damsel, patting down and extinguishing the flames.

However, removing the blanket revealed the chimney itself on fire. The girl had put it up as a screen for a couple of ducks roasting in the hearth. Grease from the frying pan had caught flame and blazed with hellish fury.

"What is to be done?" cried Mrs. Dickens. "The whole house will be on fire! What is to be done?"

The farmer Tomkins stepped forward. "Have not you a gun in the house?"

"Yes, yes, yes!" exclaimed Mr. Dickens, who had just returned with the previously-requested cream of tartar. He reached behind the kitchen-door and produced a long-barrelled Barnett trade gun.

"Is it loaded?" asked the farmer as he grasped it from the physician. Mr. Dickens nodded vociferously. "Then we'll soon have the fire out." He stuck the barrel up the chimney and fired a shot. The ladies in the parlour screamed as one. A volley of soot from the chimney descended upon the raging fire, squelching it handily. "All's safe now." He handed the gun back to our host.

"Heaven be praised!" responded Mr. Dickens as he returned the firearm to its resting place.

"But look at my ducks!" bellowed his wife. "They are as black as a boot! As I am an honest woman, they are both an inch thick of soot! Never, never, *were* the like of this seen, I am sure!"

Mr. Dickens administered to the cook's scorches, which turned out to be of a less alarming nature than we had surmised. Mrs. Tomkins and her daughter proceeded to attend poor Bridget to bed. Mrs. Dickens, with the assistance of her cousin, Miss Niobe, prepared to serve up the supper. The remainder of us returned to the parlour. Miss Jemima continued the attempt at teaching me the French riddles.

In little more than half-an-hour, Mrs. Dickens and her cousin invited us into the supper-room, where so plentiful a show of cold dishes presented themselves to our view that it almost seemed superfluous in our hostess to apologise for the absence of her fish and ducks.

At supper, a silver ornament in the centre of the table—a recent present to Mrs. Dickens—caught all of our attention and admiration. Miss Nettle spoke, "It is certainly very pretty, but if you had seen the service of plate I sat down to one day last month, at a christening dinner given by a friend of mine in Lincoln, you never would have forgotten it. I do declare I never saw so much elegant plate in one house in my life before."

"Yes, yes, ma'am, I know just whom you mean," Mr. Tomkins offered. "Mr. and Mrs. Score keep a very elegant hotel up the hill, and no doubt require a very large assortment of plate. Very good sort of people they are who shew favour, without pride, to all who have served them faithfully. I know they had a christening last month, and I have no doubt you were at it."

Miss Niobe bristled and fumed. "We don't mean the same people, sir. I assure you we don't. By no means the same people." She stared down at her empty plate.

"Well, ma'am, well, I am satisfied," rejoined the farmer. He turned to Mr. Radford, sitting next to him, and whispered loudly, "Brag's a good dog, but Holdfast's a better."

Miss Jemima had once again wheedled her way into the seat next to mine. "Pray, Mr. Brown, do you know when the players are to be here?"

Not having any idea of what she meant, I flatly stated, "I did not know there were any expected." Her excess of charms began to wear quickly upon me.

"Oh, yes, sir! Mr. Clarington gave them permission—some time previous to his death—to perform here for a month, and it was imagined that they would commence somewhere about this time."

Mr. Dickens spoke up. "I think we ought rather to make the inquiry of Mr. Tomkins than Mr. Brown for, if I mistake not, I understood that they had engaged your large barn for their theatre."

Mrs. Tomkins answered before her husband had the chance. "Why, you see, sir, players are a kind of folks that I am not over fond of, I assure you, and besides know very little about, but as our barn was standing empty, and as they say the master of this company, the manager as they call him, bears a tolerable good name and pays his way, which I understand very few people in that *show line* do, I thought we might as well make a trifle of the place as let it lie idle." She glared at Mr. Tomkins in a way to sustain his silence. "And so I made a bargain with him for a month, and on the first of November I expect him to take possession. I am sure *play-acting* is a thing that I should never fool away my money to see—there's calls enough for what one has without throwing it away in that manner—but young people, like our Jane, are fond of seeing a little of what is going on, so I made an arrangement with Mr. Jag, I think they call him..."

"Gag, mother," corrected Jane.

"Well, Gag"—she glanced quickly at her daughter before resuming vigilance on her husband—"that me and my family were to go in all the time they were here, free, gracious, for nothing at all."

"Well, it must be *uncommon* laughable to see a play in a barn," Miss Jemima tittered. "Don't you think so, Mr. Brown?"

Her eyes attempted to pierce the battlements of my countenance, but the poor thing lacked the discernment to perceive my partiality toward the male sex. "I am unable to judge by comparison, ma'am, never having seen any but those exhibited in a similar place of temporary accommodation."

"Dear, what a pity," she decried. "I am *uncommon* surprised you don't go to Lincoln to see a performance. Mrs. Maria Davison is *so divine*, you'd be quite enchanted. Oh! I do think a play is the most *uncommon* pleasant thing in the world!"

"Well, I can't say as I think so much of a *pleay*," remarked Mrs. Dickens. "I never *see* but one, to be sure, it *were* when my first goodman were courting me. He took me with him to Tetney feast, and there were a *pleay*, and we went in to see it. For my part, and I am not over shy neither, I almost thought shame of Mr. Punch's goings-on with his wife *Joanee*."

"My dearest," began Mr. Dickens, "I must be the bearer of some unfortunate news, my darling." She turned to him with a look of scorn. "What you observed was not–in point of fact–a play, but a puppet-show."

"A bloody puppet-show!?" she screeched incredulously.

"Yes, my sweetest, a puppet-show... for children..."

"My, look how late it has gotten," Mr. Clack pointed to the tall clock, whose hands nearly joined at the top. Mrs. Clack's maid-servant had just arrived with her ladies' umbrella and clogs. A few minutes later came Mrs. Tomkin's ploughboy with two pair of pattens and a lanthorn.

We all made our good-nights and god-bless-yous. Miss Jemima Clack made one more futile attempt to garner my favour by pouting her lips and batting her eyes before turning her head away abruptly. If this was what men had to endure for the likes of women, my heart rested easily in the conviction that it would one day be in the hands of another like-minded man.

Mr. Radford and I took leave of our hosts and returned to Ashbank Hall though the late-night fog.

Chapter Five:

The King of Rags and Patches

SHORTLY AFTER SUNRISE, Mr. Radford appeared in my chamber. I had awakened a few minutes prior and lay in my bed–a bed of beds, as it were–thinking back upon the events of evening last. Reflexions of potential alterations in the habits of my friends and neighbours had paraded through my head since attaining the Hall, but having the Commerce pool handed to me forthrightly and the misguided attentions of Miss Jemima Clack absolutely baffled me. I had just begun contemplating the contribution of the ill-gotten coins to Mr. Clack's poor charity when Radford appeared.

"Well, my young master, have you not witnessed the fulfilment of my predictions?" He stood at the foot of the bed, a supercilious smile bedecking his ruggedly-handsome face. "Do you still entertain an idea that you had anything prejudicial to your own credit to apprehend from your intercourse with superior society?"

I smiled at his verbalising my thoughts. "I shall perhaps appear to you more vain than I really am when I confess that I hope my advancement in acquaintance with the manners of the world will ultimately lead me into far superior society to that to which I have hitherto been introduced."

"No doubt it will"–his smile transformed to a smirk–"but your visit last night was only one of the primary steps of ascension towards the eminence which you wish to reach. I dare say your knowledge of books, if not of men, will have informed you that the passions and motives of human beings are the same in every degree of life, only softened or concealed in proportion to the education with which the feelings and manners of those whose breasts they inhabit have been refined."

"My hours with Mr. Shakespeare appears to have been well-spent, my good sir," I responded. With so much time to fill during the days before Mr. Clarington's funeral service, I frequently withdrew to the library and read from the great Bard's plays, the whole of humanity splayed out before me, written into his pantheon of dramas, histories, and comedies.

"You cannot be but flattered by the marked attentions paid to you by Miss Jemima Clack?" The ends of his lips curled upward with tempered derision.

"I consider every man to owe a debt of gratitude to those persons, however dissimilar to his taste, who evince to him that he corresponds with theirs, but I am afraid Miss Clack's case is one of those where gratitude must form the line of compact." We both gave into laughter. "That poor girl had no idea, and I believe it best not to divulge my secret to her—unless ciphered within some French hieroglyphs!"

Our childish outbursts ended abruptly with a loud knock upon the front door. We shared startled looks, then Mr. Radford rushed out and greeted our visitor. "Mr. Graveton for Mr. Brown," he announced from below.

I drew on my plain cloth banyan and descended the stairs to meet my early-morning visitor. "Mr. Graveton, such an honour to receive you at this time." I reached forward and grasped his hand. "Please pardon my informal dress. Given the late nature of the evening's proceedings, I have espoused to borrow a few hours of this morning's time."

"Glad to see you both safe and well, gentlemen." He nodded to both of us. "Very well the house was not burnt down."

"Oh, it was a trifling accident, sir," I attempted to explain, "originating in —"

"People aspiring to what they have not the means of executing, Mr. Brown," the doctor interrupted to express his unsolicited opinion. He gave his nose a titillating pinch and added, "Yes, that was the origin, sir—between you and me." A wink punctuated the judgment. He glanced at Mr. Radford, then at me, but neither of us inclined to join him in ridiculing the feast of the preceding evening. "Hem. None of the Slapp family there, I suppose?"

"No, sir. The Clacks, the Tomkins, the Dickens, and the two of us. No Slapps at all," I replied.

"So I concluded," he resumed, "Slapp's two daughters and madam Dickens are fingers and glove—never had a party before in her life without them—you may depend upon it. The reason of their not being there was that the lawyer was ashamed to shew his face in your company, Mr. Brown, after his polite remark in the churchyard on the morning of our deceased friend's funeral." Once again he looked at Radford and me, but neither of us responded. "I am sorry to say nobody is very partial to that man. I don't wish my opinion to be retailed in public, but I don't mind what I say to you, sir."

My uncle once counselled me that if I ever wanted to say something that I did not wish repeated in public, it was best to keep it to myself. Mr. Graveton, apparently, had never been privy to my uncle's sagacious advice.

"Did he, or any of his family," the doctor forged on mercilessly, "ever call upon you, sir, since your residence at the Hall?"

I turned to Radford. "Mr. Slapp left his card one morning," the steward answered, "but did not ask admittance."

"There, there, there!" squealed Mr. Graveton. "That shows me that he is conscious. How can he be otherwise? For my own part, I never saw anything violently amiss of him myself, but does not it appear that our poor, recently-departed friend had an insight into Slapp's character, though he was too nobly-minded openly to confess it, when he employed a professional man from town, in lieu of our country advocate? Yes, yes, yes! Ay, ay!" He concluded with a long pinch.

The steward and I merely shot side-glances between us.

"The true motive for my untimely entrance today—as you might be speculating—is that I wish to select a few more volumes from the library." He began to walk away. The two of us followed him into the still-dark room.

Mr. Radford proceeded to open the shutters, allowing for sunlight to bathe the chamber in glowing warmth. We stood watching as the doctor strode back and forth, pulling several dusty books with cracked covers from the shelves and placing them upon the reading table.

I looked at the growing stack of Latin classics and placed one hand on the topmost book. "How much I regret, doctor, that these volumes are a dead letter to me!"

"You know not what you lose, sir. Indeed you don't," returned the doctor. "To be properly estimated, all works, especially those of Greek or Latin authors, should be read in their own language."

On a nearby shelf, I touched a few more-recent works. "I have derived so much pleasure from perusing the translations of some of the ancients —"

"A translation, sir," the doctor interrupted me, "is but, as I may say, the skim-milk of an author. Everything, in my opinion, Mr. Brown, loses by translation, but a bishop." He laughed heartily at his own joke, snuffed the remainder of his pinch, then continued. "You are a young man, sir. It is not yet too late for you to gain a knowledge of the original. Tutors may be had, suitable to every age. You can pay, and believe me, there is not a service on earth but what is saleable."

"No doubt masters might be found," I responded, "but I should consider it so much like grown-up gentlemen learning to dance, that —"

"Well, sir," the doctor interrupted me yet again, "and nothing either reprehensible or extraordinary in that! The late Marchioness of Cholmondeley, not a hundred miles from this spot, who, everybody knows, was a farrier's daughter in Cumberland, retained a French dancing-master in her house for three months previously to her introduction at court."

"Well, sir," I replied, attempting not to allow his impetuousness to get the better of me, "I have necessarily a great deal of leisure time on my hands, and I have almost resolved upon the experiment of attempting to initiate myself into a knowledge of the dead languages."

"Books and assiduity may do much, sir," the doctor answered, "and whenever you wish to call upon an animated assistant in your labours, believe me," he puffed out his chest, "that in me you possess a friend who flatters himself that he is tolerably competent, as well as willing, to facilitate your undertaking."

"I thank you for your very generous and kind offer, sir. Please allow me to deliberate upon it."

"Of course, of course." He strutted about the room, selecting the remaining volumes to total the nineteen he lacked. During this time, which absorbed nearly one hour, he continued to lecture me upon the contents of the various works in the library, making recommendations as to which should be tackled in what order to make the most of the antediluvian literature.

After seeing Mr. Graveton to his cart, Mr. Radford greeted me at the door, and I spoke before he had the opportunity. "You have already admonished me, sir, that, as my residence is in this place, it is desirable for me to live upon terms of friendliness with all its inhabitants." I stepped inside and the steward closed the door behind me. "Mr. Slapp's having avoided meeting me at Mr. Dickens's, where it appears that he is a constant guest, evinces him ashamed of the foolish expression which escaped his lips in the churchyard." Mr. Radford cocked his head. "Having left his card with me, it fully bespeaks him desirous of a reconciliation. You have informed me that there is a new lease required for farmer Horton's land. Let Mr. Slapp be employed, in my name, to draw it out–a circumstance which cannot fail to convince him that I bear him no resentment for the past, and may perhaps be the means of preventing future broils."

"I commend you equally upon your good humour and good sense," the steward stated and smiled. "I shall draw up the copies at once."

Twenty-four hours later, an invitation arrived from Mr. Slapp for dinner at his home. I felt gratified not being at variance with a single individual in the neighbourhood.

In the course of the next fortnight, Radford and I attended dinners and suppers throughout Oldham, as each of the neighbours attempted to outdo each other with their hospitality. The time spent at the homes of others seemed to total more than that I spent in my own, diminishing my capacity to take up the reins from Mr. Radford. In a manner, it felt as though I had attained satisfactory employment with an industrious metropolitan corporation. The holding of Ashbank Hall began to feel more vocation than avocation.

One afternoon, toward the hour of twilight, while Mr. Radford and I sat in conversation over the fire, the door knocker sounded. My steward returned holding a letter.

"A strange-looking man, with whom I am unacquainted, delivered this for you and is awaiting an answer." He handed me the dispatch, I broke the wafer and found the contents as follows:

I read the curious epistle twice and handed it to Mr. Radford. He raised one eyebrow then the other.

"It makes little sense to me," the steward confessed.

"To me either. I shall be the first to admit there seems to be an insufficiency in the way of protections or safeguards for this Hall, and any common scheming burglar could make their way in here utilising very little force at all."

"Mr. Clarington never had a fear of foul play. This village, as you know, hardly ever makes use of its beadle. Mostly for crimes of indebtedness, if anything."

"The message is clearly calculated to alarm us, but what actions can we–should we–take?"

"Perhaps we could begin by questioning the messenger." I nodded my assent and Mr. Radford revisited the front door.

A minute later he returned, followed by the most uncommon fellow. Remarkably-thin, of middle stature, with a sharp and intelligent countenance, grizzly hair, and an unusually-black beard, he wore a long, drab coat that appeared of a gender between the surtout of the coachman and the lank habit of the Quaker, adorned with white metal buttons the size of crown pieces. Beneath the coat peeped out a pair of spindle-shanks cased in black worsted stockings and a couple of stubby feet,

which were almost covered with an immense pair of brass buck-
les. With many bows and scrapes, accompanied by an equal
number of smiles and grimaces, hat of a Quaker style in hand,
the extraordinary personage approached the chair where I sat.

"Pray what do you know of Simon Pure?" I asked without prefa-
tory salutation.

"Dead perfect, sir," replied the stranger. "I may with confidence
say, you will excuse me, that I don't recollect ever to have required a word from the book in my life."

Radford and I stared at each other in silent astonishment.

"You have thought of *The Bold Stroke* then, gentlemen, eh?" resumed the stranger. "Could not have made a better choice—you
will excuse me, my wife is a charming Anne Lovely, and I defy
all the world for a colonel."

Every word he uttered conveyed a fresh mystery. Mr. Radford
stated, with an assumed tone of authority, "We require you, sir,
explicitly to inform us what is the meaning of the letter which
you just now brought to the Hall?"

"Your commands, sir, are quite a paradox," returned the little
man, "you will excuse me. You intimate that you have fixed upon
The Bold Stroke for your play. Consequently, I am quite at a loss
to understand how you can have misapprehended the meaning
of my laconic epistle. Positively I am, as my name's Tom Gag—
you will excuse me—"

"What?!" I exclaimed. "Are you Mr. Gag, the manager of the
players?"

"At your devoted service, sir, as my letter intimates." He bowed
low.

"Indeed, sir, your letter intimates nothing of the kind. Please
cast your eye over it." I handed Mr. Gag the paper.

As soon as he had begun reading, he immediately burst out in a
string of apologies: "Mercy upon me! Beg pardon down to the
ground! No offense meant, upon honour! Quite an error, you will
excuse me!" He made a contrite bow between each oath. "You
see, gentlemen, this is the simple fact: When I am full of business, I pay no attention to what clothes I wear—stage clothes or
street clothes are all one to me then. In our last town, we finished
with *The Bold Stroke* and I played Simon Pure in this very coat—

and a very good property I consider it, gentlemen—quite the Quaker's cut, you see—you will excuse me, and so, gentlemen, the letter for Obadiah Prim, the one inadvertently presented to you, has been in my pocket ever since, and I gave it to your steward instead of the one which I had addressed to you. Just look at the direction, sir, if you please—you'll excuse me."

He handed me the letter and I turned it round. On the back I found it superscribed, "For Obadiah Prim, Bold Stroke, Act 5th."

"You see, sir—you'll excuse me," Mr. Gag burbled and produced a second letter from his coat and exchanged it for the stage property. This one bore the direction "John Brown, Esq., Ashbank Hall."

Please do us the honour to attend and observe the first night of our company's performance.
Signed, Mr. Thomas Gag, Manager

I handed the paper to Mr. Radford.

We all laughed out loud at the confusion and whimsicality of the late adventure. I invited Mr. Gag to join us by the fire. Radford poured the Madeira and we discussed the requested patronage.

"Of course, of course!" I responded. "I am very much looking forward to observing your players. What shall we be viewing?"

"No less than a play *and* a farce, my friends! *The Poor Gentleman*, and *No Song for Supper*." He smiled broadly.

"We should like to purchase sufficient tickets for our neighbours, tenants, and servants, so that all may enjoy your impending entertainment in the barn which —"

"*House*, Mr. Brown—I beg pardon," Mr. Gag interrupted. "House. It has *histrionically* been named the house." He bobbled his head from side-to-side. "Although, this setting is but a pit and gallery, if you'll excuse me."

"My mistake to beg pardon from you sir," I responded. "The ways of the theatre are foreign to me, and I shall attempt to educate myself upon the finer details before making its further acquaintance."

"Yes, thank you, sir." He stood and bowed. "If you shall excuse me, the hour is getting late and I must prepare myself, as I will be required to give direction for beginning the process for printing of the bills. Good-night, gentlemen." Radford escorted our merry visitor out.

The night of the entertainment arrived, and more than half the village packed into the Tomkins barn, many at my expense. An old stone foundation and walls, Tomkins had installed new thatching a few years back, and the malodourous smell of animals could hardly be observed. The troupe had reserved a section at the front of the seating area for myself and the group of people I had given tickets.

Soon after we sat, Mrs. Slapp attempted to lead her two daughters, Lucy and Maria, in the direction of our seats. Her son, Gilbert—who had been away studying at law—clasped her arm, as he was her darling. From the progression of "Owws!" and "Ooofs!" trailing behind her, I imagined she caused great inconvenience of the toes of those who occupied the seats she forced her way between to approach the spot where we sat. With many *flim-flams*, she introduced them to each other, and some of the usual sentences that follow a ceremony of this nature, the Slapp family—who had entered the place late—could advance no further and had to find accommodation in assorted unoccupied seats.

Mrs. Dickens sat to my right, and Mr. Graveton sat directly behind her. "I never saw but one actor in my life, only one—the immortal Garrick," the garrulous doctor orated for anyone who would listen. "There was not a passion in the portraying of which he did not excel. The last time I saw him, he struck me more forcibly. Indeed, I repeat, that I never was so struck by any actor in my life."

"Passion, indeed, sir, say I!" came the unexpected cry from Mrs. Dickens, who craned her head round to confront Mr. Graveton full in the face. "I think an *actor-man* that gets his living by the public, *moight* have *knowed hissel* better *nor* to have struck a gentleman like you." She pointed at the befuddled doctor.

For his part, Mr. Graveton returned a scowl and a slight inclination of his head in silence at the misapprehension. However, Gilbert Slapp, who sat near enough to have overheard what had passed, stood up and clapped together his hands exclaiming, "A hit! A palpable hit!" All eyes round him turned to see who had spoken the *Hamlet* quote—the source of which I only knew from having days prior read the script in the Hall's library. He concluded with, "Shakespeare—hem!"

A very slender moiety of applause greeted him as he reseated himself. He glanced across to Mr. Graveton, who briefly met his eyes. The doctor then rapped his knuckles on the lid of his ever-present snuff-box before taking a proper pinch.

We all went silent as the curtain rose. Farmer Harrowby entered, having just returned from a visit to London. His wife and daughter approached. The farmed hugged his girl and passionately kissed his wife, who then announced the expected lodgers had arrived early.

"Hoy, *missus*, hoy!" cried out Mrs. Dickens. "Kiss *a*fore company! Oh, for *sheame*!"

Those around us tittered, and Mr. Dickens, who sat to her right, stretched forward his head to whisper loudly in her ear, "Hold your tongue, woman! This is all *play-acting*, you know. Don't be so daft!" Mrs. Dickens pursed her lips and turned her head toward me.

From the moment Miss Lucretia MacTab appeared upon the stage, I could hear Miss Niobe Nettle—who sat to the right of Mr. Graveton—snort, sigh heavily, and gasp. When I turned to look, her wry face had frozen into a sneer. From time to time I would look upon her, and these grimaces continued.

In his interview with the Caledonian virgin, Ollapod offered, "And man-midwife too, at your service."

"Oh, what a vulgar play!" exclaimed Miss Nettle. "I never heard such stuff in my life. It is not fit for delicate people to sit and see. If Mr. Gallipot had said such a word to me, when he attended me in Lincoln, I'd never have spoken to him again."

Gilbert Slapp, who sat to Miss Nettle's right inquired, "Pray, ma'am, was Mr. Gallipot a man-midwife too?"

"No, sir," returned the irritated Miss Niobe, in a voice almost choking with rage, "he was a gentleman, and I think there are very few in the world now-a-days."

Gilbert appeared to stifle a laugh, and Mr. Graveton seemed to relax after a brief shudder.

The play somehow managed to continue with no further outbursts from the audience assembled. The broad comedy could not have approached the level of Shakespeare, but an aspect of the performance I enjoyed most was one of the handsome young players with luxurious, golden hair. From the bill, I determined his name was Frederick Cavendish.

During the interval, I could hear Miss Nettle and Miss Jemima Clack arrogating themselves the right of pronouncing a decisive opinion upon the exhibition they had witnessed, as both had regularly visited the theatre in Lincoln.

"When Mr. Cavendish pronounced, 'A pointed pain pierced my heart, A swift cold trembling seized on every part,' and Ollapod remarked, 'That is an ague,' I thought, 'What a horrid man that is to interrupt such a beautiful idea,'" opined Miss Nettle, "and so eloquently spoken too, with such grace and good sense!"

I had to agree. I, too, felt a pointed pain piercing my heart as Mr. Cavendish delivered his lines so brilliantly. If only I could find a man like him to have as my own true love.

Miss Jemima replied, "And when he recited, 'But quickly to my cost I found, 'Twas love, not death, that made the wound,' and Ollapod added, 'Damn that disease that is cured without an apothecary —'"

"Pray can any of you ladies give me the receipt?" interrupted Gilbert Slapp. "I have positively been looking for it these hundred years. Is it in your family receipt-book, or amongst your private memorandums, Miss Nettle?"

"I consider the best cure for a sensible young woman's love a beardless coxcomb," spat Miss Niobe.

"What says Miss Clack to my inquiry?" Gilbert proceeded undaunted.

"I really don't know what you mean," returned Jemima. "I was so *uncommon* intent on the play, I... I..."

"It is my belief," offered farmer Tomkins as he approached, "that Miss Jemima has been trying to shew the very actor-gentleman some of the French riddles on her fan, for she has held it before her face, with her eyes peeping over it, all the time he has been upon the stage."

"La! Mr. Tomkins," she squealed. "You are so odd! I only held it before my lips, that the smoke of those horrid lamps might not get into my mouth."

Gilbert burst into a smothered laugh and pompously exclaimed, "'She never told her love, But let concealment...' Break off—enough! Shakespeare—hem!"

Twelfth Night, I thought to myself. It was the first play of the Bard I had read in Mr. Clarington's library. The line ends, "like a worm i' th' bud, feed on her damask cheek."

"I wish the gentleman would be so polite as to let us hear a little of the play," muttered Miss Nettle.

Silence reigned till the falling of the curtain at the end of the farce.

"The poor old Scotch lady has not got a husband after all," remarked Mr. Tomkins.

"'Tis a shame the comet did not offer her a dose of matrimony," returned Gilbert Slapp. "Had any one, ten times a Lucretia, cast such impetuous glances of love at me, I must, in honour, have married her before sunrise."

"And a pretty husband she would have," said Miss Nettle.

"Oh! That is granted, *nem. con.*," answered the young student of law, affectedly stroking his chin as he spoke. "But she would seldom see me, and so I should be the greatest treat to my darling when I did *luxuriate* her doting eyes with my presence."

Gilbert then sat next to me and batted his eyelashes as if wooing. Anyone looking on erupted into a hearty laugh. He then pointed to the flour-sack in which the character Endless hid during *No Song for Supper* and remarked, "That if ever there was a lawyer a rogue, the one in the farce must be allowed to be a rogue in grain."

While I did prefer the company of the gentlemen to the ladies, under no circumstance would I have considered Gilbert Slapp a gentleman.

One fine frosty morning a few days following the theatre event at the Tomkins barn, I walked through fields near the village with my gun. About half-a-mile from the centre of the town, I observed the handsome Mr. Cavendish leaning upon a gate, earnestly perusing a volume that he held in his hand.

I had by that time made a few inquiries regarding Mr. Cavendish, and my sources spoke of him as a young man of very retired habits who never mixed in public-houses, either with his brother-performers or the inhabitants of the village. He chiefly confined himself within his own lodgings at his studies.

At this accidental meeting, his clothing, although remarkably clean and neat, did not consist of either very handsome or very new habiliments. His features appeared to convey dejection of spirits and delicate health, with a suggestion of more fortunate days behind.

I had wanted to address the actor from the very moment he had appeared upon the stage. My resolve fixed, I struck a path that led me to the gate against which he leaned. "Good morning, sir," I began. "You are, I doubt not, employed in wearing your brains for our amusement."

Mr. Cavendish moved his hat with the air of a man acknowledging a superior, but without sinking into the meanness of fawning for my favour. "No, indeed, sir. With the exception of our invaluable Shakespeare, you will very seldom find a play in my hand by choice. The book I am just now perusing is a Horace."

More like than not, a similar volume resided in the Clarington library, but I had not yet conquered sufficient skills in Latin to flash or patter. "An English translation, I presume?"

"No, sir," responded Mr. Cavendish. "It is that celebrated poet in his native language."

How impressive. My estimation of the actor blossomed even further. "Indeed. I envy you a pleasure which I am not capable of enjoying. You give me a proof, sir, that you have reaped some advantages from education, which I have not been so happy as to receive."

"Edinburgh, sir. The Scotch are remarkable for the excellent instruction which they bestow on youth."

"Pardon me, sir, but I am tempted to believe that you have not always been in the situation in which I now see you?" Well-educated and well-done, there must be bene intelligence under the rose.

"Ah, sir!" He closed the book and faced me. "How many and bitter misfortunes not unfrequently flow from one unguarded action! The stage, sir, was once my glory, my delight. It is now my necessity and my aversion."

"If you dislike your profession, why do you not exchange it for some other mode of life?" Once I had spoken this interrogatory, I then realised the gentleman may have been like I was, brought into a vocation by inheritance.

"It may appear easy, sir, in theory to do so, but the attempt is attended with incredible difficulties, the least of which is by no means the want of friends." Mr. Cavendish turned his bright green eyes on mine, and I feared I might have swooned.

This quite comely fellow had played upon my heart, and I wished to attend him. At that very moment, I could not know how to make my inclination known without incurring the risk of wounding his feelings by a too-abrupt offer of service. Before this excellent opportunity dissipated, I issued a delayed invitation. "I shall be happy if you will come and pass a few hours with me at the Hall this evening."

Mr. Cavendish did not respond immediately. His eyes moved about and he swallowed once or twice.

"I should feel gratified in an opportunity of improving my acquaintance with you." I had never attempted to welcome a man I favoured before. My heart beat wildly.

"You do me honour, sir, but we have a performance this evening, which must deny me the pleasure you design me." He glanced down, and my heartbeat ceased. "To-morrow, if convenient and agreeable to you," he began again, "I shall feel great satisfaction in accepting your invitation." When he finished speaking, he began coughing violently and placed his free hand to his breast.

"I fear you are not well." He appeared to be in great pain.

"I am suffering, sir, under the effects of a violent cold, contracted in the inconvenient, and not infrequently damp buildings, in which my present profession compels me to make repeated changes of dress, when I am heated with the exertion of performing." He coughed a few times more. "I have been labouring under it for some time past."

"And have you received no advice for it?"

"Some old women's recipes, sir, which, you know, sir, are by some esteemed very efficacious." He sported a bit of a smile. "I must wish you a good-morning, sir, for it wants only a few minutes to the hour of our rehearsal, and we are forfeited for absence, a penalty which I must endeavour to avoid."

I did not wish to further ail the man. "Dine with me to-morrow, at three o'clock, without fail." I smiled at him and he returned the smile. "Till then adieu."

Mr. Cavendish again moved his hat and, with a respectful bow, turned into the road leading to the village.

In crossing the lawn, I met up with a servant I had seen having conversations with some of the comedians. "Mr. Bennet,"–I began and he halted–"do you know whether the players make out a tolerable livelihood here?"

"The manager does, I believe, sir." His eyes rolled up and his tongue protruded slightly as if in deep thought. "The performers are very badly off, indeed. Mr. Gag pays them in what they call 'shares,' sir, and he takes so much for his own expenses, and the stock debt, that they are well off if they get a dozen shillings a-week individually."

"Poor Cavendish!" my heart pronounced silently to itself. I addressed the servant once more, "Mr. Bennet, you never see Mr. Cavendish at the alehouse, do you?"

"Oh, no, sir!" came the hasty reply. "They all say he is too proud to sit in a kitchen or a tap-room on account he was once better off in life, and on this account, none of the company much like him, I understand, sir."

"Thank you, Mr. Bennet. Sorry to have bothered you."

"No bother, sir," he replied, "no bother at all." He walked off and I resumed my travels.

Chapter Six:
Our Maladies Unseen

AS I SLOWLY ADVANCED HOMEWARD TOWARD THE HALL, my thoughts solely occupied by the conversations with Mr. Cavendish, and then Mr. Bennet, a train of reflections ran thus: "This young man has received a liberal education. He is accomplished in those parts of literature in which I am deficient. He professes himself dissatisfied with his present situation and desirous of exchanging it for any other. Why should it not be practicable for me to engage his services for imparting to me that knowledge which I so earnestly wish to acquire, and devoid of which I shall never consider myself rigidly qualified for the station which I now hold in life?"

I had reached the gate to the Hall grounds, but my mind continued to fester with these thoughts. "His words and looks appear equally to betray the indigence and hardship of his present situation. I have never met another man of such natural beauty that stirred my emotions so. It is in my power to bestow immediate comfort on him by affording him my protection and friendship and to receive, in return, at his hands, a key to the treasures which I so much covet to possess."

Yes. If, upon further conversation, I still consider him as deserving of my regard as I now believe him, I shall state to him my ideas without reserve.

Once inside the great hall, I handed the unused firearm to Radford, and he ushered me to the dining-room. Upon the table, I observed a bill for the evening's performance at the theatre. *Douglas*, a tragedy well-known to me. I had once read it with pleasure and seen it performed by a company of actors inferior to those now exhibiting themselves in Oldham. At first I had no inclination to attend, but I noticed that Mr. Cavendish would play Young Norval, the hero of the piece. As the play is set in Scotland, and Mr. Cavendish had announced his Edinburgh education, I imagined he would not fail to prove a meritorious representation of the "noble shepherd."

While I supped on roasted potatoes and cold meats, I reviewed the lines I remembered from the work: "My name is Norval; on the Grampian Hills, My father feeds his flocks; a frugal swain,

Whose constant cares were to increase his store. And keep his
only son, myself, at home."

Mr. Cavendish did not disappoint. He acquitted himself in the
character even more to my satisfaction than in any part he had
yet sustained.

Before the beginning of the fifth act, a considerably long delay
took place, and the audience became impatient. Grumbles and
mild oaths rippled through the annoyed on-lookers. A stage-
hand appeared from around the curtain, and he sought out Mr.
Dickens, who happened to be in the house, and whispered something to him. They went behind the curtain together, and a
bustle could be heard, but still a few minutes more suffered to
elapse.

At length, Mr. Gag appeared and announced, "It is with regret I
am compelled to inform you that Mr. Cavendish has been suddenly taken so seriously ill that it would be impossible for him
to appear on the stage again to-night." A few audience members
stood and turned toward the door. "However, with your permission, our Mr. Smith shall sustain his character in the remaining
act, as soon as he is dressed for the part."

The folks who had started to leave returned to their seats. Grumbling ensued once again. This time, however, intelligence buzzed
through the place indicating that Mr. Cavendish had been taken
with a fit and that Mr. Dickens had ordered him to be removed
to the Black Bull, which was the nearest house to the theatre.

It being scarcely a stone's throw, I repaired thither immediately,
at the impulse of humanity and my genuine concern for the affections of Mr. Cavendish. On my arrival at the inn, I found Mr.
Cavendish attended by Mr. Dickens, Mrs. Dobbs—the landlady of
the house—and a few other individuals. It appeared that Mr.
Cavendish had recovered from his fit, and he sat in a chair. Unfortunately, he remained incapable of either speech or motion
and his limbs trembled violently.

"He should be put to bed immediately and every attention paid
to him," the physician ordered. "His situation is more alarming
than you might imagine, I believe."

I knew his lodgings at the small cottage incapable of affording the comforts of which he at this moment stood in need. "Find him a good bed here at the inn. I shall cover the costs of his stay."

"Yes, sir, Mr. Brown," answered one of the servers. "Straightaway, sir."

Within a few minutes, the others had placed my dear Mr. Cavendish in as comfortable a bed as the inn could afford. "What do you imagine to have been the cause of his sudden indisposition?" I asked of Mr. Dickens once the others had left.

"The immediate exertion of the hour operating upon a very fragile constitution," replied Mr. Dickens. "The fit with which he is said to have been taken was rather an overpowering faintness, which debilitated his entire system and withdrew the blood from his lips."

His once-beautiful and full lips now appeared pale and dry. "Does this account of his first seizure agree with the alarm which you just now expressed as to his situation?"

"You mistook me, sir," replied Mr. Dickens, "if you conceived that I alluded to any present danger. I only apprehend that without the greatest care is paid to him at this time, a constitution so weak as his is must fall the victim of neglect."

We sat with Mr. Cavendish. I took his hand in hopes of imparting the level of care so indicated by the surgeon. At length, our patient began to revive. He opened his eyes and fixed them upon me. His lips began to move, but no sound could be heard. I could only imagine he might want to thank us for our kindness. "Do not upon any account exert yourself by attempting to speak," I cautioned. "Rely upon every care and attention being shewn you here. I will see you again to-morrow and hope to find you greatly amended." A thin smile appeared upon his lips, which had begun to regain their lost colour. I stood to leave.

"Pray, Mr. Brown, please remain for a short time whilst I run home to prepare a medicine," Mr. Dickens requested. I nodded as I sat down next to Mr. Cavendish.

Mrs. Dobbs soon entered with a glass of warm wine and water. "The doctor directed this to be administered." She handed me the glass.

With one arm, I raised the invalid's head and applied the tonic
to his lips with the other. When he drew in a little sip, I smiled
warmly, and Mr. Cavendish smiled as well. We thrice repeated
the slender draught, and his eyes gained a slight degree of animation. More colour returned to his cheeks and lips.

Just as Mr. Dickens returned into the chamber, my new friend
pronounced in scarcely audible accents, "I am better... many
thanks... I am better."

"Again, I request you to avoid the exertion of speech," I advised.
"And lest you should attempt it, once more good-night."

As I passed Mr. Dickens, I whispered, "Pray, sir, omit nothing
which can be done to restore your patient. Remember that it is
me whom you are serving."

I motioned the landlady to follow me out of the room. "Let nothing be omitted or neglected which could tend to the ease or
comfort of the invalid. He should, by no means, be left through
the night. I am answerable for every expense incurred."

She nodded her understanding, and I went down stairs. Upon
entering the bar, I found there Miss Nettle and Mrs. Dickens.

"Why ladies, what brings you so far from your house? You have
left the theatre early, for surely the performance cannot be concluded?" I inquired.

"No, it is not quite done, I believe," answered Mrs. Dickens. "We
attend the m*u*ster and will accompany him home following his
physic ministrations." Miss Nettle nodded in accord. "As I am an
honest woman, M*u*ster Brown, I must confess I got tired, and so
I *comed* away. And what is more, I don't believe I shall ever go
back again."

"How so, ma'am?"

"*Whoy*, do you know, I never found out till to-night that it was
all sham and make-believe, but I have seen what it is now as
clean as my eye." Her gaze shifted to the direction of the barn.
"You must understand, M*u*ster Brown, there was one time to-
night when the *courtain* did not fall quite down to the ground,
and as I sat on the front seat, I could peep under it. There I *see*
the fine *squire Dowglass*, as they called him, that had just been
stuck with a *swurd*–and pretended to die–jump up upon his feet
and run away as nimble as a rat, as much alive as I am." She

exhaled a heavy sigh. "Oh! I hate such *flim-flammery make-believings*! It has taken away all my pleasure, and I really don't think I shall go *no* more."

Miss Niobe smiled in silence, but I failed to suppress a laugh. "Well, ma'am, if you'll only promise to honour the theatre with your presence again, depend upon it, we'll try and persuade Mr. Smith to die in good earnest the next time he performs in tragedy."

Mr. Dickens descended the stairs and approached us. "I have discovered my patient's disorder, sir," he announced. "And I am happy to inform you that I now entertain no farther apprehensions for his safety. He is attacked by an ague, sir—a complaint which very frequently visits strangers to this part of Lincolnshire, especially those who do not enjoy a strong constitution." For some reason I could not discern, he smiled at me. "The first shaking fit is not upon him. I ran down to give you this intelligence because I guessed you might not yet have left the house, and I flatter myself I shall be able to rid him of his troublesome companion in a very short time."

The surgeon then returned to his patient, and I could return to Ashbank Hall satisfied that the fate of my intended tutor lay in good, competent hands.

Each of the days following Mr. Cavendish's indisposition, once I had completed my manor obligations, I walked to the Black Bull to inquire after his health. Mr. Dickens, being the prototype of assiduity and attention, attended my friend faithfully. He would not allow me to visit until he deemed his patient had recovered sufficiently.

Finally, on the fifth day, the surgeon announced that Mr. Cavendish could receive my attentions, but only for a few minutes.

My heart leapt with joy at being able, once more, to see my new friend. He appeared thinner and paler, but I had every faith in Mr. Dickens.

For the next week, I would visit and bring some delicious treat or other from the Hall's kitchen for the recuperating Mr.

Cavendish each day. With time, he regained his powers of speech, and we began to have regular conversations.

Eventually, I discussed my plan to have him become my Latin tutor. "Once you have finished your period of rest, you will want of proper employment, and, from what you have described to me heretofore, the life of an actor has affected your health in an adverse aspect." He shook his head in accord. "Let me suggest a scheme I have been considering that might benefit the both of us. You will have need of lodgings, and I shall have want of education. With your approval, I invite you to take up residence in my home in exchange for lessons in language."

"I shall consider your kind offer, sir," came the curt response, and I could not measure the state of his sentiment from this unanticipated answer.

My hope had been that my frequent attentions might stir within him reciprocal affections. Perhaps I had been blinded by his fetching features and tantalising talents. Would I continue to wear my heart on my sleeve, like the poor moor, Iago?

One day, Mr. Gilbert Slapp honoured us by calling. Mr. Dickens had not yet arrived, which differed greatly from his usual course. Gilbert interrogated the suffering actor with a multitude of questions regarding life upon the boards. How much did it pay? Where did he travel? Which cities played best? How many women awaited him following each performance? Did these women ever request bits of his clothing as souvenirs?

At long last, the surgeon appeared, slightly out of breath. He stood directly before Mr. Cavendish and asked, "Pray, sir, is your Christian name Theodore?"

"It is, sir," came the reply. "May I ask if you had any particular reason for your inquiry?"

"Will you, in return, consider me impertinent if I answer your question by advancing another?" Mr. Dickens posed.

"Pray proceed, my good man."

The surgeon stood upon one foot then the other as if uncomfortable with the subject matter to be discussed. "Ummm, sir, have you a pair of leather unmentionables in which your name is marked with a pen?"

"I have such a stage property," answered Mr. Cavendish without reserve.

Gilbert Slapp pulled out his pocket-handkerchief and applied it to his nose.

"I dare say," continued Mr. Cavendish, "they are in this room, as my trunk from my former lodgings and some articles which I had left in the theatre were all brought thither when I changed my abode."

Young Mr. Slapp tittered and crammed part of the handkerchief into his mouth.

"Why, sir," resumed Mr. Dickens, "a maiden lady, the cousin of my wife, who is from Lincoln, was on a visit at my house…"

Gilbert burst into a smothered laugh, snatched up his hat, and ran out of the room.

"Ah!" commented the surgeon after the student at law had departed. "I have, no doubt, seen the rogue who has been the author of all the mischief." His eyes followed the abrupt departure. "Please allow me to explain." He sat next to the bed. "Evening last—or more likely early this morning—I had just returned from ministering care to an elderly lady who was about to replenish the earth. As I ascended the stairs of my home, I smelt fire." My eyes opened to their widest. "After the recent episode at our dinner,"—he glanced at me—"I wanted no more to do with any such conflagration. A whiff of smoke escaped the door to Miss Niobe's, and I opened it using a rag from my pocket. Upon entering, I discovered the dame asleep, seated at a table, her head in contact with a burning candle. The flame had communicated itself to her wig, thus providing the combustion I had detected."

"And so soon after the burnt dinner," I added.

"Yes, indeed. I snatched the quilt from the bed and enveloped Miss Niobe's sleeping head, similar to your method in the kitchen, Mr. Brown." He smiled. "The stamping and shrieking aroused the missus, and she came a-running into the room. 'What in Heaven's *neame* is the matter?' she exclaimed. 'To be sure my husband haint been trying to be rude to thee, Niobe?'"

Mr. Cavendish and I exchanged smiles.

"I explained to Mrs. Dickens about the extinguished fire and withdrew the quilt, exposing her cousin's bald skull. Miss Niobe ran to hide in the bed-curtain. '*Whoy*, speak, I say, Niobe,' cried the missus, 'what is the meaning of all this? Up at work at this time of the night! What is this lays here that thou'st been working at?' We examined the table and discovered an old pair of leather breeches which she had been engaged in applying a new seating, employing part of the arm of a kid-leather glove."

"*My* breeches, sir?" inquired Mr. Cavendish.

"Indeed, sir. Inside of the waistband, marked with ink, barely legible, we read the name 'Theodore Cavendish.'"

"I do confess, my good doctor, I am utterly ignorant of the circumstance. Perhaps you could be so good as to search for my small-clothes in my belongings there." Mr. Cavendish pointed to the trunk beneath the window.

After a few minutes of rummaging, Mr. Dickens admitted, "No, sir, I can find nothing of the sort."

"I shall once again protest my innocence," Mr. Cavendish decried. "Perhaps that young knave who hastily departed played some role in this curious drama."

"My thoughts exactly," agreed Mr. Dickens. His gazed moved to a table on the other side of the bed. "Ho! What is this?" He walked around and picked up a jar of preserves. "I recognise this as one Miss Niobe brought with her from Grimsby. She is celebrated for her conserves and never arrives at our home without a few containers of her choicest fruits." A piece of paper slipped from around the jar. "And what is this, pray tell?"

The three of us looked on as Mr. Dickens unfolded a letter. Upon it, indited in a spidery orthography, it read thusly:

Amabel sur,

The extasys you have poured into my suseptibel sole by your malodorous vice has made me bould to dress you. I ham in the injoiment of a smal anity, the witch, if you think well and hapi to quite your presen ardus purfeshion, and unit your fate with mine, I ham reddi to fli with you to the land of luve and liberty at gretna grin, and make you the sol lord & master of me and hall I as. Slight not this, or you will desolate

"I believe it is now apparent that two of my companions have been hoaxed by Mr. Gilbert Slapp," the surgeon spoke. "If you two shall excuse me, and by your leave." He turned and withdrew.

"Well, what can we make from that?" I asked.

"I can only surmise that during my many hours of sleeping, and after the good doctor had departed, the young rogue entered this room, discovered my breeches and delivered them to Mrs. Dickens's cousin with some sort of counterfeited protestation of my affection." He turned his beautiful green eyes upon me. "Tell me, my good Mr. Brown, is she plain, this Niobe Nettle?"

A bit of a laugh escaped my lips unbidden. "She is elderly."

"Oh, my," sighed my friend. "And eagerly believing the deception, she made attempts to repair my breeches and sent a jar of preserves accompanied by a letter of troth." He cutty-eyed the doorway through which Gilbert Slapp had made his hasty retreat. "At the very least, I shall have well-mended small-clothes and some very delicious jam."

We laughed together.

When one spends so many days with a person, you begin to anticipate those times when you can be in their company once again. Over the weeks I continued to visit with my dear Mr. Cavendish, a waxing warmth enveloped my heart. My hope would be that he might feel similarly-inclined, as we had spent all these hours conversing and making better our acquaintance. However, I did not wish to inconvenience him with my budding romantic sentiments. If spoken too prematurely, it might cause him to deteriorate further, and I wished him to make his home in my residence as quickly as possible.

By mid-December, the players had quitted Oldham, and Mr. Cavendish had so far recovered his health that Mr. Dickens pronounced it as his opinion that he might quit the chamber at the inn without the fear of a relapse.

As he had no place of his own, I spoke, "If I might propose, your first walk should be to Ashbank Hall."

"Yes! Indeed. I should like to see it for myself, given all you have told me of it."

"Leave your things here, and I shall send for them later in the day."

"Shall we?" He indicated the doorway, and I watched him descend the stairs with a renewed vigour, providing to me some assurance of his recovery.

We strolled, at a bit of a slower velocity than my usual striding pace, out the high road. Radford met us at the front door, and escorted us into the library, where he had set a comforting fire against the autumn chill.

"Thank you, Radford. Could you send for some hot chocolate?" I instructed. "Mr. Cavendish,"–I resumed once the steward had departed–"Do you recall my offer requesting your tutelage in Latin?"

With a smile, he responded, "Of course. It has been difficult for me to think of nothing else. Your constant kindness and generosity shall be difficult to repay."

"Think nothing of it, sir. It has been my utmost pleasure to play some small part in you regaining your lost health." I waved a hand at the contents on the shelves of the room. "There are so many volumes a-waiting our perusal. It might be difficult to determine the proper place to commence."

"I should be honoured and flattered by such a charge. However, all I fear, sir, is that I am too young to undertake the important charge of tutor to a gentleman who has, like yourself, long passed the age of adolescence. I am only in my twenty-second year." He dropped his eyes to the floor.

"I shall not complete my twenty-first till a month hence," I replied, "but the seniority of years I regard as being of little importance in the present instance. You are decidedly my senior in knowledge, and, therefore, I desire to become your pupil." My smile most likely described the other position in my life I wished him to assume. He had, up to this point, given me no indication of his particular affections.

Mr. Cavendish glanced up at me. "Well, sir, it will, at any hour, be at your option to withdraw yourself from my tuition, should you find either my abilities or my assiduity undeserving your farther countenance."

My mind filled with fancies of sharing my very large home–and, perhaps, my very large bed–with him, as well as fulfilling my desires to find love and affection with another like-minded gentleman. His humble ways, despite all of his knowledge and talents, drew me even nearer.

I reached over and grasped his hand, shaking it cordially, but not releasing it. "You have made me very happy, and all I hope is that you will find yourself as comfortable as I am certain your society and instruction will render me." Our eyes met, and my heart went to ice.

He gently pulled his hand away. I had not even been aware that I had held it captive during my speech. His eyes lowered to the floor once more.

"Mr. Brown," he nearly whispered, "you have been ever so kind to me. Paying for my lodgings and meals, paying me visits every day, but I must now confess something to you that you might not accept with glee."

Perhaps he felt the same way but harboured uncertainties regarding me. I had tried, at every opportunity, to demonstrate my affections for him. He had shown himself to be shy and reserved. I had thought actors to be more free with their emotions in everyday life. Mr. Cavendish had certainly displayed his talents in expressing the feelings of others on the stage. What could he possibly need to express?

Chapter Seven:

An Actor's Tale

P RAY, PROCEED, SIR," I admonished, "as I believe it best if
there shall be no secrets between you and me." His eyes
remained downcast, and I sustained my hopes that,
because of my budding adoration for him, his issue would be that
of a possible devotion between us.

"My dear, Mr. Brown," he began slowly, "and know that you are
very dear to me for all of the quite liberal services you have heretofore bestowed upon me." With his face still pointing to the floor,
his intelligent eyes looked up at me. "I do believe, sir, that our
society has somehow sparked an endearing intrigue."

Yes, to be cock-sure, it has indeed. The moment I had hoped for
might soon be at hand.

"And I wish to declare, sir,"–he stumbled in his speech, very unlike his confident delivery at plays–"my undying affections for
you,"–with every pause my hopes grew greatly–"as a friend, nay,
as a brother or some such other close relative." He raised his
head level with mine. "All I fear, with the deepest of respect,
would be your disappointment in this revelation to you."

Ah! It might have been love, after all, but not the variety I had
sought. Confessing my more romantic affections to him would,
in all probability, embarrass us both. "Of course! I feel the same
with you, sir. It would have been benish folly, simply squirish,
otherwise." He smiled and sighed. "Yes, it is my fondest hope
that we continue on the same shared paths together with regard
to our mutual benefits."

"Yes, indeed." He reached out his hand to me, and instead of the
common shake, I grasped his wrist, and he grasped mine, a sign
of mutual respect and trust.

We had cleared away the brambles, but my emerging desires to
become romantically involved with Mr. Cavendish would need to
be suppressed for this prescribed arrangement to continue.

Before I could apply balm to my wounded heart, he spoke again.
"I have one thing more to premise before we ratify our agreement." He paused, but I did not respond. "The generous and

almost unexampled friendship which you have extended towards me, a stranger, would render it unpardonable, were I to withhold from you the knowledge of any circumstance which might at a future period cause you to repent the conduct you had pursued."

I gazed over at his brilliant green eyes and billows of flaxen hair wishing I could possess them for myself, but our differing realities dictated another course. Did he sense my disappointment?

He began his account, "I am ignorant who were my parents. I am also suspicious that there is a mystery connected with my birth, and upon the possibility of its tending to my dishonour or discredit, if it should hereafter be revealed, I wish you to reflect deliberately on the possibility of such an occurrence before you receive me as your inmate and companion."

My own situation is somewhat similar. The parents who brought me into this world were unknown to me, and there was some mystery as well. "It must be an illiberal mind indeed," I responded, "in whose opinion any transaction which had occurred previously to your entrance into existence could affect your reputation."

"The world is not so candid in its judgments as yourself, sir," he rejoined, "and it would hurt me more than I can express, if I should at any time become the innocent means of subjecting you to its animadversions on your choice of a friend."

How kind Fate had been introducing me to two such noble men as Mr. Radford and this new friend. Given my unexpected change in fortunes, I would have expected more the likes of rogues and scoundrels to cross my path.

"I must, however," he continued, "request that you suffer me to relate the little which I do know of myself. The events of my past life are unworthy of detail, but the relative circumstances in which it is your wish that we should be placed towards each other render it an indispensable duty in me to reveal to you every circumstance, however trivial, which is connected with myself."

Mr. Radford returned with cups of chocolate, placing one before each of us. "Would you allow Mr. Radford to join us? He should know all that I know."

"Yes, of course," responded my new companion. "I was going to relate to our Mr. Brown the events of my life so that he would be familiar with my history, should the need arise."

"Please sit, Radford. I believe I see a third cup." I smiled at the steward. He took an empty chair.

After we all took our first sips of the heartening beverage, his story began. "The name by which I had known myself, from my first dawn of knowledge till the unfortunate moment which enlisted me in the train of Thespis, is David Ferguson. The name Theodore Cavendish is my assumed title for the pursuit of my public avocation."

Radford and I shared expressions of mild surprise.

"My first memories are of my fifth year. I have no memory of my parents or whether there were any siblings, but I alone resided at the house of a matronly lady of a most respectable appearance and interesting manners in Edinburgh. She was preparing to relinquish management of a preparatory seminary for junior boys on account of her advanced age. Her name was, like my own, Ferguson, and I sometimes called her aunt, and sometimes mother, although she appeared infinitely too old to be the latter." He smiled at the thought. "Whether the affinity of blood existed between us, I am to this day unacquainted; however, it was evident that she took a lively interest in my welfare and was my only protectress. I continued to reside with her even after the other scholars had quitted her, and I was never introduced by her to any relative of my own, if she were not one."

"If I may," Mr. Radford spoke, "this Miss or Mrs. Ferguson allowed you to remain at her seminary even after all the other boys had moved on?"

"Yes. It does seem rather odd looking back," Mr. Ferguson—as I shall refer to him henceforth—responded. "The only person with whom she appeared to be upon terms of intimacy was a Mr. McCarteny, an old gentleman, who, I was afterwards informed, had seen better days, and to whom she extended every act of kindness her circumstances, which were by no means affluent, would permit. When I had arrived at an age to require more elaborate instruction, my education proceeded under the supervision of Mr. McCarteny, by whose advice I was placed in a Greek and

Latin academy. In addition to a knowledge of the Classics, I developed some insight into most branches of useful acquirement."

Even though Mr. Radford had met our visitor many times during his stint at the inn, and I had discussed my scheme to make him my tutor, I still felt the need to say, "Mr. Cavendish–I mean Ferguson rather, beg pardon–is to be my Latin tutor." Radford merely nodded.

"Often I asked my good old protectress of my parents. She always replied with evasive answers and endeavoured to turn my thoughts to some other subject. I awaited with impatience the arrival of the hour which I anxiously hoped would withdraw the veil of mystery that was now so sedulously spread before my eyes."

He paused for another sip of chocolate. "One Sunday evening, Mr. McCarteny invited me to take a walk with him in the King's Park. As we strolled along, he informed me that as I was in my fourteenth year, it was time to remove me from school and fix a plan for my future life. I told him I had given little thought to the subject, but if I ever should know my father, he might influence my choice by his advice or guide it by his authority. Mr. McCarteny cast his eyes upon the ground. I asked him if he had ever seen my father or if he could inform me who he was. He told me that he was not even acquainted with his name. It was the only secret Mrs. Ferguson kept from him all their years of society, except to say she is a distant relative of mine, and that every necessary information concerning my parentage would be revealed at a proper age."

Again, Radford and I exchanged surprised glances.

"I told him that I would consider my vocational options and give him my reply at the end of the week." He lifted his cup to take some more hot chocolate, but it proved empty.

"Mr. Radford, could we please have some more chocolate?" I asked.

"Certainly, sir." He stood, collected the empty cups and returned to the kitchen.

"On the afternoon of the following Wednesday, a half-holiday afforded myself and some of my schoolfellows an opportunity for a ramble on Leith Sands," Mr. Ferguson continued his tale. "It was a delightful day, and we lingered away the hours till the looming of twilight. As I approached my home, one of Mrs. Ferguson's servants ran up to me uttering an exclamation of thankfulness at having found me. A few hours before, her mistress had taken so violently ill that her speedy dissolution was apprehended. She and a few other persons had been searching in all directions in the hope of meeting me, as Mrs. Ferguson had repeatedly declared that she had a disclosure to make to me, without which she could not die happy."

"Perhaps she was to reveal your true parents," I suggested.

"The secret of my birth did flash on my imagination, and I rushed with all the impetuosity of a madman to the house. Mr. McCarteny greeted me at the door, mournfully shaking his head, and informing me that I had come too late."

My hand went up to my mouth. How tragic to miss out on the desired information for want of a few minutes!

"I flew to her bed, her eyes closed and every appearance of sense had vanished. I seized her cold hand and pressed it to my heart. With grief unbounded, I burst into a flood of tears. Not only had I the sudden privation of her from whom alone I had ever received maternal affection, but I suffered the disappointment at having been absent from her at the moment when I might have received the information for which my heart so ardently panted."

I reached over and grasped his hand. Hearing what he had experienced drew me even closer. Given my own history, I would have wanted to dispel the mystery of my parentage as well.

"Thank you, Mr. Brown, you are indeed a great companion." He wiped at a tear before continuing. "I eagerly inquired of Mr. McCarteny whether any expression had fallen from her lips explanatory of my birth or connexions. He replied that he had arrived in her last moments, and that she appeared to wish to make some communication, but her strength had seemed too much exhausted for the effort. All he had been able to gather from her had been some inarticulate and broken sentences: 'He shall be saved–trepanned–deceived–basely deluded–oh, Heaven! Heaven! Lend him thy–oh, my poor cou…' Mr. McCarteny suggested she might have been attempting to say 'cousin,' but the word died on her tongue, as it was her last."

"Oh, my!" I exclaimed. "It is wonderful and curious that you still retain those final words all these years later."

"I have oft repeated them to myself in an effort to make better my understanding of them. Due to the unknown ending of her final word, I inquired of Mr. McCarteny whether he had ever known any cousin whom she had possessed, and his response was that he had never known any relation of hers. His acquaintance with her had been the consequence of a connexion in trade which had formerly existed between her deceased husband and himself."

I withdrew my hand as Mr. Radford returned with the tray. His eyes quickly darted to our unclasping hands, and he gave me a stern look before serving the chocolate.

"Thank you, Radford," I said with a smile. "Mr. Ferguson just concluded that his protectress died before relating the knowledge she held of his lineage."

"How terrible!" expressed the steward.

"This, sir, is all I know, or am, I fear, ever likely to know of my mysterious existence. Although the extreme ardour I once felt to solve the enigma has, in some degree, been blunted by dwelling on the apparent improbability of such a disclosure ever meeting my knowledge, it still frequently fills my mind with anxious and unpleasant feelings."

As we took our sips, I added, "You may, perhaps, at some unexpected moment, gain the explanation for which you thirst." I raised my cup to him. "It is perhaps at the present hour only withheld from you for some happy end. The best advice which I can give you is to live resigned in that belief and in the expectation that your wishes will yet be accomplished."

Mr. Ferguson replied only with a deep-drawn sigh.

"But come," I prompted, "I must request a continuation of your adventures, as I feel desirous of hearing all that has befallen you before we met." Mr. Radford nodded.

"Notwithstanding I am conscious that I have nothing to relate which can reward you for your attention, you certainly shall, if you wish it, receive the outline of my follies and wanderings." He paused for another taste of the chocolate. "After the interment of

Mrs. Ferguson, Mr. McCarteny informed me, that with the exception of a legacy to himself, and another to her servants, she had bequeathed to me her whole property, amounting to between six and seven hundred pounds. Once again, he inquired of me what avocation I had determined to pursue. Now that I had the security of a small fortune, it provided me the opportunity to study for a profession."

"You studied drama for a profession?" I blurted out.

Mr. Ferguson laughed out loud. "No, dear friend, my choice was directed to the profession of the law. My two favourite companions were brothers, Duncan and Roderick Monro, and they had informed me that if I did select the profession of the law, they would have me received into their father's office. I placed my inheritance in a trusted friend of Mr. McCarteny who would disburse the funds as required."

"You were a solicitor?" It seemed incredible that this rather pleasant man could have ever been draped in the robes for a son of prattlement.

"Four years elapsed, during which, by my diligence, I had the satisfaction of gradually ingratiating myself into the favour of Mr. Monro, and which period of time fleeted away unmarked, except by the daily occurrences of life. With time, I learned that Duncan was naturally dull, idle by disposition, and inattentive to his father's concerns, whilst Roderick, though of an active temper and shrewd mind, which he evinced on the odd occasion for the exercise of his profession, still gave a loose to the reins of pleasure, which always made *business* a secondary consideration in his thoughts."

"How sad that these children did not wish to continue upon the golden path their father had set for them," Radford commented.

"Indeed, Mr. Radford. When Mr. Monro died suddenly, the two brothers inherited the office, and with easy means, gratified their inclinations while displaying neglect of their business affairs. The friendship with which they had treated me as schoolfellows had never abated during the lifetime of their father, and it inevitably increased as I maintained the family business single-handedly, being intimately acquainted with their affairs."

"I do hope they demonstrated to you their appreciation," I asserted.

"Yes, they did. They allowed me to accompany them to their parades in Prince's-street and their rides to Portobello, but it was the winter assemblies at the theatre that was to be my favourite place of amusement." He took another sip. "One evening, about a year after the death of Mr. Monro, the three of us attended a performance of *Venice Preserv'd*, with the unrivalled Mr. Kemble playing the role of Jaffeir. His presence so moved me, that I unconsciously burst aloud into an apostrophe of admiration. The words, I recollect, were, 'I should think myself the greatest and happiest man upon the earth if I could sustain that character like its present representative!'"

With a smile at his enthusiasm, I wondered, "It must have been something amazing, I should imagine."

"The following morning at breakfast, Roderick said, 'From your exclamation in the theatre yesterday evening, you are undoubtedly become a very great stage-amateur, and I should not be surprised to see you shortly sporting your figure in a private theatre.' I laughed mockingly, 'That you will never do, depend upon it,' came my reply. 'But I see you as great as Kean or Kemble,' Roderick returned with a laugh. After some consideration, I responded, 'If a man of talent would study for the stage, why should he not rise to the eminence in that profession—much like the two celebrated heroes of the buskin whom you have just named—as well as in physic, law, or divinity?' Our conversation was here broken off, but I think, Mr. Brown, I have said enough to convince you that my soul had imbibed all the wild romance of theatrical knight-errantry."

"But I do believe, my dear Mr. Ferguson, there is so much more to this particular tale," I observed. "Wherefore else would we be sitting here now discussing the events which brought together our quite disparate lives?"

"You are quite correct, Mr. Brown. My visits became insensibly more frequent to the theatre. A short time after the Kemble performance, Roderick and myself were invited to a public dinner at which we met some of the principal members of the Edinburgh company. In the warmth of wine, he introduced me as a stage-struck amateur, which led to conversation between myself and the comedians, interlarded with many persuasions on their part for me to make an experiment of my abilities. Subsequently, I frequently passed my evenings in the public rooms to which theatrical performers and admirers of the drama resorted. At length, I consented, for the benefit of a Miss Benjerfield—a considerable favourite in the Edinburgh company—to make my appearance on the boards."

"I can only imagine how magnificent your first appearance. If only I could have attended," I mused.

"Given the opportunity to make my own choice, I fixed upon my favourite Jaffeir. After many tremblings and quakings in rehearsal, at length arrived the night 'big with my fate.' I moved from the green-room to the stage like a felon to the stake whilst the performers crowded to the wings to witness the event of my temerity."

"How brave you were to appear in public so," I commented. "I do not believe I could ever be capable of such an act."

"Think me not vain, for I consider it one of the greatest misfortunes that could have befallen me, when I inform you that my *début* was crowned with every token of approbation which could communicate triumph to the heart of youth." Mr. Ferguson paused for a bit of chocolate.

"I only wish I could have been there to witness your initial success." I also took another draught.

"But, alas! With my success, I found that pens and parchment, if they employed my hands, were no longer capable of fixing my mind. I felt the office a restraint and experienced an anxiety for company and conversation." He looked away as if far-off voices had called in his ear. "From that time, I began to concentrate more on my life upon the boards than at the office. It was about six months later that Roderick left me a note saying he decided to close the business and that he had quitted Edinburgh with Miss Benjerfield, whom he intended to marry." He turned back with a smile. "However, he did compliment me profusely, considered me born for the stage, and gave me every wish for my prosperity and happiness."

"How marvellous for you!" I chimed.

Mr. Ferguson sported a pout. "At first, the excitement carried me, but whenever I made an attempt to hire on at other houses of law, I was confronted with the knowledge of my exhibitions in the theatre, which conduct proved a serious disadvantage, as well as having been associated with the Monros. With my small sum of money and collection of dresses, I joined with a company under the direction of a Mr. Ferretter using the assumed name of Theodore Cavendish. We played at Aberdeen, Banff, and Inverness, but instead of increasing my fortunes, I found my purse growing ever thinner."

"Such a reversal of fortune, say I."

"Indeed."

Mr. Radford stood. "Young master, shall I inquire the cook as to your supper?"

I looked across at Mr. Ferguson. "Are you staying the night?" He nodded with a grin. "Yes, thank you, Radford." He began to walk off. "Oh, and please do us the honour of joining us."

The steward smiled and exited to the kitchen.

"That is quite the tale, Mr. Ferguson. I am gladdened that you have decided to remain here with me. We can begin our studies in the morning."

"If you can abide me, I have one more adventure to share before our meal," Mr. Ferguson entreated.

"What? More?" I roared with a great smile. "Play on, sir, play on!"

"We wintered in Inverness, a miniature London, if you will, and the weeks rolled by. One February afternoon while sitting in my lodgings, a letter was brought by the town post. My landlady handed it to me while suggesting it might be a Valentine, as it was the fourteenth of February. Once she had left I looked at it closely. The seal bore the impression of two doves and a scroll inscribed with the words, 'Dinna forget.'"

"And forget you 'dinna.'" I laughed at my own joke.

"Yes, well. When, upon opening the paper, to my surprise, as you may easily imagine, out dropped two fifty-pound banknotes."

"A hundred quid?!" I exclaimed.

"Indeed. If this be a quizzing correspondent, she pays well for her amusement, I thought, and is welcome to repeat it as often as she pleases. I shan't share with you the entire contents, but just know that the lady expressed her appreciations for my performances but proved too shy to approach me in person. She begged me to accept the enclosed trifle and that she did not trust herself to write me again. Assuring me that it was utterly impossible for me to discover who she was, she signed herself, 'my devoted Alicia.'"

"My! A secret admirer. And one who pays well! Huzzah!"

"Suffice it to say that my brain was on fire to discover my Alicia, whom I already loved by instinct. When on stage, I endeavoured, but in vain, to single her out from amongst the numerous lovely females who adorned the semicircle of the boxes. When in the street, I cast a scrutinizing eye towards every female as I passed but read nothing in the countenance of any one which could render me suspicious that I beheld my correspondent. At length, I inquired of my landlady whether she knew any woman, either in the town or neighbourhood, whose Christian name was Alicia. As she had been the principal monthly nurse for thirty-five years thereabouts, she would have known all of the rising generation. Unfortunately, she could not recall any young lady who bore that name."

"How curious," I offered. "If anyone could have assisted you in your quest, it should have been her."

"Thus passed on five weeks of torturous suspense, when, as I was one evening quitting the theatre enveloped in a plaid cloak and bearskin cap, with two or three silk handkerchiefs wound round my neck as precautions against my increasing a cold and sore throat, a person in a large, buttoned-up driving-coat with a deeply-verged hat drawn over his face addressed me directly with my own name. I acknowledged my identity and he thrust a small parcel into my hand before he ran out of sight in an instant."

"How curious."

"I rushed into my lodging with a rapidity which made my old landlady stare. I lost not a moment in examining the parcel. I saw it had been directed to me with the same handwriting as Alicia. Inside, I discovered a small box which held a handsome gold watch, chain, and seals, but beside them lay a billet. It was from my dearest, and she informed me that she would be setting out for Edinburgh in a few days for the benefit of medical advice.

90

The trinkets were to be the last gift and a token of remembrance.”

My face became a grimace. “How frustrating in her to disappear like that. I can only imagine your longings.”

“Every possible inquiry which I could make of private individuals, at livery-stables, of post-boys, or at inns, were insufficient to gain me intelligence of any family who were about to quit Inverness for Edinburgh. When a fortnight had elapsed in these vain attempts, I concluded that she must have departed, and I sunk into a state of ‘melancholy musing’ which my acquaintance, both in and out of the theatre, did not fail to rally me. How true their conjectures when they pronounced my malady love.”

“With no foreseeable cure,” I suggested.

“One evening I overheard the conversation of two gentlemen standing in the *arcana* of the theatre. They discussed a Mrs. Mandover as a decidedly cut, frequent attendant in the stage-box. The accusations included lots of rouge and a large plume on her jetty *tête*. A certain Colonel Percival approached and their conversation halted. He was a tall, handsome man of about forty years of age. In his company were two ladies. One was a completely dashing woman of *ton*, an imposing and well-turned figure, whose age appeared to be between thirty-five and forty, and whom I surmised as the before-mentioned Mrs. Mandover. Accompanying the Colonel, a timid bud of a girl, shrinking beneath the gaudy lustre of the other woman. Small of stature, with a lovely countenance, she did not appear to pursue the rules of *ton*, either in dress or conduct. Even so, I found her one of the most enchanting women I had ever seen, and, I believe, if she had not been married, and Alicia had never written to me, I should have been sufficiently arrogant to have wished her mine.”

I smiled. “Ah, love.”

“A few weeks later I received a missive, in Alicia’s hand, suggesting we might meet at last. The letter stated another post would follow on Saturday with instructions where to meet on Sunday. As you can well imagine, Saturday could not arrive fast enough. When at last the billet appeared, it instructed me to proceed to Primrose Bank at three o’clock. Well, I could not sleep at all that night, and in the morning I made inquiries as to the location of

Primrose Bank. I paid utmost attention to my toilet and made sure I carried the gold watch she had gifted me.”

Mr. Radford returned. “Gentlemen, dinner is served.”

The three of us walked to the dining room, and I sat at the end of the table with the two men on either side of me.

“Mr. Ferguson was in the midst of a tale of conquest seeking a mysterious lady named Alicia,” I informed the steward. He merely smiled and nodded.

After a few slices of meat, Mr. Ferguson continued, “I found Primrose Bank to be a neat cottage *ornée*, embossed in a small shrubbery, with a flower-garden in front. A gravel-path led to the door of the house, and with a tremulous action, I sounded the knocker. Much to my surprise, instead of a servant, the person who appeared was the stylish woman from the theatre, Mrs. Mandover. You may guess my astonishment. Unable to conceal my feelings, I stared at her, and I felt instantly convinced she had observed the action. With the easy manners of a woman of the world, she introduced herself and advised me not to mistake her for my correspondent. What a relief! She then explained that I was to meet an intimate friend who had been invited to dine. Mrs. Mandover led me to a parlour that had more the nature of a boudoir than that of a drawing-room. At one end stood a harp surrounded by music tables piled with compositions. Another table was covered with the materials for drawing, and near it, rested against the back of a chair, a landscape in water colours, prettily touched. Paintings adorned the walls, handsome vases and busts ornamented the mantelpiece, and, in a recess, on shelves of cedar, reposed the works of all the lords, earls, baronets, gentles, and simples who have rendered themselves conspicuous within the last half-century for their oblations to the muses.”

“Such an elegant setting,” I mused. “I would imagine it could be quite intimidating.”

“Yes. All the trappings of an elegant mind. Mrs. Mandover then expressed a condition for the meeting of my beloved Alicia: We would confine ourselves to commonplace subjects of conversation. She warned me that if a tender syllable dropped, she would no longer espouse my cause. Also, if she should happen to leave the two of us alone without chaperone, the sin of sighing would then be upon our own heads, as she could not be responsible for our good behaviour when absent. As I reflected upon the conditions she had expressed, Mrs. Mandover led me to a dining-room. A lady whose back was turned stood with her face directed to a window at the farther end of the apartment. My hostess introduced the stranger as Mrs. Percival, and my breath stopped. Indeed, it was the lovely creature from the theatre. Can you fail to imagine that at that moment I conceived myself the happiest of men?"

"It must have been quite a shock, I imagine," I said.

"She received Mrs. Mandover's introduction with a polite curtsey and took her seat at the table. The young lady displayed not the slightest emotion, as if she considered me as an utter stranger. Thanks to the ease and volubility of Mrs. Mandover, the dinner-hour passed off with less confusion on my part than I had anticipated from the awkwardness of my situation. What most surprised me was where Colonel Percival could be engaged whilst his friend, Mrs. Mandover, was so kindly employed in introducing me into the society of his wife."

"Yes, that does strike one as odd," Mr. Radford contributed.

"About half-an-hour after the withdrawing of the cloth, a servant delivered a note to Mrs. Mandover. She announced that a tiresome dowager, Lady Winkle, wanted some numbers of the Mirror of Fashion. Our hostess excused herself, and I reconsidered in my mind the admonition regarding the sin of sighing. I fell upon my knees before the object of my adoration, and in terms most incoherent, most foolish, I am certain, I thanked her for her condescension, her liberality of sentiment, the interest which she had displayed in my fate, *et cetera, ad nauseum*. She interrupted me to explain that she had no idea as to what cause she could be indebted to, and she entreated me to quit my position and resume my seat. As I rose, youthful indiscretion commandeered my decorum, and I threw one of my arms round her neck, catching her other hand in mine, imprinting a trembling kiss upon her cheek."

"Oh, my! How cheeky!" I could not resist saying.

"At that instant, the door of the apartment was thrown open, revealing Mrs. Mandover and Colonel Percival. Mrs. Mandover exhibited a ghastly look of surprise and shock. The Colonel uttered some angry, unrepeatable words regarding his wife's infamy, and Mrs. Mandover ordered me to quit her house immediately, accusing me of villainy and disgrace. As I departed, I cast one last glance at Mrs. Percival, who had concealed her face behind a handkerchief."

"What a blow, what a blow," I felt so sorry for my dear friend. "The fat's in the fire now, I'm afraid."

"When I returned to my room, I reconsidered the unaccountable scene in which I had just been concerned. I could only draw one decisive conclusion, which was that Mrs. Mandover had been traitorous to the cause which she had pretended to espouse."

Mr. Radford spoke. "That seems a reasonable postulation, sir, given what you have related."

"Well after dusk, the landlady brought me a letter. When I inquired as to who had brought it, she said it were an old gentleman of respectable appearance of whom she had no recollection. Once she left, I lit the candle and perused the letter. The writer assumed the character of a concerned stranger who had been observing me for some time, and who had knowledge of the day's events at Primrose Bank. His advisement was to quit the town before the assizes commenced Tuesday a fortnight hence, as a trial against my actions would most likely ensue. The final words indicated himself as a sincere friend who would support me in any emergency. Three tenners were enclosed."

"Thirty quid?" I shrieked. "It seems people are after sending you money. At least some of your cards are trumps."

"Given the nature of this extraordinary, but consolatory, epistle, I felt gratitude at having a 'friend in need.' I heeded the imparted advisement and made preparations to depart Inverness. However, the next evening, the landlady produced yet another letter, delivered by the same gentleman as before. This new missive proved even darker than the first. It now appeared that Colonel Percival wished to pursue legal recourse for my actions with his wife. However, my unknown benefactor had obtained an interview with the Colonel, and the aggrieved husband would drop all charges if I consented to leave Scotland altogether. Enclosed with the letter was a hundred pounds."

"My word," I blurted out, "it seems you have earned more at playing the scoundrel than at the stage."

"I explained to the landlady that I would be departing immediately, and she told me she knew of the circumstances, as the scandal-loving world had rapidly circulated reports of my indiscretion. We settled my account, and she agreed to forward my trunks to Edinburgh. I bid her a cordial farewell, wrapped myself in a plaid cloak, within the folds of which I concealed a small bundle containing a change of linen, and set out, shaded by the friendly gloom of a misty night."

"Gentlemen," Mr. Radford said as he rose, "speaking of gloom and night, the hour is late. Perhaps Mr. Ferguson can continue his adventures over breakfast."

"Oh, yes, please, sir," I beseeched. "You have me sliced and wrapped." I turned to Radford, "Please show our guest to the room next to mine."

The steward bowed slightly and led my dearest friend, David Ferguson, up the grand staircase.

Chapter Eight:

A Ghost Reappears

FOR MANY AN HOUR I LAY AWAKE after entering the cloth market that was my bed. The event-filled nature of Mr. Ferguson's history charged me with renewed excitement. A man of law, a man of drama, a man of mystery.

In the morning, I noticed the door to his room stood ajar, I looked in and found it empty. People of the theatre were supposed to be notorious nightingales, creatures of the small hours. Perhaps he had readjusted his time clock while recuperating at the inn.

I threw on my banyan and hurried down the stairs only to find Mr. Radford and Mr. Ferguson sitting by the fire in the library. What an agreeable sight to have my two most favoured men together again.

"Good morning, young master," Radford called. "Mr. Ferguson has just caught me up on the bits of his saga I lacked."

"And there is more, to be sure," I winked.

"To be sure," concurred Mr. Ferguson.

Mr. Radford stood. "Please sit, young master, and I shall bring in the morning coffee." He exited, and I sat next to my dear friend.

"Did you sleep well? Did you sleep at all?" I inquired.

"Oh, yes. On both accounts." He grinned. "The bed at the inn might be satisfactory for one or two nights, but it lacked in luxury compared to the mattress here. And yourself?"

While I wished to open my heart and confess abiding love to him, much the way he attended his dear Alicia, I silently acknowledged our different desires and held my clapper. "Very well. Thank you."

We sat in silence for a few minutes. His countenance shifted among numerous emotions, and I could only guess he had drifted into several reminiscences.

Mr. Radford returned and poured coffee for all.

"Well, Mr. Ferguson," I prompted, "did you wish to continue your fascinating voyage?"

"If that is you wish, sir." Radford and I nodded. We all took a taste of our hot drink. "My journey back to Edinburgh proved easy enough, and I procured an engagement with a manager who was going to open the Berwick theatre, preparatory to race-week. As the months flew by, not a day passed when I did not reflect upon Mrs. Percival with increasing wonder on the extraordinary circumstances which had attended, if I may so name it, our acquaintance. One evening, I received a note from a gentleman who claimed to know me from Inverness and who wished to meet me at the Crown subsequent to the performance. It turned out to be a Mr. Fraser, the junior partner of a mercantile house, with whom I had been particularly acquainted. He told me how happy he was to see me, as they all believed I had been spirited away. Once he saw my name on the playbill, he wrote the note to me."

"I imagine it was good to see a friendly face from Inverness," Mr. Radford stated.

"Yes. When I asked after the town and what they said of my abrupt exit, he told me it was universally believed that I had gone off with Mrs. Percival, who had left the same day I did."

"What coincidence! And how could you have known?" I wondered.

"There is some mystery in this affair which I cannot fathom." He paused for another sip. "Mr. Fraser then told me they attributed her fall to the artifices of Mrs. Mandover, who herself had been in love with the Colonel. This corroborated my beliefs that the older woman had a hand in the whole affair. He produced a clipping from an Inverness newspaper announcing the marriage, by special licence, Lieutenant-Colonel Frederick Blagdon Percival to the honourable Mrs. Mandover, widow of the late Eugene Mandover of Bayford Park, Hants. I cannot say that my astonishment was very great, and many were our conjectures relative to the present situation of the divorced Mrs. Percival, which we did not hesitate to conclude her. How sincerely did I, at that moment, desire to know her fate!"

"How cruel your own fate, sir," Mr. Radford consoled.

"My concerns at the time were more with her consequence than my own, but I do appreciate your words, Mr. Radford." Mr. Ferguson smiled at the steward before continuing, "I convinced myself that my wishes were too presumptuous, my ideas too aspiring, and I endeavoured to smother and subdue them. As it was, the Berwick company manager reduced the performers from salaries to shares, and our individual incomes suffered. In the course of the ensuing winter, the drafts which I was obliged to make upon my purse were so frequent that I became uneasy at the diminution which my little capital was undergoing. That was when I first wrote to Mr. Gag, in whose company I was first introduced to your notice. He promised to make my salary fifteen shillings a-week, and I joined his troupe. Unfortunately, I was in Northumberland and Mr. Gag in Yorkshire, a distance of nearly sixty miles. It was the latter end of February, and a deep snow covered the ground. I sent forward my trunks by the stage wagon, and, as the seats had all been occupied, I resolved to walk my journey."

"In February? In the northern lands? Could you not wait for the next coach?" I inquired.

"When I did inquire into subsequent conveyance, I was told that due to the inclement weather, the next wagon would not depart until after I was expected in Yorkshire."

I added, "It seems you had little choice. I imagine you were quite pitch-kettled."

"I know not whether you will deem the incident which I am now about to relate as worthy of a place in my memoirs, if I may so name them, but it made so strong an impression on my mind, that I hardly think it will ever be obliterated from my memory."

"Perhaps we could all move to the dining-room to hear the next chapter of your 'memoirs,' as you have named them, Mr. Ferguson," Radford suggested. "I believe I smell the cook's fry-up."

The three of us rose and walked to the dining table. I sat at the end, and Mr. Ferguson took the chair next to mine. Mr. Radford continued into the kitchen.

"The first night of my journey I passed at the house of a farmer whose sons I had contracted an acquaintance. They prevailed upon me to prolong my visit another day, but I had determined to be punctual with my new manager. The weather remained calm and I covered much territory. As the moon was full, I considered to keep on walking through the evening."

Mr. Radford returned with the breakfast cart, and we received our plates full of meats and eggs.

Once the steward had taken his seat, Mr. Ferguson resumed. "Suddenly, a foggy denseness began to overspread the atmosphere, the brilliancy of the moon became obscured by thick and fleecy clouds, a keen wind arose from the east. Shortly thereafter, a heavy fall of snow and rain, which, in the course of half-an-hour, increased to a hurricane that swept with violence across the open plains, along which I was journeying."

"How frightful!" I remarked. "I am certainly glad you have survived this tempest and can regale us with your exploits."

"According to the imperfect calculations which I was able to make, it was about nine o'clock in the evening, and I was still seven miles distant from the village where I had intended to pass the night. The moors of Yorkshire are thinly scattered with habitations, but had they abounded around me, the increasing darkness of the night, added to the blinding influence of the driving sleet, must have rendered any object at the distance of a mere yard impenetrable to my sight."

"It sounds simply dreadful!" Mr. Radford exclaimed.

"I found that I had strayed from the road and was wandering on an uneven and untracked ground. Uncertain how best to proceed in this dilemma, I stopped a moment in reflection, and once more cast around my eyes. In the distance, I beheld the momentary gleam of what I considered to be a lamp. I instantly moved towards the spot from whence it had proceeded. Presently, I reached a building which seemed to be formed of earth and flags, covered with ivy. Its form was circular, and I moved around it, hoping to discover the easement from which the light had proceeded, but found none. After a time, I arrived at an arched porch and knocked upon the door."

When Mr. Ferguson paused to take a few bites, I asked, "A circular cottage in the midst of the Yorkshire moors? What a blind squeak."

"Indeed. I heard a deep, manly voice ask who was there, and I replied I was a benighted traveller who entreated shelter from the inclemency of the weather. The man bid me to enter freely, and I advanced into a rude apartment. Seated in a wicker chair, beside the cheering blaze of a wood fire, was one of the most extraordinary beings I ever saw. Somewhat past the meridian of life, habited in garments of an almost indescribable fashion, of which the single colour was white, a white hat covered his head, his white beard fell upon his breast, and at his feet, upon one of which its head rested, lay a milk-white goat."

"The White Man!" I shouted.

"You know of him?" Mr. Ferguson returned.

"Quite! He appeared here in Oldham the day before Mr. Clarington's funeral service, and upon the sad day's morning, he stood right there!" I pointed out the window, much the way Mr. Groveton had done.

"What a striking coincidence," observed Mr. Radford.

"Please continue. I am anxious to learn every particular," I requested of Mr. Ferguson.

"Of course. On the opposite side of the fire to that on which my entertainer sat, stood another wicker chair, similar to the one which he was himself occupying, and pointing to it, he requested me to repose myself and dry my clothes, without ceremony, at the fire. When I was seated, he rose, taking a small flask, a stone jug of water, and a drinking cup of horn from a recess in the wall. He placed them before me and invited me to mix myself a draught of brandy and water. He apologised for the lack of luxury but was thankful for the necessary comforts. I was not the first traveller who had sought repose within his humble walls, or so he told me."

"I do remember him being more of the humble sort."

"His voice, his language, his manners were that of a perfect gentleman, and I could not forbear regarding him with astonishment. When he had resumed his seat, he indicated a pallet of straw and asked if I would stay the night. The tick-tick-tick of time inside my head dictated that I must press on if I were to make my journey's goal, and I politely declined his gracious offer. He reminded me that even if the storm were to abate, the moon would be down, that I had strayed two hundred yards from the main road, and in the dark it would be impossible to regain. I perceived the truth of his observations, and I reconsidered that by declining his invitation, I might appear to cast the obloquy of distrust or dissatisfaction upon hospitality so benignantly extended. With many thanks, I consented to be his guest for the night, and he threw an additional log upon the fire. Then he drew forward a small table, white as his garment, upon which were a loaf, some cream cheese, and dried beef. He stated it would give him pleasure if I could make a comfortable repast. The grace of my entertainer's hospitality sweetened my meal, and I ate heartily."

"Do eat up, sir," Mr. Radford cautioned, "before your breakfast becomes too cold."

Mr. Ferguson took a few bites before continuing. "A considerable time passed, during which occasional observations on the weather and some instructions which he gave me for the progress of my journey in the morning, were the only subjects of our conversation. At length, I stated that his habitation stood in a very sequestered spot, to which he replied that it was like himself, removed from all intercourse with the busy world. I pointed to the goat and asked if that was his only companion. His answer included praise for the irrational animal because it had allied itself with him spontaneously. He also instructed me to draw aside a woollen curtain behind me. When I did so, I was betwattled upon seeing a negro, of the deepest jet, stretched on a pallet furnished with comfortable bedding. My host informed me that his human companion had been unwell for some days past, and that he had administered an opiate for pain, which held him securely bound in the folds of sleep. I asked whether the black man was his servant, and he chided me by telling me my conclusion was that of a man who judges according to the opinions of the world, and that he called the other fellow friend and equal."

"You had spent all that time with a sleeping negro nearby and never knew it?" It seemed difficult to believe.

Mr. Ferguson nodded. "We then discussed our mutual distaste for illiberal beings who believed that diversity of colour from their own was cause sufficient to sink a man into the brute. He continued on his own lecture as to wherefore the black man, with equal justice, may condemn us as his inferiors for the fairness of our complexions. His belief was that Heaven had not deigned to declare which was the preferable race, that all who live were his children, and that no one was sufficiently presumptuous to deny those for his brethren whom the Eternal has affirmed to be so."

"A very liberal mind, indeed," I said. "The brief conversation I had with him did not range that far a-field."

"At the conclusion of our colloquy, he then announced it was past the hour he was accustomed to seek repose, and he requested me to retire to the pallet. My host drew a wooden bolt across the door by which I had entered and went into a recess at the extremity of his dwelling, which I concluded to contain his bed. Given the highly unusual nature of my surroundings, sleep did not come quickly to me. As I lay in reflection, I gazed upon the sleeping negro, and I could see that his features were formed infinitely more like those of a European, even though his skin was of the deepest black. Fatigue finally overtook me and I slept. When I awoke, I found that it was daylight, and that my host had prepared me a comfortable breakfast. The woollen curtain had been drawn once again, and I could not determine whether the black man still slept as before. When my meal was concluded and I arose to depart, my hospitable entertainer offered to expedite my journey with his own purse, as I had indicated the importance of speed. As I had more than sufficiency in my pocket to carry me conveniently to the end, I resolved not to encroach unnecessarily on the liberality of so noble a heart."

He did not seem so noble and generous with me upon his visit, I thought to myself.

"With many thanks for his hospitality, I bid him farewell, but he insisted on guiding me back to the high road. He took up his staff and preceded me out of the hut. As we walked I stated my well-wishes for his friend, and he said he expected the fellow to be perfectly recovered when the effects of the opiate had died away. When we arrived at the main road, he pointed the way to me, and bade me a friendly farewell."

"Then you have never, since that hour, seen this extraordinary being again?" I asked.

"No, I have not," answered Mr. Ferguson.

"Nor heard of him?"

"You will not doubt that I made every inquiry concerning him at the village," responded Mr. Ferguson, "but all I could learn was that he and his companion had inhabited the hut for a considerable time and were strangers to the townspeople. The majority considered them inoffensive beings, and they esteemed the kindnesses with which they conducted themselves towards their humble neighbours and the occasional acts of charity which they extended to the needy. Some of the more vulgar folks believed them to be wizards. Even so, they were treated with respect, although, in the minds of the few, that respect was perhaps the effect of superstitious fear."

I then spoke, "How often have I desired to know where this extraordinary being resided, that I might see him and endeavour to obtain from him a knowledge of the motive by which he was actuated in his visit to this village at the period of my benefactor's interment. Yet, now I am acquainted where he might be found, I am awfully, impulsively withheld from putting my inclination into effect by the impressive mandate with which he quitted me: 'Attempt not to follow me,' he charged, 'the shade of your father commands you to obey me!' What a strange declaration! Inexplicable prohibition!"

"You cannot object to receive back the advice which you but a few hours since gave me," Mr. Ferguson taunted, "'You may, perhaps, at some unexpected moment, gain the explanation for which you thirst.'"

"Yes, yes. All is plummy," I cried. "You need not continue repeating my own words back to me."

The three of us ate in silence for a few minutes.

"I say sorry for my rude outburst, sir," I apologised. "Pray continue your story, as I wish to know how it concludes."

"Very well. During the months I spent with Mr. Gag's company, my distaste for the profession daily increased. My health declined rapidly, impaired alike by fatigue, disappointment, and apprehension for the future. When we had arrived in Oldham, my feelings were in a state of nervous debility which I can scarcely describe. I had drawn my last shilling from the Scottish banker, and all that remained of my worldly goods was the watch, chain, and seals, which had been presented to me by my precious Alicia. I truly believe that the illness with which I was seized in the theatre during my performance of *Douglas* was the result of the horror with which I looked forward to the miseries of a destitute sickbed."

He ceased his narration and stared out the window with a gloomy expression.

"Mr. David Ferguson," I began, "I heartily accept the terms of our agreement, and as of this moment, you are officially my tutor in the Classics." I stood and shook his hand. "Welcome to Ashbank Hall."

How I marvelled at Mr. Ferguson's chance to have spent time with the secretive and mysterious White Man. How curious that his choice of human companion was a Black Man. If only I could have set aside the advisement against following him, which he had admonished me upon his short visit.

Our lessons began with the basics of the Ancient Greek and Latin languages. Aside from having to commit the curious alphabet of the Greeks to memory, I had little difficulty tramping through the mire of vocabulary and syntax.

The more time I spent with my Mr. Ferguson, the more I felt closer to him. There were times when I wished to forgo the lessons for want of some physical contact, even as much as a silly little kiss, a proper buss, or even a bit of a smack. Yet, I knew that Mr. Ferguson did not share my want of male companionship, and if I should have breached this dear friendship, it could have meant the end of our society and the loss of a close companion.

Once I mastered the complexities of the ancient tongues, Mr. Ferguson had me read directly from the dusty old books in the library. From what I could gather, the Ancient Greeks had a system they called *pederasty*, where young men would partner with father figures for the purpose of sexual pleasure, as well as education and tutelage. This is what I had sought with Mr. Radford upon at first, and perhaps it was the nature of his relationship with Mr. Clarington, who had been so many years his senior.

Mr. Ferguson would occasionally catch me gazing at him moony-eyed, and I would have to catch myself, be economical with the truth, merely stating how stimulating I had found his knowledge and skills.

During this time of learning and studying, I rarely left Ashbank Hall. Prior to my taking up residence in the manor, I would spend a few nights a week at the Black Bull, nursing a pint, listening to the local lads crack and crow, watching the whist fellows argue over proper card play. I should have made a better effort to attend an evening or two, but the more I learned from Mr. Ferguson, the less I felt like going back into the unruly pub-house.

One morning, before commencing our daily lessons, Mr. Ferguson stated, "My dear Mr. Brown, I do believe that you are now intimate with the volumes of literature and science contained within these books." He gestured about the room. "It is my belief–my firm belief–that you should now contemplate studying the still more elaborate volume of mankind."

"I thank you for the complimentary words and flummery, sir, but my belief–my firm belief–is that the tutor has borne the bulk of the endeavour." Without Mr. Ferguson's assistance, I would still be a beetle-headed barber's boy in a big house.

"Shall we just go snacks, as they say, and share equally in the prize?" We smiled at each other, but I felt that my reasons for smiling differed from his.

"What is the assignment for your student, then?" I asked. "How shall we study the 'volume of mankind' that you have so indicated?"

Mr. Ferguson made a swallow loud enough that I could hear. "I propose a journey to London –"

"London!?" I jumped up. "It has been my fondest wish to travel to the heart of our great British nation."

"To London," he resumed, "so that you can meet other people, more sophisticated people, mix with them in society and receive further enlightenment."

"Radford!" I called out. "Mr. Radford, if you please."

A moment later the steward appeared in the doorway to the library. "Yes, young master. I believe I heard you bellow for me."

"Yes. Sorry. Yes. Please excuse my exuberance, but Mr. Ferguson has suggested that he and I travel to London to further my education. What say you?"

Mr. Radford took a pause for reflexion before speaking. "While I would hesitate to send you up to town on your own recognisance, Mr. Ferguson is well acquainted with the ways of a large city, and I must confess there is little here in Oldham to maintain your interest and curiosity much longer."

I stood and hugged him. "Thank you, Radford, you are the tip-top, bread-and-butter best!"

"Please do be careful, young master," he coughed, "you don't want to squeeze the life out of me."

"No, of course not," I let him go. "I am so excited by the prospect." My smile grew so wide, the muscles of my mouth began to hurt.

"The only difficulty which I foresee on our arrival in town," remarked Mr. Ferguson, "is that of procuring an introduction into such society as it would give you satisfaction to mix with. The constant visiting of public places can, after a time, afford little pleasure, when compared with that which is to be derived from enlightened conversation."

"Our good friend, Mr. Graveton, might be able to assist you, young master," Mr. Radford advised. "His late wife—who has now been so many years dead, that I much doubt whether you can recollect her—was the sister of a baronet who is considerably looked up to in the fashionable world. Sir Julius Maberly is his name. Now, although something like a coolness has lately appeared to actuate the doctor's conduct towards you, in consequence of Mr. Ferguson having recovered from the ague without his assistance, and your having made acquaintance with the Greek and Latin languages unaided by his tuition, he is so proud of his relation, the baronet, that if you think proper to ask for an introduction to Sir Julius, his vanity will not only influence him to regard you with all his former complacency, but you will also readily obtain the grant you request."

"Mr. Radford,"—I moved to hug him again, but he held up a hand, and I deferred—"you are the best friend—and steward—a man could ask for."

"Perhaps we should send him some... motivation," the steward suggested.

"What did you have in mind?"

"Aren't the peaches in the hot-house ripe and juicy? I believe the good doctor has a partiality towards that particular fruit."

"You are a genius, sir!" I commended. "Have the stable boy take a dozen–no!–a basketful of peaches to the Graveton house. I will write out a note to go with them. Mr. Ferguson and I shall call later in the day."

"Very good, sir."

That afternoon, my dear Classics tutor and I walked into Oldham. At the home of Mr. Graveton, I sounded the knocker, and the doctor himself opened the door.

"Mr. Brown and Mr. Cavendish! A pleasure to see you both. Do come in." He opened the door and led us to a small sitting-room off the main hall. Once inside, he indicated chairs for us. "Mr. Brown, you have done me a double honour. The peaches are succulent and sweet, and you also wish to make the acquaintance of my distinguished brother, Sir Julius Maberly."

"That is correct, Mr. Groveton. By the way, my companion here only uses Cavendish while on the stage. His actual name is Ferguson."

"Ah, Ferguson. All good, all good. Can I provide you gentleman with a beverage? A little brandy, some coffee, tea?"

"No, thank you, sir," I responded. The less time I spent with Mr. Graveton, the better. My plan had been to get a letter of introduction quickly and then depart.

"Ah, well," the doctor seemed momentarily deflated, but that swiftly passed and he resumed his air of gratified importance. "My brother, Sir Julius Maberly, will–you may rely–do honour to any introduction which he receives, either personally from me, or through the medium of my pen. I shall be most happy to request that he will rank you amongst his acquaintance." He retrieved his snuff-box, gave it three sounding raps and took a long pinch. "Yes, sir, my brother, Sir Julius Maberly, has a most extensive knowledge of all persons of rank and fashion. He is himself rather an eccentric character, but a most agreeable one. His society is universally courted, his conversation entertaining to a degree. I don't know when I feel myself so happy as in the society of my brother, Sir Julius. Indeed, I am not convinced that I shall not take a trip up to town this year myself."

He snuffed the remainder of his pinch and moved to his writing-table. A few minutes later, he furnished me a letter that expressed even more in my favour than I could have expected it would have contained.

"Thank you very much, Mr. Graveton. I appreciate your patronage, and I hope you have been enjoying the volumes you have chosen from the Ashbank library."

"Yes! Oh, yes! Splendid books, indeed. However, I believe I would prefer to have had the continued society of the late Mr. Clarington; however, the addition of his volumes to my own personal library is but a pale substitute."

We bid our host a good day and returned to Ashbank Hall. We showed the much-appreciated letter to Mr. Radford, and he responded, "I knew very well how it would be. I was certain that you could not please him better than by an application which proved that you considered sir Julius a man of consequence."

"You are quite wise, and once again, let me state my admiration for your continued service." I made a curt bow. Mr. Radford had certainly demonstrated himself the trusty Trojan.

"And," the steward continued, "I have a sister who is married and resides in Oxford-street. Part of her house is handsomely furnished and let as lodgings. I shall send a letter inquiring whether you could obtain the use of them during your stay in London."

Yet another pleasant surprise! "Yes, that would be most welcome, Mr. Radford. Most welcome indeed!"

Mr. Ferguson and I returned to the library to continue our lessons, but it proved difficult to concentrate on anything other than our impending voyage.

Chapter Nine:

Furthering My Education

A WEEK LATER, MR. FERGUSON AND I began our journey to London, via the Lincoln mail. The travel continued all-the-night, and I remember little of the dark countryside through which we passed.

But in the morning! Bright, promising London approached before us. Oldham had been the only city I had ever known, and now it seemed infinitesimal in comparison to our great capital. So many houses! So many streets and avenues! So many tall and grand buildings!

From the General Post Office, we hired a hansom to drive us to the home of Mr. Titmus, Mr. Radford's brother-in-law, in Oxford-street, past Regent Circus, with all its colonnades. As we traversed the crowded streets, overflowing with people and their wares, I could not help but gawk at all the new and marvellous sights.

The Titmus house appeared quite plain from the outside as it sat between two glorious marble structures. Radford's sister, Mrs. Titmus, greeted us at the door, with many apologies, and ushered us through a dark corridor into the cosy but comfortable-looking parlour, where a handsome breakfast had been prepared.

"Many apologies, Mr. Brown, Mr. Ferguson, but the lodger who currently occupies the rooms you shall have only agreed to quit the apartments after breakfast. Your rooms should be ready by the dinner-hour."

"Mrs. Titmus, am I to understand that you have requested someone to vacate on our behalf?" I asked, incredulous at the unanticipated action.

"Yes, sir. My dear brother asked me to accommodate the two of you rightly, and it was the only way. Many apologies," she replied.

"The apologies should be ours, not yours, my good woman," I responded. "Your income should not diminish on our account."

"Quoz," she blurted. "My brother's friends are family to me, and family always comes before profit. Eh, Mr. Titmus?" Her husband grunted loudly. "Mr. Titmus is a pastry-cook and confectioner. You shall not starve in this house."

"Thank you, Mrs. Titmus. Thank you very much indeed." What else can one say in such a situation? I planned to discuss the matter later with Mr. Ferguson as to how we could somehow recompense our hosts for the lost revenue from the lodger.

The elder of their two daughters, Bet, poured the tea. "I *'sure* you, sir, as you are my uncle's friend, *mar* gave warning to one of the genteelest gentlemen I ever knowed." Her funny manner of speech amused me, but I restrained myself from laughter. "He is a *barrow-night*, and such a dashy, handsome man."

"Handsome that as handsome does!" exclaimed her father, who appeared to be a plain, well-meaning man dressed in dark, woollen cloth. "Whatever he is, gentlemen, he has been here eleven weeks and I have never seen the colour of his money. If you had not been coming, he shouldn't have stayed here eight days more—I can promise him—without coming to some settlement. I don't see that I am likely to get a shilling out of him by *civil* means."

"Well, I'm sure he's a man of quality. His very *h*air and department bespeaks him that," responded Bet, "and you'll shew yourself very vulgar and very *h*ignorant if you go for to be any ways *obstropolous* with a man of his station."

"Ay, she thinks *as how* it is though," her younger sister Charlotte hollered with a sarcastic leer as she brought in a tray of sausages.

"Come, Miss, don't let's have none of your *h*impertinence, I desire," exclaimed Bet. "It *h*ain't nothing to you what I think."

"I have as much right to meddle with that as you had to tell my Mr. Dobby, last Sunday, when I'm sure he was *as smart* and *as dandyish* as the tailor could make him, that he looked like a footman out of livery," Charlotte asserted with some pride.

"Well, well, hold your tongue about my affairs and keep your pawnbroker to yourself," returned Bet.

"As you *'ope* to do Sir Frederick," mocked Charlotte, "but for all you think he's in love with you, if my *'ead* never aches till he marries you, I —"

"I'll tell you what it is, you husseys,"–interrupted their mother, half-rising from her chair–"if you don't hold your tongues, I'll take and rap your knuckles for you, or turn you out of the room." She pointed toward the door.

The two sisters sat in sullen silence.

"So, tell me gentlemen," Mr. Titmus turned to us, "what is the state of the country in the North? Are the times bad? How are the prices of eggs and flour? Is the mail service as horrid as here in London?"

Not knowing any of the correct answers, I faced Mr. Ferguson, who spoke, "My good sir, things in the North, as you put it, are much the same as everywhere else these days. The main difference, as I see it, is that here in town, you needn't walk as far." He smiled.

"Ah! 'Course, 'course," our host muttered into his plate.

At the conclusion of the quite delicious meal, Mrs. Titmus directed us to our rooms upstairs with many apologies. I found the lodgings quite generous for the size of the building. Mr. Ferguson and I each had our own chamber, and we both drifted to the Land of Nod after the fatigue of travelling all-the-night.

Upon rising, my pocket-watch showed three o'clock, and sunlight streamed through the small window. I quit the fairly comfortable bed, which was about one-quarter the size of the huge palette I had at Ashbank Hall, and arranged the business of my toilet.

I discovered my handsome companion seated in a nearly-as-handsome drawing-room. Just as I entered, a gentle tap sounded on the door.

"May we come in, gentlemen?" came the voice of one of the Titmus daughters.

"Undoubtedly," I responded, and the two sisters entered, now linked arm-in-arm.

"I 'ope, gentlemen," the one named Bet spoke, "you won't think us troublesome or *h*intrusive, but we have *such* a favour to ask."

"Without reservation," I responded, and Mr. Ferguson nodded.

"Why, you see, sir, Sir Frederick Lambert–that is the gentleman *h*as I told you had lived in these here rooms," Bet explained, "has got some *h*orders for the boxes at *H*ashley's *H*amphitheatre to-night, and he has given one to me and another to Charlotte, and we have both such a mind to see the *'osses* ride."

"And Mr. Dobby," Charlotte added, "would come and meet us, for we'd let him know as how we was a-going."

Bet continued, "But we are so afraid that our *mar* won't give us leave. In short, sir, it all rests with you."

"How so?" I asked, half not grasping what they were asking, and half not grasping what they were saying.

"Why, if you would but have the *monstrous* kindness to say as how you *'ad* a mind to go to *H*ashley's yourselves, and that you'd *ax'd* us to go with you, because you were strangers in *Lunnan*," Bet explained. "I dare say *par* and *mar* wouldn't have no objection at all, because they'd think us quite safe with you. *Par* wouldn't allow me to go with Sir Frederick, if he knew it, on account of the trumpery bit of money he owes him, as if he wasn't able to buy him and his whole shop, if he chose it."

"And *mar* wouldn't like me to go into public with Mr. Dobby because he's called *sich* a rakish young man, but I am sure *'e* never was rude to me in his life," Charlotte went on.

"I do believe," Mr. Ferguson responded, "I have heard of Astley's Amphitheatre, and it is just possible that Mr. Brown and myself are a bit curious about its programmes. The gallopers are well-renowned."

"Indeed they are, Mr. Ferguson," Bet chirped with a wink. "So you'll 'company us, then, Mr. Brown?"

"Of course, Miss Titmus, of course." How could I have returned a flat denial to their request? They are Mr. Radford's nieces, and their parents had expelled a non-paying lodger for our convenience. However, I resolved to avoid their society after that day, at least in public.

"Oh, thank *ye*, thank *ye*, sirs!" the girls squealed and flew down the stairs.

Later in the day, Mr. Ferguson suggested dining at a local tavern before escorting the young ladies to their *beaux*. As we descended the stairs, Mrs. Titmus intercepted us.

"And where might the two of *ye* be *'eading* off to?" Her quizzical eyes danced from face to face. "Were you thinking of going elsewheres for your meal? No, no! I insist you follow me down these stairs and dine with us."

Mr. Ferguson and I glanced at each other and shrugged. "Of course, Mrs. Titmus. We thank you for your generous offer and could not think of turning you down," I responded.

"Good!" she exclaimed, "because I have just sent our Mr. Cooke for some wine." She turned, descended a few steps, stopped, turned, and continued, "My stores afford a variety of soups, excellent pigeon pie, tongue, tarts, jellies and sweets of every description. Oh, and our Mr. Cooke had just returned from Covent Garden with a quart of green peas!"

We enjoyed a marvellous repast with the Titmus family. Once the parents had left the room, Bet spoke to us in a low voice, "*Mar*, gentlemen, begs you'll step down into our parlour and take a cup of tea before we go to the play." She looked about and then continued, "Excuse me for *'urrying* you, but if we *hain't* there before the curtain draws up, our *horders* won't be admitted."

"Perhaps we should proceed in a coach," I offered.

"Oh, no! Do pray, if you please," Bet decried, "let us walk because Sir Frederick is to meet us on the bridge, and we shall miss him if we ride." She stood and tripped away, stopped, looked back and invited us to follow.

We entered the parlour and Mrs. Titmus greeted us with, "Many apologies, but Mr. Titmus is busy in the shop. Please sit." She began arranging the tea equipage.

Charlotte leaned over and whispered to me, "Mr. Brown, I've let Mr. Dobby know as how I'm a-going, and he has lent me this here necklace to wear to-night." She indicated the jewellery about her neck. "*H*ain't it a beautiful one? It's one of his unredeemed pledges. He wears a great many of them himself, and that makes him look so genteel and stylish when he goes into public." She smiled daintily.

At length, we set out, and I realised it was my first time as a pedestrian in the streets of London. I marvelled at the various buildings we walked past with wonder and admiration. Such an amazing collection of architecture, the likes of which I would never have seen back in provincial Oldham.

A dark shadow loomed before us, and I recognised it as the Houses of Parliament with the famous clock tower. I scanned the scattering of people rushing about, looking to see if any of them might be members or peers.

As we crossed the Westminster Bridge above the roiling Thames, Bet, who had been leaning on my arm, stopped and pointed. "Oh la! There *is* Sir Frederick, I declare!"

I glanced in the direction of the pointed finger and beheld a tall young man, of an excellent figure and handsome person, fashionably and elegantly dressed, advancing toward us.

"Mr. Brown, this is Sir Frederick," Bet introduced us. We shook hands gently.

"Why Miss Titmus, you grow more resplendent with every day. I can hardly maintain myself in your presence." He bowed slightly and took her hand to his lips.

Oh, how I wished to attain such demonstrative tenderness, quite the diametrical opposite to myself. Of course, I would not have minded if such a gentleman greeted me with such pleasure.

Mr. Ferguson and Charlotte then came up. "Mr. Ferguson, Sir Frederick Lambert," Bet introduced.

While it might not have been obvious to all, I did notice a smile of recollection pass over both their features as they reached out their hands.

"How do you do, Mr. Ferguson?" Sir Frederick said as he took the offered hand. "I am very happy to see you, upon my honour!"

"I hope I see you well, *Sir Frederick*," returned Mr. Ferguson, rather coolly and with a slight emphasis upon the fellow's name.

The five of us proceeded across the remainder of the bridge, entering Lambeth, and on to the Amphitheatre. The looming shadows of the night grew longer and more foreboding.

We had scarcely taken our seats in the house when Miss Charlotte exclaimed, "Well, if '*ere h*ain't our Mr. Dobby already! Lord, how good of '*im* to come before 'alf-price! For, as '*e h*ain't no *h*order, it's cost '*im* four shillings '*ard* money clean out of '*is* pocket."

Mr. Dobby entered our box, smart with rings and things, a fine array as could make him.

"Everyone, this is Mr. Dobby," Charlotte stated. The gentleman bowed as low as the tight lacing in which his slim form permitted. "Ah, Mr. Dobby! You can't think *'ow* much I *ham* obliged to these *'ere* gentlemen. For, if it *'adn't* been for their *axing*, I don't believe *mar* would *'ave* let us out. Wouldn't that *'ave* been cruel?"

"*Werry* se*w*ere," replied Mr. Dobby. His manner of speech proved even more difficult than that of the Titmus family to apprehend.

"And of all things," Charlotte continued, "it is so provoking to be kept shut up at *'ome*, when one knows one might be so pleasant abroad."

"*Werry* se*w*ere indeed!" answered Mr. Dobby.

"If *mar* finds out now that you and Sir Frederick met us *'ere* to-night, I dare say *'ow* she'll lead us the life of a dog for it, for Lord knows *'ow* long."

"How monstrous se*w*ere," returned Mr. Dobby.

As the orchestra took up the music, the ladies consorted with their *beaux*, leaving an opportunity for conversation with my companion.

"You know Sir Frederick Lambert, it seems," I whispered to Mr. Ferguson.

"For one of the greatest liars and swindlers that ever walked about unpunished," Mr. Ferguson spat back in hushed tones. "But more of than anon. We'll walk into the lobby by and by, and I'll tell you what I know of him. He is no more Sir Frederick than you are. His name is Harry Glara. A few years ago he was the light comedian of the Edinburgh company, and I have frequently met him in public parties when I was in the employment of the Monros. But he does not know that I ever trod the boards, as he had quitted Scotland before I was seized with that fit of insanity."

The performance seemed more like a carnival than a proper drama. People in fancy costumes chased animals in fancy costumes, the animals chased the people, and horses trotted around the great enclosed circuit. At the end of the first act, Mr. Ferguson said to me, "It appears that Glara and Bet, Mr. Dobby and Miss Charlotte are occupied with the entertainment, or with each other. This might be a good time to move to the lobby."

We stood and made our way out, through the heavy, deep red velour curtains, into the spacious atrium. Other patrons scraped about or stood, indicating we were not the only ones looking to lounge.

"And so this pretended knight or baronet, whichever he may please to denominate himself is, in fact, but a poor player 'who has strutted his hour upon the stage?'" I inquired of Mr. Ferguson.

"But he is perhaps the man of all others who is most capable of supporting the title he has assumed. He is by birth a Hibernian and possessing a more than common share of that effrontery which is some degree the characteristic of the inferior orders of his countrymen, added to an understanding, and an education, both rising above mediocrity, and seconded by a person which the female world have universally, as I have understood, allowed to be resistless," my friend responded. "There is nothing which he hesitates to attempt, and very few attempts in which he fails. When he first came to Edinburgh, he gave himself out as the *lady-killer*, and indeed his words were very near being verified."

"Oh, dear," I sighed. Spying the tea cart nearby, I suggested, "Shall we take some tea?"

As we walked, Mr. Ferguson continued, "He had not been above a month in the place when, on the very day on which he was to have become the husband of a girl whom he had seduced from her friends in Glasgow, and whom, in order to close the lips of scandal, he probably considered it politic to marry, arrived, in quest of him, a wife from Yarmouth, and another from York."

What shame! This Sir Frederick, or Glara, or however he wished to style himself, sounded like the very worst sort of scoundrel.

"The Glasgow girl shed torrents of tears at the apprehension of losing the beautiful swain upon whom her heart doted. The Yorkshire damsel stormed and raved in a dialect, which in Edinburgh was almost unintelligible. The Yarmouth lady, who was supposed to be the only one who had an actual claim upon him as husband, quietly swallowed a draught of laudanum. This action cost him a harder day's work than he had probably ever gone through in his life, as he found himself under the necessity of keeping her in constant exercise for nearly sixteen hours, by the direction of the physician who had been called in to her assistance, in order to prevent her from falling into a sleep which might have proved fatal to her existence."

I wanted to mill the bloody bugger myself for his fly-by-night scraps. What kind of man can gleefully accomplish these types of foul, unconscionable acts worthy of Old Nick himself? And now, Miss Bet, Mr. Radford's niece, is partial to the bogland blackguard.

We had reached the tea, and I purchased a cup for each of us.

"How did he contrive to disentangle himself from this treble net?" I felt compelled to inquire.

"Oh, most ingeniously!" Mr. Ferguson responded. "To the Glasgow fair one, with every appearance of regret and disappointment, he pleaded the inviolability of a prior engagement for retracting the promise which he had made to her. To the Yorkshire lady, he solemnly declared that he had never been united by any ties which were binding by law, and, by pretending a regard for her character, induced her to return, at his expense, to the South—whither, it was whispered, he had privately engaged in a short time to follow her. For his neglect of his real wife, for such he confessed the claimant from Yarmouth to be, he apologised by declaring that whilst performing the preceding year in Bath, he had received intelligence of her death from her own father."

"What an improbable tale!" I offered.

"But that is not all." Mr. Ferguson took a few sips of tea, and from his expression, I could tell it was not of the highest quality. "He is notorious for ducking out of his obligations at the very last moment by diabolical fetches and nefarious tricks. Moments before consummating an agreement that he never had intention to fulfil—such as a duel, a loan payment, or rental due—a message would arrive, or a servant would announce a caller, and the fellow excused himself to handle the artificial situation."

"Never to return, I presume?" The tea tasted as bad as Mr. Ferguson's expression had indicated.

"Exactly so. He would disappear behind a curtain, lock himself in a trunk to be sent by mail, or even disguise himself–sometimes in women's clothing–and walk away without a care."

"What a consummate –" I had begun to say, but my companion quickly checked me by pressing his arm upon mine just as he saw Sir Frederick advancing toward us.

"Well, upon my honour"–the imposter began with the air and voice of a perfect man of the world–"I am extremely happy to see you again, Mr. Ferguson. How are they all in the North? How long have you left it?" He leaned in before a response could be made and whispered, "I dare say you were devilishly surprised when I was introduced to you by the name of Sir Frederick Lambert. I am a lucky dog. I inherit the title from a distant relation of my father's to whom I have been proved heir at law."

Before responding, Mr. Ferguson reviewed the fellow with his eyes. "I thought I recollected your name to have been Henry."

"Oh, yes, so it is," answered Sir Frederick, not an iota abashed, "but it was a whim of the old man's that his heir should call himself Sir Frederick after him, and it makes no kind of difference to me, you know." His eyes lit with a cunning light.

"I hope you have succeeded to wealth as well as title," my friend added.

"Nothing to brag of. Tolerably decent–between two and three thousand a-year–sufficient to buy toothpicks at all events." The hypothetical baronet laughed engagingly.

"Oh, mercy!" exclaimed Bet. "If there isn't that *'orrid* wretch, Mr. Tunks! I *'ope* he won't attempt to come this way, for I can't *a-bear* the sight of *'im*."

When I looked in the direction Miss Titmus had indicated, I beheld an ordinary, middle-aged, formal-looking man dressed in a suit of clothes that, however good or fashionable, conferred no credit on the wearer. With a downdrawn countenance, expressive of sensations the opposite of satisfaction, he made repeated stiff bows toward Bet, who had so ungraciously pronounced aloud her disapprobation of his civilities.

Charlotte tittered and told us, "That Mr. Tunks is a very rich wax and tallow chandler in the Borough. He was my sister's *beau* till she got acquainted with Sir Frederick, and now she's turned *'im* off, and he's fit to break *'is 'eart* about it."

Bet herded us back to our box to avoid an undesired intersection with her former *beau*. She meandered us through the throng so as to best hide from the poor benighted soul.

Once we all sat, Charlotte resumed, "'*E* sent her word last week that if she would but consent to *'ave 'im*, as *'ow 'e'd* keep *'er* either a dennet or a tilbury, which ever she liked best, but she won't *'ear* a word *'e* has to say."

Whilst Charlotte amused us with this explanation, Mr. Tunks had stolen, unperceived into the box and seated himself behind Bet, to whom he began offering oranges, cakes, and sweetmeats, carefully wrapped up in a white cambric pocket-handkerchief.

"No, no, no, no!" she replied to each offered gift.

The unhappy bachelor sighed, and in scarcely audible accents pronounced, "Oh dear, Miss Betsey, angel!"

Such a ludicrous scene played out before us and left us scarcely capable of refraining from joining in the laugh at his experience. Miss Charlotte and her Mr. Dobby seemed to be spurring the poor fellow on with unblushing indulgence. He grasped her hand and proclaimed, "Miss Titmus, would you promise to join hearts with me at the altar of love?"

At that, Mr. Tunks touched Bet gently on the shoulder with his hand, and when she for an instant vouchsafed to turn towards him with disdainful eyes, he produced a sigh of treble the length of those which he had previously heaved with his melancholy countenance.

"Oh dear, Miss Betsey, angel!" he proclaimed, directed to the stage. "Why is it that you and I cannot be happy as this couple before us?" He placed his handkerchief to his face.

I turned to Mr. Ferguson. "Did you ever see the like?"

"No," he replied, "but I have, if I may be allowed the expression, read a *fac-simile* of this desponding man. Every time he has sighed, 'Oh dear, Miss Betsey, angel!' I have been diverting myself with regarding him as the prototype of poor Dummie Dykes, whose sole address to the object of his passion was, you will recollect, 'Ah, Jeanie, woman!'"

The fall of the last curtain prompted us to assist in protecting our female companions through the crowd in quitting the house. I, once again, proposed the accommodation of a coach, but the sisters again declined. The young ladies evidently wished to be accompanied home by their admirers.

We had skirted Mr. Tunks, and the six of us set forward in pairs, with Miss Bet and Sir Frederick leading the van. This afforded the two of us the opportunity to drop back and converse unheard by the others.

"I have been puzzling my brain, but to no purpose," Mr. Ferguson began, "to divine what benefit the mock baronet can expect to derive from the marked attentions which he pays to that girl. That interest is the spring by which his conduct is actuated. I cannot for a moment doubt, but still cannot imagine how, even with his peculiar skill in manœuvring, he can hope to reap advantage from his present proceedings. It appears a decided matter, that a worldly, wary man, like old Titmus, who has probably acquired his all by indefatigable application to business, would never be induced to give his consent to his daughter's union with a man whom he describes as being unable to pay him the amount of a few weeks lodging. If he marries her without, he burdens himself with an individual for whom it is impossible for a man of his ideas to have any regard."

"From the examples which you have given me of his management and address, I long to see the conclusion of this enigma," I remarked.

"Depend upon it," returned Mr. Ferguson, "that if I perceive her, or her family, in actual danger of becoming his dupe, I shall consider it my duty to give her father some insight into his real character."

We had just arrived in Oxford-street when Charlotte suddenly stopped and exclaimed, "Oh lord, gentlemen, to be sure there must be a fire somewhere. Only see 'ow red the sky looks before us!"

"*Werry* red indeed!" returned Mr. Dobby. "It's either a fire, or a sign of *var*. They say as how the sky always looks red before *var*."

I raised my eyes to the fiercely illuminated atmosphere and beheld the bright crimson. Just as I was about to express the coincidence of my opinion, I heard the sound of wheels rolling rapidly along.

"Oh, there is a fire as sure as a gun," cried Mr. Dobby, "for here comes a *hingine*!"

Chapter Ten:
Love in a Blaze

DOES ANYBODY KNOW IF IT'S *WELL* LIT?" asked a rugged fellow in a long, scarlet jacket with tall, leather boots. He stood next to what appeared to be a vat of water on a cart being pulled by other similarly-dressed gents. Some of the men looked quite fit and eye-catching, but I realised this was not the moment to be distracted by their native beauty.

"Oh, famous!" came a reply from the assembled mob, "quite a *blazer!*"

"Firemen!"–cried another voice from the crowd along the pavement–"Whereabouts is the fire?"

"At the corner of Portland-street, a little higher up here in Oxford-street," the fireman answered.

"Oh, mercy upon us! What? So near our house as that!" cried Charlotte. "Oh, do pray let us make 'aste 'ome, for *par* and *mar* will be in *such* a fright!"

"Wherever it is, it is evidently raging with great violence as the redness of the sky momentarily increases," I observed.

"Oh, do pray let us make '*aste*," repeated Charlotte.

Proceeding with hurrying steps, we shortly overtook Sir Frederick and Bet, who had hitherto been moving in advance of the party. As we drew near the scene of conflagration, the tumult and pressure of the crowd rendered it necessary that the ladies be housed as quickly as possible.

"We shall guide the Titmus sisters back to their father's home," I yelled to Mr. Dobby and Sir Frederick. With considerable difficulty, Mr. Ferguson and I, at length, reached the door, which stood open, Mr. and Mrs. Titmus huddled in the archway.

"Oh, thank *ye*, thank *ye*, Mr. Brown for bringing our daughters safely back to us." The parents hugged their children.

"How dreadful a sight!" remarked Mr. Ferguson, casting his eyes toward the flaming mass, which was nearly opposite to the spot on which we stood.

"I'll tell you what it is, sir," spoke Mrs. Titmus, "it's more than dreadful. There is one house burnt to the ground, another in flames, and a third which has just caught fire. In the upper story, they say there's a young person that must be burnt to death for nobody can't get up there. We've heard shrieks for help, and the mother raving like mad about, 'Poor dear! Poor dear!' in the street."

Having witnessed a few fires back in Oldham myself, I recalled the horrible consequences. "I cannot be an idle auditor of such distress," I exclaimed. "Come, Ferguson, let us endeavour either to afford help to the sufferer ourselves or to spur on those to exertion who are better acquainted than we are how to render assistance upon these occasions."

Mr. Ferguson required no second admonition to obey the call of humanity. He seized my arm and we forced our way into the crowd. In a short time, we beheld the youthful form, of whom Mrs. Titmus had spoken, at an open window of the third story. The flames quickly ascended, rending the air with shrieks.

"Can't be saved. Impossible!" pronounced a bystander.

"Why don't they try to raise the ladder again?" inquired another.

"Nobody can ascend it if they do," came a reply, "on account of the flames which are issuing from the windows of the room below."

"Why not jump?" cried another of the crowd.

"Poor dear soul! Every bone would break," answered another.

As we forced our way nearer the house, my ears rang with the cries of the mother, "Oh, save my child!" In frantic accents she exclaimed, "I conjure you, save my child! I'll give anybody a thousand pounds to save my child! In God's name, save my child!"

At that moment, the memory of a similar rescue back in Oldham crossed my mind, although none of those homes had three floors. "Stick close by me, Ferguson, and I think I see how preservation may be effected." I looked about for a blanket. Not seeing one, I raised my voice to its highest pitch, "Who'll bring me a blanket? I'll give any person ten pounds who procures me a blanket!"

"Here, sir! Here! Here!" vociferated the distracted mother. "Here! Where I am standing, there is bedding of all kinds just thrown out from the second story of my house."

I rummaged through the jumbled collection of bed-clothes and selected one of the largest, sturdiest blankets I could find. Taking one of the corners in my own hands, I directed Mr. Ferguson to take another. I then called out to the crimson-costumed firemen, "Two of you come hither this instant and lend me your help!"

We held up two sides of the blanket, and a few of the masculine fellows perceived my intention, rushed over and took up the remainder of the blanket in their hands. As one, we manœuvred the cloth beneath the window above and pulled it taut.

"In the name of Heaven," I screamed up, "seize the only means which present themselves for your preservation. Spring fearlessly down, and trust to our exertions for preserving you from injury!"

The youth looked about with an agony of countenance indescribable. The flames now surrounded the window.

"Jump down! We shall catch your fall!" I called up, while the mother stood nearby praying.

A momentary crash came from the upper part of the house, and I conjectured that the floor of the chamber just behind the window had fallen. In the next moment, I could see the youth clinging, for support, to the window frame. Climbing with trembling limbs upon the ledge, the poor stranded creature shouted, "God have mercy on me!" and leapt forward.

The blur of a body falling through the rising smoke induced fears of failure. However, the prayer had been answered, due to the adroit management of our team. Such a fall caused temporary unconsciousness, but I could see the form of a beautiful young man, barely clothed, resting in the nadir of the blanket. What lovely strawberry hair! Such creamy skin! Here appeared the embodiment of love before me, like a wingless angel just fallen from Heaven, to be rescued. While I could not designate any certain number to an age, his whips of nearly-translucent facial hair indicated some maturity beyond adolescence.

Following my momentary rapture, I began gently lowering the blanket to the ground, and the others imitated my action.

"Oh, my child! My child!" cried the enraptured parent, as she knelt. "Alive, I tell you! Alive! Oh, my love! My only one! Do I once more clasp you to my heart? Oh, God be praised for his mercy towards you!" Her tears began to flow. "And to you, sir," she addressed me. "How can I thank you? How testify my gratitude for your noble, generous conduct?" She wiped at her moist face. "Excuse me, pray excuse me, for I am so agitated, so bewildered, that I cannot speak to you as I wish. I am sure Heaven sent you to the preservation of my dear child."

I hoped that Heaven also sent her dear child to me as a preservation as well. "Your fears being relieved, madam, allow me to extricate you from this scene of danger, and conduct you to some place of safety." Again, I looked down upon the angelic form of her sleeping child, just fallen from Heaven above.

"Oh, sir, you are too good, too kind!" she returned. "I am scarcely able to think for myself just now, but I have a friend in a neighbouring street who will gladly receive us, if we can but make our way to her house." She looked down upon her offspring. "My poor child, I fear, will catch death in the night-air, for he was in bed when the fire broke out, and has nothing but that night-gown to defend against the cold."

I quickly responded, "If you will accept my friend as *your* protector, madam, entrust your son to me. I will wrap him in the blanket which effected his preservation and bear him in my arms to the spot you wish to reach." The scene I had just described of the hero carrying off his love interest reminded me of one of the dramatic performances Mr. Ferguson had enacted.

"Oh, sir!" returned the mother, "how can I ever repay such goodness, such humanity, so —"

The end of her pæan fell not upon my ears as I carefully enfolded the still insensible, but beautiful, burden. With a hand signal, I directed Mr. Ferguson to force a passage through the crowd. The lady pointed out the way to her friend's house. Once we passed the first few layers of people, the crowd thinned and we could walk more naturally. I bore my bundle with glee, flights of fancy winging their romantic ways through my lovelorn skull.

When we arrived at the house a few streets over, the maid informed us that the lady to whom it belonged was at the opera, but every moment expected to return home. She appeared to recognize the weeping mother and admitted us entrance, guiding us to a large drawing-room. As I set the blanket upon the sofa, the young man's mother began to narrate the events of the night.

Suddenly, the boy's eyes opened. With faint breath and wildly ranging eyes, he asked, "Where am I?" His voice sounded angelic yet slightly masculine.

A paler shade of blue I had never seen in a man's eyes before. The excitement I had felt upon first observing him only heightened. My desire for this lad grew with every passing moment.

The child's mother fell to her knees and hugged her boy to her breast and then applied generous kisses.

"Oh, that fire! That dreadful fire!" the youth pronounced feebly but fearfully.

"You are safe, far from it now. Quite safe," replied the mother, and a second round of kisses began.

In my heart of hearts, I kissed the boy as well, hugging him to my breast, and murmuring words of succour into his enchanting ear. If only I could learn his name.

Now that the emergency had passed, and not wishing to seem overly-enthusiastic, I merely offered, "As strangers, madam, we cannot doubt that our presence must at this moment be a restraint. Wishing, therefore, that no ill effects, either to your child or yourself, may succeed the accidents of the night, we will retire, hoping, ere we depart, to be favoured with your permission to make personal inquiries after your health in the morning."

Mr. Ferguson stepped forward, "I can assure you, madam, that Mr. Brown is quite astute at his medical visits. He faithfully called upon me each and every day during a recent infirmity."

"Sir," the lady addressed me directly, "I am the doting mother of an only child. To you I owe the preservation of his life, and next to him, I must in future ever esteem you."

She caught my hand in hers, raised it and impressed on it her lips. I felt a moist tear fall from her eye. She then stood, moved to an inkstand, and in a few moments presented me with a card on which she had written: "Mrs. Allingham, Mayfield Avenue, No. 11."

I took the presented card. "I have no card to give you, Mrs. Allingham, as we are newly entered to London. We are staying with some friends in Oxford-street, and I will bid you a pleasant night and call tomorrow."

"Oh, yes, please!" the lady responded. "We shall be expecting you. A pleasant night to the two of you as well."

How I wished to burst out with Romeo's famous, "Good night, good night, parting is such sweet sorrow, that I shall say good night till it be morrow," but I knew to keep a civil heart I would need to keep a civil tongue.

On the homeward walk, I could think of nothing else but the visage of the young man we had quickly captured from the fire who had quickly captured my fancy. What could be his name? In my heart, it was Cupid, Eros, Himeros, Pothos.

Mr. Ferguson might have been conversing, but I heard none of it until we reached Oxford-street once again, and he pulled me in the correct direction. We gazed up at the burnt-out remnants of the good woman's home across the way. A few stray flames could still be observed, but the major flares had abated.

"Excuse me, good sir," Ferguson inquired of one of the firemen, "has anyone been injured in the fire?"

The handsome, dark-haired fellow with blazing brown eyes turned to us. "No. Not my knowledge. The people here were very lucky, they were. This time." He appeared to be looking off to another incident, in another place, on another day.

The Titmus family anxiously awaited our arrival, with understandable apprehension. Due to the length of our stay with the mother and her adorable son, I could tell they wondered if some misfortune might have befallen us.

"Tell us! Tell us what happened!" the sisters demanded, and Mr. Ferguson and I recreated our adventure as simply as it had occurred.

"If I may ask, is anyone with the family name of Allingham known to you?" I inquired after the tale had run.

Mr. Titmus glared at his family to induce silence, and then he spoke, "Although I am not acquainted with the lady herself, I knew her first husband very well. His name was Evelyne, and he had been a pawnbroker of considerable eminence, in Tottenham-court-road. At his decease—which was about thirteen years ago, now—a Mr. Dobby, the father of the youth who aspires to become my son-in-law," he shot a side-glance at Charlotte, "purchased the goodwill of the business, and the shop of the widow, who was reputed to be very rich, and who had–within the last two years–once more entered into the marriage state with a gentleman of the name Allingham, but who or what he is, I know not."

I had to ask, "The young person whose life I have this night been instrumental in preserving is then Mrs. Allingham's child by her first husband?"

"Yes," Mr. Titmus replied, "and I understand that he is reckoned a very accomplished and very striking young man."

To the latter, my heart had already confessed. Mr. Ferguson and I bid our hosts good-night and retired to our rooms.

"Ferguson, I must express to you my anxiety and impatience to behold the youth again," I began. "I have not encountered such beauty in my entire life." I could never express my similar longings for him so directly.

"I confess," returned Mr. Ferguson, "from the slight glance which I had been afforded, I thought him a charming fellow as well."

"Charming, yes." I could not decide whether to fully describe my fervent attraction to the young man we had rescued. Mr. Ferguson had certainly bared his innermost secrets to me. My belief was that I should be able to tell him what motivated my own emotions. "But I should probably make clear to you that my interest goes beyond mere outward appearance."

"You are experiencing some emotional attraction to the youth?"

Not having the words within me, I nodded and kept my face directed downward.

A warm hand clasped my shoulder. "Mr. Brown, please do not suffer yourself with your feelings. I already know that you prefer the company of men above woman."

"You do?" I looked up at the face of my closest friend.

"Of course. Why else would you have visited me every day at that blasted inn?" He smiled warmly. "It was my fondest wish that I could have only returned your affections in a way that would have satisfied you."

"You knew?" I squeaked. "And it does not cause you offense?"

He chuckled. "Pray, do not forget that I have spent the better part of a year in the company of actors. Many of them have the same predilection, but none have been as gentlemanly as you." He squeezed my shoulder. "If only I shared your tastes, I believe we could have been a most marvellous and happy couple."

The colour rose into my face as if the temperature of the room had doubled. I wanted to turn away but could not. "Thank you, David."

"And your secret is safe with me, after all," he continued, and I nodded. "No one else need know about this. But I would caution you, if you wish others not to discern your tastes, be careful with your glances. They could unmask you."

"You are, indeed, a good as friend as I could have ever wished for. We are quite the cater-cousins, you and me." I reached out and clasped his arm.

"But beware not to fall too deeply into Cupid's snare at his first attack upon your heart." Mr. Ferguson cautioned. "For recollect, my friend, that, according to the regulations by which you have often repeated to me, you are bound to remain a free and single man for a full four years passing before you can venture to assume the title of a Benedict."

"Fear not," I replied, "that I should ever wish to infringe upon the injunctions of my benefactor, but may I not, when I see perfection, worship it, as the Indian does the sun, at a respectful distance? If I find my adoration accepted, may I not treasure in the silence of my heart the anticipation of future bliss?" Even though I had experienced 'love at first sight,' I needed to maintain my air of independence. "I shall be a much better judge after our promised interview to-morrow. Now let us to bed, for the morning, I imagine, is already very far advanced. Look at your watch. I have not mine upon me."

Mr. Ferguson placed his hand upon his fob and, with a look of the utmost chagrin, exclaimed, "I have it not! I have been robbed! It was that given me by the divine Mrs. Percival, and I can never sufficiently lament its loss."

"I am saddened to hear that, as I know how much the precious timepiece has meant to you."

His face dropped precipitously. "The natural consequence of entering a London crowd, I do imagine," he stated sadly.

"It shall be advertised," I suggested, "and a sum offered for its restoration, which will, I doubt not, place it again in your possession."

"You have found beauty, and I have lost the sole relic which remained to me of the only woman whom I ever prized in my life. So much for the adventures of our first night in London. And now, as you say, let us to bed, and if we sleep, I am sure we cannot be deficient in subjects for our dreams."

The words of William Shakespeare filled my head. Like the great Scot, Macbeth, I had to wonder, *Have I a heart to love, and in that heart, courage, to make my love known?*

Due to the lateness of the hour we laid ourselves down, it was nearly eleven o'clock when I awoke. I found Mr. Ferguson at the dining-table eating his breakfast.

"Well, good morning, my friend!" he greeted me. "Did you sleep well? And did you sleep at all?"

I grinned at his turning my own questions to him upon me. "It did take me some time to fall asleep, but when I did, my head filled with visions of angels."

"Strawberry angels?" he chided.

My stern glance soured his sweet smile. "I shall be keeping the subject of my reveries to myself, it appears." Mr. Cooke poured some hot beverage into a cup in front of me on the table. "Thank you, my good sir." I took a sip and found it to be very weak coffee. Not wanting to be an ungrateful guest, I continued to sip at it, but very, very slowly. "I wish to get an early start upon our morning call to the Allinghams," I announced to my friend.

He reached over and grasped my hand in his. "My dear Mr. Brown, I know you are anxious to reunite with the subject of your rescue and preservation from evening last, but in London town, things run upon a different sort of timeclock."

"Oh? How so?"

"I wish I had a better explanation for this, but when a person requests a *morning* call, it generally means three o'clock in the *afternoon*."

My eyes sprung open wide. "You mean we will have to wait almost four hours before making our call?"

"Yes, my friend. Don't be so impetuous." He held up an open hand. "Upon the heat and flame of thy distemper, sprinkle cool patience."

"Pray do not quote the Bard to me, Mr. Theodore Cavendish!" The use of his stage name may not have been enough to make my light-hearted intention known. I smiled to let him know of the jest.

"Oh, if'n it's Shakespeare you're a-wantin',"–he put on a silly accent–"How 'bout a bitta Harry Five: 'He's of the colour of the nutmeg, and of the heat of the ginger. He is pure air and fire; and the dull elements of earth and water never appear in him."

"I believe in that speech they spoke of a mount, not a young man."

Mr. Ferguson laughed out loud, perhaps the first time I have seen honest amusement in my friend's face in quite a while. "Well, if that is the case, Mr. Brown, I suggest you keep a tight hold on those reins!"

We both slapped at each other and laughed merrily until Mrs. Titmus entered the room and glared at the both of us.

At the appropriate time, we began our leisurely stroll back to the home of Mrs. Allingham's friend, where we had left her and her son in safety. A servant admitted us directly and guided us to a drawing room where we found the mother sitting with another woman.

Mrs. Allingham stood and approached us. "Gentlemen, it is so wonderful to see you both again, and in good health I trust?"

"Yes, madam," Mr. Ferguson responded, "good health. And you?"

"Oh, yes! The very, very best if it were not for your heroic actions." She indicated the other woman. "Please allow me to introduce my friend, Mrs. Ansel, who has graciously consented to our temporary residence."

We stepped to our hostess and took her hand in turn. Mrs. Ansel proved more worldly, her ensemble indicated refinement with experience. Her deep burgundy velour house dress hung modestly but well above the ankle.

As I shifted my head about, searching the apartment for the object of my affections, Mr. Ferguson spoke the question in my mind. "Excuse me, Mrs. Allingham, are we to have the pleasure of your son's company?"

Her head angled and faced the carpeted floor. "I am afraid my child has been too agitated by the events. He will not quit his bed due to a fever and headache. I will, however, deliver your generous regards."

How poor are they that have not patience! Iago screams in my ear. Despite waiting for hours to be reunited with the young man, he has taken to bed. I could have offered to sit with him, but I decided that would have been his mother's job, and I did not wish to offend her in any way.

As Mrs. Ansel had been to the opera while we enacted our own drama, we reconstructed the sequence of events for her. At the conclusion of the tale, Mrs. Allingham heaped praises upon me, energetic overflowing gratitude, which did bring some blush upon my face.

Mrs. Ansel turned to me. "Mr. Brown, I trust that you are not offended by my friend's ebullience. Perhaps she could refrain from pursuing this subject further." She turned to Mrs. Allingham with admonishing eyes.

"Well, well, I understand what you mean," she replied, "and I will hold my tongue if I can." She faced me. "Mr. Brown, I do hope you will excuse me for giving utterance to my sentiments, but they force their way to my lips, in spite of my efforts to control them." Her head swivelled to our hostess. "For I am either so vulgar, or so unfashionable, call it which you please, as to feel gratitude where it is due, and not to be ashamed of confessing it."

"Now, now, my dear," Mrs. Ansel chuckled, "with Mr. Allingham away in Newmarket, and the catastrophe of evening last, you are to be excused from all transgressions of society."

"Newmarket," Mrs. Allingham muttered with gritted teeth.

We proceeded to the gate of entrance and quit the little park. My mind continued to envisage the antics of the slight and lithe creatures, wondering if that might inescapably be the eventual flavour of my existence.

Chapter Eleven:
Sir Julius Maberly's Tutelage

SLEEP, ONCE AGAIN, PROVED DIFFICULT. Given the deficiency from the prior evening, due to the rescue and preservation of Mrs. Allingham's little angel, whose given name still eluded me, my need for proper rest remained unsatisfied.

Having observed the fay antics of the 'mollies,' as Ferguson had called them, brought to my mind the question of my own interest in the male sex. My thoughts wandered to wondering if I would have to give up my own way of life and adopt theirs if I were to continue seeking the company of another man.

While I did not condemn the poor creatures for their peculiar habits, their style of behaviour seemed foreign and unnatural to me. I just wanted to be true to myself and my regular nature. Concerns began to consume me that I would have to succumb to a well-established, but unfamiliar, culture in order to fulfil my desire to bond with another gentleman.

I found Mr. Ferguson sitting in the small drawing room, dressed and awaiting the day to come. His gaze hovered upon my countenance, and its initial joy became a look of concern.

"My dear Mr. Brown," he uttered, "did you not sleep well?"

Rather than speaking, I shook my head in the negative.

"I am distressed to hear that. Is there something I can do to remedy the situation?" His genuine concern warmed my heart. Why could not he be the one to return my affections? Again, I just shook my head in response.

"Was it something that happened yesterday?" he inquired.

Yes, indeed it was, and I nodded in the affirmative.

"Ah, I think I know." He stood and approached me, placing one innocent arm about my shoulders. "If I may be so bold as to conjecture, I believe it was the tribe of mollies that has distressed you so."

How could he know such things? This man truly grasped my heart. Once again, I nodded as tears began to form.

"My friend,"–he spun me so that we looked face-to-face–"that is but one way to conduct oneself. There are many men like yourself that give no outward appearance of their proclivities. If your worries come about from the belief that you would have to behave in such an eccentric manner as the mollies, please, banish them at once!" He clasped both my shoulders and squeezed firmly.

"Really?" I managed to squeak.

"Really!" he emphasized. "There are no rules requiring that a gentleman behave one particular way or another. Pray remember that I have lived in the company of other men who are like you. Some of them do exhibit effeminate behaviours, but most do not." He cocked his head. "As a matter of fact, some of them seem... overly masculine."

The clouds parted, and my smile appeared. "Thank you, David. This matter has been troubling me, and you have helped to dispel it in good haste."

"Excellent! Now, if you are as hungry as I am, I suggest we descend to breakfast before it is no longer!"

Following our repast, we made ourselves presentable and departed for the home of Sir Julius Maberly, brother of Mr. Graveton. We walked out Oxford-street, past Grosvenor Square, to Upper Brook-street, near the edge of the great Hyde Park.

His house appeared rather impressive from the outside. A stone and marble façade with many ornaments gave the sense of wealth and importance. The handsome young man who greeted us at the door, dressed in fine livery, bowed low and requested the favour of our names.

In my former life as a mere barber, I could have seen myself happy with a fellow such as this servant. Well-groomed and well-behaved, his, ruddy, round face appealed greatly to me. However, as a noble landowner, it would cause scandal to fraternise with ordinary service staff.

"Mr. John Brown and Mr. David Ferguson to see Sir Julius, by the direction of Mr. Graveton of Oldham, the baronet's brother," Mr. Ferguson made the introduction for us while I continued to gather wool.

"This way please," the fellow requested and led us to an apartment on the first floor. I could not help but notice how well the costume fit his well-developed body. He opened the door of a library, where an elderly gentleman sat writing at a table.

He appeared about fifty-eight or sixty years of age. His dress was of the plainest kind and by no means of the most modern fashion. A simple linen jacket hung limply about his torso. What hair he had left had been considerably thinned by the hand of Time, lightly-powdered, and a few scanty locks descended beneath the nape of his neck confined by a rosette.

"Mr. Brown and Mr. Ferguson, as per Mr. Graveton, sir," the attractive fellow announced and then quit the room, but not before I could catch one last glimpse of his impending, departing beauty.

"Gentlemen," the baronet addressed us as he stood, "I am extremely happy to see you. Your *avant-courier* arrived here upon paper on Saturday last. Please to be seated, and allow me, in the first place, to thank you for the pleasure which you have conferred on me, by introducing yourselves to my acquaintance."

I could not help but notice that his eyes lingered upon the face of Mr. Ferguson, but not in the way one does upon making a surprise recognition. The gleam in the older man's eyes described desire, and I could understand this as my companion well surpassed me in the arena of handsomeness.

"Pardon me, sir," I returned, "but I conceive the gratification to be conferred upon us."

"Negatived!" answered the baronet. "The doctor informs me that you are novices in the great world. I am old upon the town. I have seen the shadowy wonders which it contains, and observed all the whims, eccentricities, and vagaries of the full-grown babies who inhabit it, till they no longer afford me any amusement in the contemplation." He indicated two chairs next to his, and we sat. "My pleasure is now transferred from gazing and listening to seeing others affected with the same admiration and surprise which I once experienced myself. I pledge my word to you, gentlemen, that I shall derive an unexpected treat from shewing you *the lions.*"

We could not have expected a more flattering reception from a near stranger, especially as it appeared to proceed from the heart of the speaker. His animated and expressive countenance, while interesting and imposing, did little to conceal his unaffected manners.

Thirty minutes of desultory conversation passed, mostly concerning the status of Mr. Graveton's family, health, and medical practice. Sir Julius had never met Mr. Clarington, but his brother had mentioned him frequently in his writings.

"What do you purpose doing with yourselves the rest of this day?" asked Sir Julius.

"We have not at present formed any plan, sir," I answered, but could barely keep my thoughts from straying to young Mr. Evelyne.

"Of course, then, you have not any engagement," returned the baronet. "Therefore, if agreeable to you, I'll order my carriage, and we'll go and pass an hour or two at the exhibition of paintings in Somerset House."

I turned to Mr. Ferguson, and he nodded with a smile. "Yes," I responded to our host, "we should have great pleasure in attending with you."

"But I have a condition to annex, without which I cannot be your companion," Sir Julius announced as he stood. "You must promise to return and dine with me." He smiled, showing his brown-stained teeth. "I shall enjoy your company ten times more if you will accept this friendly bidding than if your first visit to me were paid upon formal invitation. I pledge my word to you, I have lived long enough to be weary of overstrained ceremony and all the restraints which it imposes."

While his grand request seemed most magnanimous, I could not help but think he had some ulterior motive, most likely the continued company of Mr. Ferguson, upon whom he appeared to be doting. "Your sentiments are greatly in our favour, sir," I responded.

"Settled!" continued the baronet, "and now I'll order the chariot." He turned, took a step, halted, and turned back. "But stay, I always take a luncheon about this time of day, which consists of a sandwich and a glass of Madeira. What will you take?"

"If anything, a biscuit and a draught of ale," I replied.

"Approved!" exclaimed Sir Julius. "Excuse me, but I predict sir, that you and I shall be very intimate. You speak as I like to be spoken to: plainly, and with no artifice." He turned to Mr. Ferguson with a gleam, "And you sir, what will be your choice?"

"I am so excellent a breakfast-eater, Sir Julius, that I believe I shall reserve my appetite for dinner." He bowed his head.

"These are windy words, my lord," the baronet said with a grin. "Recollect that it is a long while to six o'clock."

"With your permission then," Mr. Ferguson responded, "I'll take a biscuit with my friend, and a glass of Madeira with you."

"Agreed!" replied Sir Julius. "*In medio tutissimus ibis*, as the Roman poet expresses it. By-the-by, I have not kept up a very intimate acquaintance with any of those ancients since I quitted college. I remember once getting very angry with them, though, by all the rules of common sense, they ought to have suffered no share of the blame because, at a certain period of my youth, I discovered that I could write better Latin than I did English, and I have never since considered it a folly for boys to be compelled to study the dead languages before they are complete masters of their own."

"Mr. Ferguson has tutored me in the ways of Greek and Latin, if you please, Sir Julius," I indicated my friend," and I do believe I had sufficiently mastered our King's English before taking up the dead languages, as you have called them."

The baronet smiled broadly at my friend, displaying even more teeth. "Ah, Mr. Ferguson, you are full of surprises I can tell."

He led us to the dining-hall, where we continued our light-hearted banter over sandwiches, biscuits, ale and Madeira.

The carriage ride across London gave me a chance to observe the city's denizens. While Mr. Ferguson and Sir Julius nattered on about this or that, I kept my gaze out the window and watched well-dressed people and well-dressed buildings pass us by.

Just within the gallery's entrance, Sir Julius took my wrist and said, "I shall only be your preceptor by halves if I do not point out to you observation characters of notoriety, as well as inanimate objects of curiosity." He gestured about with his hands. "And to begin my instructions, what should you suppose that person to be, whose eyes are so attentively fixed upon the painting of Macbeth with the daggers?" His finger pointed to a not-very-handsome man in a military great-coat with his right arm suspended in a sling.

"I should suppose him a wounded officer who had retired upon half-pay," I guessed.

"That is exactly the opinion which he wishes to be entertained of him," Sir Julius began, "but he never bore arms in his life. A few years ago, he was one of the most noted gamblers, and—I may, without scruple, add—blacklegs, in the kingdom, and Bath was his principal scene of action."

My attention turned to the indicated gentleman again. He presented no sense of evil or cunning. I returned my gaze to my mentor.

"One evening, being engaged at cards with a party of gentlemen at a tavern in that city, the knave of clubs, the hero of the game of Loo, which they were playing, was missed from the pack, and one of the party positively asserted that it was concealed under the hand of the person before you, which was spread on the table. Upon his refusing to raise it, the accuser snatched a fork from the sideboard and pinned the fellow's hand with it to the table."

My face grimaced in pain as I imagined the feeling of having one's hand pierced by a fork.

"An examination of the gentleman's grounds for this precipitate action, of course, immediately took place. The card being found beneath his palm, he was consequently kicked out of the room, and never again ventured to appear in the place. He has, as I have understood, a small annuity upon which, with occasional lending his name and protection to members of the frail sisterhood, he contrives to live."

How vulgar and dishonest! I needed to keep reminding myself the world is full of people who are constantly attempting to better themselves by treachery and lying than by honest work.

During Sir Julius's recital, my friend had separated from us. We stepped toward him.

"I am in raptures," Mr. Ferguson said, "with this painting, which represents a lady feeding swans."

The sheer number of works of art hanging on the walls overwhelmed me. From floor to ceiling, from corner to corner, frames competed for every last inch of space, with some slightly overlapping. Even though we stood quite near the painting indicated, it took me several seconds to locate it due to the overabundance of similar pieces surrounding it.

"Coincided!" chimed Sir Julius, "but still I pledge my word to you, that closely as you may have imagined yourself to have examined it, I think I can direct you to the discovery of a curiosity, if not a beauty, which has escaped your scrutiny."

He moved a few steps nearer to the portrait, and we followed.

"You observe the portrait of a young countess, commissioned by her elderly husband. Examine the expanded wing of the swan nearest to the female figure. Fix your observation upon the third feather of that wing, and moving your eyes slowly downwards, tell me whether you cannot perceive the profile of a face, of which the leading feature is a large Roman nose?"

"Yes! I see it!" I shouted, and the echo reverberated through the large gallery. A few heads turned in my direction but just as quickly turned away.

"That is the likeness of a young aide-de-camp, which the painter received a *douceur* to insert," the baronet continued. "The lady's tender motive for having caused it to be drawn there is obvious to all her acquaintances except for her venerable husband, who is content to caress his young family and bless Heaven for having given him a progeny at his advanced age."

We spent the next few hours gawking at various walls overflowing with art. At times, Sir Julius would point out one thing or another, but I had difficulty comprehending his prittle-prattle.

Every time I observed the depiction of an angel, my thoughts strayed to Master Evelyne, the young fellow with whom I desired a reunion

As we prepared to quit the rooms, the baronet suddenly arrested our steps and pointed to a very attractive young lady at the end of the hall. "Observe that lovely and unaffected girl who is examining the case of miniatures near the window. This is the siren songstress Catherine Stephens of Covent Garden." He paused to lick his parched lips. "It is said that, a few months ago, a letter was one day delivered to her in the green room from a middle-aged but noble earl, requesting her to name upon what terms he might enjoy the happiness of calling her his. In reply to which, she took her pencil and, having written upon a blank space of the letter, 'As your daughter,' returned it by the bearer." He glanced quickly at his pocket watch. "But come, although no epicure, I like my dinner hot. My cook knows my punctuality, and at six precisely, it will be ready to come upon table."

As we entered Upper Brook-street, an open barouche carrying three particularly dashing and gaudy ladies passed us. Sir Julius flinched at the sight of them.

"Did you remark that carriage and the painted Jezebel in it?" he inquired. "I believe there can be no scandal in pronouncing that woman the greatest demirep in existence, for the flagrant act by which she had lately procured herself a second husband and made him master of a large fortune is so notorious, that even many of her own order of *extra*-fashionables have considered it decent to withdraw themselves from her acquaintance. You must excuse my talking any more with an empty stomach, but after dinner, I will recount to you what I know of her history. I pledge my word to you, I think it will entertain you."

While we dined, Sir Julius regaled us with endless details of his exploits and society connections. Again, I found it difficult to concentrate, as my thoughts strayed to Mrs. Allingham's beautiful boy. However, when the name "Percival" jogged my concentration, I gave our host my full attention.

"Percival, you say?" Mr. Ferguson questioned.

"Yes," the baronet replied, "the name of the lady whose artifices I am going to relate to you is now Percival, the honourable Mrs. Percival. Have you some acquaintance with her, Mr. Ferguson?"

"I should say I do, indeed, Sir Julius. Pray continue before my heart leaps from my chest."

Our host waved a hand to a servant to refill the goblets. I looked over at Mr. Ferguson with a sympathetic eye.

The baronet took a sip of fresh sherry. "Mrs. Percival is by birth a Scotchwoman, the daughter of a man of considerable fortune and consequence, whose wife, having forfeited her existence in giving birth to her infant, placed no bounds to the indulgence of his child. Her juvenile revels were principally confined to the sister kingdom till after her union with the honourable Mr. Mandover."

"Mandover?" Mr. Ferguson exclaimed. "It was a certain Mrs. Mandover whom I encountered at Inverness a while back. Do you suppose it could be the same woman?"

In Ferguson's tale, it was Mrs. Mandover who invited him to meet his beloved secret admirer who, as it turned out, was the bride of Colonel Percival. The malevolent woman had trapped my dear friend as a means to cause the Percivals to divorce.

"I am uncertain, as she was only about twenty years of age when she first visited London with her father, where, subsequent to her marriage, her residence was fixed." He paused for another sip of sherry. "She had always been accustomed to the best society, and she possessed a certain quickness of faculty and subtlety of disposition, by which she contrived, very shortly after her arrival in town, to rank herself with the leaders of the *ton*, and to become of importance in the circles of fashion."

Sir Julius stood and waved us to follow him. "Perhaps we should retire to the sitting-room, as this portends to be a lengthy tale."

Mr. Ferguson jumped up and moved quickly, and I followed in their shadows. Once we had seated ourselves in the comfortable padded leather chaises, Sir Julius continued.

"Soon after the marriage, her father died and bequeathed to her several thousands, which she had so adroitly played her cards previously to his death as to have induced him to secure indivisibly to herself. Her new-found extravagance and folly now spurned the barriers which common sense and decorum would have opposed to her pursuance of her unheeded course. As Pope says, 'The love of pleasure, and the love of away are the distinguishing feminine passions.' Although I cannot agree with him as to the general truth of his observation, there are, undoubtedly, many partial instances daily to be seen of its veracity, and Mrs. Mandover, as she was known then, was one of its most striking examples." Sir Julius sipped on his sherry before continuing. "Mr. Mandover, in every sense of the expression, an accomplished gentleman, doted upon his wife; however, she regarded him with all the indifference of a discarded doll."

Mr. Ferguson's expression changed to one of complete surprise. His eyes opened widely and his jaw hung slack.

"Oh, yes. Despite his fervent attentions and useless attempts to rescue her from the baneful vortex into which she was sinking, she remained unfeeling and dedicated to her fashionable *dishonourables*. The poor fellow sought false solace in the glass"—he held his goblet up for effect—"and he gradually metamorphosed into a careless and inanimate sloven. At the early age of thirty-two, he sunk into the grave, the victim of his wife's indifference."

My hand went up to my mouth to express the shock of hearing how this woman destroyed an honest man. I peered over at Mr. Ferguson, who sat frozen in contemplation.

"Within a year, the stone-hearted widow made the acquaintance of Colonel Percival, a handsome man of engaging manners." The baronet took another sip.

"Pardon me, Sir Julius," Mr. Ferguson interrupted, "but the Mrs. Mandover I previously had encountered in Inverness introduced me to a Mrs. Percival who impressed me as a shy and demure woman, nothing like the fashionable society *bonne vivante* you have just described."

"You have knocked me for six, sir!" the baronet exclaimed. "But, pray, let me continue, and, perhaps, all shall be revealed."

We nodded our heads in consent.

"I imagine that it must be almost unnecessary to inform you that a woman like Mrs. Mandover felt regret at the death of her husband only in proportion as the event for a time withheld her from appearing in public. She waited for as long as she could tolerate—approximately four-and-a-half months—before reacquainting herself with her society circle. Soon after, she encountered a handsome colonel of engaging manners and of a disposition for pleasure, exactly suited to the taste of the dissipated widow."

"Was this Colonel Percival?" Mr. Ferguson inquired.

"Why, yes. At any rate, it was clearly perceptible that she had very little attractions for the colonel, but the colonel had very little actual property besides his commission. He led a life of gaiety, which naturally produced many drafts upon his pocket, which he was frequently at a loss to answer."

"And how was it that they met, Sir Julius?" I asked.

"The widow was at that time the mistress of a faro bank, and whenever the colonel played, he was certain to become a winner. For the replenishment of his purse, he repaid the indulgent owner of the concern with his affected smiles and caresses."

Mr. Ferguson asked, "You mean to say that Mrs. Mandover forced the colonel's luck to maintain his patronage?"

"Yes, indeed. Although Cupid is represented blind, the keenest-sighted of mortals are those in love. The widow continued to build her suit with the gentleman, but one day she learned of a rival for the colonel's attentions, Miss Jessy Campbell, an orphan, but a lovely, innocent, and accomplished girl. Upon attaining her twenty-first year, she became the mistress of seventy thousand pounds. Mrs. Mandover, now approaching the age of thirty, could not compete with Miss Campbell's youth, and the colonel made public his engagement with the younger woman." Sir Julius smiled broadly. "Accordingly, one evening after the announcement, the overly-confident colonel ventured six hundred on a card, and he was not a little surprised to find himself a loser. Mrs. Mandover hastily closed the bank on some pretext."

"What an unabashed sore loser," Mr. Ferguson observed.

"If you suppose, gentlemen," the baronet continued, "that the *ne plus ultra* fashionables are more delicate in expressing their sentiments, or more chaste in the selection of the phrases in which they give vent to their offended feelings, than those whom they consider as crawling at the very foot of that ladder of *ton*, to the most exalted step of which they imagine themselves to have ascended, you are, I pledge my word to you, most egregiously mistaken," he pointed an admonishing finger in the air.

"And so the colonel married Miss Campbell?" My curiosity had been piqued.

"At their very first opportunity. Mrs. Mandover continued to associate with the happy couple, all the while scheming to pry the two love-birds apart. A few years back, the shrewd one devised a ploy whereby she drew the attentions of a young gentleman to the Percival home on the pretext of Miss Jessy being a devotee. Mrs. Mandover manufactured a tableau in which the colonel caught the unsuspecting fellow in a compromising position with his wife, thus leading to a divorce. Once the dust had settled, the viper struck and finally claimed the colonel for her own, and she is now known to all as Mrs. Percival."

Mr. Ferguson held his handkerchief to his face. A smothered exclamation burst from his lips.

"Dear me, sir. Are you unwell?" inquired Sir Julius.

When he did not respond, I announced, "My friend is possessed of a very susceptible heart, and I doubt not, sincerely sympathises with the unfortunate victim of treachery whom you have been describing to us."

"Sympathise!" echoed Mr. Ferguson, starting from his seat and pacing the room with the steps of a madman. "Sympathise," he repeated. "Oh, God! Is there a term in language sufficiently eloquent to express the horror with which my soul is affected as I reflect on the cruelty, the injustice, exercised against that loveliest of human beings, the wronged Mrs. Jessy Percival? Oh, that I possessed the power of crushing into annihilation, of exposing to the universal abhorrence of the world, the infamous beings by whom her spotless reputation has been calumniated, her innocence blackened with the imputation of guilt!"

"Pardon me," remarked Sir Julius, "but it appears you have had more than a passing acquaintance with the ill-starred, first Mrs. Percival."

"Sir," returned Mr. Ferguson, "short as our acquaintance has been, I have perceived you to be equally the gentleman and the man. To your honour, therefore, I feel no hesitation in confiding that I am the individual who was made the instrument of Mrs. Mandover's infamous plot."

"Indeed!" replied Sir Julius. "I had understood that the gentleman was an actor, and his name Cavendish."

"I almost blush, sir," answered Mr. Ferguson, "to confess that a theatrical mania had at that time drawn me by its irresistible force to the stage." He then related the tale of his time in Inverness, the letters and gifts, and the scene of Mrs. Mandover's nefarious plot. "From the moment of my quitting Inverness, I have never seen or heard of Jessy, as you call her. Perhaps, sir, you can acquaint me what has been her destiny?"

"Acknowledged!" answered Sir Julius. He tipped the glass to his lips to remove the last dregs. "Mrs. Mandover had young Jessy sent to Glasgow and placed under the care of a humble relative. In the course of a few weeks, an account appeared in the daily prints of her imputed offence, and her consequent repudiation from her husband. The treachery of which she found herself the victim communicated shock to her feelings, driving her almost to madness, which gradually subsided into the deepest melancholy. I have been informed, that it is now about twelve months, she put a period to her wretched existence by throwing herself into the Clyde."

I turned to see tears of anguish burning the cheeks of my dear Mr. Ferguson. "Sir Julius, please pardon me, but I must depart for Oxford-street now. Thank you for your hospitality."

The expression of the baronet's eye fully convinced me that he had penetrated into the state of Mr. Ferguson's heart. "I admit, that the pillow is often an excellent soother, as well as adviser. Although I had anticipated you both would have supped with me, I will not attempt to detain you longer than till my chariot is ready to convey you home."

As we alighted from the baronet's coach in Oxford-street, Mr. Ferguson reached absent-mindedly for his pocket-watch. "Heaven be praised that I have lost the blessed timepiece! It was the vile gift of that infernal murderess! Oh, Jessy! Jessy! Oh God, revenge the innocent." He sighed but spoke no more that night.

Chapter Twelve:
Angels' Flight

MR. FERGUSON RETIRED DIRECTLY upon entering the Titmus residence, but as I ascended the stairs leading to our shared drawing room, I arrested my steps upon hearing the voices of our hosts. The conversation arose from their parlour, and I entered, observing a weeping Mrs. Titmus.

"Oh, Lord-a-mercy," she exclaimed upon seeing me. "What is to be done?" She glanced at her husband. "We 'ave got such a misfortune to tell you." A hand went to her forehead. "Would you believe it? Betsey slipped on 'er 'at and shawl after we finished our *breakfasses*, said as 'ow she was only a-going to step to the *millinder's* over the way, and I'll tell you what it is, sir: She's never been a-near 'ome since."

"And I tell *mar*," Charlotte spoke, "that as sure as can be, she's gone off with Sir Frederick."

"*E's* an infernal scoundrel! That's what 'e is!" burst out Mr. Titmus. "And if I can catch him, I'll 'ang him, if the law *hallows* me."

"Oh, Lord, *par*, don't talk so," advised Charlotte. "Why, if 'e's married to Betsey, 'e's your son now, you know."

"Damn such sons," her father reacted. "If I don't clap 'im up in gaol, if I ever get 'old of 'im, but I dare say 'e will take pretty good care to keep out of the way when the girl's money is spent."

I did not realise that the family had any money at all. "Had Miss Titmus money at her own disposal?" I asked.

"Yes, sir," replied the father, "she 'ad three 'undred pounds left 'er by a godmother placed in the 'ands of a banker in the city. I find it was drawn out, by an order from 'er, about two o'clock this *hafternoon*."

After hearing Mr. Ferguson's tales of villainy this reprehensible scoundrel had previously executed, I considered it would be only unnecessarily increasing the grief of the parents to confess that I had any cause for entertaining suspicions of the fairness of the pretended Sir Frederick's character. "I am so sorry to hear of this. It would be my fondest wish to be able to somehow affect repairs.”

“Oh, I could take and break me *’eart* about it!” exclaimed Mrs. Titmus. “So well as she might *’ave* been married, and settled in the world, if she *’ad* but considered things in a proper light.”

“Ay, indeed,” observed the father. “There sits the man that would *’ave* made her as *’appy* as a queen. That’s what *’e* would.”

I turned my eyes toward an obscure corner of the room to which the extended finger of Mr. Titmus directed them. There sat a male figure barely lit by a single candle burning on the table nearby. His silhouette did not stir my memory, but in an instant, all mystery resolved when a dolorous voice sighed forth, “Oh dear, Miss Betsey, angel!” thus announcing the disappointed Mr. Tunks.

Not wishing to continue my participation in this oversentimental family scene, I spoke thus, “Would that I could remain and converse, but I am compelled to compose letters of thanks to my day’s host and his brother, who so kindly introduced us.” I hurry-scurried up the stairs and spent the rest of the evening writing to the doctor Graveton and his brother, Sir Julius, conveying my gratitude for their assistances.

On the following morning, I found a message from Mr. Ferguson stating he would take his breakfast in his chamber as he was not perfectly well and wished to pass a few hours in solitude and hoped to join me for dinner. The poor fellow! Hearing that his object of adoration had taken her own life had placed a darkened cloud over his head, and I would have to respect his wishes for privacy until such time as he felt open to my unremitting company.

On the other hand, I myself had many pleasant things to look forward to that particular day as I was to visit Mrs. Allingham and her fair son. Following my own meal, I returned to my chamber to prepare myself for the joys ahead.

A knock on the door revealed Charlotte with a note. “This just came for you, Mr. Brown.” She handed me the folded paper and curtseyed slightly. I had to keep reminding myself that the Titmus family had not known me as the town barber’s nephew, only as the distinguished lord of the manor, Mr. Brown, and they will continue to treat me as such. It was my hope that I would eventually adjust to such treatment.

"Thank you, Miss Charlotte." I smiled blandly at her as I took the letter. She disappeared quickly down the stairs.

The spidery handwriting proved to be from Mrs. Allingham. She had written to inform me that due to yet another exchange of apartments, she would be unable to enjoy my society that day. An invitation for myself and Mr. Ferguson to dine with her at the future residence in Berners-street on the morrow followed her sincerest regrets. Dinner would be at five, but she desired us to pay our call earlier for a more friendly visit.

Once more I was denied the company of the angel whom I rescued from a fiery death. I refolded the paper and slipped it into an inside pocket. As I contemplated my plight and marinated in my anxiety, a loud rap sounded at the door.

"Mr. Brown," began Mrs. Titmus, "I just came up *'ere* to inform you that no tidings from our dear Betsey *'ave* as yet been procured. Neither any word of Sir Frederick Lambert *'imself*, under *'ose* protection there is no doubt she has placed *'erself*. That fellow *'ad* been an utter stranger to us when *'e* first *h*engaged lodgings with us, and we are completely *h*unawares of any friends or connexions *'e* might *'ave 'ad* in London. No one ever visited *'im 'ere* that I rightly know of, and –"

Another thunderous clamour from below interrupted my jabbering hostess, for which I was quite grateful. Sir Julius Maberly quickly hobbled up the stairs announcing, "I am unfashionably early in my call, Mr. Brown, but I have already told you that I am by no means a strict adherer to useless forms, and I am anxious to inquire how your friend does this morning." He turned to Mrs. Titmus and stuck out his hand, "Hello, madam, I am Sir Julius Maberly, friend to your lodgers, Messieurs Brown and Ferguson."

Mrs. Titmus glanced at me with saucer-sized eyes and blanched cheeks, then at our guest. She took his fingertips in her hand, curtseyed slightly, blurted, "Charmed, *h*I'm sure," and raced down the stairs.

"What a fascinating creature!" remarked Sir Julius. "However, I am certain that the concern which your friend evinced at the fate of poor Mrs. Percival was from the heart, and I really found myself interested in his feelings."

I motioned for Sir Julius to enter our sitting room and offered him a chair. "I really can't tell you much more than what I know, which is very little indeed. Upon reaching our rooms, Mr. Ferguson disappeared, and I have not seen him since. He left me this note," which I picked up and handed to my guest.

Upon finishing reading, Sir Julius looked up at me. "Mr. Brown, I consider myself peculiarly fortunate in finding you alone this morning." He handed me the note and I placed in on a table. "Sir, I am going to take a freedom with you which I am almost tempted to apprehend that you will consider an unwarrantable liberty on my part. I therefore beg your excuse before I commit my offence and throw myself upon your lenity for obtaining it."

After all he had done for us, I had no reservation. "From the lips of Sir Julius Maberly, it is impossible that I can anticipate a willing offence. Pray, sir, express yourself freely." I sat in the other chair.

He seemed to be studying my face before continuing. "Sir, at the time of Mr. Clarington's death, I read in the newspapers an account of his extraordinary will and your good fortune. I pledge my word to you that the circumstance has, since that period, cost me many an hour of serious reflection."

His words concerned me. "From what cause, sir, could that arise?" I asked.

"I will tell you, sir, but as a necessary introduction to what I wish to relate to you of others, I must first intrude upon you a few words concerning myself." He coughed lightly into one hand. "Like you, sir, I was not born exactly in the sphere of life in which I am now moving. We have both, if I may be allowed the use of the expression—in reference to the nine days of wonder which a few years ago amused the world—been 'fortunate youths.'" Again, he scrutinised my countenance. "The family from which I am descended is old and respectable, but wealth is not always the accompaniment of those qualities. My father, who was a clergyman of the Church of England, being the parent of twelve children, for the sole support of whom he enjoyed only a living of four hundred and seventy pounds a-year, a plain, but a good and general education, in the rudiments of which he himself grounded us, formed by far the most valuable part of the fortune which he could flatter us with the prospect of ever expecting to derive from him." He glanced at the pitcher on the table. "Could I trouble you for something to soothe my dry throat?"

I poured a glass of barley water, which he greeted with raised eyebrows. After a sip, he continued. "The only male relative whom my father was conscious of possessing was a first cousin, named Sir Julius Maberly, after whom I had been christened. He was a whimsical and cynical old bachelor, and I had little anticipation of either inheriting his title or his wealth. When I was about nine years old, he came to pass a few days with my father. He had not seen me since the time he had appeared as one of my sponsors at the baptismal font, when I had received the title of Julius the Second. At this visit, he professed himself greatly pleased with me, called me *his* boy, and declared his intentions of giving me a college education at his own expense."

He took another taste of the water. From his wrinkled expression, I imagined he had been hoping for Madeira.

"Under his auspices, I was first placed at Eton, and, at a proper age, removed to Cambridge. Nearly the whole of my vacations passed with him at his seat in the neighbourhood of Shrewsbury."

As I listened, I dreamed I could have been placed in public education and received a proper upbringing, unlike the marginal instruction I received in Oldham.

"My most intimate companion, and indeed only chosen friend at the university, was a young man, somewhat my junior in age, but our dispositions, our manners, and our pursuits were so congenial to each other's feelings, that we were almost inseparable. We both studied law, and my friend's parents, as I understood, were residing in Asia, where he was to return when an opportunity offered for introducing him to advantage at the Eastern bar."

Once again, he raised the glass of barley water to his lips and screwed up his face. "Would you prefer something else to drink, Sir Julius? Tea, perhaps?" I offered.

"No, my boy. This shall be quite sufficient for the earliness of the morning." He sat the glass down. "I was myself the fifth and youngest of my father's sons, but the mandates of death, which do not regard the rules of primogeniture, had left me the sole male descendant of my house. About the period of completing my twenty-fifth year, by the sudden death of my relative, Sir Julius, I found myself not only the legal heir to his title, but the bequeathed inheritor of his large fortune."

"How... fortunate for you," I reacted.

"Yes, so to speak." He smiled a bit. "When my friend and myself quitted Cambridge, we had repaired to London and became occupiers of contiguous apartments in the Temple district. Our hours of recreation being, as they had invariably been, ever since our acquaintance had been first formed, passed in each other's society." A look of wistfulness and longing passed over his face. "With the intelligence of my namesake's death, I had received a summons to appear immediately in Staffordshire. My friend, at once, turned melancholy. When I inquired as to his shift in disposition, he told me he expected we would no longer be fellow-students, as my new-found fortune negated the need for pursuing a profession. I assured him that I had every intention of returning as soon as I had settled my affairs and the forms of decorum would permit. Even so, I was of the opinion that I should determine to leave the field open to those who have more occasion for the emoluments to be derived from its practice than I could expect to experience."

"And you never completed your degree in law, Sir Julius?"

He held up a cautioning hand. "Not so all-a-gog, Mr. Brown, the story has yet to fully unfold." Another sip of the distasteful water shifted his countenance. "In the course of about two months, I had made arrangements in favour of all those to whom I was bound by the ties of blood—including my sister who married your Mr. Graveton—and repaired back to London, proceeding immediately to the Temple in quest of my friend. In his apartments, I found another inhabitant who informed me that he had, in the most sudden manner, left London without explaining to any individual whither he was going or the cause by which he was actuated in his hasty proceedings. Every inquiry which I set on foot after him proved futile. Every exertion which I made to discover his retreat—ineffectual. From that moment, his fate has to me remained an impenetrable secret." He turned and examined my face again.

"Is something the matter, Sir Julius?" I inquired. "You appear to fix your attentions on my face for some reason I cannot make out."

"Oh, I apologise, dear boy. Please forgive my rude behaviour. But now, sir, mark the cause of my having related these particulars to you: The name of the friend whom I have been describing to you was Oliver Clarington."

Oliver Clarington? Could it possibly be the same considerate gentleman who had left me his considerable fortune?

"At the death of your benefactor," Sir Julius continued, "I was immediately led to reflect whether Mr. Oliver Clarington, just deceased, could have been a relative of him whom I so sincerely esteemed. Having heard that the Mr. Clarington—whose extraordinary disposition of his property caused him to be the subject of conversation—was supposed to have amassed the wealth of which he possessed in India. I could not doubt that he was the father of my lamented friend, and from the bequest which he had made of his property I felt an indubitable conviction that my friend, if indeed my friend *had* been his son, must have ceased to exist."

I observed a welling tear in the gentleman's eye. He must have truly loved his friend, perhaps in the same way I have felt affection toward other men. "The circumstances upon which you ground your opinion, sir, appear indeed very strongly to coincide."

"Granted!" he blurted. "Granted beyond a doubt. And now, sir, on an entirely different matter, give me leave freely to ask you whether you actually believe that you are not in any degree related to the gentleman to whom you have fallen heir?"

"Of that I think I can declare myself without hesitation," I answered. "To be positive, my mother was a native of the village of Oldham, where Mr. Clarington lived, and in which I now reside. My father, who was a serjeant in a marching regiment, died at Cork."

"Well, it is very extraordinary," he again fixed his eyes, with a steadfast gaze, upon my countenance. As he continued to scrutinise my face, I had to accept that it might not have been Mr. Ferguson's company he favoured, but mine. While it warmed my heart to a certain extent, I felt no similar attraction to one so aged and time-worn.

"Was your friend married?" I inquired to return the topic of the conversation to Mr. Clarington.

"Not that I was ever acquainted with," returned Sir Julius. "Nor, to my knowledge, a father. What he might have become after our separation from each other, I cannot answer for." A warm smile spread across his face. "Well, I have relieved my mind by unburthening it to you. I could not overrule the inclination which I felt to propose to you the plain questions which have just been the subject of my inquiries." He extended his hand toward me.

I placed my hand in his, and the baronet pressed it while saying, "Permit me, in future, to regard you as my friend, and you will confer on me an indescribable satisfaction."

Just as I began my reply, the sound of footsteps advanced toward the apartment. "Hush!" cautioned Sir Julius. "Someone approaches, and there is no occasion to acquaint a third person with what has been passing between us."

I smiled in reply to the delicacy of the baronet's observation, and in the same moment, Mr. Ferguson entered the room.

"Ah!" the baronet exclaimed, "I am happy to see you well this morning, sir."

"Yes, Ferguson, as am I. Sir Julius paid me a call just as I was preparing to visit with Mrs. Allingham, but this note arrived." I retrieved the folded paper and handed it to my friend.

"Mrs. Allingham!" repeated Sir Julius. "Are you speaking of that Mrs. Allingham whose lovely child so miraculously escaped with life from the fire which took place nearly opposite to this house last Saturday night?"

"The very same, sir," I responded.

"Why, can it be possible–and yet I know not why–but I could pledge my word that you are the two gentlemen whom the daily prints record as having been the instruments of his preservation?" inquired the baronet.

"We had indeed, sir, the satisfaction of lending our assistance to the escape from the peril which you have ascribed," came my answer.

"And have you seen the little angel since?" asked Sir Julius.

"Well..." I began, "we have made several attempts, but at each turn we are blocked by chance circumstances mainly attributed to the current vagrant nature of the mother and child. However, this note"–I pointed to the paper in Mr. Ferguson's hand–"indicates that we are to dine with them on the morrow at their new place of residence in Berners-street."

"Take care of your hearts, gentlemen," Sir Julius advised, "for I pledge my word to you that the young August Evelyne is a most interesting and captivating child. He is one of my particular favourites."

His admonishing words seemed unnecessary as I had already felt the sting of the blind god's arrow. However, he did make use of a name unfamiliar to me. "August? Did you say the young man's man was August, sir?"

"Affirmed!" replied the baronet. "He was born in that month, as I have understood, and it was a whim of his mother's to have the child christened by that name." A smile crossed his face. "Mrs. Allingham is an excellent woman, one whom I can with sincerity declare that I believe to be truly amiable. She undoubtedly has her foibles–what human being is without them?–but hers mostly rank on the side of goodness, and the casual caprices of the head, in my opinion, deserve to pass uncensored where the tenor of the heart is uninterruptedly good." He placed a palm upon his chest. "Mrs. Allingham calls herself a distant relative of mine."

Given his large family and familiarity with so many people, it gave me pause to wonder if almost everyone we should encounter would be somehow connected with Sir Julius. "Indeed, sir," I pronounced.

"Her third and present husband, Mr. Allingham, has, like herself, been married before, and his first wife was my eldest sister. I shall leave it to you to judge whether this relationship is distant or non-existent." He tapped the side of his swollen nose. "Between ourselves," he spoke in more hushed tones, "I fear her union with him has, ere this, proved an event which by no means affords her satisfactory reflections. He is a man whom, to say no worse of him, I very much dislike, yet a man in every respect calculated to insinuate himself into the good opinion of an unsuspecting stranger. A gamester by nature, and I may add, by profession, for, when in town, his days and nights are passed in those infamous receptacles, the disgrace of St. James's, where the vicious and desperate meet for the express purpose of destroying each other's means and expectations." His eyes rolled up. "When not in London, a parallel line of occupation draws him to Newmarket. Why he married her is obvious: she possesses a handsome jointure and has—or at least *had*—also considerable property at her own disposal. It is one of the foibles of Mrs. Allingham, who was, at an early period of her life, considered beautiful, not to be capable of so clearly perceiving the ravages of time in her own person, as they are perceptible to her acquaintances. I can only surmise that she became blinded to his views and real character. That and the triumph of her vanity at being once again addressed in the terms of love."

Sir Julius did not hold his tongue in matters of personal history. This revelation of the Allingham family presented further concerns. "Is Master Evelyne entirely dependent upon his mother, Sir Julius?" I felt it important to know for my own security.

"You are inquiring, methinks, upon very slender acquaintance, into the state of affairs," the baronet smiled and laughed. "This reminds me of the good old times, when marriages were announced to the public in the form of 'Squire So-and-so had led to the altar the accomplished and beautiful Miss Such-and-such, with a fortune of fifteen thousand pounds.'" His hand went to his smiling lips.

I could not help but smile myself, and I turned toward the window in hopes of avoiding the scrutinising eye of the baronet.

"Although I do not believe that your question was advanced from any mercenary feeling, it may not be unpleasant to you to learn that he has ten thousand pounds in his own possession, left by his late father." He tapped his nose again. "My little friend, August, is a treasure, with those sparkling eyes and dimpled chin." After a glance at his timepiece, he announced, "But I dine out ten miles in the country to-day, and must return home first to dress, so adieu. I shall be all impatience to hear your sentiments of Master Evelyne after your visit to-morrow." He rose and strode to the door. "Your heroic efforts will do much to gain you the favour of both mother and child, Mr. Brown." With a wink, he began descending the stairs.

I turned to face Ferguson and he looked up from the letter and grinned at me as if saying, "Please be cautious in your matters, my friend."

Yes, my heart had been pierced by infatuation, but time had been testing my resolve by constantly postponing the reacquaintance with Master Evelyne, my August. And as Lysander cautioned us in *Midsummer Night's Dream*, "The course of true love never did run smooth." Even so, the scheduled dinner could not have arrived soon enough.

Chapter Thirteen:
A Scoundrel in the Suds

FOLLOWING OUR LUNCHEON, Mr. Ferguson suggested we take a walk about the surrounding area. Believing this exercise might help to repair my friend's heart break, I heartily accepted the invitation and we made our way down the stairs and into Oxford-street. We had just reached Bond-street when we heard voices raised in alarum, calling out for assistance.

"Help!" someone called out from the opposite corner. "Murder!" screamed another.

We moved toward the spot and beheld a gentleman in the clutches of two men, and a woman of inferior description, who appeared to have pursued and overtaken him. A crowd had rapidly assembled, as–I have experienced–is the custom in the streets of London.

Mr. Ferguson asked one of the fellows observing the affray, "What is the matter, sir?"

"Oh, I don't know what, sir," came the reply. "The gentleman is drunk, and he seems to be got into bad hands."

"Then why has not somebody stepped forward to his relief?" my friend inquired.

"You had better not interfere, gentleman," the other fellow responded. "You don't know what mischief you may get into yourselves."

"That consideration will not deter either of us from lending our assistance to an ill-used person," I shouted as Mr. Ferguson and I approached the squabble.

We could hear two men, one of whom detained the besieged gentleman by the collar of his coat, demanding of him payment, in the coarsest language–which was not repeatable in pleasant company. They charged him with having that evening incurred a bill in the house of the woman, who–with all the opprobrious violence of a vulgar and exasperated person, was corroborating the statement which they made, loading him with epithets of the bitterest and foulest nature.

The benighted gentleman cried out denials, which could barely be understood as he seemed quite boosey, clipping the King's English with his entreaties, thoroughly soaked. "Watch!" he cried out. "Watch!"

At first I thought he might be pleading for us to observe the proceedings, but as a small group of blue-suited gentlemen rushed to the scene, I realised he had been attempting to summon the watch, a group of beadles who patrolled the streets of London.

The female ally of the ruffians shouted out, "Let us skedaddle, mates. Here come the blues!"

As the watch drew nearer, the crowd began to dissipate. We breached the circle and disengaged the hapless soul from his tormentors as the two of them and their woman accomplice ran off to evade their pursuers.

"They beat me an' abused me," the drunkard slurred. "An' I know not whyfore." His eyes closed and then opened quickly. "Please. Please conduct me to my lodgings."

"And where might that be, my good sir," Mr. Ferguson inquired.

"Where I am staying, of course!" the inebriated fellow cried out. "Wait! I do believe I am at Short's hotel in Bond-street."

I glanced at Mr. Ferguson who nodded. We each drew an arm of his through one of ours. At a deliberate and broken pace, we managed to lead him to the spot which he had named.

Upon reaching the hotel, waiters immediately ushered us into a dining-room. The politeness and alertness of the house staff plainly indicated they knew the stranger well and respected him. He dropped into a chair and promptly fell soundly asleep.

One of the waiters inquired into the situation and I recounted what had passed. "I shall do myself the pleasure of calling upon the gentleman in the morning, to inquire after the state of his health, as I am very apprehensive, from the rough treatment which he experienced, that he may have sustained some injury, of which he is at present unconscious. For whom shall I inquire?"

"Sir Malcolm Brockelsbie, sir," the waiter replied.

Brockelsbie? I took a second glance at the person sleeping before me. He had first cast a shadow upon my life when he abruptly appeared at Ashbank Hall the day of Mr. Clarington's services.

Rude, brash, assuming himself to be the sole heir of the recently-deceased's estate, the baronet had strut about like a flouncing peacock, foul in his language and dismissive in his attitude. I scarcely recognised him in his current state.

I directed my gaze to Mr. Ferguson, nodded my head toward the door, and we quitted the room. As we stepped into Bond-street, a voice arrested us.

"I beg your pardon, gentlemen, but I am Sir Malcolm Brockelsbie's servant, and having just heard the essential service which you have rendered him, I am certain that he would never forgive me if I omitted to request your address."

At first, I considered refusing to divulge such information as I wanted little to do with pathetic rogue who had besmirched the funeral of my benefactor. If he discovered my identity, he might want to pinch and snaffle whatever he could from me, still claiming my lawfully-assigned estate as his own. Then, upon further reflexion, determined no sufficient reason existed for withholding it.

"I have not a card in my pocket. You may say Mr. Brown and Mr. Ferguson. If you provide some paper, I shall write the address out." He directed me back inside to a desk with writing accessories and I quickly scratched out our particulars. After I gave the slip to Brockelsbie's servant, we hastily departed.

Once we had moved out of the hearing of the waiter who had conducted us to the door of the hotel, I said, "London is so full of adventure, my friend. Is it always thus?"

He smiled and replied, "So it seems, my friend. So it seems."

"Well, what think you of this new adventure? Is it not a singular circumstance that I should have been a party concerned in the rescue of the only man who envies me my inheritance?"

"Oh!" Mr. Ferguson's face registered surprise. "Is that the fellow you have told me who descended upon your dear benefactor's home, claiming to be rightful owner, and then disparaged nearly the entire town at the gravesite?"

"One and the same, I am afraid."

"If a single spark of generous feeling exists in his heart," replied Mr. Ferguson, "he must, I think, more than blush for the sarcasm which he so unjustly cast upon you in Oldham churchyard."

"Nay, I can plead an excuse for him. It was certainly a great provocation to be summoned to witness the instatement of another into that inheritance which he had, doubtless, from his birth, been taught to consider as his own."

We ambled along Bond-street as Mr. Ferguson continued. "Supposing you a stranger, he will, of course, seek an introduction to you, under the present circumstances."

"I should imagine such would be the case," I returned.

"And how do you intend to act?" he asked.

Following a moment of reflection, I replied, "You very well know how repellent it is to my feelings to perform either a proud or an unfeeling action. My conduct shall be regulated by that which he observes towards me."

Mr. Ferguson smiled and shook his head gently at my response. "If you ever have an enemy, I am positive that it is what you will never merit."

"I call that man an enemy who is guilty of a premeditated wrong, not him who is hurried, by the circumstances of the hour, into the utterance of a harsh expression. Reverse our situations at the moment the offence was given, and I should most probably have acted the same. You know, 'to err is human –'"

"To forgive divine," Mr. Ferguson concluded as he pressed my hand with his.

Every time my dear friend performs a physical act of affection, demonstrating the very depth of his friendship with me, I silently curse Cassius, who expertly counselled "The fault, dear Brutus, is not in our stars." How I have prayed that my dearest David could somehow transform his heart and find me the person of his tenderest desires. Sadly, I suspected this would never happen.

I glanced down at our clasped hands. "Yes, I acknowledge that it is so, when the heart is averse to yielding forgiveness, and yet constrains itself to grant it." I looked ahead. "But it loses all merit with me, as it is for my own happiness that I seek to be at variance with no one."

We smiled at each other, but for very different reasons, I was quite certain.

At our return home, we found Mrs. Titmus standing in the door-way of her parlour "like patience on a monument, smiling at grief," as Viola might have described her. As we passed, she informed us, "We still *hain't 'eard* one word from our *h*undutiful daughter, Mr. Brown, Mr. Ferguson. Not one word! I verily believe you will find no one more *'eartsore* than Mr. Tunks and meself."

Not knowing rightly how to respond to her persistent anguish, an old phrase popped from my mouth, "Well, hope for the best, they say."

Constrained by grief, "Fear the worst, they also say," she grumbled as she watched us ascended to our chambers.

I knew full-well that she entertained a mood to discuss the subject nearest to her heart the live-long night with anyone who might join her in conversation. However, I had personal heart-near subjects to dwell upon in the privacy of my room.

On the following morning, whilst we sat at breakfast expatiating on the extraordinary adventures which had already marked our brief stay in London, Mrs. Titmus entered the apartment and closed the door after her with some degree of caution.

"Mr. Brown, sir, there is a gentleman below *as* calls *'imself* Sir Malcolm Brockelsbie," she announced in a quiet voice, "and requests for to know whether *'e* may be permitted to see you?" As I opened my mouth to respond, she continued unbidden, "*h*I'll tell you what it is, sir, just now there comed a loud rap at the knocker, and the servant *'appening* to be from *'ome*, and the maid busy about the *'ouse*, I went meself to answer the door." She placed her hands upon her wide hips. "There stood upon the step quite a genteel gentleman, as *axed* if Mr. Brown lived *'ere*? And I made answer, and said as *'ow h*indeed *'e* did." Her head moved up and down in a curt nod. "Says I, '*e* and the other gentleman, that comed with *'im* from the country last week, are both at their *breakfasses* at this very minute.' – 'Oh, from the country, is *'e*?' cried *'e*. – 'Yes, sir,' says I, 'from *Hol*dam, in Lincolnshire, and one of the first reckoned gentlemen in *'is* county. Me brother is *'is* steward, sir,' says I. – 'From *Hol*dam, is *'e*?' *'e* repeated. I thought to meself that 'e looked quite surprised like. 'What, Mr. *John* Brown?' 'e *axed*. – 'Yes, sir, just the very man,' I made answer and said. So 'e looked, as I thought, quite confused, but *h*after a minute or two, 'e said, says, 'e, 'Pray tell '*im*, with me compliments, as '*ow* Sir Malcolm Brockelsbie requests to know if 'e may be permitted to see '*im*?'"

I glanced over to Mr. Ferguson, whose blank expression gave me no direction. "Of course, Mrs. Titmus," I turned to face our land-lady, "please shew the gentleman up here immediately."

She scuttled down the stairs, and in a few seconds Brockelsbie entered the room. "Mr. Brown," he said in an unctuous tone, "upon my soul! I don't know how to express what is at this moment passing in my mind. I am conscious of having once offered you an unmerited affront. I am also sensible of having received from you the greatest service. I can only declare myself devil-ishly sorry for the former, and, without words, to acknowledge my gratitude for the latter."

He bent at the waist slightly and extended his hand. Such an avowal became an infallible passport to my heart, and I pressed the offered hand in mine with the warmth of an old acquaintance.

Sir Malcom then addressed Mr. Ferguson, "To you, sir, also. I am a debtor in the scale of gratitude, but excuse me for having acknowledged the obligation first to your friend because I stand convicted to myself of not having merited his services."

I placed a chair for him as I spoke. "Let me beg of you, as a favour, never again to revert to a subject which it will impart the greatest satisfaction to my feelings to bury in oblivion."

"Upon my life, sir," he exclaimed, once again taking my hand. "You appear to me to be the finest fellow I ever yet had the pleasure of being acquainted with!" Sir Malcolm offered a smile to Mr. Ferguson as well. "I consider you"–he squeezed my hand–"more worthy of the good fortune which has fallen to your lot–damme if I don't!–and heartily wish you a long enjoyment of it." His semi-permanent grin widened to a full smile. "Excuse me, I am a devilish odd fish, I can't help speaking my mind, but I mean no harm–upon my soul I don't! I often play strange tricks with my head, but very seldom with my heart, unless I get hard pushed,

grow restive, and turn out of the course, and then I am apt sometimes to kick devilishly, till my fit's off again." He dropped my
hand as he sat. We followed suit.

"I congratulate you sir," Mr. Ferguson spoke, "as it appears you
have received no material injury from the fray in which you were
heretofore engaged."

"I have good luck, and better friends, to thank for my escape," he
answered, smiling at both of us in turn. "I am most devilishly
ashamed to say that I have always been so devoted to the turf–
and the green cloth–that I have paid very little attention to the
science of self-defence." Sir Malcolm held up slightly-balled fists
as an example. "It is a damnable scandal for a man, in my station
of life, not to be up to the bleeding of a brace of pups like those
that bullied me last night. I shall put myself under the tutelage
of a pugilist directly." He glanced at us quizzically. "Have you a
man to recommend, eh?"

Mr. Ferguson and I looked at each other and shrugged. "I must
confess, Sir Malcolm, both of us are unfamiliar with that particular sport."

"What, never been at the Fives?" Sir Malcolm appeared surprised. "Never traversed the country after a match and been
driven by the *beaks*?"

"The *what*, sir?" inquired Mr. Ferguson.

"The magistrates," replied Sir Malcolm with a smile. "The *beaks*,
as the fancy call them, to be driven by them, I say, from common
to heath, and from heath to common, for half a day, perhaps,
before the backers can fall in with a spot for the mill."

Again, Mr. Ferguson and I passed puzzled looks.

"Oh, it's devilish good sport–upon my soul it is! I'll take pleasure
to shew you all these kinds of knowing things, if you'll honour
me with your society."

I smiled and bowed, Mr. Ferguson followed suit after a second.

"You've heard, no doubt, of the extraordinary bet I made at the
last York meeting?" Sir Malcolm peered at us expectantly. When
neither of us responded, he went on, "The devil you haven't! I
thought every living animal, man, woman, and child, had heard
of that. I'll tell you how it was." He nodded convincingly. "I laid
an even five hundred that I would guess the number of living

souls on the race-stand. It was a devilish chance-go—damme if it wasn't! I named a hundred and seventy-four. It was found to contain only a hundred and seventy-three. I was accordingly cast for the loser—and must indubitably have come down with the dust—if it hadn't been for the humanity of a farrier's wife who, from a fright which she received from the breaking down of the carriage on her way home, immediately gave birth to a young squaller, who having, beyond all dispute, been a living soul in the stand at the time of my making the bet, by his sudden entrance into life, constituted me the unexpected winner, by a decided majority of the voices of the Highflyer Club!"

He grinned at each of us, ostensibly expecting some sort of congratulatory response. However, Mr. Ferguson and I remained silent. As for me, I knew not how to reply to such a far-fetched piece of flummery. Instead, I returned to the subject of last evening's attack. "Were you acquainted with your assaulters?"

"If I don't know them by name, I do by nature," Sir Malcolm returned, seeming a bit deflated. "Confound them for a set of infernal filchers. But I'm not without my hopes of sending them over the herring-pond for their frolic, I can promise them." He pointed a bony finger downwardly. "It's a devilish long story, and I should like to tell you all the particulars, but—upon my soul!—I have not time this morning, for there's a sale at Tattersall's, at which I am going to put up three hunters and a race-horse." His finger now pointed upwardly. "I must be there poz or I shall get quizzed by the dealers, but I tell you what—this is the arrangement I have made in my own mind—I take no denial to your eating your mutton with me this evening at Short's, and then you will hear all about it, as I expect a gentleman to be of our party whom I mean to employ in the business. There'll be only ourselves, and six the hour. I dine early on purpose that we may enjoy a social glass to our better acquaintance after dinner."

My mind immediately recoiled at the invitation, as we were to dine with the Allinghams that evening. "Sir Malcolm," I began hesitantly, "your invitation is most generous, but I am afraid Mr. Ferguson and I are already engaged to dine with friends this evening."

"Bring them along!" Sir Malcolm invited with cheer and a wave of his hand.

"I do not believe that would be wise, sir, as they have recently experienced great distress, and it is my unassuming belief they would not be right for the company you have described."

"Well then, shall we make it for to-morrow?" His smile beamed friendship.

I turned to Mr. Ferguson, who gave no indication of conflict. "Yes. I believe we are not engaged to-morrow, and to refuse your invitation would be most discourteous."

"To-morrow it is! Six the hour."

"We shall be punctual, Sir Malcolm," I stated, and Mr. Ferguson nodded.

The baronet moved to quit the room and suddenly stopped at the door. "You don't want to buy a hunter, do you?"

The question caught me off-guard. "Why, before I leave town it is my intention to purchase one, sir."

"It shan't be one of mine, then," Sir Malcolm placed his finger archly on his nose. "I never take in my friends. Mine are all hollow concerns, made up for the market, to diddle the flats. Well, remember to-morrow, six o'clock. Nothing but a rump-steak and oyster-sauce. Adieu, my dear boys!" He turned and descended the stairs rapidly.

After he had gone, I turned to Mr. Ferguson with a bit of a smile. "Well, my dear friend, I apologise that you had to be a witness to all of that, but consider how he might prove very instrumental by introducing us, as occasional visitors, to various societies into which we possess no passport."

He nodded. "This makes me wonder what our other new friend, Sir Julius Maberly, might have in the way of opinion upon your previous tormentor."

"Perhaps we can pay him a call on our way to dine with the Allinghams this evening," I suggested.

Following our luncheon, Mr. Ferguson and I made our way toward Upper Brook-street to seek the counsel of Sir Julius upon the slightly-improved Sir Malcolm we had just encountered. As we walked, Sir Julius darted upon us from a bookseller's shop across from Grosvenor Square.

"Gentlemen!" the baronet exclaimed. "What a pleasant coincidence. What brings you here?"

"We came in search of information upon a person just re-introduced into my life by the name of Sir Malcolm Brockelsbie. He has invited us to dine with him on the morrow."

"Brockelsbie?" queried the baronet. "Ah, yes, the name is familiar to me; however, I am not personally acquainted with the gentleman, if I may even be permitted to use that ill-fitting label."

"You know of him, Sir Julius?" Mr. Ferguson asked.

"Concurred!" he responded enthusiastically. "While I cannot speak of him either in favour or prejudice, I do regard him as a commonplace member of the fashionable horde of drivers, boxers, gamblers, loungers, and such, who are regularly to be seen upon the Bond-street *pavé*." His head wagged disapprovingly. "There is one inference which I consider myself enabled to draw, relative to his character, and that arises only from an association of circumstances. You are acquainted with the old proverb, 'Birds of a feather...'?" We acknowledged our familiarity. "Sir Malcolm Brockelsbie is, I have heard, one of Mr. Allingham's most favourite associates, and thence, I think, I may fairly conclude that he is fond of play." An admonishing finger pointed. "Take my advice, whatever *sights* you go to see, be satisfied to remain spectators only. Take no lessons in any art. You comprehend me, I dare say."

He observed our mutual expressive smile and nodded accordingly.

The three of us continued on to the baronet's home in Upper Brook-street. Sir Julius halted and loitered in front of a grey-haired old man, decently, but shabbily, clad. The baronet drew some coins from his waistcoat-pocket and slipped them into the other fellow's hand. The charity produced an expression of the most impressive gratitude.

"That honest and now indigent creature," Sir Julius testified upon rejoining us, "is the victim of infidelity. He had lived above fifty years in the joint service of the late Marquis of Marlborough. The present marquis, his son, had married a very young and uneducated girl, who also suffered from a lack of morality. This servant informed his master of several instances of infidelity he had unwittingly observed, and the new marquis precipitously discharged the old fellow on the accusation of having attempted to disseminate the seeds of discord between the marquis and his wife. *Ainsi va le monde!*"

I then remarked, "It appears, I think, to be a very dangerous matter to speak the truth sometimes."

"Acknowledged!" replied Sir Julius. "Yes, sir, I pledge my word to you, that in the modern circles of fashion, especially in the more exalted ones, it requires a very considerable degree of courage to speak the truth, as, in most cases, it exposes the utterer to unforeseen hazards, privations, and difficulties. I consider a close and steady observation of the falsehood and folly of the world, capable of effecting more towards the formation of a real philosopher, than all the pedantry of scholastic knowledge can accomplish. Men may ruminate in the sequestered scenes of life, but a correct and comprehensive knowledge of this mazy globe, and the enigmatical beings whom it contains, can only be gained by an extensive intercourse with mankind. The citizen of the world is the only true philosopher. He examines without prejudice—he judges from experience—he sees things as they exist."

We had conducted the baronet to his residence and bade him farewell. After the door to his residence closed, we began walking eastward toward Berners-street.

"It is curious that Sir Julius knows of that Malcolm fellow," Mr. Ferguson declared.

"Sir Malcolm, you mean to say."

"I believe he is as much a baronet as the counterfeit Sir Frederick. Much of what he has said bares closer scrutiny, and I am only telling this to you because you are my closest friend." He looked directly at me.

There were so many things about Sir Malcolm Brockelsbie that did not ring true; however, I wished to give him every opportunity to demonstrate his transformation. "I believe that tomorrow's dinner will give us a chance to examine him once again, my friend." My midsection produced an audible rumble. "I say, all this walking has fostered my appetite. Let us please turn our attentions to this evening's meal with the jolly Allinghams."

Mr. Ferguson nodded as we turned into Berners-street.

Chapter Fourteen:

An Evening in Heaven, an Evening in Hell

WHEN WE ARRIVED at Mrs. Allingham's latest lodgings, she met us at the door and guided us up a narrow stairway and through a tight hallway to a small sitting room decorated in light-coloured velours and darker Morocco leather. The chair I sat in felt more like a book cover than a seat. Mr. Ferguson took the high-backed chair next to me, and Mrs. Allingham sat next to her son on a love-seat across.

"Well, Mr. Brown, Mr. Ferguson. How delightful to see you both again. I trust that you have been enjoying yourselves in London."

My ears paid little attention to our hostess as my eyes partook in the loveliness of August Evelyne. He sat next to his mother with an unaffected simplicity of manner that invited confidence and secured esteem. Fair and finely formed, with hair of a light auburn, his beaming eyes of blue conveyed a sensibility that bespoke the purest and most gentle affections.

"We have been kept busy, my lady," Mr. Ferguson offered when I had not responded.

A gentle cough in my direction prompted me. "Oh, yes, quite busy. I trust that you have settled into your temporary home adequately."

I faced the boy, but it was the mother who answered. "These are fine, little apartments, and I must apologise for delaying our little reunion, but here we are!" She smiled at me and then followed my gaze to her little boy. "August, pray demonstrate your appreciation to our guests."

The angel rose from his seat as if lifted by little wings and drifted across the room to us. "Mr. Ferguson," he said with a soft and delicate voice as he hugged my friend briefly. He then turned to me and spoke my name, which caused some brief stirring in my breeches. For some reason I could not understand, I stood to accept his greetings. When he reached out to hug me in turn, my manhood betrayed my feelings, and I could tell he felt the solid bulge between us. "Perhaps I should hold you for a bit longer so that you may conceal your affections," he whispered into my quickly-reddening ear.

Unfortunately, hearing him speak thusly to me made the situation even more difficult to handle. I thrust my free hand into a pocket and adjusted my disobedient piece as best befitting the situation.

"Better?" he whispered before easing his grip. When he kissed me lightly on the cheek, it felt as though I might have discharged my mettle and embarrassed myself even further. "Mr. Brown,"–he continued as he rejoined his mother–"I have heard that you are the true architect of my well-being, having devised the very clever mechanism for my escape from the conflagration." A sly smile appeared.

How I wished I could kneel and shout, "Hear my soul speak. Of the very instant that I saw you, Did my heart fly at your service," as did Ferdinand confess to Miranda in *The Tempest*. However, given the situation, I could only provide polite intercourse. "Think nothing of it," I babbled as I sat once again, hoping the position would hide my arousal for the best. "Back home in Oldham, we had used a similar ruse, and your situation merely jogged my memory."

We sat in silence for a minute or two, taking turns smiling at each of the other people in the ever-shrinking room. At length, Mrs. Allingham clasped her son's hand and shook it gently. "August, perhaps you could entertain our guests with some music." Her head turned toward a harp that had been standing unnoticed in the corner.

"Yes, of course, mother." He stood and asked, "Do you gentlemen have any particular pieces that you would enjoy hearing?"

My little angel could play the harp! How could this story improve any further? "I must confess that I have no knowledge of music for the harp, sir. Please perform at your leisure. I'm sure that your talents shall enthral us immensely."

August took up the instrument and plucked at its sinewy strings with his lithe, slender fingers as if he were performing balletic dance steps with his delicate hands. Mr. Ferguson observed the performance with rapt attentions.

Following a series of instrumental pieces, the young man began singing along with the divine strings as he plucked them. I had no idea what tune he played, but I imagined it similar to the siren song of the Odyssey.

Following a lovely ballad August invited, "Please sing along with me, gentlemen, I would enjoy this all the more."

I turned to my friend, "Mr. Ferguson, I believe this is your specialty, sir."

"My good Mr. Brown, I beg that you forgive my inability to partake in the entertainments."

"But you are an actor, sir!" I retorted.

He smiled lightly. "An actor, yes, but not a music hall singer. Go on, John, pray demonstrate your talents."

"Oh, yes, Mr. Brown," the young man's dewy eyes enticed. "Do sing with me. I am certain you know this one." He began to play a quite familiar tune. *"Drink to me only with thine eyes, And I will pledge with mine,"* he sang.

I stood and joined him, *"Or leave a kiss within the cup, And I'll not ask for wine."* He sang harmony at the end, and our blended voices brought a tiny tear to my eye.

Mrs. Allingham then led us to a small dining-room with a table set out for a light repast. Young August sat to my left, and Mr. Ferguson to my right. Mrs. Allingham's friend, Mrs. Ansel, joined us for the meal, sitting directly to her right, and quite closely, I noted.

From time-to-time, I did observe surreptitious glances pass between the two men seated on either side of me. Polite conversation ensued, and hours passed before any of us realised the hour.

When we had quitted the house and entered the street, Mr. Ferguson spoke, "My dear friend, I can hardly describe how anxious I am to express to you that I hope my conduct this day has not excited either your anger or jealously?"

"I am utterly at a loss to comprehend your meaning," I returned.

"Your own happiness then has so exclusively engrossed your feelings that you have not observed the earnest and wistful glances which I have found it impossible to constrain myself from casting at young August."

"I certainly did once or twice perceive you to regard him with particular attention," I replied, "but believe me, that to entertain a suspicion of jealousy against you could not for a moment enter my mind. You have made it clear to me that you prefer the company of women, such as your attachment to Mrs. Percival, of whose fate you have only so very lately acquired information."

"My attachment to Mrs. Percival is the cause of the conduct for which I am apologising to you," he answered with voice faltering as he named the lamented individual of whom he was speaking. "For the strong resemblance which Master August bears to Mrs. Percival is almost incredible. It can only be estimated by one to whom they have both been known, and from this circumstance I was led to regard him with an emotion of surprise, which I own that I found the greatest difficulty in suppressing within the bounds of politeness."

"It does appear extraordinary, I confess, but pardon me, you are gifted with the power of discovering resemblances at first sight. Recollect the likeness which you believed yourself to trace between the mysterious White Man on the Yorkshire moor and his Negro companion."

"And I do, upon my honour, think that my eyes did not, in either case, deceive me," Mr. Ferguson returned.

A thought then struck me. "Did I not, whilst I was engaged in conversation with the agreeable August, overhear you expressing another resemblance with which you had been struck, by telling Mrs. Allingham that you considered her son to bear a strong likeness to her?"

"I certainly did say so," answered Mr. Ferguson, "but my mind was so fully occupied by the ideas which were privately passing in it, that, scarcely able to withdraw my thoughts from myself, and yet compelled not to be silent, I made the observation at random, as an apology for something better to say."

"Why, indeed I should imagine that you cannot seriously think a similarity exists between their persons," I returned.

"Very far from it," Mr. Ferguson replied. "I feel no difficulty in crediting what Sir Julius Maberly told us, that the mother has once been handsome, but it must have been a very different style of beauty from her son's. The mother's charms must have been entirely of a nature to please the eye–she is greatly deficient in that interest of countenance, that sweet sensibility of smile, which, in Master August, makes so forcible an impression on the heart."

I knew not what to reply but merely exhaled a soft sigh of pleasure, acknowledging the truth of my friend's reflexion.

"But did you remark the answer which Mrs. Allingham made in return to my observation?" he continued.

"I did not. What was it?"

"'Like me, sir!' she exclaimed," Mr. Ferguson made an attempt to perform the part, placing one hand lightly upon his breast. "'Oh, no, no! Dear August will never be like me! I wish he were so. Sincerely should I delight in his resembling me.'"

"And did she speak this as if her wish proceeded from personal vanity, as conceiving her offspring inferiorly gifted to herself?"

"No, upon my word, she did not," answered Mr. Ferguson. "An emotion of tenderness appeared to accompany her words, which excited my surprise. The feeling was not a little increased, by my observing her friend, Mrs. Ansel, to be directing at her a look which I considered as intended to enjoin her not to pursue the subject."

"It is somewhat odd indeed," I remarked.

"It struck me as being so, I assure you. My own reflections did not entirely prevent me from observing the character of Mrs. Allingham. You, I dare say, were too much engaged with the son to permit your thoughts to wander to the mother, and I think she bears every appearance of possessing all the amiability of heart with which the old baronet represented her as being endowed, but I must also consider her as a weak, although a good, woman," Mr. Ferguson returned.

We strolled down Oxford-road in silence enjoying the beautiful moonlight upon the moist cobblestones. As we neared the Titmus house, my mind considered the possibility that Mrs. Allingham and Mrs. Ansel might be more than just friends.

✳

The following evening, Mr. Ferguson and myself proceeded to Short's Hotel, as directed by Sir Malcolm. A waiter ushered us toward the same dining-room that we had previously occupied. As we approached, voices could be heard through the partly-open door.

"I hope you will, sir, if it is only forty or fifty pounds, it will be of infinite use," spoke a man unfamiliar to me. "Indeed, I expected you would have kept your word, as I heard you had a sale at Tattersall's recently."

"It went to the devil," replied the distinct voice of Sir Malcolm. "I lost twenty pounds by it, by God! I'll be damned if I didn't! But upon my soul and honour, I'll do something for you to-morrow. I expect an old fellow here about raising me some money immediately, and if –"

"Mr. Brown and Mr. Ferguson for Sir Malcolm, if you please," announced the waiter as he opened the door, interrupting the conversation. Sir Malcolm stood and advanced to meet us.

"Welcome! Welcome, my friends," he greeted us and shook our hands vigorously.

The other fellow, a plain but well-dressed man, left the room without introduction.

We sat around a table. As time glided on, our discussions included popular topics of the day, as Sir Malcolm seemed particularly interested in every detail of our stay in London so far, especially the rescue of young Master August from the blazing building. I tried to keep in my mind the admonition of Sir Julius regarding the humbug nature of our present host.

From time-to-time, Sir Malcolm examined his watch. The degree of impatience on his countenance increased with every examination.

When a clock struck seven, he sprang from his chair and rang the service bell. "Dinner upon the table, directly," he ordered. "I shan't wait another minute for the old fellow," he said to himself. "He's only a lawyer who transacts all my business. A very convenient sort of a person, though, to apply to, on many occasions– as rich as the devil but as greedy as a hawk," he said to us.

The waiter placed a good meal for us, but no one spoke during its consumption. As the server removed the cloth from the table, Sir Malcolm's servant entered.

"A gentleman from Mr. Briefwit's office wishes to speak with you," the fellow reported.

"Is it Mr. Slapp?" asked the baronet.

"Yes, sir, it is."

"Waiter! Put some more glasses upon the table and set another chair." To his servant he said, "Desire the fellow to join us."

After his man had withdrawn, Sir Malcolm spoke, "Slapp's a devilish keen young fellow, a thousand to one more likely to ferret into my cursed affair of the other night than his deliberate, hesitating old master. I am glad he's come. I'll pour a few glasses down his throat and put him upon scent directly."

The door to the room opened, and in stepped Gilbert Slapp, the mischievous son of our neighbours back in Oldham. I seemed to recall that his mother had a relation in the Minories named Briefwit.

"Bless my soul!" Gilbert exclaimed as he saw me. "Have I the happiness of seeing, Mr. Brown? And Mr. Cavendish too? I declare!"

"It's Mr. Ferguson, sir," I explained. "An unexpected accession of good fortune since you saw my friend last has caused him to change his name."

"Good fortune could not have come to a more deserving fellow," responded Mr. Slapp in a tone that suggested resentment.

"What the devil?" cried Sir Malcolm. "You know each other already, do you? Oh, damme! I might have guessed that. You're an Oldhamite yourself, I recollect, and I suppose the last time you toddled down to see the old ones, you got acquainted and all that." His eyes darted from face to face to face. "Well, I say, Slapp, my boy, what does the old dog say? Am I to have the stuff?"

Sir Malcolm's attentions to Mr. Slapp gave me pause to consider the nature of their relationship. From the peer to the pickpocket, everyone treats those whom he makes useful to himself with condescension–and even with flattery. The baronet's continued palaver made things more and more obvious.

"He desired me to tell you," Mr. Slapp announced, "that he is very unwell and does not think he can attend to business for a day or two, that he has had some considerable losses since he saw you last, which have pressed very hard both upon his mind and his finances, and almost all his ready cash is placed out where he can't possibly withdraw it at present. Poor man, how I pity him!" He displayed an arch leer at the baronet.

"Confound the old devil!" cried Sir Malcolm. "I wish I had the squeezing of his sovereigns out of his lying old throat. He only wants me to offer him a higher premium, but he may be... which way does the wind blow? I mean, but I won't put myself in a passion, by..." He swallowed a bumper, perhaps to check rising bile. Following a brief pause he continued, "Well, but Slapp, what is to be done? Damme if ever I understand that infernal old uncle of yours! Do you mean to say that he is resolute?"

"'Very like a whale,' Shakespeare–hem!" replied the knowing Gilbert. Polonius, from *Hamlet.* I had forgotten Gilbert's penchant for the Bard. "Trust all that to me, Sir Malcolm."

"Well then, explain. You may have the use of my private box tomorrow at Drury-lane," replied the baronet.

"Much obliged to you, 'pon my honour!" Gilbert smiled. "We'll talk of your affair with my uncle by-and-by, Sir Malcolm, or tomorrow morning. You have friends with you just now." He indicated Mr. Ferguson and myself.

"Very true," Sir Malcolm said, but his eyes appeared to be gazing far off. "Besides, I want your advice and assistance in another damned quizzical business. I was robbed of a gold watch, chain, and seals, a few nights back, and nearly pulled to pieces in the bargain. Curse me if I'll be queered so without redress." He turned to us, "Wasn't I prettily handled, gentlemen?"

Mr. Ferguson and I exchanged glances, and then I explained the events regarding our rescue of the benighted baronet.

"I say, old chap, this affair ought to be investigated. Sir Malcolm, please–if you can–recount every particular connected with this business that you can recall.

The baronet immediately complied, but his details proved more verbose than I deemed the subject to require. In brief, he claimed that a couple of fair ones had lured him into a house and caused him to tally a bill for wine and refreshments amounting to nearly twenty pounds. Sir Malcolm discovered he did not have such funds, and the woman of the house insisted on detaining his watch till he fulfilled the payment. He did, however, discover three five-pound notes stashed in a private pocket that he offered on condition of his watch being returned to him, but the proprietress refused. At that point, Sir Malcolm forced his way out, only to be followed by two of the gentlemen-retainers and the woman we had encountered. He claimed they were attempting to keep his watch and remove the fifteen quid as well.

"Say I am only half-bred if I don't tell you the house at once," exclaimed Slapp. "Mother Mackinflore's, in Liquorish-court, not a hundred miles from Vere-street chapel. Was that not the situation, Sir Malcolm?"

The baronet blinked his eyes a few times. "Yes, as nearly as I can recollect, I believe it was, now that you mention it."

"And what will you bet me that I don't bring you your watch and appendages back in less than an hour's time without leaving a single shilling in their stead?" asked Gilbert.

"You don't imagine so?" cried the baronet with a hint of artfulness.

"I am sure so. Will you bet me five pounds I can't do it?"

"I will," returned the baronet.

"Done!" replied Gilbert.

"Done!" repeated Sir Malcolm.

"Done!" echoed Slapp. "And these gentlemen are witnesses, but as I don't exactly like to go alone, as I may want proof hereafter of what passes, will you allow your servant to carry a line for me to be a friend of mine who lives close by and whom I wish to accompany me?"

"I shall pen such a note for you straightaway," agreed the baronet.

✳

For the better part of the next hour—or the worse part, perhaps —we sat with Sir Malcolm as he regaled us of his far-fetched conquests, his preposterous strokes of luck, and his self-centred laudations. Were it not for the constant replenishment of the libations, Mr. Ferguson and I would have left soon after Mr. Slapp and the servant.

"Huzza!" came the cry from the young lawyer as he burst exultingly into the room. "'The deed is done!' Shakespeare—hem!"

"The devil it is!" Sir Malcolm called out as he stood.

"Who says I am not the boy to come the go when I set about it?" Gilbert boasted with flushed face and gleaming teeth. "Who says I am not up to gammon?"

"Come then, shew us the ticker," directed the baronet.

"Shew us the five-pound," countered Gilbert, apparently encouraged by his triumph to be even more familiar than usual. "Shew us the five-pound!" He placed an outstretched palm before Sir Malcolm.

"We will settle all that by-and-by," the baronet replied as he sat down, arms folded across his chest. "As long as she is safe, I don't care a whistle who has her."

"Here she lies, as snug as may be," answered Slapp, clapping his hand upon his side-pocket. "Cannot you hear her sing?"

Sir Malcolm cocked his head slightly and raised his eyebrows. "But how did you contrive to nab her?"

"Oh, by a very concise method," answered Slapp. "You shall hear." He sat with us. "Your valet and I went boldly into the house and called for a room and a bottle of wine. After I called for a second, in the middle of all that, I announced we desired to see Mrs. Mackinflore. In a few seconds, in came the old abbess, curtseying down to the ground. 'Very good wine, this of yours, ma'am. Take a glass yourself.' Down it went to our better acquaintance, and five minutes more emptied the bottle—only half-pints, you know, racked off into hollow-bottomed decanters."

What a horrid business! Selling shorted bottles of wine to unsuspecting customers. I hoped fate would somehow make things right.

"'Eighteen shillings, if you please, gentlemen,' she requested, and I put some coins on the table. 'There is the money, ma'am.' She thanked us and hoped to see us soon again. Now comes the grand flourish: 'I am sorry to trouble you, ma'am, but as you sell wine, I have called upon you, by order of the Board of Excise, to inspect your licence.' My eye and Betty Martin, what a caper!"

He let a jolly laugh escape, and Mr. Ferguson and I caught each other's gaze momentarily.

"She offered us ten pounds a-piece, and the freedom of her house, to hush up the matter. So, when I found that I had brought her to her pins, I told her that if she would deliver me up safe the gentleman's watch which she had detained a few nights before for a wine bill, I would engage the business should drop. My terms were immediately complied with, and the article in question delivered into my hands." Gilbert took a gold watch, chain, and seals from his pocket, displaying them to us all. "And here she is, safe, sound, and handsome." With a delighted grin, he dropped the timepiece upon the table before Sir Malcolm.

"Why, what the devil is this?" cried the baronet. "This is not my watch."

"Not yours!?" returned Gilbert in amazement.

"No, by all the powers of devilry, it is not mine!" replied Sir Malcolm, "but it is a handsome concern, as you say, though." The beady-eyed baronet examined the watch with all the scrutiny of a horse-buyer.

"Permit me to see it," Mr. Ferguson requested. Sir Malcolm picked up the piece and placed it in my friend's hand. "Upon my word,"–he stated without a moment's hesitation–"this is the watch, chain, and seals that were pinched from me upon our first night in London." His eyes glowed in recognition of the prized pocket watch.

"This is an extraordinary sort of business," remarked Gilbert Slapp as he took a second look at the piece in Mr. Ferguson's hand. "This discovery appears to prove Mrs. Mackinflore a *cove* in addition to her other branches of business."

"A what, sir?" inquired Mr. Ferguson.

"A receiver of stolen goods, sir."

"I should very much like to know by what means these articles can have come into her possession," my friend remarked as he continued to study the dear objects.

"Well, sir, with the hold I have upon her, that can very easily be inquired into, and probably with success." Mr. Slapp seemed drunk upon his recently-gained victory. "I shall certainly pay her another visit to-morrow for the purpose of endeavouring to recover Sir Malcolm's property. Night is a bad time to visit an academy upon a business like yours or mine, but in the morning, if you please, to accompany me thither. It is but an hour or two thrown away in viewing the scenes of life, if even your investigation should not be satisfactorily replied to."

"Yes, I believe I should be happy to attend you," Mr. Ferguson answered.

The thought of my dearest friend entering this wretched business concerned me greatly. "What can be your motive for desiring to know by whom your watch was purloined? You have most unexpectedly regained it, and I should imagine it could be of little consequence to you now who was the thief."

"I have a motive, be assured," Mr. Ferguson replied, "but lest I should criminate an innocent person, I will not explain it till after our inquires have taken place to-morrow."

"Well then, let us meet in the coffee-room of this hotel at twelve o'clock to-morrow morning, and from thence we shall proceed to Liquorish-court to visit Mrs. Mackinflore," Mr. Slapp proposed.

"Devilishly sorry, dear chaps, but I am compelled to appear in Cambridgeshire for the Huntingdon races where I have entered a favourite horse to run." Sir Malcolm dashed from the room without placing any money upon the table.

I turned to Mr. Slapp. "The baronet was supposed to have been our host for this evening's supper, but he seems to have disremembered to pay for the services. Are you able to cover the amounts?"

Gilbert's smirk of satisfaction transformed into a grimace of grief. "I suppose it should fall to me to carry this particular burden." He then glanced up at me with a wink. "Methinks I shall merely append the charged amounts to his account. 'Time shall unfold what plighted cunning hides.' Shakespeare–hem!" He stood and quit the room.

Mr. Ferguson appeared focused on the timepiece, which now indicated the hour of midnight.

I stood and touched his arm. "Shall we?"

He nodded silently, slipped the watch into his pocket, and we made our way out to the street.

"How striking an example"–I said when we had begun our way toward the Titmus residence–"is poor Sir Malcolm, that men of pleasure are the enemies of their own happiness! Is it not pitiable to see a man of his rank and income at the mercy of creditors and lawyers clerks?"

"I have often heard it remarked that profligacy carries its punishment along with it, and I think that the dashing baronet whom we have just quitted is indeed a melancholy proof of the truth of the proposition." A small smile spread across Mr. Ferguson's face. "Oh, fashion! What a restraint art thou upon the manners–what a bane to the morals of thy votaries!" He paused before continuing. "And now, as I believe you are well aware that I have no secrets from you, I will inform you why I wish to become acquainted with who was the predator that robbed me of my watch. From the esteem in which I know you to hold your steward, Mr. Radford, you would, of course, be happy in rendering a service to those with whom he is connected, and I consider that it would be a most material benefit conferred on the poor Titmus family if their unfortunate daughter could be released from the entanglements of the despicable Harry Glara."

"I should certainly experience a great satisfaction if I could, by any means, be instrumental in restoring her to her parents," I responded. "But I do not perceive the point at which you are aiming."

"Have you no idea how a knowledge of the purloiner of my watch might lead to a discovery of their daughter?"

"Indeed, I have not," I replied. "Pray explain."

"Then, to be candid with you, I do most shrewdly suspect that they were the agile fingers of the daring Harry Glara which beguiled me of my watch. On reflecting upon the robbery I had sustained, on the very night it had occurred, I remembered feeling a hand pressed upon my fob when we returned to the box in which we had left the party after our stroll in the lobby." His gaze appeared far-off. "At the time, there was not an individual near me but yourself and him. The circumstance passed unnoticed by me at the moment, but it has, since that period, frequently been the subject of my thoughts. From this association of ideas, I am of opinion, that if the affair of the watch could be brought home to him, that, by the same means, the poor deluded girl, who has no doubt been his dupe and victim, might be traced out and restored to her friends."

"Good Heavens!" I exclaimed. "Can you suppose it possible that he can have descended to the mean villainy of a pickpocket?"

"I can believe a man whom I know to have committed the frauds which I am acquainted with his having practiced to be capable of repeating his crime in any shape, where a temporary advantage excites him to the hazard." His eyes lowered to the walk before us. "For my own part, should I prove him guilty, I shall leave him to the chastisement of his own conscience. My only motive, as I have already told you, for endeavouring to elucidate the affair, arises from the sympathy which I experience in the distress of Mr. Radford's relatives."

We had arrived at the darkened Titmus residence and attempted to make the least noise possible as not to disrupt their slumber. As we ascended to our rooms, I reviewed Mr. Ferguson's indictment of the sham Sir Frederick and reminded myself that malevolent people worked their nefarious intrigues in murky circles all about us.

Chapter Fifteen:

Mysterious Business

THE FOLLOWING MORNING, I found a letter waiting, addressed to me in handwriting resembling that of Mr. Radford. It had been sent through the general post, and, having no word from Oldham since our journey began, I decided to read it before proceeding down to reunite with the Titmus family.

I broke the seal and occupied one of the sitting-room chairs. The date was from a few days earlier.

My Dearest Mr. Brown,

I trust this letter finds you in the peak of health, and that you are enjoying your time in London with Mr. Ferguson. Let me assure you that all is well at Ashbank Hall and you have no cause for alarm.

A circumstance occurred to me yesterday morning, which has since occasioned me a considerable degree of reflection, and the principal reason of my now addressing you is to communicate the same to you. As I was walking in the six-acre field, which, you know, is this year sown with wheat, and through which there is a public path into the village, I was met by a stranger, a middle-aged man of genteel appearance, in a riding-dress. He complimented me on the condition of the wheat crop with a gentle inclination of his head. I responded that the weather has been very favourable, and it promises to be a fine crop. He then asked if I were Mr. Radford, to which

I responded in the affirmative, then he inquired into your health, sir. I informed the gentleman of your current station in London, and he asked that I pay his respects to you. When I inquired as to how he knew you, he replied, "I have seen him, and with some of his connexions I have been intimately acquainted." I asked whom shall I have the pleasure of informing him that inquired after him. "No matter. I do not imagine that he would know my name if I were to leave it with you." He asked if you were going to be in town for a while, to which I replied yes, and he bid me a good-morning.

I followed after him a bit later, finding that he had a horse waiting at the Black Bull. The fellows told me he had made the same inquiries which he had advanced to me. One remarkable thing was that I saw a mourning ring upon his finger, the one I believe you gave to that extraordinary being whom we have always distinguished by the appellation of the White Man.

My best wishes for your stay in London. Please rest assured that all is well at Ashbank Hall. Your servant, J. Radford.

I perused the letter again, with an interest natural to the perplexing affinity which appeared to bear some hidden link of my destiny. Then I sunk into a train of bewildered reflections, curiosity, and astonishment strongly blended with each other.

A while after, and I know not how long the cloud of confusion hung over me, Mr. Ferguson entered. I handed him the letter.

186

Just as he began to read it, a clatter from down below arose, and up the stairs toddled Sir Julius Maberly.

"Good morning, sir. Good morning!" the baronet began.

"And to you, sir," I replied with a bit of a dry throat.

"Please pardon my early call, but I come to invite you both to a friendly dance in honour of my favourite, August Evelyne, at my house this day fortnight. I give no crowded routs, balls or masquerades. I invite only those whom I am happy to see, and whom I believe to derive pleasure from visiting me. I do not publish myself *at home*, to make my house an open-doored receptacle for a mob of idle and dissolute beings, whom I probably never saw before, and am quite as likely never to see again. No, no. I like such society as constitutes sociability, not multitude, and to such a party, I invite *you*." He smiled genteelly.

In that moment, I wished I had gone for coffee before the arrival of Sir Julius. His delightful banter proved too zestful for my peepy head.

"Shall I tell August that you are engaged?" he inquired enthusiastically. "You can lead off the first dance at my hop, for I won't dignify my little entertainment with the name of a ball."

"I shall, beyond all doubt," I began, "be most extremely happy to –"

"Well, I have ventured to say so already," interrupted the baronet. "So that point is settled. I shall supply a sufficient number of guests; therefore, all must dance. How often have I, in a fashionable ball-room, experienced an almost uncontrollable desire, when I have observed a dozen or two of puppies, leaning on their sticks, and quizzing through their eye-glasses the other attendees, ready to snatch their hedge-stakes out of their hands and apply them to their backs!" He laughed gaily. "If you have nothing better to do, come and dine with me to-morrow, for I must leave you now because I am my own card-bearer and consequently have several calls to make this morning. I am glad you approve of my having engaged you, and so, farewell for the present."

As he hobbled down the stairs, Mr. Ferguson and I caught each other's eyes.

"Don't you dare say a thing, Mr. Ferguson!" I cautioned him, and we both broke forth in laughter.

We arrived at Short's Hotel minutes before the noon hour prescribed by Mr. Slapp. He sat waiting in the coffee-room.

"A good day to you, gentlemen," he greeted us, and handshaking went all about. "Shall we?"

He led the way up Bond-street toward Liquorish-court. Upon reaching the Mackinflore house, the door stood open and discordant voices emanated from within. Given the nature of the place, I supposed it to be some common *fracas*, and we entered without hesitation.

The quarrel ceased upon our entry. Mr. Slapp looked about and exclaimed, "I say, not a countenance do I recognise." He turned to us, "Neither Mrs. Mackinflore, nor any other person whom I had seen the preceding evening are now present."

One of the women, a tall figure, fashionably but tawdrily dressed, held in her grasp a short, squabby, red-haired girl in the attire of a servant. "Tell me, you dirty drab!" the taller woman shouted. "Tell me this instant where your infamous mistress and her vile beau-trap Lambert are gone to? Tell me, I say, or I won't leave you a breath of wind in your body!" She raised her free hand as if to strike a blow.

"Haud yer hans aff me, ye dirty quean!" returned the shorter woman in a thick Caledonia-bred accent. "Am I no telling ye they're baith rinned awa, and I ken nought about them, neither the auld wife, nor yer Sir Frederick as ye ca' him."

"Stand clear of the wench a minute, if you please, ma'am, and let *me* speak to 'er," ordered a man whose air and voice suggested him a bailiff. He interposed himself between the two combatants. "Come, come, we knows very well as 'ow all you're telling us is only a flam, what you've been put up to to save your missess's flash man. So look you, do you 'ear? Do yourself a good turn, put us up to the rig, and we'll give you ten 'og and a pint of *blue ruin*. Come I say, 'old your *daddles*, and take the *stuff*."

"As I tell you, I ken nought!" protested the Scotch girl.

"I say, Carrotty Jean, you're a flat for yourself!" A meagre, pale-looking cut-down-gentleman sort of a fellow advanced as he spoke and stood to the side of the bailiff. "Peach, you soft fool! I'll be two *Georges* to you out of my own pocket to boot."

"And if you're such a *h*ass as to be *h*obstinate," added the bailiff, "why we must take you up to the *h*office in Bow-street to be *h*examined on suspicion of confederacy."

The taller woman threw up her British lace veil and waved a gloved hand in front of her nose. Her face, while tolerably handsome, appeared figured and flowered with dyes and cosmetics. Mr. Ferguson looked at her and the two locked gazes. She stepped toward my friend and spoke, "Lord bless me, sir! I little expected to see you here. It adds to my distress, I assure you, sir, to encounter you at a moment of this kind."

"Miss Benjerfield, if I mistake not," replied Mr. Ferguson. "Or shall I say Mrs. Roderick Monro."

"It is on Mr. Monro's account entirely, I assure you, sir, that I am here," she answered. "He has at this time the misfortune of being confined in the Fleet. I have been so imprudent as to lend considerable sums out of my own pocket to a deceitful fellow, who, I am informed, is well known here. Now I am in want of money to supply the emergencies of Mr. Monro, the shameful conductress of this house shields the unprincipled rascal from me, but I will have my due of him yet, if there is a law in the land."

A dirty lad, almost out of breath, ran up to the bailiff exclaiming, "Why what the *'ell* are you doing *'ere*? You're always upon the wrong scent! I *seed* mother Mackinflore and that there sir not five minutes ago in a *'ackney*-coach, right agin St. Gile's Church, a-going for the city."

"Come along then," cried the bailiff. "We mayn't be too late to trap him yet."

As the two departed, Mrs. Monro shouted after them, "Do all you can, and I'll reward you, see if I don't." She turned to Mr. Ferguson. "I hope, sir, to have the pleasure of seeing you again, when my mind is more at ease. There is my card, sir." She took a slip from her reticule and handed it to Ferguson. "Come, Mr. Nabber, let us proceed to your house," she instructed the thin, sallow fellow. "Good-morning, sir! Gentlemen all, good-morning!" She tripped away, followed by the aforementioned remnant of a gentleman.

Of the original occupants of the room upon our arrival, only the red-haired girl, called Carroty Jean, remained.

"Miss Benjerfield, No. 5, Queen Anne-street east," pronounced Mr. Ferguson, reading aloud the card which he had just received from the hand of the lady.

"Oh ho! I guessed as much," remarked Gilbert Slapp. "Indeed I might have been positive at first sight."

"Of what?" asked Mr. Ferguson.

"Tell me where you live, and I will tell you who you are," replied the young lawyer, "is a general rule, with very few exceptions, when applied to the inhabitants of London. Fitzrovia, I believe." He glanced over at the Scottish girl. "I think we might contrive to pump this person upon your business and mine, although she was proof against the attacks of the Philistines."

"Allow me," Mr. Ferguson replied in a whisper. "I anticipate that I shall have more weight with the person in question than any-one present." He stepped toward Carrotty Jean. "I hope, ma bonnie woman," he assumed his Scottish accent, "I hope yer na sair hurt. It would fash me to see a kintriewoman o' my ain a sufferer."

"Am shure am happy te see ye, sir, syne yer a kintrieman," re-turned the girl. "There's few o' them comes this gait."

"That," decried Gilbert, "is because her countrymen have more wit, and less money, than most other pleasure-hunters." Both Mr. Ferguson and I shot warning glances in his direction.

"This is no a very cannie place for ye, ma lass, I think," resumed my friend.

"What can I dee, sir?" replied the girl. "When me mother deed, and a come awa te Lunnon town to seek a service, the auld wife that keeps this house met me at the waggon I rode in by, an promised me sae fair, that I hired myself till her, an whan she got me haim, an I wadna dee her wicked biddings, she made me a downricht slave. An ye see, if a seek after anither service, there's naebody wull tak me because I stopped i' this shamefu' place. But is yer name Ferguson, sir?"

"Ay, it's that, but what make ye speer?"

"Because then am thinkin, that it was as muckle on yer account, as on the account o' the execution, that our folks rinned awa."

"What execution, ma woman?" asked Mr. Ferguson.

"They were threatened wi' an execution i' the house this afternoon, at four o'clock," Jean replied. "Gin they didna raise five hunner an fifty pund agin that time."

"And are ye positive that the man that's awa wi' yer auld mistress is ca'd Sir Frederick Lambert?" Ferguson inquired.

"Oh, ay, am shure enough o' that," she answered. "I ken plenty o' him, and his ways te."

"Weel, ma woman, it gans till ma heart te see yen o' my ain kintriewomen sae badly used, as ye represent yersel te be, and I'll mak ma endeavour to see ye into some respectable service, upon my ain recommendations."

"A Lord, sir"–Jean curtseyed–"Am shure Heaven wull bless ye for yer guidness, for it was hae broke the heart of my puir mither gin she'd lived to ken how I was situate."

"Ye may depend on't I'll no deceive ye," replied Mr. Ferguson. "But I maun first hae ye to answer me a few questions aboot the folk we hae been speaking o'."

"Am unco sartain, sir, ye'll find me willin to oblige ye as far as lays i' my pour," answered Jean. "Am bound no to refuse ye, for as yer a Scotchman, and, I dare say, by yer tongue, an Edinburgh man."

"Indeed I am."

"And am the same, as I may say." Jean stood proudly. "For am frac Leith, a canna doubt yer word, an therefore am willin to serve ye as muckle as am able, in return for yer kind promise to me."

The ensuing conversation proved as obscure to me as that of the renowned Delphic oracle of old to its interrogators, owing to the language in which it occurred. Both my friend and the Scottish woman spoke at length in their dialect, most unfamiliar to me, and so I provided here the pith of their discussion.

Between the pretended Sir Frederick Lambert and Mrs. Mackinflore there existed a league founded on mutual interest, although its nature could not be clearly understood. Notwith-standing the vast sums of money that were daily taken in the house, it had for some time past been threatened with an execution, which was to take place that very afternoon unless the aforesaid five hundred and fifty pounds could be produced. A few days before, Sir Frederick had brought to the house a lady from whom he had received a considerable sum of money, who, in return, expected marriage from him. We surmised the unnamed lady to be none other than the missing Miss Titmus. Instead of being immediately led to church, Sir Frederick informed her that the condition upon which alone he would make her his wife was that she must consent to furnish him with instructions, which he might communicate to a certain set of *craftsmen* with whom he was acquainted, for entering and robbing her father's house. Once the act had been accomplished, he would, without delay, give her a legal title to his name. The lady declared she would never agree to become a party concerned in so nefarious a transaction against her own parent, and she attempted to fly from the house. Sir Frederick and Mrs. Mackinflore forced her into an upper chamber, where she remained confined.

However, on the previous evening, about half-an-hour after Gilbert Slapp had left the house, Sir Frederick and Mrs. Mackinflore began a violent quarrel. In the course of the squabble, Sir Frederick loaded his partner with the most virulent epithets. The words "ruin," "hanged," and "transported" could clearly be heard throughout the house.

Just before our party had arrived at noon, Mrs. Mackinflore alerted Sir Frederick that she had espied the arrival of Mr. Slapp, stating that he had been the one to whom she had given the watch the previous night. Sir Frederick looked out the window and exclaimed, "And Ferguson with him! He will be my ruin!" Jean remarked that was the reason she knew his name without introduction. The two villains quit the building through a back door, taking Miss Titmus along with them.

Within minutes, Miss Benjerfield and her party made their appearance in search of Sir Frederick. That is the point at which we joined the proceedings.

"Is there anyone else about?" I inquired.

"There's naebody bides i' the house but the mistress an my fellow-servant an myself," responded Jean.

"Do you ken that Miss Benjerfield that was here the now?" asked Mr. Ferguson.

"I never seed her afore, but a ken the man that's wi' her." She nodded. "He's ain o' they chaps as pretends to be husbands to the lassies and frights the gentlemen out o' their siller, but a ken little about their ways, except what a've hered frae my fellow-servant. She's an auld han at their tricks."

"An whar *is* yer fellow-servant?" inquired Mr. Ferguson.

"Why, ye see, when Sir Frederick cam here last nicht, he cam in a cotch, an he brought wi' him an elderly man like, vary weel pit on, but a seed that they'd blinded him and they led him straight up te the garret, an there they hae kept him ever since. My fellow-servant is hading watch o'er him that he disn't flee awa."

Mr. Ferguson asked, "An de ye ken what for they made a prisoner o' him?"

"Not richtly, but I guess, frae an expression or twa that they made use o' at their breakfast this mornin, that they wanted to coax him to pay their debt an free them frae the execution."

"Oh, damme," Gilbert Slapp exclaimed, "let's see the prisoner!"

"I'll let ye see where he is, gin ye follow me," Jean announced, and she led the way to the worn, old stairs. On reaching the garret, she thundered lustily on the door with her fist and exclaimed, "Here Loora, Loora, Loora, woman! I say, open the door, am telling ye. The mistress has rinned awa and here's some gentlemen must come ben."

A hoarse voice boomed from within, "Me no open door. Me see ou dam first!"

Jean turned to us and whispered, "Promise her drink an she'll dee ony thing."

"I would be happy to provide you some… liquor to slake your thirst if you should be so kind as to assist us, ma'am," Gilbert shouted.

The door snatched open, and out reeled a huge black wench, her glaring eyes fixed on the assemble party. Whiffs, like the dregs from an empty swizzle barrel, followed soon after, causing my nose to wrinkle. While a plain, draped cloth covered her torso, a brightly-coloured bandana circled her head. "Well, where liquor?" she exclaimed. "Me glad company come, me promise ou. Dam stupid company him,"–she pointed into the darkness behind her–"no like neder bingo nor fair sex, an me do all me can entertain him too."

Mr. Ferguson and I pushed past and proceeded into the almost empty chamber, seeing only a miserable bed without hangings. We beheld the form of a human being wrapped in a coverlid extended upon the mattress.

"Where me liquor?" cried Loora from the doorway.

Upon hearing us approach, the person raised his head, and, in tremulous accents, pronounced, "Oh dear, Mr. Brown! Oh dear, Mr. Ferguson! Heaven be praised! Heaven be praised! Oh dear, gentlemen! Oh dear! Oh dear!" We had once again discovered the unfortunate Mr. Tunks.

"Rise, sir, rise," I directed. "You are safe. Depend upon our protection and banish all apprehension of your foes. Come, sir, rise!"

"I can't, sir. I can't rise," Mr. Tunks intoned in misery. "They have stripped me to the skin for fear I should attempt to run away. I can't rise. Oh dear! Oh dear!"

"Is him quite naked," Loora professed as she approached us. "Him so shame let me see him. Lor help him silly head, buckra man all go naked in him own country and tink no shame neder."

I motioned to Gilbert to remove the intrusive woman, a hint which he immediately complied with. Once Loora faced away, Mr. Ferguson removed his great-coat and covered poor Mr. Tunks with it.

Once again clothed, Mr. Tunks stood up, stretching and shaking his arms and legs.

"My good fellow, how did you come to this situation?" I asked.

"Oh, dear. Oh, dear." He turned to my friend. "Thank you, Mr. Ferguson, for the loan of your coat. I shall return it most hastily. Oh, dear." He turned back to me. "You see, I received a letter a few evenings ago... Oh, dear. I thought it was from my Miss Betsy, angel, and I followed the stranger who delivered it as he promised to take me to where she was." He wrapped the coat around him a bit tighter. "Oh, dear. Once we had walked a few steps, the mysterious fellow suggested taking a coach, as it was

a considerable distance. After we boarded, two other men immediately followed and commenced to tie a bandage across my
mouth so I could not call out. Then they threw a cloak over my
head so I could not see wherever it was we travelled. Oh, dear."

"That sounds dreadfully frightful, Mr. Tunks," Mr. Ferguson attempted to console the hapless fellow.

"Indeed it was, Mr. Ferguson. Oh, dear. When the bizarre journey ended, they brought me to this garret where you have found
me. One of the men told me I would only be allowed to leave if I
gave them a draft for two hundred and fifty pounds. When I refused, they stripped every rag off me, tossed me into that horrid
flock-bed"–he pointed an accusing finger–"and set that dreadful
woman,"–he indicated Loora–"with a bottle of brandy by her
side, to watch me. Oh, dear. What a night I have passed! Oh,
dear. Oh, dear…"

"Miss Jean," I called out, "could you search for Mr. Tunks's clothing, please?" She nodded and ran off.

"Thank you, Mr. Brown. And if I may ask, if you could convey me
to my home immediately. I am afraid the fright and cold to which
I have been exposed will verily be the death of me." He looked at
me with his forlorn eyes. "Oh, dear. When I do get home, Heaven
only knows what I shall do, poor lone creature that I am. For my
old maid, Sukey, left me yesterday, and I have nobody to make
my gruel and warm my bed."

"Take me, massa, for ou maid," Loora roared. "Ou know me offer
ou every complaisance last night, only ou so dam saucy to Loora.
Take me, massa. Me make ou nice gruel, put him in drop brandy,
and keep ou as warm in bed as ou like." A toothy smile appeared.

"Oh, dear, gentlemen. Oh, dear!" cried Mr. Tunks, retiring into
a corner of the room. "Pray see me civilly treated. Don't let her
come a-near me. I am sure you wouldn't wonder I was afraid of
her, if you knew all. Oh, dear. Oh, dear!"

Mr. Ferguson drew the fellow aside. "You know, sir, there is another female here whom you might do well to take on. She is a
good, Scottish girl, from Edinburgh, like myself. Until just now,
she had been working here under the wiles of the old proprietress, who is now gone. Believe me, sir, you could do much
worse."

At that moment, Jean entered with a pile of clothes. "These were in Mrs. Mackinflore's chamber, sir, beggin pardon." She dropped the wrinkled package on the bed before curtseying.

"Oh, dear. Is that her?" Mr. Tunks asked.

Mr. Ferguson nodded. "Yes, indeed." Mr. Tunks's face brightened. "Would you like me to arrange her service with you?" The older gentleman's bristly head bobbed up-and-down enthusiastically. "Jean, how would you like to work for Mr. Tunks? His previous maid has just left him, and he is in need."

Jean scurried over and took the hand of Mr. Tunks. "Thank ye, sir. Thank ye, indeed." His face reddened at the attentions. "Ye will nae be sorry."

"Oh, dear!"

"Perhaps we should give Mr. Tunks some privacy so that he may dress," I suggested, and the party retired to the landing outside the dingy room.

"Gilbert, would you have any interest in taking on Mr. Tunks to aid his attempts at retribution for the crimes committed against him?" I figured it might be a good job for my fellow Oldhamite.

"Most definitely!" he replied. "Yes, I shall make a good job out of this yet."

The door opened, and out stepped a dishevelled, but calmer, Mr. Tunks.

"My good sir," I began, "Mr. Slapp, who is an excellent legal representative from the house of Briefwit, will serve you in your case, if you so wish."

"Oh, dear. I had not given the matter any thought, but you are correct. I should pursue legal remedies for my inconvenience." He stretched out a dirty hand. "If you are willing to work with me, sir, I am willing to work with you." They shook hands briefly.

"Perhaps you could conduct, Miss Jean and Mr. Slapp to your residence to begin the work."

He glanced at his two new companions in turn. "Oh, dear. Yes, yes. Do come."

I turned to the lawyer, "Gilbert, perhaps you could meet us back here after your visit."

He nodded, and the three of them descended the flimsy stairs.

This gave me great satisfaction, as we had rescued several people that day. Back home in Oldham, my humdrum life did not include such acts of heroism. London had proved to be a wonderful opportunity for me to discover my previously-unknown capabilities.

Chapter Sixteen:
The Rascals Carry On

MR. FERGUSON, LOORA, AND I stood on the landing. "Shall we go down," I suggested, and we returned to the ground floor, the room where this unpleasant episode had begun.

"If missy Mackiflore gone, oo run de house?" Loora asked, surveying the empty herd of tables and chairs.

"You shall, my lady," answered Mr. Ferguson.

"Me, massa?" Her eyes opened to their fullest.

"You, ma'am. And please refrain from calling me your master. You and I have no such relationship."

"What I call ou den?"

"Mister Ferguson will do nicely."

"Oh, yes, massa Fersun." She smiled and my friend closed his eyes. "Dey no bingo. How work wit no bingo?"

"Is there no storeroom?" I asked.

"No storm, but bingo cross street," Loora explained.

"Loora, please bring three bottles," Mr. Ferguson ordered. "Two for the customers and one for you. I believe Mr. Slapp promised you a bottle for assisting us."

"Yes, ee did, ee did." She bobbed her head up-and-down. "Me go get bingo."

After she quit the room, I asked, "Do you truly believe her capable of running this establishment single-handed?"

He smiled. "She probably did most of the work anyway, and, besides, she cannot do a worse job of it than her predecessor."

The sounds of a scuffle came from outside the door. I could hear Loora proclaim, "No my bingo, by gam! Ou be quiet, let my bottle lone. Dis gentleman bingo."

A man's voice replied, "I don't care if it's the devil's bingo, I will have a pull–for luck."

"No! No!" cried Loora.

Mr. Ferguson and I stepped toward the entrance as the man spoke again. "You can fill it up with pump-rhenish, you know, my pretty powder-puff, as you have served many a hundred bottles before that you've tapped on their way home."

"Give me de bingo!"

"But tell us now, Loora Lilly, do you positively mean to say that Lambert and my aunt have taken leg-bail together?"

"Dey gone devil, and ou go after dem," Loora roared. "Dam thief, drink my bingo, cuse ou!"

"No doubt Lambert will be punctual with me to our appointment," the man's voice trailed off.

We reached the door just as Loora entered. "Who was that you were speaking with?" inquired Mr. Ferguson.

"Ee beau-trap," answered Loora. "Bully-rook, quaintance of my missy Mackiflore."

I ushered her to the bar so that she could set the bottles down. "He said something about an appointment with Sir Frederick Lambert. Do you know anything about that?" I asked.

"Me no reconnect."

Mr. Ferguson stepped to the bar and uncorked the already-opened bottle. He took a glass and poured a modest quaff. "Come, take a glass, Loora."

"Me fraid me get slubbery, massa Ferson."

"It might refresh your memory." He held the glass out to her and she drank thirstily.

"Ooh! Good bingo!" She slapped her large tongue about her large mouth. "Me member now. Massa Lambert say he take dis fella dinner in Issiltin... or mebbe Pettonil... for is servesses."

Gilbert Slapp returned at that moment, and I told him what we had just learned. "Shall we begin our search, gentlemen?"

"Loora," Mr. Ferguson purred, "please keep the house going while we are away. We shall return in a few hours."

"Yes, massa Ferson. I keep de house good." She smiled.

Outside, we signalled for a hackney-coach and instructed the driver to take us to Islington. After asking at a few houses that had no reservation for Lambert, we headed to Pentonville, where we found our fellow located in the Belvedere Tavern.

"Mr. Slapp, have you any ideas as to how to proceed?" Mr. Ferguson asked.

"Indeed I do, Mr. Ferguson," Gilbert grinned. "I propose we take possession of another apartment in the tavern. Then we send a waiter with a message saying an acquaintance of Sir Frederick Lambert requests the pleasure of seeing him."

"Should we bringing some officers with us to strengthen our hand?" I suggested.

"Most assuredly not!" He responded, "For hawks like Sir Frederick know every officer in town, and if he sees you in company with these Philistines, he'll smoke the joke, depend upon it, and, more likely than not, slip through our fingers at last."

Gilbert marched into the house and returned a minute later.

"Gentlemen, our good proprietor, Mr. George Gammond, has managed to get us the room directly opposite that of Sir Frederick." He held up a key. "Shall we proceed?"

As we walked cautiously into the ground floor hallway, I could hear the distinct voice of Harry Glara speaking gaily with the fellow we had heard in conversation with Loora earlier.

Once inside our room, Mr. Ferguson spoke to the publican, who had escorted us. "My good sir, please bring us a bottle of English Burgundy, and then go to the opposite room and say that if there is any person there of the name of Sir Frederick Lambert, a gentleman begs to see him here."

Mr. Gammond quit us and we all crept to the wall, attempting to listen to what sounds might have emanated from the other room. Our efforts proved ineffective.

Some time later, Mr. Gammond returned with the bottle and glasses. After he poured, the fellow cocked his head toward the door and said, "My waiter has been in that room with those gentlemen this half-hour, sir. I can't think what he's after. I was just going to call him out."

The landlord departed, leaving the door slightly ajar. Gilbert moved to listen. All appeared quiet in the opposite apartment, nor did any sounds of mirth, similar to those with which we had heard a while ago, meet my ear.

All in a sudden, we heard a momentary scuffle that terminated in an unknown voice exclaiming, "I have caught you–you pay all!"

Mr. Gammond then blurted, "Why, James, what the deuce are you at? Are you mad or drunk? And where are the gentlemen that dined here?"

When we stepped across the hallway, I could see a man, un-doubtedly the waiter, in the act of taking a pocket-handkerchief from his eyes.

"What! Are they all gone?" the waiter screamed. "Damn it! They've done me nicely, that's for certain, the rascals!"

"Yes, and if you've let them slink off without settling their bill, you might well say *I* was to pay all, you careless puppy!" the ir-ritated landlord replied.

"I can explain," the red-faced fellow sputtered.

Mr. Gammond stood with crossed arms and a glowering expression.

"You see, sir, the gentlemen had rung the bell, you see, and when I arrived to receive their orders, they were all laughing heartily at some joke, you see. They called for a couple more bottles of claret, which I procured, you see. After a glass, the fellow at the head of the table asked me if I was fond of fun, and you have instructed us, sir, to be agreeable with the patrons. I told him that I was willing to do anything to oblige them, you see. So, that fellow"–he pointed at the end chair–"told me they couldn't decide which of them was to stand treat, as they called it, and therefore they had agreed that I should be blindfolded, and that whoever I caught was to pay all. He led me into the middle of the floor and blinded me, you see. They must have slipped out one of the windows. Now that I think about it, they set them open just after dinner."

I felt so badly for the poor fellow that I offered to pay half the bill as it was most likely our fault that the party departed early. Mr.

Ferguson had remarked upon Sir Frederick's keen sense of smell, and perhaps he had sniffed us out.

On the return carriage ride to our lodgings in Oxford-street, we resolved to withhold all knowledge of what had passed from the Titmus family. Anything we might tell them would farther aggravate their sufferings. As to Mr. Tunks, we likewise resolved to maintain silence till we had heard what report he should himself make of his unfortunate adventure, aware that we might communicate either more or less than might be consonant to the feelings of that distressed gentleman.

Over the next few days, I called regularly upon the Allinghams at their temporary residence in Berners-street. August and I became more acquainted, and from time-to-time, he would play his lovely harp. He taught me some of the ballads he knew, and I introduced him to some of our Lincolnshire tunes. Every additional hour I passed in his society strengthened the favourable impression I had, from the first moment of our acquaintance, made upon my heart.

One particular afternoon, Mrs. Allingham left the room, leaving August and I unchaperoned. He turned to me with an impish smile. "When did you know, Mr. Brown?"

"Know what, Master Evelyne?" He could have been inquiring upon several different subjects, but I would prefer he specify the category rather than me answering the wrong question.

"That you preferred men to women, of course." He lowered his chin and smiled again.

"Ohhhhhh," I drawled, hoping to give myself more time to form an acceptable response. "As long as I can remember, I guess. And you?" It seemed only fair to return the question.

"Oh, yes, much the same. Thank the heavens that Mother has grown to accept me rather than attempt to alter me."

"Yes, thank the heavens." I said with a wildly-beating heart. "Can one be altered?"

August laughed in his angelic way, light, mirthful, and twittery. "I should hope not, Mr. Brown! I should hope not!" His piercing blue eyes caught mine. "I do hope, Mr. Brown, you are aware of my feelings."

I swallowed hard. His gaze could be intense. "I... I... I believe we are of one mind, Master August."

"Yes! We must be," he rejoined. "After all, you and I would not be sitting here today if it were not for your clever manœuvre in rescuing me from the fire." He blinked a few times and smiled. "I honestly owe to you my life, and you are my hero!" He raised his eyes to the ceiling and hugged himself loosely.

At times he seemed slightly effeminate, but not to the excessive degree of the mollies Mr. Ferguson and I had encountered in the park. "Are you aware of a group of men that calls themselves, 'mollies'?"

His head turned to a slightly different angle. "Mollies? Why I have never heard of such a thing. Sounds positively fascinating! What can you tell me?" He leaned forward in anticipation.

Before I could continue, Mrs. Allingham returned, and I silently thanked whichever guardian angel had intervened, relieving me of having to describe this tender subject.

On the morning of Sir Julius's ball, I called as usual, and, for the first time, made the acquaintance of Mr. Allingham, who was just arrived from Newmarket. His elegant manners exactly corresponded with what Sir Julius had represented; however, during the few minutes for which we conversed together, I discovered in him symptoms of the ambiguous character of which the baronet had likewise painted him. While he assumed an air of ease and gaiety, there appeared to be an actual gloom overspreading his spirits, which I could not forbear attributing to some recent loss sustained either on the turf or at play.

When he had left the room, Mrs. Allingham's assumed smile disappeared. "Mr. Allingham has been such a rake," she said in a soft voice with one hand to the side of her mouth. "He tells me that he is eager to enjoy a little country air and solitude. We are therefore to return to our home at Turnham-green to-morrow."

"Do you know where it is? Were you ever there?" asked August of me.

"Never," I replied, "but I shall make it my early endeavour to discover the spot."

"I hope so—indeed I expect so," returned Mrs. Allingham. "You must be assured—at least I trust you are so—that there is not a person upon earth whom August and myself have so much pleasure in seeing as you. We must both be ungrateful beings if we did not respect you above all the world beside."

It felt good to hear those words. As the days had progressed, August had become the very centre of my little universe, and I could not bear to depart from his society. "My dear madam, revert no more to the subject of thanks, I beg of you," I stated. "I have long since had your promise to that effect, and I also hoped that I had convinced you, that if there is a debtor on the score of happiness in the case, it is myself."

"God bless you both!" she exclaimed. "I hardly know which of you I love best." Small tears began to trickle down her cheeks.

August, meanwhile, employed himself in turning over the leaves of a music-book, but with an agitated hand. Could it be that the lovely being I idolised was affected with an equal degree of sensibility toward me?

Before I could gain a solution of Mrs. Allingham's words, morning visitors arrived and put a period to my attempts. I felt compelled to take my leave, and I resolved to make an open declaration of my passion to the lovely August that evening at the dance.

At the entrance hall to the house, I encountered a person familiar to me.

"Sir Malcolm Brockelsbie calling for Mr. Allingham," he informed the doorman. Upon seeing me, he exclaimed, "Ah, Mr. Brown! You are the very man I wanted to stumble upon. Where the devil have you hid yourself these thousand years?" I opened my mouth to speak, but before I could utter a single syllable, he carried on, "I say, I sacked the dust at the Huntingdon races—dished the knowing ones, by God! Devilish good wit, wasn't it? But I'll tell you what I wanted you about. The Duchess of Silvertongue gives a masquerade to-morrow night—quite a first-rate kind of thing, I promise you." He poked my shoulder pointedly. "I have the disposal of six tickets, and I mean to introduce you and your friend. Dine with me at seven at Short's, and we'll all go together. Shall I expect you?"

Perhaps I had misjudged the old fellow hastily. I could only imagine Mr. Ferguson murmuring words of caution into my ear;

therefore, he would want to attend if only to prove his apprehensions. "I shall accept your invitation with pleasure"—I bowed slightly—"and will likewise take upon me to answer for my friend, as it is a species of amusement which we have never had an opportunity of seeing, and feel much inclined to witness."

"All's right then," returned Sir Malcolm. "Good morning! Excuse me, I'm in a devil of a hurry just now." He shook my hand briefly and rushed past me into the house. On my walk back to Oxford-street, I considered the various reasons for such a magnanimous invitation from such a duplicitous person.

At length arrived the hour for us to repair to the little fête given by Sir Julius, at which Mrs. Allingham had been invited to preside. Mr. Ferguson and I strode to Upper Brook-street in different moods, it seemed.

"I cannot understand it, Brown, why you have accepted the invitation of that scoundrel," Mr. Ferguson said following a long silence.

"Can you not grant me, my dearest of friends, the possibility that he is trying to make good for his past indiscretions?" My step appeared more bouncy in contrast to his flat-footed march.

"No! And I cannot believe that you are willing to walk into what seems a pretty well-laid trap," the colour rose in his face. "I truly believe that man will not rest until Clarington's properties are entirely within his possession. I urge the utmost caution in dealing with this gamester. He is a blacklegs of the foulest sort, I do believe."

"And that is why I have invited you to join me in this venture, my friend." I clapped him on the shoulder. "It shall be your duty to keep me from all harm."

A slight scowl covered his countenance, but I smiled in return. I had looked forward to tripping it on the light fantastic toe. The evening provided an opportunity for me to breath forth my soul to the object of my adoration in hopes of receiving sufficient encouragement; although, my gentle August had shown himself timid and modest, not given to speaking freely.

Mr. Ferguson and I each danced with ladies unknown to us, some older, some closer to our own ages. At my first opportunity,

I sought out Master Evelyne, who had been practically holding the skirt of his mother the entire evening, as if afraid to be swept off by the gaiety and merriment all about.

When I finally managed to pry him away, in a deceptive attempt to procure refreshments, I spoke to him softly. "August, I have been waiting anxiously, patiently, to speak with you alone." An angelic smile crossed his glowing face. "I do believe you are aware of my fondness toward you." He nodded and then kept his chin lowered. "I only wish to know if you can reciprocate my desires. If they are not equal, then we shall part friends."

"Oh, no!" he gasped. "I could not bear to be parted from you, Mr. Brown. After all, I would not be standing here this very moment if it were not for your heroic efforts. Because of this, I believe my life is yours." He looked up and I could see the moisture on his eyes. I wanted to hug him and kiss him to prove my love, but given the situation, we would have to wait for a more private moment. "But I do know that such mutual affections are... challenging to pursue in this society. We cannot risk being found out, for the punishments are rather severe." Tears began to well.

"But I have already witnessed such affections between men without repercussions. If handled discreetly, none would bother us. We could live on my estate in Oldham together most comfortably," I told him. "The previous occupant was similarly inclined, and his romantic interest resided with him until the death." I did not wish to admit that Mr. Clarington's lover was also his steward. "However, according to the terms of my late benefactor's testaments, I must remain free from romantic entanglements until I have attained the age of twenty-five."

We had taken the beverage glasses and were returning to where Mrs. Allingham sat. "It sounds lovely, and my mother absolutely adores you, but your heart may change over the course of the next few years." He looked away.

"It cannot!" I blurted foolishly. "From the moment I first looked upon your eyes, I knew that you would be the one person I would most want to spend the remainder of my days."

He turned back to me. "And what about your precious Mr. Ferguson." His tone began to take on the inflections of a jealous lover.

A laugh burst forth from my lips. "My 'precious' Mr. Ferguson is well-smitten with a woman who is presumed dead and lying at the bottom of Glasgow harbour." August's head snapped in my direction. "His inclination is toward women, dearest one. You have nought to fear from him."

A smile replaced his frown as we rejoined his mother's party. At last I had made my feelings known and found them reciprocated as well. The difficulty ahead of us would be waiting until I achieved my twenty-fifth year.

Once we had dispatched the refreshments to his mother and Sir Julius, the two of us took to dancing with various young ladies, all the while glancing across the floor from time-to-time to catch each other's eye. After a half-dozen dances, I began to feel light-headed and took a seat near our host and Mrs. Allingham. They must not have observed me as they began speaking with each other in a personal manner, yet loud enough for me to overhear their conversation.

Mrs. Allingham began, "I hope you will excuse me, Sir Julius, indeed I feel satisfied that you do, or I would not have hazarded the communication which I have made to you. You must clearly perceive, that, in a perplexing case like this, I have no individual amongst my own immediate connexions to whom I can, with safety, unburthen my heart, and, likewise, ask advice from in return. I must confess that I have also been considerably biased in my choice, by the partiality with which I have ever considered you to regard my poor August. I think I am not wrong in supposing him a favourite of yours, eh, Sir Julius?"

"Granted!" exclaimed the baronet. "I pledge my word to you that I am very fond of little August—very fond indeed—and shall experience a real satisfaction in rendering any service in my power to you both. When shall I see you? Shall I call upon you at your lodgings in town to-morrow, or defer my visit till you are settled at Turnham-green?"

"No, no, do not come to me," Mrs. Allingham sounded flustered. "Suffer *me*—the first morning I can invent an excuse for coming to town alone—to call upon *you*. When an opportunity offers, I will send you a note the evening before apprising you of my intention. If you were to come to Turnham-green, and we were to be in private conversation together for any length of time, the circumstance might give rise to inquiries which I should find my-self at a loss to answer."

"Admitted!" returned Sir Julius.

The dinner bell sounded, and our host began to rise.

"You will keep my secret?" Mrs. Allingham whispered in his ear.

"You have placed your confidence in me," he replied, "and I pledge my word to you that you shall not repent having done so."

The heart of love is ever anxious, fearful, and suspicious, especially that of new love. What could compel Mrs. Allingham to seek the advice of Sir Julius? Could it be relative to any circumstance connected with the happiness of our dear August? Perhaps she might have entertained the idea of Sir Julius proposing himself to her as a husband. What *was* the reason? A question I could not forbear to ruminate, impossible to answer, and, moreover, in all probability, ever destined to remain unrevealed. It would have been impossible to advance an inquiry on the subject without me confessing having been an unsuspected auditor of the conversation, although I had become so without any premeditated effort on my part.

Throughout the remainder of the evening, I said nothing to either August or his mother regarding the overheard interaction. When Sir Julius announced the lateness of the hour, guests began to shuffle out.

"Shall we see you to-morrow, then, Mr. Brown?" asked Mrs. Allingham.

"Most assuredly, ma'am." I smiled politely at August. "I would not forgo the chance to see you both before you depart for Turnham-green."

"Until then," she smiled and walked off, August in hand.

"Did you have any fun at all, old man?" inquired Mr. Ferguson as he approached me.

"Fun?" The question had startled me. "Oh, yes. Fun. And you?"

"I am willing to wager that you had more fun than I did. Were you able to get an answer to your question?"

"Question?" Again, a startling interrogatory. Then I realised he could not have been referring to the conversation between our host and Mrs. Allingham. "In point of fact, I did manage to achieve a few minutes alone with young August."

"And...?"

"It does appear that our interests are, indeed, mutual." When I spoke the words, they felt colder than I had intended. The uncertainty of that conversation, and the impending intercourse between Mrs. Allingham and Sir Julius, hovered above my heart like a pregnant storm cloud.

"Excellent!" decried Mr. Ferguson.

"Yes, excellent," I replied, attempting to sound enthusiastic.

"Gentlemen!" interrupted Sir Julius. "Perhaps you did not hear me remark upon the lateness of the hour. You need not return to your lodgings, but you most certainly cannot remain here." He pointed to the doorway.

"Of course, Sir Julius," I responded. "We both thank you for your more than generous hospitality. Until to-morrow." I put out my hand, and he seized it gently.

His eyes sparkled as he looked at us both. "You two are like the sons I never had." As he dropped my hand, he remarked, "It will not be soon enough that I see you both again. A good-night."

On our return walk, Mr. Ferguson described his evening, the ladies with whom he had danced, and the invitations he had received—but declined. However, my head had become so full of nervous calculations as to what might have been the subject of the conversation between Mrs. Allingham and Sir Julius that I could not properly hear my friend's report.

The following morning, I reported to Berners-street at my earliest opportunity only to find the carriage which was to convey August and his mother to Turnham-green already at the door.

"Do us the pleasure and honour of calling for a visit in a few days, Mr. Brown," declared Mrs. Allingham.

"Yes, please do," murmured August.

I reached into my pocket and found one of the mourners' rings, which I handed to the object of my affection, saying, "Hold this as a token, and I shall reclaim it upon the next time I behold you."

A flush of colour ran into August's pale face as he accepted the piece. "Until I behold you again," he replied with his head pointed down bashfully. He and his mother climbed into the conveyance.

From the walk next to the house, I stood and watched the carriage depart, not knowing when I would see my beloved August again. At the very least, my heart knew it could never be soon enough.

Chapter Seventeen:
Many, Many Masks

F OR OUR COSTUMES, Mr. Ferguson and I chose a set of old domino dresses that Mrs. Titmus had packed away. They fit well-enough, and we brought them with us to Short's for our appointment with Sir Malcolm. Following the anticipated dinner, we would don them before departing for the evening's merriment.

When we arrived at the hotel, a waiter ushered us to a dining-room where the baronet and several gentlemen sat. Following the meal, and the removal of the cloth, the glass circulated freely, and a lively conversation ensued. Various toasts to a round of beauties had been proposed, and then Sir Malcolm filled his glass to the brim, stood, and proclaimed, "The delightful Master August Evelyne, a treasure of youth!"

As the others emptied their glasses, Mr. Ferguson and I locked eyes with furrowed brows. I called to mind the admonition given freely by my friend regarding Sir Malcolm's presumed schemes upon my pending inheritance.

Our host stood and approached me. "Damn it, my dear fellow," he declared, laying his hand on my shoulder with familiarity. "I believe fate has ordained that I am to be indebted to you for every happiness which I enjoy in the world. A few days ago you rescued me from being torn to pieces by a mob, and I now understand that you preserved my ward from being burnt to death."

"Your ward?" I choked on the word.

"Yes, my boy," a wicked smile appeared. "I have consulted the Allinghams with regard to lightening their financial burden. Master Evelyne, who has proven to be a costly encumbrance upon his family, shall soon become my enchanting protégé. The matter is now in the Court of Chancery, and we expect a positive outcome within the week."

My heart dropped. The baronet must have learned of my affections for August and made arrangements to remove him from my grasp. Not wanting to give him any further advantage, I bit my lip and proclaimed as blandly as I could, "I had the happiness of being instrumental in the preservation of Master Evelyne, sir."

"You can't think how devilishly I respect you," returned Sir Malcom. "I hope we shall in future be sworn friends—upon my soul I do! But mum, my dear boy! Don't broach the subject here. I have not mentioned it yet to an individual but yourself." He put a finger to his thin lips. "Mum!"

As he walked away to converse with other guests, I almost resolved withdrawing from the Duchess's masquerade, having no interest in frivolity. After a few moments of reflection, I altered my opinion and resolved to attend as planned. Given our last intercourse, I felt that August had pledged his life to me, and any rivalry for his attentions would be mine in the end.

"You look rather down-hearted, my friend," Mr. Ferguson offered as he clapped a hand on my shoulder. "What ever can be the matter?"

I looked up into the eyes of my closest companion and regained the strength to continue. "Sir Malcolm just confirmed your suspicions of his underhandedness. Whilst I cannot reveal the content of the conversation, please understand that he has proposed to remove my dearest August from his family and my life."

Mr. Ferguson squeezed my arm. "Then I propose it is in our best interests to attend this evening's festivities as a method of maintaining our watch upon him."

I nodded sadly, unable to free my mind from the prospect of losing my dearest. We donned our dominos dresses and walked with the others to the home of the Duchess.

Her apartment, though elegant and stately, at first seemed too small for the number of guests occupying it. While the décor gave the impression of wealth, signs of decay and wear caught my eye in the quick glance I had made upon initial survey. As we got hustled about the room, I caught a few titbits of intriguing conversation.

"I know you," claimed one fellow dressed as an Elizabethan prince. "You don't know me," came the response from a feathery bird.

One gentleman wearing a chimney sweep's garb asked, "What's o'clock?" only to have a dance-hall moll answer, "A timepiece which tells the hour of the day and night. Are you such a fool as not to know that?"

A fellow dressed like a common lady mop squeezer grabbed the arm of a make-shift judge. "Maid of all work, your honour!" only to be rebuked. "I've been at work all day, my dear, and mean to rest to-night."

Mr. Ferguson and I had paraded the gay scene for about an hour when a light figure in the dress of a haymaker began to follow us directly. The person appeared slim and effeminate, perhaps a woman who had exchanged her outward attire for the semblance of the opposite sex. We stepped to the side of a pillar and the made-up haymaker approached me.

"How do you do, Mr. Brown, sir? I hope you are *wery vell*."

At first, it surprised me that one of this motley group would know me. However, I had taken off my mask, due to the warmth of the apartment.

"It's *wastly 'ot*, ain't it, sir?" the character continued without giving me the time to reply to the previous inquiry.

"Oppressively so," I replied.

"Oh, *werry sewere* indeed!" That phrase caught my attention, as I had heard it pronounced just that way only recently. "To be sure you must know me, sir." The haymaker leaned in to my ear and continued in a half-whisper, "I'm Mr. Dobby, sir, as you see at *H*ashley's play along *v*ith Miss Lotty Titmus." Oh, yes, the purveyor of the two-to-one shop. "I shouldn't have made bold to speak to you in public, Mr. Brown, sir, but only in these *'ere* places nobody knows *v*on another, and everybody speaks together just as it *'appens*."

"I did not expect to meet you here to-night," I confessed.

"Oh, bless you, sir!" Mr. Dobby burbled. "I'm forced to be *'ere*, and so is *par*, *v*ether *v*e likes it or not, but I likes the frolic *werry vell*, I assure you, sir. I thinks it quite *h*entertaining."

"How do you mean forced," I asked.

"*V*y, you see, sir, you know the line of life *v*e's in, don't you, sir?"

"Yes, I think I have understood that you lend money on property."

"Yes, sir, yes, *v*e's pawnbrokers," Mr. Dobby said proudly. "Vell, sir, only I *v*ould not *v*ish it to be mentioned because people like *v*e, in business, shouldn't tell tales of their customers, they say.

The Duchess of Silvertongue, as gives this 'ere gala, has all her plate laid up in our 'ands, and ve've let it out to her to-night, at so much per cent for the hevening, and so ve've both comed 'ere to make certain that ve gets it all safe back again."

This intelligence confirmed my first impression of the hostess's faded wealth. "Indeed," I nodded my ascent.

"I vish I could have brought Lotty vith me, but I couldn't get a ticket for her. If I could, I could have dressed her as fine and expensive as any lady in the land, vith diamonds—and vatnot be-sides—as father and I has got in our varehouses."

At that moment, my attention had been drawn to two persons carrying constables' staves in their hands. They appeared to be the most active characters in the fantastic scene before me. I asked Mr. Dobby, "Do you know those masqueraders?" I pointed in their direction.

"Vat, them constables, sir, as is running after the dandy and the flower-girl?"

"The same," I responded.

"Vy they ain't masks at all, sir," came the response. "They are right real constables, in good hearnest."

"Real constables?" I said in confusion.

"Oh, bless you, sir, there wouldn't be no keeping peace—nor vatches neither—vithout them. There's as many shy-cocks get hadmittance into these 'ere dashy places as if they vas open at 'alf-a-guinea a 'ead."

"I find that difficult to believe, Mr. Dobby."

"Oh, you see, Mr. Brown, sir, the people as gives these 'ere kind of feets don't care a straw who's at 'em, so as the newspapers does but represent them to have been crowded to excess. For there's queer vork amongst the great folks. If you knew all, Mr. Brown—there isn't nobody upon earth as does such mean actions as them that sets the fashions and cuts the greatest swell—oh, dear sir, you vouldn't believe the 'alf on't!" He wiped the side of his mouth with a gloved hand. "Vy sir, it vas only last vinter as a respecta-ble tradesman, a tailor by trade, sir, vas robbed of his vatch at a public masquerade, by a character in the dress of a sweep. The next morning, ven he vent to vait on von of his customers—a young buck of the fashion—he seed his vatch upon the table vere he *v*as at breakfast, and the sweep's dress hanging up in the room."

How horrible! I thought. A man's pocket-watch can be quite an intimate article. "And what was the consequence?"

"*V*y, it *v*as never known exactly how the matter *v*as settled, but there is little doubt that the tailor *v*as satisfied to take back his *v*atch and pretend that he considered the affair as a joke. For if '*e 'ad* not, to a certainty, *h*all the bucks *v*ould have joined together to knock up his trade."

The beckoning hand of a domino across the room summoned me. "Please excuse me, Mr. Dobby." I began to move toward Mr. Ferguson. "And thank you for the information."

He tipped his haymaker's hat. "An *h*onour, sir."

I made my way through the labyrinth of guests, bowers, saloons, and tables to find Mr. Ferguson signalling me from a side room that had metamorphosed into a grotto. Along the walls, tables held a spread of refreshments, but the centre of attention proved to be an individual of an extraordinary and splendid appearance. His dress blazed with diamonds and valuable jewels of every description. A crowd had formed about the gentleman.

"What an amazing dress," I whispered to Mr. Ferguson.

"Not dress, my friend," he replied, also in a whisper. "The fellow is a sable potentate who has lately arrived from his own country on a visit to the British Dominions."

His face seemed magically symmetrical—he wore no mask—and as we got closer, I could tell the magnificent garb turned out not to be a masquerade at all. The excellence of the handiwork left little doubt of its not being a disguise.

"I believe I know him," Mr. Ferguson spoke even softer. "He appears to be one of the fellows I had encountered on the Yorkshire moor. When I last saw him, he was a-sleeping."

A woman holding a platter and dressed as a Savoyard addressed the gentleman freely, "As I understand your highness comes from Otaheite, you must, of course, be a friend to the... *Sandwiches.*" She presented the platter—which contained some slices of bread and ham—to him with a witty smile. With an elegant inclination of his head, the fellow declined her offer.

Another woman, this one bedecked as a Sultana stepped forward. "I am told that you have been sent over to England by your father, who is an Asiatic king, for your education. Pray, sir, are you the Prince of Wales in your own country?"

The handsomely-garbed man turned to the speaker. "In the nation to which I belong, no such dignity exists."

"Oh, how delightfully he talks English!" exclaimed a shepherdess. "I must have a few words with him myself." She manœuvred between some of the other guests by parting them with her tall crook. "Pray, your highness, have you any military in your country? If you have Royal Lifeguards, the same as we have here, I would give a joint off one of my little fingers to be the wife of a colonel. It would be so extravagantly odd!"

With a noble tilt of his head, the gentleman replied, "I would advise you, then, for the sake of your reputation, if not your peace of mind, to pursue a more honourable method for engaging *your* colonel's hand than was adopted by your friend in securing *hers*."

"Brute! Savage!" cried out the Sultana. She grabbed the shepherdess by the wrist and retired from the spot.

A woman's voice behind us caught our attention. "Did you hear that? See how the sarcasm has stung her!"

We turned round to see a couple splendidly dressed as Elizabethan courtiers. "It is something new indeed to witness her betray any systems of feeling," responded the fellow accompanying her.

Mr. Ferguson turned to the man who had just spoken. "May I take the liberty of inquiring who the lady is of whom you have been speaking? Do you know her?"

"Who does not, sir?" replied the courtier with a roll of his eyes and a jaunty hand movement. "I believe there are few indeed in town who do not know the *exquisite* Mrs. Percival." He took the hand of his companion and they strode off to one of the side refreshment tables.

At the mention of the name, I could feel Mr. Ferguson's heart wince. If this sable prince did, indeed, come from Asia, how could he have become acquainted with the history of the current Mrs. Percival, and by what cause could he have been prompted thus severely to tax her with her crime? I turned to speak with my companion, but he had fled the chamber. Upon reaching the hallway, I caught sight of him pursuing the faux Sultana and her shepherdess. They stopped at the entrance of a narrow avenue of artificial jessamine, which led into an orange bower.

As I approached, I heard the Sultana proclaim, "It's intolerably hot. I shall go home directly," to which the shepherdess responded, "I am sure it must be very late. Will nobody tell me what's o'clock?"

Mr. Ferguson stepped between the ladies, snatched the watch from his pocket and thrust it in front of the Sultana's face. "Consult this watch, if you please, madam. I believe you will find it speaks truth."

The woman's eyes landed first upon the watch, then upon Mr. Ferguson, and her countenance indicated that she recognised them both. A dreadful, almost satanic, expression took possession of her features. In broken and scarcely articulate accents, "Merciful God! Can it be possible?" burst, from her lips. "Wretched vill–" She halted abruptly, seized her companion's arm and darted through the crowd with an energy that appeared the effect of a momentary frenzy.

"Heaven be praised," muttered Mr. Ferguson. "If I have had it in my power to communicate a pang to thy abandoned heart in retribution for thy murder of the innocent Jessy!"

"I wonder if *he* is here as well..." I spoke, mostly to myself.

"To whom are you referring, my friend?" Mr. Ferguson must have heard my musing.

"Oh, the White Man, whose hospitality you enjoyed on the Yorkshire moor and who visited me at Ashbank Hall after the interment of Mr. Clarington." I pointed back to the grotto room. "If you recognised the Asian prince as his companion, I must believe that he is about here someplace, and I should wish to address him again."

Mr. Ferguson smiled. "I believe it would be most difficult to bring a white goat into this crowded establishment."

"Difficult," I mused, "but not impossible."

During the following hour, we searched for the Asiatic Prince and the White Man. Finding neither, we soon after took leave of the festivities and braved the brisk night air of London. Upon our return to the Titmus home, the residents inquired into every aspect of the masquerade, and Mr. Ferguson and I regaled them with our experiences. It felt like the least we could do for lending us their domino dresses.

The following morning, I hired a hackney-cab to whisk me to the Allinghams residence in Turnham-green. I needed to speak with August and his mother to discuss the overheard plans verbalised by Sir Malcolm, a most undeserving ward guardian.

Upon reaching their home, a servant informed me that Mr. Allingham did not allow for visitors while he remained in residence. The servant did make it known, however, the gentleman had plans to quit the home three days hence.

It would be three days of agony and expectancy. Mr. Ferguson made vain attempts to give me cheer by taking me to various theatrical events, but nothing could lift the unwelcome gloom from my spirit.

On the appointed morning, I borrowed a horse and rode the distance out to Turnham-green, only to discover that August and his mother had gone a few miles into the country to dine with a friend. As I mounted for the return journey, Sir Malcolm Brockelsbie, likewise on horseback, advanced in the opposite direction.

Once he recognised me, he drew in his horse's head and rode up to my side, extended his hand, and shouted, "Mr. Brown, I am devilishly glad to meet you! Upon my soul, I am!" After we shook hands politely, he continued, "It is the most fortunate thing that possibly could have occurred, for I have a subject of the greatest moment which I wish to discuss with you, and as I also wish that it should remain an inviolable secret, I repeat that, by God, nothing could be more fortunate than our happening to meet here!" He pointed back in the direction I had been moving. "Let us step into a house I know in nearby Hammersmith and have a little private conversation together. Pray don't refuse me."

I could imagine no subject which a private conversation with this dishonourable man would benefit me. However, if Sir Malcolm had gained the knowledge that I also had an interest in August Evelyne, it might have appeared cowardly in me to refuse his invitation. Not wishing to seem unhandsome, I nodded my ascent and followed him to an inn not far away. We dismounted and gave our charges to the hostler.

Sir Malcolm entered the house ostentatiously, as if it were his own, and called for a bottle of sherry and sandwiches. The house woman led us to an unoccupied table in a corner.

"Mr. Brown,"–the baronet began as we sat–"except that you have lately allowed me the honour of calling you friend, we are comparatively strangers to each other, and the liberty I am about to take with you, at this moment, may, I fear, appear to you a most unwarrantable one."

As I listened to him, remembering Mr. Ferguson's warnings, this adventure had resemblances to the snake in the Garden of Eden. Every word seemed crafted to bring advantage to Sir Malcolm and detriment to me.

"If it does so," he continued, "I can only rely for pardon on that charitable spirit with which you are so eminently gifted, and which has already so benevolently displayed itself towards me."

Against my apprehensive instincts, I spoke, "Pray, Sir Malcom, speak freely."

"My dear fellow," he reached across the table and caught my hand, pressing it in his. "I am a fool–a madman! I am, by God! Nay, if possible, worse. I have not a friend in the world to whom I dare disclose my sentiments, and the feelings which at this moment agitate my mind."

The house woman arrived with a tray of sandwiches, two glasses, and a bottle of sherry. She placed them on the table and scurried away. Sir Malcolm uncorked the sherry and poured two bumpers.

"Fashion, Mr. Brown–fashion, dissipation, and play, those devilish, alluring, damning qualities, have led me into a net of difficulties from which I apprehend that I shall never be able to extricate myself." He stood and hastily swallowed his glass, resumed his seat and continued, "I have sold my stud, mortgaged my estate, and overwhelmed myself with promissory notes. By Heaven! Except the trifling value which I can attach to my wardrobe, and a few trinkets that I possess, I know not where to look for existence a week hence."

He poured a second bumper, stood and swallowed that in an apparent effort of desperation.

My pitying heart wanted to offer assistance to ease his suffering, but his recent words and actions had amplified my scepticism. However, my mother had raised me to be a good Christian, and I felt compelled to say, "Believe me that I truly commiserate your feelings. Tell me, frankly, if there are any means by which I can act towards their relief."

He cast his eyes downward. "I do not deserve this concern from you, sir. I know devilishly well that I do not, and you increase your own merit by bestowing it on me." His gaze moved up to mine. "Damn it, my dear fellow! If I have been wild, dissipated, and committed ten thousand other follies besides, I can discriminate, and sometimes have sense enough to wish that I resembled those whom I have hitherto been so unlike." He licked at his lips nervously. "But to the point, for I shall annoy you by speaking too much of myself. You ask me if it is in your power to grant relief to my feelings? Indubitably, instantly."

It sounded very much like sort of trickery in which I would get bobbed, but I still felt the need to offer. "Mention the means, sir."

"Dare you accept my bond for the sum which would extricate me from my present difficulties?"

"Name what that sum is," I answered, "and believe me, that if I perceive the ability to be mine, the will is cordially so."

"Damn it, you are a fine fellow! By Heaven, you are!" he exclaimed. As I gave him no response, he proceeded, "My difficulties are great, inordinately so. Nothing less than ten or twelve thousand pounds can extricate me from the dilemma in which I am at this time placed!"

Ten or twelve thousand pounds?! The audacity of such a request caused my throat to burn, and I coughed involuntarily.

"Drink up, my boy." The baronet pushed a glass toward me.

I took a sip to quench the fire before speaking. "My dear Sir Malcolm, you must surely be convinced that I cannot be in possession of such a sum. You heard the will of my benefactor, and must therefore be acquainted, that till I attain my twenty-fifth year, I am allowed only an annuity of one thousand pounds."

He stood and paced about. "But are you not aware that upon the security of the large property of which you will then come into possession, it would be in your power to raise any sum you choose?"

In my mind, I could not help but picture the serpent in the Garden slithering up a tree and undulating its forked tongue in my direction. "It may be so,"–I replied, attempting to maintain a calm composure–"but there is a clause in Mr. Clarington's will which forbids me to be in debt more than one hundred pounds before I attain my twenty-fifth year, on pain of forfeiting the inheritance which will otherwise become mine. Perhaps this was a point unknown to you?"

Sir Malcolm turned away quickly, as if I had caught him unawares. He turned back with a tight smile and a light in his eyes. "Oh, no. I had heard of it, but what of that, my dear fellow? Money affairs can be so secretly transacted in London, by the means of proper agents, that it is an impossibility they should transpire."

"Indeed, sir," I returned, "it is a contingency to which I cannot for a moment think of exposing myself."

"If you'll only consent to let Slapp have the management of the business, I'll be answerable for his secrecy with my life–I will, by God!"

The bile within me rose at such a trespassing request, and it took me a moment before I could respond calmly. "Believe me, in one word, that I am determined not to risk the hazard which might arise to me from such a transaction. No method of agency which can be pointed out shall induce me to swerve from my resolution. Had I attained the age when I shall be able to render a benefit of the nature you require a friend, upon my honour, it would have given me pleasure to have stepped forward to the relief of your mind." His countenance darkened noticeably. "Whilst I have inhabited Ashbank Hall, I have not lived extravagantly. Consequently, I have a few hundred in my possession which are my own. If you will accept the loan of those, they are heartily at your service. Sincerely do I wish they amounted to the sum of which you stand in need."

Sir Malcolm rose, slapped the palm of his hand in agony to his forehead, then placed himself opposite to me. "My dear sir, my dear fellow, the sum you offer me, instead of relieving, would only serve to involve me still farther. Yet I thank you—sincerely I thank you." During a pause, he touched a finger to his temple. "No, so trifling a sum, I repeat it, would but serve to involve me still farther. I have then but one resource, and that is a wretched one—a devilish one it is, by Heaven!" When I did not make an inquiry, he continued, "Shall I candidly tell you what the resource is—what is my only alternative to being shut up in a gaol, from which I have no chance of escaping for five years to come? But drink, or I shall really imagine that you have taken offence at the liberty I have used with you."

"Then you will think unjustly of me, indeed."

We emptied our glasses, and he confided, "If you are truly unable to satisfy my need, my only alternative, then, is to set in motion a course of events which begins with my obtaining an innocent ward through the Court of Chancery."

He must have been referring to my dearest August, after the rapturous manner in which he had previously toasted him. "Is it possible for you to disclose such course of events to me, Sir Malcolm?"

He stood and paced the room with hasty and impatient strides. "No. It is not possible."

Once more, placing himself opposite to me, and fixing his eyes steadfastly on mine, he purred, "Perhaps yet, by Heaven! I consider your disposition too noble, too generous, to be capable of so mean a suspicion. Perhaps you entertain an apprehension that, as the next heir-in-law to the late Mr. Clarington, it is my wish to entrap you into a debt to benefit by the treachery which I should practise. Surely you cannot think thus of me?"

As I continued to look upon his face, it began assuming a green, scaly appearance, he pupils narrowed to vertical slits, and a moist, forked tongue slipped from between his lips. "Indeed, I do not," I managed to reply.

"Is there any oath by which I can convince you that I wish every torture of the damned to assail me, if so base an idea ever entered my mind?"

"I have already said that I do not suspect you," I responded, attempting to maintain calm. "Therefore, I cannot require a confirmation of the nature you mention, upon a point on which I have already positively assured you, that my resolution cannot be shaken."

"Well then, to Chancery, to Chancery, to Chancery, alone remains to me!" he exclaimed wildly. The baronet raised another bumper to his lips and extended his other hand to me, which I immediately accepted. "Heaven bless you, my dear fellow! Though you have most devilishly disappointed my high-raised expectations, I sincerely thank you for what you did offer me."

How pitiful he sounded! I still felt compelled to assist. "Will you still acc–"

"No, no, no," he interrupted. "You know what I have already told you. Too insignificant to quell the storm already raised. The possession of a few hundreds might tempt me, as a relief from my devilish feelings, into actions that would eventually only swell the hurricane. Well, God bless you! When shall I see you again?"

The fact that he protested my offer made me consider that, perhaps, he might not have been the swindler I had taken him for. However, Mr. Ferguson's cautions still remained. "We shall see each other soon, no doubt."

"To convince me that we part the friends we met, give me your honour that you will not divulge to anyone the conversation that has just passed between us." His eyelids appeared half-closed. "It could avail you nothing to expose my circumstances to a sneering world or to feed its spleen with a repetition of the expressions which I have dropped relative to my forced actions."

"Upon that you may rely," I assured him. "Upon my honour, what has passed between us shall remain buried in my breast."

"You are a devilish good fellow! Upon my soul you are!" bellowed the baronet. "Damn me if you ain't!"

I settled the bill, knowing that Sir Malcolm had no such intention, and we ordered our horses. We rode together to Hyde-Park-corner, where we parted.

As I walked my horse slowly up Park-lane, my mind filled with the most perplexing reflections. Had Sir Malcolm Brockelsbie intended to draw me into a snare, or had the vehemence of his entreaties arisen solely from the actual distress of his feelings? He has previously shown himself as a wild, inconsiderate man, by no means an unprincipled one, and I wished to consider him so still. Doubts remained which I could not divest myself. I could only assume that his anticipated ward would be none other than my precious August. The transaction of the morning sat altogether as an enigma that I could not divulge, owing to the promise I had made to Sir Malcolm, and I could not receive an opinion from my friend upon the subject. I could only trust to future events–and observations of my own–for the development of the truth.

Chapter Eighteen:
A Time of Treachery

SOME DAYS HAD ELAPSED since I had last seen Sir Julius Maberly, and I realised the path back to my lodgings had drawn me near to his home. Considering that he might be able to provide some perspective upon my situation with Sir Malcolm, I resolved to pay him a short visit. A servant informed me that his master was at home and ushered me into the library.

Sir Julius leapt up upon seeing me. "My dearest, Mr. Brown! A pleasure." He grasped my hand and gazed into my eyes. "It is a great honour to see you, but, if you could, please, grant me a few minutes to conclude a letter I wish to send on the five o'clock post." He directed me to a chair at a desk with a large folio upon it. "Have a gander at this." He opened the large book. It contained a collection of prints. "This volume is on loan for my inspection. Please let it keep you company whilst I complete my correspondence."

Sir Julius returned to the table where he had been writing, and I sat upon the directed chair. Just as I began perusing the folio, I caught sight of some unexpected motion. Directly in front of me hung an extremely large mirror in which I could see my countenance. However, in the reflection behind me, I observed a set of folding doors, one-half of which opened slightly, and the head of a man projected from them. I immediately turned round my head, but in the moment of action, the door closed, and the visage disappeared.

The countenance seemed familiar, but I could not immediately recollect where I had beheld it before. Although fleeting, it made a lasting impression in my mind.

Sir Julius looked up. "Go on examining your prints and pay no attention to that gentleman. It is only an old friend of mine from the country who occasionally pays me a visit. He dislikes the society of strangers, and, seeing you, retired."

"I am very sorry, sir, you did not intimate to me that you had a friend of that description with you," I replied. "I should not thus long have detained you from his society."

"No apologies, no apologies," the baronet cried. "He and I are no strangers to each other, I pledge my word to you. But you are not going. I insist upon it that you do not hurry away on my friend's account."

I pulled my pocket-watch and saw the hour. "Pardon me, Sir Julius, but I promised Mr. Ferguson to return home to dinner, and he will be expecting me."

"Well, then, let me see you soon again," rejoined the baronet. "I have a particular reason for wishing it."

"Of course, of course," I responded before quitting his library.

Along the ride to return the horse, my eye accidentally fell upon a white goat led by a young girl. My mind immediately flashed upon the memory of the stranger in Sir Julius's library. Of course! The reflection in the mirror must have been the White Man himself, divested of his beard and slouched hat. The probability of this increased with the knowledge that his companion had appeared at the masquerade a few evenings before.

By what means had so extraordinary a character become known to Sir Julius Maberly? I considered returning directly to discover the answer, but then recalled Iago's forewarning, "How poor are they that have not patience!" I promised myself to make it a point of inquiry at our next visit.

Our dinner passed with little conversation. I kept reflecting upon the fleeting image of the White Man, now civilised, in Sir Julius's library. As much as I wished to divulge my intelligence to Mr. Ferguson, I thought it best not to discuss the matter until I had spoken once again with the baronet to determine the nature of his relationship with the White Man.

The following morning, I arose before my friend, dressed quickly and quit the house. With no particular destination in mind, my feet took me to Westminster Abbey. The tombs of our former monarchs, Edwards and Henrys, Mary and Elizabeth, attracted me immediately, but I was especially drawn to that of Edward VI, who lived but 15 years. He had the weight of our great nation thrust upon him at a very young age. After only five years, he succumbed. While my age is greater and my inheritance much less, I prayed that my comparable life would last somewhat longer than his.

Upon my return to the Titmus residence, Mr. Ferguson engaged me in a discussion. "Do you have plans for the evening ahead, Mr. Brown?"

"I think I shall occupy myself with writing to Mr. Radford. He has requested my instructions with regard to some new tenants whom I am going to receive upon the estate." This business, while not pressing, provided a reasonable excuse to remove myself from my friend's presence. "Whilst engaged in contemplating novelty abroad, I do not consider it just to neglect the concerns of my old friends at home. What will you do with yourself?"

A bright smile spread across his face. "You have often heard me mention the infatuation which first took me to the stage. I see, by the play-bills, that Charles Kemble acts Jaffeir to-night. I am determined to go and ascertain whether my early opinion of his performance is still the same."

Following a pleasant meal, Mr. Ferguson set out for the theatre, and I placed myself before the writing-desk. Composing the correspondence proved difficult as I had great difficulty concentrating on my task as the ghostly image from Sir Julius's library made frequent appearances in my mind.

Somewhere after nine o'clock, one of the servants knocked upon the door. "Mr. Brown, sir, there's a person below 'oo requests to see you *h*immediately on business of great *h*importance."

"Please shew him up directly, thank you."

A well-dressed young man entered the apartment and approached me. "If your name is Brown, sir, I am sorry to inform you that your friend, Mr. Ferguson has fallen into a quarrel with a gentleman at the theatre. They are gone to a tavern to adjust the dispute, and Mr. Ferguson desires to see you as soon as possible."

"May I ask who you are, sir?"

"I am, sir," he hesitated momentarily, "one of the waiters of the tavern where Mr. Ferguson is expecting to see you."

Given this information, I grabbed my hat, put on my coat and quit the house with the young man. Once we had reached

Oxford-street, he spoke, "It is a long way from hence to Covent-garden, sir. I would advise you to let me call you a coach."

Although I had already walked past that district earlier in the day, the darkness of the hour and the immediacy of the situation indicated the wisdom of the suggestion. "Yes, of course."

The fellow stepped out and hailed the nearest coach. He held the door for me but then sprang upon the box, by the side of the coachman. As the ride continued, I began to get agitated, as it appeared to be longer than expected.

At last, the vehicle stopped, and the young man opened the door for me. After I settled with the coachman, I followed the young fellow up a narrow street that suddenly turned into a paved alley, similar to those which I had observed surrounding the theatres.

"I am taking you to a back-door, sir, by which you can enter the tavern and see your friend without any other person knowing that you are in the house," he informed me.

The fellow conducted me through the door he had alluded to and into a stone passage. On the floor stood a lamp, which the young man took up. "This way, sir." We passed through many turnings and windings, ascended a narrow, dingy, and dirty staircase, at the top of which, we turned through a door to the right. My guide threw open a second door immediately opposite to that which we had just passed. "In here, sir."

Upon entering the indicated room, I found myself in a moderately furnished apartment. Upon a table in the centre, two candles burnt, furnishing the sole illumination. "Please to sit down, sir, and I will send your friend to you," the fellow instructed before he turned and left, closing the door behind him.

A considerable time elapsed without the appearance of anyone. At length, an approaching foot-step sounded. The door of the apartment flew open and in stepped a tall, slender, foreign-looking male figure with a lank visage, sallow complexion, and immense black whiskers, clad in a shabby brown surtout, a black cravat, and a pair of what had once been white trousers.

"*Serviteur, monsieur!*" he said.

I stood. "I came here, sir, expecting to see a friend of mine. Where is he?"

"*Un ami!—vat ami?*" returned the man. "I know no *ami* vat you got here but myself. I am your *ami,* to serve you mit every *ting* vat you please to order and vant."

"What?!" I exclaimed. "Have I been trepanned into some snare? Shew me immediately the way out of your house, sir, I command you."

"*Dat* is impossible, *monsieur,*" he responded. "I am *expressement* commanded to keep you in my house."

"Stand aside, sir," I shouted, dashing toward the Frenchman (as I shall call my gaoler, based on his accent). "Allow me to pass or you shall repent your denial."

"Oh, you may pass," came the reply. "You may pass here, *monsieur, s'il vous plait,* but you cannot pass the next door on the top of the stair."

I stepped past and experimented with the handle of the door, discovering his words had been true. "If you are determined on making me your prisoner," I rejoined, "only let me know the cause for which I am detained."

"I would do *dat, monsieur,* only you got no patience—no patience *du tout.*" He reached into a side-pocket and presented me a folded paper. "You read dat *lettre.*"

The text read as follows:

> Mr. Brown is requested not to entertain the least anxiety for his personal safety, as he may rely that no injury is intended him. He is earnestly desired to make himself perfectly easy till to-morrow, when the occasion of his present detention will be fully detailed to him, and the means of emerging from captivity be immediately placed in his power.

Even though I knew I could overpower the Frenchman, the door behind him had been fastened beyond my ability of opening it. For the first time in my life, I felt a prisoner. No one had ever denied me free passage before, and I began to panic.

"Shall you drink the glass of *vin*? I have very good *vin* at your service, and a *bon* souper too, so you shall please to eat." He smiled weakly.

"My feelings are not just now directed to any idea of that nature, I assure you." With my stomach in knots, the thought of eating distressed me. However, a stratagem occurred to me. "As you have made me an offer, give me leave to make you one in return. A bribe has doubtless constituted you my gaoler. If you will mention to what amount you have been rewarded for undertaking the office, I will double the sum, on condition of your confessing to me who are your employers."

"Impossible, *monsieur*!" responded the Frenchman with a haughty attitude. "*Mon honneur, monsieur! Mon honneur!*"

How curious that my gaoler could hold honour above money. What admirable fortitude! My belief had been that a thief (or a Frenchman) would have leapt at the chance to make such a gain. My attempt to grease his fist fell flat.

With a bit of a sneer, the Frenchman snatched up one of the candles and indicated that I should follow him. He led me into a second apartment, which turned out to be the bed-chamber.

I continued to scrutinise the countenance of my detainer, observing for an expression belaying his dislike of the business on which he had been employed or complete ignorance in acting amiss in the conduct he pursued. It then occurred to me that a few glasses of *vin* might open his heart.

"Perhaps I might adjust better to this unwarranted imprisonment after a few bottles of wine," I suggested. "Pray, remain and favour me with an hour or two of your company. If we are to become friends–or *amis*, as you would say–it would help us to become better acquainted."

"*Bien sûr, monsieur*," he replied blandly. From a side pocket, he retrieved a small bell, which he rang. A few moments later, footsteps could be heard on the stairway beyond the locked door at the head of the stairs. The Frenchman retrieved a tray and brought it into the sitting-room.

I made every attempt to be *bon companion* to my gaoler, in an attempt to draw out his soul, but he appeared wary–or even timid in the extreme–of committing himself. He seldom drank, and when he did, took but small sips. After two hours passed in irksome society and futile attempts, I finally accepted my fate, that I should not be permitted to quit my prison that night.

The Frenchman stood. "If *monsieur* would dispense with my service till *de* morning, I *vould vish* you *var* good night."

By that time I had wearied of his company and wished to be left undisturbed to reflect. "Yes, of course."

Once the wretched fellow had quit the room, locking the door behind him, I waited until his footsteps on the stairs no longer vibrated on my ear and tested every wall for a weakness and each door for egress, but to no avail. The window-curtains hid long, narrow casings with iron bar grates so close I could scarcely insert my arm between them.

The sky shone full of stars, and my eye could penetrate a considerable distance; however, I could perceive only the pointed roofs of houses, stacks of chimneys, and occasional party-walls extending between the different ranges of buildings. Given my lack of acquaintance with the metropolis beyond, I could form no conjecture as to where my prison might have been situated.

As I further examined my temporary lodgings, I noticed the battered wainscoting with tattered and dim cloth above. Now swarthy and unrecognisable, it might once have been tapestry, now robbed by the hand of time of all pretensions to its former title. I passed my hand over all parts, hoping, like the hero of some Gothic romance, that some sliding panel or concealed outlet might eventually meet my touch.

To ease my frustrations, I pounded upon each wall and door in hopes of rescue. After a few minutes of silence, I accepted the hopelessness of my condition and threw myself into a chair. The hour for sleep had passed some time back, but in my current state of agitation, Morpheus had no power over me. Even considering the sentiment from Cymbeline, "He that sleeps feels not the tooth-ache," had no direct effect.

The furniture proved comfortable enough, and I began to contemplate my situation. Mr. Ferguson would most likely be the first person to realise my absence, but how ever could he find me? I didn't even know where I was. Somewhere near Covent Garden, I presumed, but with all the fabrications, I could have just as easily have been whisked all the way to Whitechapel.

My thoughts drifted to Turnham-green and the realisation that I had not seen my beloved August since I revealed my feelings to him at Sir Julius's ball. My two previous attempts at visiting had been thwarted, and now my present condition prevented any further efforts.

I stood and began to perambulate the apartment, my mind being terribly ill-at-ease, hoping that some exercise might bring relief. After only a few turns, I heard the single beat of a distant clock. Some of the strokes must have been drowned either in the passing breeze or in the sounds produced by my own footsteps.

At that point, I resolved not to retire to regular rest considering that if any evil were intended me, I should be better able to contend with it consciously than if suddenly awakened from the folds of sleep. In the excessive stillness of the night, my spirits began to sink, and I considered whether I had done something to provoke the displeasure of Him to whom I owed every mercy. I prayed with a fervour recompensed by a tranquillity of mind that prepared me to encounter any disaster.

Again, I threw myself into the chair I had occupied previously. When I tilted my head back, I gazed upon a small door in the roof of the apartment, composed of wainscoting corresponding with the panels of the apartment, apparently fastened by a single bolt.

I bolted out of the chair and drew the table directly beneath the door above. Atop that, I placed the armchair in which I had just been reclined, and upon that, a wooden stool I had found in the bed-chamber. As I climbed up toward the ceiling, I considered that if my detainers had planned for all contingencies, they would have taken every precaution to render my prison cell impregnable to my escape attempts. Then I realised that I had no reason not to make such an attempt, and any outlet or chance of communicating with my fellow-beings could only be obtained by means of this trap-door.

With little difficulty, the bolt yielded to my hand. On lifting the trap, I perceived a reflection from the light of the stars, suggesting this upper region had been furnished with a window. I climbed down, collected one of the candles, and cautiously ascended again to explore the place above by its light.

The space proved to be a garret filled with lumber. As I looked about, I imagined I heard a person sigh. I paused a few moments in silence, but the sound did not repeat, and I proceeded to the window. It did not have any barricades, like those below, and seemed large enough to admit the body of a human being to pass through it.

About three feet beyond the window, I beheld a glass lanthorn, of a spiral form, at least twenty feet square at the bottom. A brilliant light appeared to surmount some apartment beneath. I opened the window, rested my hands upon the sill, and vaulted over the ledge. The descent appeared less than I had imagined it, but my feet encountered some flowerpots, which broke under my weight, and due to uncertain footing, threw me some paces from the spot on which I had alighted.

No injury from the fall had I received. As I raised myself from my recumbent position, a loud and boisterous laugh struck my ear. The tyrants of my fate must have discovered my attempted escape and exulted in their power of frustrating my endeavours. I stood for a while in that breathless silence in which the harassed mind hears only the palpitations of its own heart, but the sounds did not repeat, and I became reassured once more.

As I cautiously approached the glass lanthorn, attracted by the vivid flame within, a yell, more discordant than the fiends of Pluto could have supposed to send forth, rose from the space beneath, and, for a few moments, checked me from pursuance of my purpose. Silence again prevailed, and I knelt down, approaching my face to the glass. The scene beneath petrified me with horror, dreading that I might have been seduced to the spot for the purpose of becoming a victim, similar to what I observed below.

In a large and handsome chamber, brilliantly illuminated, I beheld dozens of persons, many in the most fantastic habits, masked and dispersed through the apartment in every attitude and position. Scattered among the various costumes, I observed extensive crinoline petticoats, decorative waistcoats, and fine laced shoes. Many were the milkmaids and shepherdesses with green riding hoods. Others had their faces patched and painted beneath befurbelowed scarves.

At the upper end of the room blazed an immense fire, in front of which four people garbed as demons held a barely-clad wretch at the threshold of the scorching flames, nearly setting the person's long, curly locks a-fire. Others stood about pretending to flagellate the poor victim with thongs and whips. The more piteous the cries and shrieks of the victim, the more boisterous the mirth and applause of the fantastic and inhuman forms assembled to behold such agony.

The scene below terrified and repulsed me, but I stood, transfixed, in observation of this hellish ritual. The demons then dragged the victim—who, for some indecipherable reason unknown to me, seemed to be smiling in heavenly delight— to a low table where someone dressed as a vicar stood. I could now determine the long-haired person to be a man, as his robe had partly opened, clearly displaying his male anatomy. Some of the others produced a wedding-dress, tattered and stained, a high-waisted, frilly thing that appeared to have been dredged from the Thames. They slipped it over the poor victim's body and made him stand next to a gnarled-looking fellow wearing a threadbare, high-collared jacket that Beau Brummel might have created for our former Regent many years back. Onlookers gave a make-shift trumpet voluntary as the ceremony progressed. A partier dressed as a domino placed a tatty lace veil atop the wife-to-be.

The vicar began speaking words that reminded me of the ceremony of marriage. This confused me as both participants happened to be of the male sex.

He then addressed the make-shift bride. "And now that you have been properly 'prepared' by our 'fire brigade,' Mary, dear," he paused when the crowd erupted in laughter. "Are you, Miss Mary Contrary, ready and prepared to consent to an unlawful marriage with this particularly handsome chap?" He turned to the supposed groom, who, by my measure, appeared anything but handsome. A person standing behind the "bride" grabbed the back of his head through the veil and forced a consenting nod.

To the "groom" the vicar asked, "And are you, Mr. John Thomas Wood, sir, ready and prepared to consent to an unlawful marriage with this"—he turned to the one he called "Mary"—"this... this!?"

The crowd once again burst forth with raucous laughter. It upset me greatly to observe such a wanton riot. Can the hearts of men be thus steeled against each other? Is it possible, in a civilised country like our own, such inquisitorial enormities like these are practised, unknown to, or unheeded by, the otherwise vigilant legislature?

"By the celestial powers vested upon me by Mary, Queen of Queens, I now pronounce you married both!" He slipped some sort of crude ring on each participant's finger. "Those whom Queen Mary hath joined together let no man put asunder."

In that moment, my heart froze as I considered that my capture might have been for this purpose, to be initiated into a band of illuminati for such rituals as I could not imagine. The note presented by the Frenchman stated that to-morrow would be when the occasion of my present detention will be fully detailed, and the means of emerging from captivity be immediately placed in my power. It would, indeed, be a horrible fate if my voluntary participation in their preposterous ceremonies predicated my release.

When I gazed once again at the proceedings below, I saw that the small table had been cleared and the "bride" placed, face-up, upon it. The "groom" then initiated simulated copulation, even though both participants remained clothed.

The surrounding crowd began slowly approaching the couple, chanting and shouting expletives, such as, "Give it to her, good, Wood!" "Plant it deep!" "Oh, Mary, you tart!" With time, I began to realise that all the people in the apartment below happened to be male. Not one woman appeared visible. Those who dressed like women displayed hints of their male-ness by beard hair protruding through their make-up or bulges in their dresses where bulges should not appear.

I recalled the walk through the park with Mr. Ferguson when we encountered a gay group of fellows putting on effeminate airs and wearing women's clothing. He had called them "mollies." Perhaps this is a similar gathering. Again, I balked at the idea of being compelled to participate in such rituals were I to take another man as a lover, but then I remembered Mr. Ferguson's expression from his experience that not all man-lovers are "mollies."

The scene below continued to play. A person dressed like a midwife stood next to the splayed-out "bride," holding the person's wrist with an over-dramatic look of worry. The vicar approached with a wrapped bundle in one hand. He reached up the wedding-dress with the hand containing the bundle and circled the other over the poor, distressed person's abdominal region. A few moments later, he jerked his hand from between the legs of the victim and opened the cloth to reveal a wooden toy doll.

"It's a boy!" the vicar announced triumphantly, and the crowd gave loud cheers. "I christen thee... Willie Wood." The assemblage resumed its revelry as the vicar attempted to wave them into silence. "It is time for the baptism. Good people, will you welcome this child and uphold them in their new life in the service of Mary, Queen of Queens?"

As one, the crowd chanted, "With the help of Good Queen Mary, we will."

"May I have the father hold the baby." I watched in horror as the "groom" took the wooden doll from the vicar and another grotesque ceremony began.

The vicar spat upon his thumb and moved it about the forehead of the wooden doll. "Mary, Queen of Queens, claims you as her own. Receive the sign of Queen Mary!"

A raucous uproar rose in response. At that moment, the candle I had left in the garret extinguished, removing my means of safe movement through the small room.

I stumbled over some of the flowerpot shards and bumped into a dark human form whose murky eyes reflected the glare from the blazes below.

Chapter Nineteen:
At the Mercy of Foreigners

I N SUCH A PRECARIOUS POSITION, I did not wish to raise an alarum, and I whispered as loudly as I could, "Who is there?"

"Who me?" came the response. "Who ou? Dam odd how ou came here, whoever ou be! Let me look at ou. Me tink me know ou. Do ou no reconnet me?"

A familiar aroma of fusty spirits reached my nostrils, and I realised at once it was the dark woman, Loora, from Mrs. Mackinflore's house. Before I could respond to her inquiry, she brought her face quite close to mine, as if examining a piece of jewellery, inclining her neck one way then the other. The stench of her breath made me want to turn away.

"By gum me member ou! Ou and other gentlom give me bottle *bingo*, when ou come see mother Mackiflore in Lickorie-court. Me Loora. Ou no member Loora. Take care massa Tunks?"

"Yes, yes, I do remember you," I replied, turning my head away slightly so that I could breathe. "In the name of Heaven, conjure you to tell me where I am, and to become my friend in my present exigency, for which rely on my generosity."

"Me dam but me serve ou if me can, massa," Loora answered. "Dough me no know what brought ou here. What devil did bring ou here, eh, massa?" Again, she inclined her head at different angles. "You no fraid tell me, poor Loora sober nuff now. Cussa him Frenchman!"

"What!? Do you live with the Frenchman?"

"Liv wid him?! No, me starve wid him, massa. Dam him! Give poor servant no vickel, but *beef lemo soup* and *frigatee* salad."

"How absolutely horrid! Perhaps we could move somewhere else so that we may speak without fear. I am being held in a room below. Do you think you can manage to climb in at this window?"

"No need climb. There hole." She began moving off and I followed. About a foot to the side of the casement, she crawled through a small aperture capable of admitting a person. I must not have seen this opening when the candle was a-lit.

I scrambled to the table where I had left the now-extinguished candle. It had not burned down totally, and I but needed a way to re-light it. "Loora, I have a candle. Can you light it?"

"I *ax* ou how ou came here," she said while fiddling through her pockets. A second later I heard scraping and saw sparks fly from a flint. Once the candle took flame, I could see Loora holding a large, dangerous-looking blade and a small stone. "Tell Loora now. How ou came here, massa?"

I pointed to the trap-door opening. "The Frenchman is holding me prisoner in the apartments below. I discovered this door and climbed up." I remembered some wine remained. "We can go down and talk there."

The ladder of my own invention held steady as I descended, and I braced it when Loora followed. Only a small amount of the wine remained, and I poured it into the glass used by the Frenchman and handed it to my guest. The dark, red liquid disappeared almost instantly.

"Me never get no *bingo* now, massa," Loora purred, tears starting in her eyes. "No, poor Loora get no bumbo now, very little wage, and very little meat, massa. Him Frenchman dam rascal. What ou tink he do, massa? Poor black *ax* him drop *bingo*, one day, to put in her teapot, when she tired death mit work. What ou tink him do, massa? Put quid bacco in teapot and call him *bingo*. Dam nasty dirt Frenchman!" She ran a long, dark finger around the inside of the glass to catch the remaining drops and suckled.

A memory crossed through my mind, and I inquired, "I thought we left you in charge at Mrs. Mackinflore's house. How did you come to be here?"

Her eyes grew, as if frightened by something horrible. "Dam missy Mackiflore come back Lickorie-court. Chase Loora away. She say bad tings Loora. Very bad tings, she say." She trembled noticeably. It might have been fear or, perhaps, the wine.

"It is most fortunate, indeed, Loora, that I happened upon you." I smiled in an attempt to be reassuring. "Earlier in the evening, a man came to call at my lodging, informing me that my friend, Mr. Ferguson needed me. Accomplices brought us to this place, and the Frenchman maintained my detention shall be explained in the morning. Do you have any idea who he is and what this place is, Loora?"

"I very bad at *talk French*. Him name very, very long. Hard for Loora member. Downstairs tavern, bad place, very bad place. But they have dam *beef lemo* me must eat.

Her eyelids began to droop, and I couldn't help but think my own were not far behind. However, I could not risk having her here when my captor returned. "Loora, have you any idea where this house is situated?"

"Loora no read, massa. Sign no talk me. But me tink we in place call-a New-git causa I hear de Frenchman say he quite at home in New-git." She held the glass up to me.

"I am sorry, but there is no more wine." I picked up the bottle and shook it. She grabbed it from my hand and began sucking at it. "Have you any idea why I might be detained and made prisoner here, Loora?"

Her head rotated from side-to-side, and then she removed the bottle from her lips. "No idee, massa. No priznuh ever here afore."

"And where is your bedchamber?"

"Far way. Utter side of de house." She waved a hand to demonstrate the distance.

"What brought you up to the platform upon which we just met?"

Loora looked up and away, as if dreaming of a more pleasant climate. "Some time, after hard work, tired, me go up there, spend time wid Irishman, Dennis O'Dottlety. He de man take care of de boot and knife here." She patted her pocket where the blade rested. "No can talk him during day, only night. Me go there affa dark. Nother hole in wall up de stairs go me room." A smile graced her face. "Me find de hole when dust de carpet. But me no go near him to-night, for it almost morning, almost quite light. So what ou got say, massa, ou must say as quick as can be."

Perhaps I could escape through the woman's own chamber. "Loora, is it possible you could admit me into the body of the house through your own room?"

"No, no, massa. De dam Frenchman keep all de key to all de door, and de window has de bell—make ding-ding if open."

"Could I get to another house from up above, where we met?" I had to ask about every possibility.

"Maybe yes, but other house no good. They prig and teef. No good. Kill you fast." Her eyes bulged.

"Well then, will you, if I give you a couple of sovereigns for your pains, carry a note for me into Oxford-street, to the gentleman who treated you with the bottle of brandy?"

"Me dam if me don't," she answered. "And tank ou kindly, too, massa." Her smile reappeared.

"If, on your return home, your French master should turn you away, on account of your having been for a few hours absent from your service, I will either take you into mine or provide for you elsewhere."

"Me no fraid dat, massa. Me no forget how nice him gentlom vat buy me bottle *bingo* provide for Carrotty Jean. Me no care if cussa French massa turn me way so soon me come back."

A few sheets of writing paper and a few pencils sat on the nearby desk. I scribbled down a few lines to Mr. Ferguson and handed the note to Loora with two sovereigns.

"Me take good care ou, massa, but must go now. Light soon."

"One moment more and I have done," I exclaimed. My curiosity had urged me to ask, "Can you inform me who and what those extraordinary beings whom I beheld in an extensive apartment, through the glass lanthorn, where I just encountered you?"

"Oh, me no know dat." She shook her head. "Dat grand secret, massa. Nobody go in dat room. Dennis and me often tink dere be some bad work in great ball-room, vat dey call, but me never see inside of him, or Dennis either, massa."

"Then what induces you to believe that there is evil going on within those walls?"

She looked down as she spoke. "One time, Dennis in bar, do work, and utter man, from Oper House, come in. He ask about meeting in de ball-room. Bar man tell him only if he had de courage he can go in. He say he had de courage. Dennis never see him again!" She pointed up at the trap-door. "Massa, I must go now. Must go!"

"Of course. You know where to deliver my message?"

"Yes. Me help ou. Two big coin. Me help. Now ou help me." She pointed to the device she need to climb.

I assisted her to reach the trap-door, and she disappeared. Once she moved past my sight, I shut the trap and drew the bolt. Upon returning to the floor of my room, I disassembled my scaling-ladder, extinguished the candles, and threw myself upon the bed, hoping, praying, that my liberty would come soon.

Not knowing the time, I reached for my watch, only to recall that I had left it upon the writing-desk back at the Titmus home. I had been engaged in sealing my letter to Mr. Radford when the pretended summons to assist Mr. Ferguson arrived, and, in the hurry of the moment, I left the watch behind, a circumstance I now regretted. Although the sun had risen above the bottom of the window, I remained ignorant of the hour.

Soon after–perhaps nine o'clock or so–the Frenchman made an appearance. Following behind him, a boy carried a tray, and the two of them spread the contents of the table for my breakfast. Because I had sent a message via the services of Loora, I felt no need to further engage my captor regarding the terms of my release.

"I 'ope you will enjoy dis meal," the Frenchman pronounced with all the *politesse* imaginable. "Should *monsieur* require any addition dat might gratify his palate, *s'il vous plait*, make de request."

"My request is that you leave me alone."

While I ate the not unpleasant food, I considered that Oxford-street must have been some distance from Newgate, and I resolved that I should not expect to see Mr. Ferguson, or any friends deputed by him to effect my rescue, until past the middle of the day. The Frenchman returned to clear the table, and I asked of him, "Pray, *monsieur*, am I at liberty to write letters?" I indicated the paper and pencils nearby.

"Oh, *qu'oui!*" came the response. "*Monsieur* has the *liberté* to write all the *lettres* he please, *mais*, but, *pour moi*, I am not permit to deliver dem."

I laughed aloud at the sarcasm delivered most seriously by my captor.

Before leaving me alone once more, the Frenchman opened a drawer of the writing-desk and removed an inkstand, which he placed next to the small stack of paper. After he had departed, I withdrew the slip of paper he had delivered to me the preceding evening and re-read:

> to-morrow, when the occasion of his present detention will be fully detailed to him, and the means of emerging from captivity be immediately placed in his power.

Whilst I ruminated upon this subject, the Frenchman returned with another letter in his hand. He presented it to me and departed in silence.

The direction listed my name, and the wax seal bore the simple impression of a wafer-stamp. I broke the seal, unfolded the paper, and cast my eye first to the signature, which, to my astonishment, was that of Sir Malcolm Brockelsbie. It read as follows:

> My Dear Sir,
>
> My affairs are at so alarming a crisis, that nothing upon earth can increase the desperation of my situation. At the conversation which we had together yesterday, I was too much of a coward to confess to you the cause for which I asked the loan of the ten thousand, with which I then solicited you to accommodate me. I beg that you will, in the benevolence of your heart, extend your merciful hand to save the life of an avowed criminal. I trust that the generous spirit which I am acquainted animates your heart will not steel itself against the miseries into which the rashness—nay, insanity—of a deluded fellow-

being have plunged him. I appeal to your heart—with the soft voice of mercy—to judge me with Christian lenity. I have forged a bank-bill for ten thousand pounds! The matter is, at present, unrevealed, and the bill lies in the hands of a banker in the city, but if it is not taken up before twelve o'clock on Monday next, the fraud must be discovered. I need not point out to you the consequences that must inevitably follow.

You will perhaps ask why I have placed the restraint upon your liberty, whilst I make to you the dreadful acknowledgment contained upon this paper? I intended to have made the confession of my guilt to you at our last interview, but my courage failed in conversation, and I resolved to explain myself to you in writing. Conscious as I was, that, in the rectitude of your soul, you would not voluntarily oppress a sinking man by a public denunciation of his guilt, still I feared that the secret might involuntarily escape you. In solitude I desired you to reflect on the horrors of my mind, to dwell upon that appeal to your feelings which supplicates you to save a fellow-being from an ignominious death.

Should you accede to my prayer, you will, of course, forgive the means which I have pursued to procure your assent. Should you refuse to save me, the minor fault arising from the unlawful restriction which I have for a while

The paper fell from my hands, and I sat, silent and alone, lost in a maze of thought inexplicable. The more I reflected, the more my ideas became perplexed. I scarcely knew in what light to consider this extraordinary epistle, much less to decide what part it befit me to act in consequence of the still more extraordinary appeal which it contained to my feelings.

With no clear path in my mind, I resolved to defer all proceedings till the arrival of Mr. Ferguson. However, the hours crept on, and neither Mr. Ferguson, nor any emissary commissioned by him, appeared. I had to consider that he might have been absent from home at the time Loora arrived. Most likely, the evening might have set in before she could have been able to see him.

The Frenchman arrived with my dinner, and we both maintained silence during that time. I did not wish to be careless of addressing my gaoler, and he appeared unwilling to converse freely with me or make advances toward the purchase of his favour.

Later that evening he appeared with an unanticipated inquiry, "Would *monsieur* like coffee?"

"Oh, yes, please," I responded, glad of any occupation that afforded a temporary relief to the irksomeness of my situation.

When the Frenchman returned, he brought not only coffee, but a plate of strawberries, the first I had seen that year. He placed the treats before me, with a gracious smile and bow. "It gives me de happiness to be able to offer dis kind of delicacy to a gentleman, like *monsieur*. I consider no indulgence to be too great."

I favoured him with an appreciative smile. *"Merci beaucoup,"* I said, trying to remember my rudimentary French. Perhaps this display of courtesy he had disclosed lessened my doubt that the fellow could be moved to assist me in regaining my freedom. However, till I saw how the plan I had already set on foot for my release prospered, I resolved to maintain a distance between myself and the gaoler, no matter how tasty and sweet the strawberries.

The shades of night soon began to fall to the earth, and still, no one arrived to effect my rescue. I would have to exert more patience and hope a little farther. This left me a-waiting the hour at which I had, the previous night, discussed with Loora, and at which I now endeavoured to console my feelings by persuading myself that she would, most probably, again visit me and bring some intelligence from my friend.

In the course of the day, I had discovered a small bar at the bottom of the lock upon the door. Fastening this device would relieve me from the fear of interruption when I returned to the garret above.

When, at length, the brilliancy of the starts indicated that midnight approached, I set the bar on the door and formed the scaling-ladder. After I slid the bolt and opened the trap-door, I remained for a few minutes at the aperture, eagerly listening whether any sounds floated on the air, announcing the proximity of human beings. A deathlike silence prevailed, and my curiosity—aided by a desire to breath the fresh air—prompted me to climb up and creep through the small opening that had been pointed out by Loora.

The sheets of lead on the roof felt colder than before. I approached the lanthorn, anxious to behold whether the extraordinary forms had returned to exercise their apparently-unhallowed rites in the apartment beneath. This night, the room proved all darkness and silence. As the air had turned cold and raw, I saw no reason to remain. In a very short time I returned to my room, leaving the trap open, in the expectation of soon hearing Loora approach. I threw myself upon the sofa from where I could command a view of the aperture. With my hopes raised, an almost breathless anxiety came upon me. The unbroken silence now prevailed, rendering distant sounds that in the busy hum of day would not have been audible. Distinctly, I heard a clock, the same, I imagined, that struck my ear the previous night, proclaim the first hour of the morning.

With no intention of doing so, I became drowsy and insensibly slunk into a restless slumber. Some time later–precisely when, I could not be certain–a voice at the mouth of the trap aroused me.

"Sir," came the speech in an under tone, "I say, your honour. Hist! Sir, your honour. Hist!"

I instantly started upon my feet. "Who is there?" Glancing up, I saw a shadow at the trap and asked, "Is it Loora?"

"No, it is meself, your honour, meself," replied the speaker. The head and shoulders of a tall, raw-boned ragged male figure, about half-a-century in age, appeared through the aperture.

"And who are you?"

"Sure, your honour," the fellow replied. "Did not you hear Loora spake of me? Did she not tell you nothing at all, at all, about one Dennis O'Dottlety?"

"Oh, you are Dennis, are you? Do you come commissioned to me by Loora?"

"No, I wish I did, your honour," Dennis replied. "Blazes fly away wid her foolish self! No, your honour, I come to comfort you for her undutifulness."

"Why? What of her? Where is she?" I began to panic once again.

"Divel and herself only knows where she is, your honour," he answered. "Curse the foot she has put into this house since she went out of it in the morning!"

"What!? Not returned yet?" I exclaimed.

"You may say that, your honour."

"She acquainted you then with the business upon which I employed her?"

"Sure and she did do that thing, your honour, but it is just as sacret, depend upon it, as if she had never opened her lips to me." The more he spoke, the more I could catch his Irish accent. "Her and me, your honour is only both like one, as the saying is."

"You had better come down into this room," I invited. "I should be glad to have a little conversation with you, and I am afraid of speaking at this distance from each other, lest we should be overheard."

"I'd be mighty glad to oblige your honour wid me company below," Dennis stated, "but I'm lame of a leg, and that same accident makes me very bad at climbing, and meself's afraid that if I come down, I'll never be able to get up again, so we'll just spake here, if your honour's agreeable."

"Then don't hazard it," I responded. "I will stand here and talk to you." I moved the table into position and stood upon it as to lessen the distance between us. "What can be the reason that Loora is not returned?"

"Meself's afraid, your honour, that the fault is all your own."

"Mine?!" I exclaimed. "How so?"

"Why, if I may make *bould* to *ax*, sir," replied Dennis, "didn't your honour perhaps give her a tenpenny or two for her trouble before she set out?"

"I gave her a couple of sovereigns," came my answer.

"Oh, the *proker!*" he shouted. "She'll not be back dis week. She's a good soul, that's what she is, is Loora, but she's too fond of the *crater*. Every tenpenny she gets, she never leaves the change-house till it's all gone. I guessed how it was, begging your honour's pardon, and so I thought I'd make free to come and have a little information wid you about the subject, as meself was tinking you'd be very dull upon the occasion of not hearing from her."

"But don't you suppose that she would deliver my note before she stopped to regale herself?"

"That's all a chance, your honour," answered Dennis. "If she met wid any *ould* companion upon the road, the odds is mightily against her going straight forward about her business."

"Good heavens!" My hope evaporated. "How unfortunate that I should have confided in her!"

"Not at all, your honour. A day's but a day, and I comed here on purpose to tell your honour that if you'll only be after writing that same bit of a letter that you intrusted her wid over again, meself will carry it for you in de morning as straight as a hook."

My heart breathed once more. "I shall be happy to reward you handsomely for doing so, depend upon it."

"And to shew you that I *mane* to be faithful to your cause, your honour, don't pay me a *harper* of me wages till I come back, and den there'll be no fear of me staying by the way." He smiled down at me. "So, if your honour will pl*a*se to step down and write that letter…"

"I will immediately," I interrupted him. "But first, I wish to ask you a question or two. Is there no possibility of your assisting me to effect my escape out of this house?"

Dennis shook his head mournfully. "The d*i*vel himself could hardly make his way out of dis house if they were determined to keep him in it." He shrugged. "Do you think dat dirty spalpeen of an ugly-skinn'd Frenchman, me master, would trust himself so often as he does wid you alone in that room there below, where you are now standing, when he knows you might upset him like a teetotum, and afterwards break open the room door with your fist, if he wasn't *sartin* that you could not make your way out when you'd done so? No, no, dere's too many locks and bolts and bars here for that manner of work, your honour."

How confounded the business of this place! "To what purpose is the house thus secured?"

"Why, your honour, the *beef alley mode*, and all that in the *winder*, is only a flam. It's a gaming house, your honour, where high and low, rich and poor, especially *forinders*, meets to ruin one another. All dem locks and tings I've been sp*a*king of is to keep out de *bailies*."

"And what are those extraordinary beings whom I last night beheld through the glass lanthorn out on the leads?"

He tilted his head in thought then responded, "Oh, dey are harmless *craters* enough, they are, except for de noise they make. It's a molly meeting, and I guess late last night they had some merry-makings."

My suspicions had been correct. I had observed some harmless pranks and larks. Still, I felt uneasy with the conduct I had witnessed. A question occurred to me. "Do you know any persons of the name of Sir Malcolm Brockelsbie? Does he frequent this house?"

No response came.

I repeated the inquiry, "Do you know…"

Dennis placed a finger across his lips to enjoin silence. A few moments elapsed, and then he said, "I thought I heard a footstep, your honour, but it's only dem divils the rats and mice, I'm after thinking. There's plenty of them in me bedchamber. I *ax* your pardon, but what was it your honour was inquiring of me, if you pl*a*se?"

"I asked if you know any persons of the name of Sir Malcolm Brockelsbie who might frequent this house."

"No," he replied without hesitation. "No, meself is not in acquaintance with the p*a*rson you sp*a*ke of, at least not to me knowledge. So now, if your honour will be pl*a*sed to write the bit of a note, as I *tould* you before, O'Dottlety's the boy that will s*a*rve you honestly, that's what he will."

I climbed down and took up a piece of paper and the inkstand provided by the Frenchman. On the dinner tray, I spied a bottle of wine. As a gift, I handed it up to the Irishman for his amusement. Returning to the task at-hand, I penned a note similar to the one I wrote the preceding night. While my mind exclusively concentrated on the subject that employed the pen, my reverie immediately ended as the wine-bottle fell back into the apartment, shivering into atoms on the floor.

At the first moment, I imagined that its contents had been too powerful for Dennis, but then, three seconds after, a groan came from above followed by an exclamation, "Oh, J*a*sus! They have found us out!"

When I looked up, I could see and hear O'Dottlety being dragged away from the aperture. Immediately after, a substance of immense weight was drawn over the trap and nails driven into the floor above, followed by a bustle in the garret.

It now appeared my trap-door could no longer facilitate my eventual escape, and I sunk into a dark, dark mood.

Chapter Twenty:
A Glimmer in the Dark and a Shock of Despair

HALF-IRRITATED, HALF-DESPONDING, I threw myself on the sofa. I expected that neither Loora nor the Irishman should find an opportunity of visiting me again. If she had stopped to regale herself with her dearly beloved *bingo* before proceeding to the execution of her commission, all my hope then rested with the Frenchman.

In the midst of my occupation with these reflections, I heard the lock turn, and the door of the apartment rattle vigorously. "Who's there?" I demanded.

"*C'est moi, monsieur*," replied the voice of the Frenchman. "Nobody but *moi*. Me *tought* me heard you call, and me be *ver* sorry to be inattentive to *monsieur*."

"You mistook," I replied. "I did not speak."

"Beg pardon, *monsieur. J'en suis désolé. Bon repos.*" Footsteps faded away but then grew louder. "*Monsieur*, no mind troubling me, whether day or night, so I may do any ting to serve *monsieur*." The sounds of his steps upon the stairs diminished to silence.

Artful villain! I mentally exclaimed. Perhaps he believed that, at the moment of my disappointment incurred by the detection of my conversation with the Irishman, my heart would be open to treat with him for indulgence. On this account, he endeavoured to throw himself in my way. My feelings still smarted under the occurrence, but for this night, at least, his expectations should not be gratified.

At that point, I accepted that incessant watching would only incapacitate me for any exertion to which the next day might subject me, and I resolved to enter the bed. It seemed both clean and comfortable, and I soon fell into a profound sleep.

In the morning, I arose refreshed by my slumbers. In consequence of some reflections that I had made on the pillow, I took to the writing-desk and composed the following note to Sir Malcolm Brockelsbie:

Sir,

Although you undoubtedly estimate my feelings correctly, that they are by nature attuned to sympathise with the distress of my fellow-beings, they are not still devoid of discrimination.

Had you not, sir, selected me as the confident of your guilty confession, I should not have deemed it my province to have reflected on the enormity of your crime, but I now adjure you to let the reflection of the dreadful precipice on which you have stood operate on your feelings with sufficient force to withdraw you for ever from those scenes of iniquity and folly, of which the acuteness is tenfold increased by the consciousness of their being self-inflicted.

My own circumstances have already been so fully unfolded to you that I must deem it utterly unnecessary to repeat that I cannot myself stretch out a helping hand to the amelioration of your case. However, if you will but immediately come and give direction for my enlargement from the unwarrantable and illegal restriction which you have placed upon my liberty, I shall interest in your favour a sincere friend of my own, upon whose secrecy I am confident that you could rely. I would propose him as a mediator in the present delicacy of your case, between yourself and the threatening authority of the law, and I will make it my immediate business to introduce you and state your unhappy situation.

I conclude by saying that the sooner you resolve to be guided by my advice, the sooner your mind will be restored to comparative ease, and I shall be relieved from the state of anxiety to which my sympathy in your heart-rending reflections and horrid anticipations has subjected me.

Yours, &c.

John Brown

I re-read my writings and, feeling satisfied that it contained the exact sentiments I wished to convey, folded it and used left-over bits of wax from Sir Malcolm's letter seal it. My thoughts then turned into another channel of reflection: whether I had, in my benevolent anxiety for preserving the life of a fellow-being, perhaps ventured too far with regard to the promise I had expressed relative to the friend I had announced my intention of introducing. Many instances had convinced me that Sir Julius Maberly's heart had been cast in the mould of nature's mildest benevolence, and I might place implicit faith in the honour of his principles.

Sir Julius had, from the first commencement of our acquaintance, avowed for me, and the unfeigned warmth he had ever directed me to command his friendship emboldened me to the resolution of imploring his assistance in the unfortunate case of the misguided Sir Malcolm. To such end, I must request his assent to enter into a verbal arrangement–a secret that I well knew I could confide in him without the slightest apprehension of its ever being divulged to a third person–of becoming responsible for the sum necessary to be advanced the moment I had attained my twenty-fifth year.

This plan seemed sanguine, and the anticipation of relieving the culpable, yet pitiable, being–in whose behalf I had formed it from the horrors of his present situation–communicated a satisfaction

to my heart. At all events, I considered, were it possible that Sir
Julius should prove averse to assisting my charitable design, or
be unprovided with the requisite sum, I consoled myself with the
knowledge that the few hundred I had in my possession would
prove sufficient to carry the unfortunate Sir Malcolm beyond the
reach of justice.

Mid-afternoon, the Frenchman came to make preparation for my
dinner.

"Pray, *monsieur*," I instantly addressed him. "Is Sir Malcolm
Brockelsbie at present in your house?"

"Oh, *que non, monsieur*," replied my captor, "*mi lor n'est pas ici.*"

"But he very frequently is here, I imagine, as you must naturally
be upon terms of great intimacy with him, to be made the agent
of the illegal restraint which he is at this moment exercising
against me."

Without reacting to the remark that concluded my sentence, he
merely replied, "Oh, *non, non, monsieur, mi lor* Malcolm *n'est
pas jamais ici*, never, never, *monsieur!*"

I lifted the sealed paper. "I wish this letter to be delivered to him.
How soon can I expect an answer?"

"In *deux heures*, or little more," he answered. "I tink you may
depend."

"Let no time be lost in its delivery, *s'il vous plait.*"

"*Monsieur*, I promise attention to your request," the Frenchman
responded as he took the letter from me and left the room.

He returned a few minutes later with my meal, and no conversation passed between us while I ate my dinner. The Frenchman
cleared the things and retired.

Over the course of the next few hours, I ruminated upon the current circumstances and the various outcomes possible. Given the
unpredictability of all the actors involved, any sense of hope
waned.

The sun had all but disappeared when the Frenchman returned,
well past the two hours promised. "I have been expecting to see
you before this," I proclaimed. "It seems that double the space of

time is elapsed that you led me to suppose I should receive an answer to my letter."

"I *ver* sorry, *monsieur*, disappoint you," he answered. "*Mais mon garçon* vat did carry your *lettre* is only this moment return, and he bring *intelligence* vat *mi lor* Malcolm *est non pas chez lui*, not at home, but that he is expect about nine or ten of the clock this evening."

With a slight inclination of my head, I acknowledged hearing the information delivered. Again, the reliability of those effecting my capture proved deficient.

The Frenchman kept moving leisurely about the room, employing himself in the arrangement of immaterial trifles. Occasionally, he cast expressive glances at me, appearing once more desirous of entering into conversation.

My disappointment must have been patently obvious, as he made a feeble attempt to chat. "I am *ver* sorry dat *monsieur* is so *solitaire ici*. I am hope it will not be for long."

"Have you any idea then that my captivity is about to cease?" His statement aroused my hopes.

"Me no acquaint mit any ting about dat, *monsieur*," he replied.

"Perhaps you begin to repent of having been a party concerned in this affair and feel some inclination to grant me my enlargement?"

My suggestion met with silence.

"I promise you that if you are resolved to become the means of my release, you shall never be arraigned for your adjunction in an act which, you must be aware, if subjected to the recognisance of the law, would expose you to a heavy punishment."

He looked at me directly. "I am promise protection already, *monsieur*."

"By Sir Malcom Brockelsbie, of course,"–I mumbled to myself– "who being a principal party in the iniquitous transaction, has not the power of defending even himself against the vengeance of the law."

The Frenchman maintained silence, and it appeared that some point agitated within his skull, reflections upon which he seemed not altogether well pleased.

"Perhaps those who led you into the error of assisting their designs did not explain to you the hazard to which you were exposing yourself by consenting to forward them?" I seized upon the moment of presumed doubt in his mind.

"Why, *monsieur*, it is *ver* bad time. I have de *grande famille*, de great expense, and..."

He had paused, and I picked up his thought, "And so, for a present advantage, you determined to risk the probability of a future evil?"

"I could not, *monsieur*, refuse *mi lor* Malcolm any ting, *monsieur*. I should have been worse off, so I had oppose *sa volonté*."

"You are bound to him, then, by some private tie, which renders you fearful of opposing his commands or inclinations?"

The Frenchman fixed his eyes on the floor, but did not speak.

"If you are not," I continued, "induced to serve me by what, if you were to form a just estimate of your present perilous situation, you would perceive the most essential bribe which could be offered to you, namely, the promise of burying in oblivion the conduct of which you have been guilty, I will stimulate you still further by pledging myself to throw fifty guineas into the scale, with the lenity of which I have already given you my assurance."

He merely shook his head but did not raise his countenance from the earth.

"Well then, the better to meet your feelings. Tell me, candidly, upon what terms we can agree, and I will immediately inform you how far I am inclined to accede to them."

After a short pause, the Frenchman looked up at me. "Well den, at *von* vord, if *monsieur* will grant me two hundred pound, I will *instantment* open to him my door, but I cannot do noting under dat, for if I cannot raise *de l'argent* to dat amount, I am ruin man. I am, indeed, *monsieur, par mon honneur!*"

Two hundred pounds! A great sum to demand, but my situation necessitated extraordinary measures. At first, I decided not to comply with the terms of an extortioner who appeared prepared to defy every hazard for the lucre of gain. Sir Malcolm would most likely visit or reply to my letter at an early hour in the

morning, the consequence of which would be an immediate enlargement from the restraint. It seemed prudent to defer
responding to the Frenchman's offer till the morrow, at least.

"I shall consider what you have said," came my response. "In the
morning I shall deliver my reply."

The Frenchman made one of his obsequious bows and retired.

With the sealing of the trap-door above, it seemed improbable
that I should receive a night-time visit from either Loora or her
Irishman. As Mr. Ferguson had yet to make an appearance, I
decided to enter the bed once again, and in a short time, I resigned myself to the influence of sleep.

I woke before the sun rose fully. Rendered restless by the events
which I anticipated would mark the progress of the day, I rose
from the bed and paced about the small room. Something upon
the dressing-table caught my eye: a slip of paper I had not left
there previously. I immediately took it up, and read the
following:

DO NOT DESPAIR — YOU HAVE A FRIEND WITHIN THESE WALLS

"A friend!" my heart repeated. Who could that friend be? By what
means could the paper have been introduced into the chamber
whilst I slept? At first I thought it must have been the Frenchman, whatever the motive. No one but himself appeared to have
access to these apartments. Even the boy who occasionally
attended him had never been permitted to step beyond the
threshold of the door.

It could have been a stratagem of my Gallic gaoler to urge me to
the conclusion of terms. However, in my own opinion, the conduct of Sir Malcolm would, in the course of a few hours, render
such a treaty unnecessary.

I tore the paper to shreds and scattered the fragments out the
window, determined not to give the slightest intimation to the
Frenchman that I had ever observed it.

Within minutes, my breakfast tray arrived with a letter. "It was
arrivé, I believe, *von* half-hour before, but I do not deliver till I
hear *monsieur* walk about the room for fear I should disturb your
bon repos."

I hastily broke the seal, glanced at the signature of Sir Malcolm Brockelsbie, and eagerly proceeded to peruse the contents:

Sir,

I must indeed be lost to every generous sentiment which animates the heart of man. With the most sincere gratitude, I therefore thank you for the interest which you have expressed in my welfare, and the plan which you have projected for my preservation. But I can only thank you—for a long and harassing deliberation with my own mind has convinced me that I can submit to any inconvenience in preference to permitting my unfortunate case to be deliberately detailed to any human being in existence beyond yourself.

I have therefore resolved precipitously to avail myself of the only method which now remains to me of escaping the dreadful fate which I am threatened. Previously, I hinted to you that it was in my power to secure myself wealth by taking on an available ward. By your decision not to become yourself my preserver, and thus to lock the secret of my shame within your own single breast, you have decided me to petition for the affluence present so indispensable to my protection.

A very, very short period of time will now seal my fate, and within an hour after the Court of Chancery has granted me the ward, I shall set out for a foreign country from whence

His negative return to my proposition left me feeling disappointed and chagrined. Yet another field for apprehension and reflection opened to me that pressed with infinitely greater weight upon my mind. Was it possible that the ward of whom Sir Malcolm spoke could be my beloved August? The thought of losing him for ever sickened me, and for a few moments I believed myself almost capable of bursting through the walls of my prison and rushing to ascertain the truth.

Thankfully, calmness, produced by the recollection of his angelic smiles, and the promise of fondness I had won from his lips, helped me quickly to reassume possession of my senses. I then needed to consider how to best regain my freedom afore Sir Malcolm's legal plan could proceed. I believed it soundest to renew the argument of my liberation with my gaoler.

By my best reckoning, the day should have been Friday. Sir Malcolm's first letter had informed me that the forged bill must be taken up before noon this Monday to prevent detection of his crime. That meant he would as soon as possible remove himself from the scene of danger, and, in all probability, he would petition the court this day or the next. With every hour, the probability strengthened that Loora had recovered her recollection and seen Mr. Ferguson. Given these reflections, I resolved to submit one night more to captivity.

The hours passed more drearily and uncomfortably than any of the preceding ones, and, as the evening advanced, I almost resolved, upon the Frenchman's approach, to tamper with him for my liberty. Doubts, apprehensions, and surmises racked my imagination, and I began to reconsider the price at which my freedom could be purchased, as I felt compelled to rescue my dearest August from the grasp of Sir Malcolm.

Whilst pacing the apartment, in an agitation of mind that I felt
unable to subdue, the Frenchman unexpectedly entered and presented a large paper packet directed to me. I instantly opened it
and found another letter from Sir Malcolm and a second letter. I
directed my attention to make acquaintance of the baronet's
epistle first.

Sir,

I called this morning at your lodgings wishing to see Mr. Ferguson, your esteemed friend, and explain to him, as far as the delicacy of my situation would permit my unfolding myself, that you were well and would, in the course of twenty-four hours, rejoin him. Mr. Ferguson, I understand, has been for some days absent from home, and consequently, I did not see him. Your landlady ushered me into your apartment, where I perceived a letter directed for you lying upon your writing-desk, and I immediately resolved to forward it to you, anxious to convince you how much it would hurt my feelings to cause you any additional anxiety or privation to those which you have already experienced on my account. To apologize for my past conduct is now in vain, but sincerely do I implore you to pardon what I have done. Little did I, two hours ago, imagine that I should have addressed myself to you again. At this hour to-morrow I shall receive my gift from Chancery, and you your liberty. May prosperity attend you! Farewell for ever!

Macolm Brockelsbie

How enigmatic that Mr. Ferguson should have been absent for several days from our lodgings. I could not account for this save the cause of his absence being a fruitless search after me, which ill success had not tempted him to relinquish.

I then took up the other communication, one written by a tremulous writer, most likely female, I suspected, also one not much accustomed to the use of the pen. The signature read Elizabeth Allingham, which little surprised me.

Oh, sir! Oh, Mr. Brown! What can have induced you to act in the cruel and dishonourable manner in which you have conducted yourself towards my child and me? After having inveigled away his heart, deceived him by the falsest of promises, and fixed his affections, is it not base to have addressed yourself to him in the unfeeling and unmanly manner in which you have done? Without a cause assigned, carelessly to state that a change in your opinion of him had taken place--that you had consequently felt yourself under the necessity of breaking off your association with him and leave town in the course of a few days. Although convinced that I ought only to despise you, so great was the esteem in which I once held you, that I cannot forbear expressing to you the astonishment with which your conduct has affected me. I confess that I experience a severe disappointment in no longer regarding you as a future family member, as I would have thought of you as another son. And, oh, Mr. Brown! You know not what a treasure you have lost! What a treasure you have rejected! A treasure which it is now impossible for you ever to win again. I have resolved to place my dearest August into the hands of a more steady and honourable protector, beyond your ability ever to aspire to a reconciliation. It is unknown to him that I write you, but worlds should not have withheld me from candidly avowing to you the sentiments with which your strange, your unfeeling, and your ungentlemanly conduct have inspired me. I now place my reliance, for the future happiness of my beloved child, on a being

whose character I apprehend to be the immediate reverse of yours.
To-morrow the Court of Chancery makes August his ward and thus
allies him for ever.

Elizabeth Allingham

A thunderbolt could not more effectually have stunned my sense than the perusal of these lines. Desperation and anguish preyed upon my heart and drove me almost to madness. It seemed evident that a letter bearing the contents mentioned by Mrs. Allingham had been sent in my name to August, my beloved. By whom, or from what motive, could I have imagined it to have been forged but by Sir Malcolm Brockelsbie himself for the purpose of alienating August's affections from me, and thus securing the supposed Allingham fortune.

"Villain! Villain!" I exclaimed aloud, though no one else occupied the room. To-morrow, Mrs. Allingham's letter informed me, the court would make her son the ward of another, and Sir Malcolm had also mentioned his petition for a ward would be taken up at Chancery to-morrow. This coincidence appeared to strengthen my belief beyond all possibility of doubt that my beloved August was the destined ward of the guilty baronet.

"Like a poor prisoner in his twisted gyves," Juliet reminded me. I resolved to accede, without hesitation, to the terms of the Frenchman. The moment I obtained my liberty, I should proceed directly to Turnham-court to procure an interview with the idol of my heart and explain the deception that had been practised upon him.

The half-hour that intervened between the formation of my determination and the arrival of the Frenchman with my coffee I considered the longest I had ever passed.

At length he entered, and, unable to brook a moment's delay, I instantly announced, "I am prepared to comply with the terms you have proposed for my liberation."

The Frenchman made a polite bow. "I should be *ver* happy to accommodate *monsieur*," he answered.

"I have already given you my honour that I will never arraign you for the part which you have taken in my late imprisonment. We have, therefore, I believe, no farther preliminaries to settle."

"Will *monsieur* chance to have de two hundred pound upon him just now?"

"Certainly not," I responded. "It is not a likely sum for me to carry in my pocket, but I will give you a cheque upon my banker, which will place you in possession of the money to-morrow morning."

He shrugged. "I dare say *monsieur* is *ver grand gentilhomme*... and *ver bon gentilhomme*, but *monsieur* is *tout-au-fait* a... stranger to me. I must be certain dat *monsieur* did *non pas* mean to deceive me before I run *tel grand hasard*." He shrugged again. "I dare say *monsieur* is *bien honnête*, but it is *impossible* vat I could be *assure* of dat... or dat *monsieur* had two hundred pound at dat *moment* in de hand of de *banquier*. I cannot, upon any term, conclude de bargain except dat of de *l'argent* being in my possession before *monsieur* quit de house."

Such a response most unexpectedly damped my highly-raised expectations. The circumstances aggravated me even more as I could devise no ready means of overcoming the difficulty. By that hour, all banking-houses had shut. I considered it as more than hopeless were I to dispatch a note to Mr. Titmus requesting the loan of the sum, that he should be provided with it in his house. Almost on the point of yielding myself up to despair, I conceived the idea of addressing a few lines to Sir Julius Maberly requesting the accommodation of which I stood in need.

"In the alternative, I have an acquaintance, nay, a friend, it is my intention to write for the funds which he would immediately provide. You could yourself be the bearer of the note."

"*Mais, non, monsieur*," returned the Frenchman. "If your *ami* is as you represent, he has an interest in your welfare, and I doubt he would fail to question de bearer of such note as you propose to send, *monsieur*. Further de more, might he not deem de request as—how you call—extortion, and he could detain me for examination. *Ah, bien*, my hopes, my character... *poof!*" He made accompanying movements with his hands.

"We could commission someone else to be the bearer of the note."

"*Alors, monsieur*, I know no one I can trust." He shrugged.

"I could couch my request in such terms that no suspicion would fall upon you. I would even grant you free permission to peruse the note and even to alter any expressions it contained that you might consider objectionable."

His head shook back and forth. "*Monsieur*, you must have de *politesse* to wait till de morning. If you will write me a cheque upon your *banquier*, I would *instantment* go in person and ascertain if it were answerable. Upon such proof, *monsieur* would *promptement* be restored to *sa liberté*."

"Perhaps you do not understand the urgent necessity of my procuring my liberty to-night." Desperation got the better of me. "I can *double* the stipulated sum if you would only accept my cheque for the money."

My gaoler stood, gaze fixed upon me. After a minute or so had passed, he announced, "I wish you *bon repos*," and he hastily quit the apartment, closing and locking the door after him.

I stood, transfixed, for several minutes on the spot where I had just been conversing with my nefarious gaoler, the effigy of mute despair. The die of fate appeared now to be cast, and my poor, beloved and deluded August destined to be torn forever from my arms. In an agony of grief unutterable and unassuageable, I cast myself upon the sofa with a state of mind similar to that of a criminal who is conscious that the sentence of capital punishment has been passed upon him beyond all hope of recall.

Chapter Twenty-One:

Escape!

THE STRONGEST PAROXYSMS OF GRIEF subsided gradually into calmer feelings, and after a time I began to deliberate on the circumstances and persons connected with my present miserable situation. I doubted not that my gaoler had been bribed by Sir Malcolm to tamper with my feelings down to the present hour.

By encouraging me to passiveness, and by the hope of being my friend–and willing to assist in effecting my escape–I might the more patiently submit to my confinement until the baronet had concluded his horrible business at Chancery. How many lies, how many fabrications, how many inventions had Sir Malcolm devised to accomplish his escape from legal prosecution?

Had he even called upon the Titmus home? It seemed plausible that he had not paid such a call. Should he have attempted such a visit, he might have been subjected himself to those inquiries as to his concerns regarding my friend.

Equally extraordinary, why should Sir Malcolm so far have interested himself in the trifling comforts of a man of whom he had taken an eternal farewell as to have dispatched to me Mrs. Allingham's letter, especially considering that I would have been restored to liberty in the course of a few hours and received the communication without his interference? There lay a mystery in the whole transaction that I could not fathom, and the more enignmatical I regarded the circumstances surrounding me, the more I panted for an opportunity of penetrating the cloud that wrapt them.

In such a wretched and unsolaced state of mind, in tediousness indescribable, passed on the heavy hours till the voice of the distant clock that had before occasionally sounded on my ear proclaimed midnight. The Frenchman had yet to visit at such a late hour, and all hope of my enlargement that night appeared lost to me. A stagnation of utter despair seized upon my faculties.

A faint rustling noise, followed by a foot-step, roused me from a trance of thought that had rendered me scarcely conscious of existence. "Pray, sir, don't be alarmed," came a whisper. "It is only me. Don't you recollect me?"

I raised my eyes to the sound and beheld a person approaching through the door to the bed-chamber. His countenance I instantly recognised as the young man who had conducted me from our lodgings to my current spot of immurement. "What brings *you* here?" I exclaimed hastily as I started upon my feet.

"Did you not this morning, sir, find a paper on your dressing table informing you that you had a friend within these walls?" replied the fellow with a query.

"I did—I did."

"It was I, sir, who placed it there," he continued. "I am the friend it mentions, and I am now come to make you proposals for effecting your escape."

I had not discovered any passages in or out of these apartments save the door to the stairs and the trap-door above. "By what means did you enter my chamber in the night, and how have you now gained access to me?"

"By a secret door behind the old tapestry in your bed-chamber, sir, known only to the Frenchman and myself," came the reply.

"Are you not afraid the Frenchman should discover your being here now?"

"No, sir. If you agree to accept the friendship which I offer you, I set him for ever at defiance." He made a tight smile.

"And you say that you can effect my immediate escape?" I found this to be quite a coincidental opportunity, and I remained dubious.

"Beyond all doubt I can, sir," he responded. "Although constrained to act the deceptive part which lured you hither, I resolved—from the first moment of my being employed in the transaction—if I found you willing to remunerate me for my services to tender you my assistance in escaping from the toil into which you had fallen." His head bobbed slightly in a curt nod. "Believe me, sir, I could not have found an opportunity of so doing at a more critical moment to your fate than the present one."

After having a better chance to observe my potential rescuer, I found him not much older than me, dressed rather plain, and not unattractive. "Pray proceed. You find me a willing audience."

"Believing me devoted to their interests, I have been an auditor of several conversations between Sir Malcolm and my master, the Frenchman, both before and since you became an inhabitant of this house." He glanced back toward the bed-chamber fleetingly. "But I must be brief in what I have to relate. My master is now absent from home, and I have availed myself of that interval for this communication with you. However, in the course of an hour or less, he may return, and all my plans be defeated."

"For Heaven's sake, then, proceed quickly!"

He made another nervous examination of the other chamber before proceeding. "The sole cause of your being detained here is to prevent your unmasking the numerous falsehoods by which Sir Malcolm has supplanted you in the heart of your... umm... companion, August Evelyne. To-morrow morning, the baronet makes his appeal to the Court of Chancery for wardship, and you will then be enlarged without any redress for your injuries."

"Oh, let us then, I implore you, be gone this instant," I exclaimed. "My generosity –"

He held up a hand to interrupt me. "I do not doubt your generosity, sir–upon my life, I do not!–but I beg of you, for a few moments, to take into consideration the hardness of my case and the hazard which I am encountering to serve you." Another glance over his shoulder. "Young as I appear, sir, I am the father of seven children, and the husband of a wife pronounced to be in a dying state. When my master discovers that you are fled, it must be evident to him that I alone can be the person who has been instrumental to your escape. Consequently, after this night, I must quit his service for ever, and–but for you–become destitute. Grant me a sufficient sum to enable me to remove my family to some distant county, and should you wish to produce evidence against either the Frenchman or Sir Malcolm Brockelsbie, I will in that respect also be devoted to your service." He made a slight bow.

How sad that one so youthful be encumbered with such hardships. Seven children and a wife close to the grave. "Only name what will satisfy your wants."

"Will you, sir, consider it too great a reward to bestow on me the two hundred pounds which my unprincipled master has been bragging to me that you this day offered him for a similar purpose to that which I have promised to enable you to effect?" His eyes grew large.

"If you are willing to accept a cheque upon my banker to that amount, which you can get cashed by ten o'clock to-morrow morning."

"Willingly, sir." He bowed again. "I owe you my eternal gratitude for your benevolence."

My heart began to race, and with a trembling hand, I took out my pocketbook. As I examined its contents, I made a startling discovery. "I find I am mistaken in having supposed that I had some blank cheques upon me." In alarming fear I searched every pocket of my garments without success.

"It is immaterial, sir," he replied. "Pray do not agitate yourself on that account. Merely give me a memorandum to the effect that you will not permit me and my helpless family to become sufferers for the exertions which I am making in your cause, and I shall be satisfied."

Surely a promise to pay would be as solid as a bank cheque. However, there still remained one other option. "If you will accompany me to my lodgings, you shall receive part of your reward to-night, as—to the best of my recollection—I have fully a hundred pounds now lying there."

"You must be well aware, sir, that I cannot be seen in any location where Sir Malcolm, or his many minions, might observe," came his unforeseen response. He tore a slip from a sheet of paper lying on the table. "Permit me, sir, to write a few words, which I hope will meet your approbation. Whilst I do so, for Heaven's sake, endeavour to compose your feelings, as you know not what difficulties you may have to encounter before the expiration of the succeeding twelve hours. You must not lose a moment in proceeding to Turnham-green to prevent Sir Malcolm from advancing his nefarious scheme."

Whilst speaking, the young man had also employed the pen. He presented me the paper for my approbation:

"There, sir," he added, "if you will only please to place your signature to that and permit me to call upon you to-morrow at your bank, for the specified sum, I swear to you by Heaven, that in less than five minutes you shall have quitted these walls."

"Of course, but I am unacquainted with this part of the city," I stated. "Promise also to conduct me to a coach that will convey me to Oxford-street."

"I shall," he replied.

"Very well. I thank you and readily accept your services. Give me the pen." I affixed my name to the slip of paper.

"Thank you, sir! Thank you very, very much!" He placed the note carefully in a pocket and pointed to my hat. As I donned it, he blew out the candle. Then he took my hand. "Please, sir, be silent and trust me to your safe conduct without fear."

Having no alternative, I nodded; however, in the darkness, I doubted whether he could observe such motion. As a silent signal, I squeezed his hand gently twice. How soft and warm it felt.

My rescuer led me into the bed-chamber and from thence through the secret door concealed behind an old tapestry. Subsequently, we descended a long flight of steps then traversed several dark and narrow passages. To my excessive joy, I found myself once more in an open street. My conductor placed a finger to his lips, enjoining me to maintain silence. He hurried me to a stand of coaches, engaged one of them, and assisted me in entering.

"I shall see you at the bank later, shall we say 15 minutes before closing time," he whispered into my ear directly. "Best of wishes with your… companion." He then sprang upon the box as he had done on the night of my abduction.

Various sensations and ideas crowded upon my brain on the progress toward Oxford-street. The most prominent reflection was the triumph I would enjoy in exposing the artifices of Sir

Malcolm Brockelsbie to the Allinghams. It would be my infinite bliss to experience in being once more with my beloved August.

At length the coach stopped opposite the Titmus house. The coachman opened the door and lowered the step for me. As I alighted, I looked up to thank my liberator, but did not see him.

"I say, sir," I asked of the coachman, "where is the young man who accompanied us from our point of departure?"

"Oh, *'im*, sir?" the fellow replied with a slight bow. "*'E* suddenly jumped down about a mile back, sir. Seen no more of *'im*, sir." He lowered his gloved hand in expectation of payment. I found a few coins in my pocket sufficient for the fare.

The fellow to whom I owed my freedom had mentioned that he would see me at the bank later in the day. At that moment, I realised I had not given him the name of the institution. Perhaps Sir Malcolm or the Frenchman knew of it and passed the information along to his subordinates.

The coach pulled off and I approached the house. A window from above opened, and a servant asked, "Who is it who goes there at this hour of the night?"

I looked up and responded, "It is me, John Brown." When I arrived at the door, the servant had opened it for me and permitted me to enter. "Is Mr. Ferguson at home?"

"No, sir," replied the servant. "The gentleman has not returned since the night you yourself disappeared."

Another disturbing titbit! Could he have been the dupe of an artifice similar to that under which I had been suffering? I had not the remotest idea why anyone would want to deprive him of his liberty. In that moment, however, it must be a secondary consideration with me, as a tie still nearer and dearer to my heart demanded my keenest exertions.

Another question surfaced in my mind. "Have you observed Sir Malcolm Brockelsbie at this house during the period of my absence?"

"No, sir. Not at all," the servant responded.

"Did he not call and inquire for Mr. Ferguson?"

"I do not suppose that to be the case, sir, as if I had been from home when the baronet made his call—and I do believe that I have quitted the house for but a quarter of an hour at most—one of the others would have mentioned such a visit."

"I see." How queer. Sir Malcolm insisted he had called. "One last question: Had there been any letters left for me during the period of my absence?"

"Certainly not, sir," came the answer.

"Thank you and a good night to you," I spoke without thinking. Other matters had absorbed my thoughts. Either Sir Malcolm received the letter from Mrs. Allingham's own hands or it would prove to be a composition of his own forming. My impatience to unravel this link of the chain of mystery swelled.

In my chamber, I donned some more respectable dress and provided myself with money for the expedition ahead. In the dark of the night, I quit the house once more and proceeded to the livery-stables where I had frequently hired horses. At that hour, the gates stood closed, and I had to knock rather loudly to attract the attentions of an assistant.

At length, a half-dressed yawning groom appeared in response to my summons. "Beg pardon for the early hour, my good sir, but I am in the direst need of a chaise."

"Pray give me ten minutes, sir," responded the sleepy fellow. As he walked away, I could hear him mutter, "Bloody —"

In somewhat less than a half-hour, the welcome sound of "All's right" announced the approach of the chaise I had requested.

"Turnham-green," I instructed the postboy before springing into the carriage. We left the stable-yard, and as we passed Hyde-park-corner, the clock at the turnpike informed us all of the hour: a quarter past four o'clock. Once we were well past Hammersmith, I projected my head from the window of the chaise and provided the address to the postboy.

Minutes later the carriage arrived in view of Mr. Allingham's cottage *ornée*. It had been my expectation that the house would be darkened at this early hour; however—to my great surprise—almost every window shone bright with the light of candles. Again, the situation boggled me.

The chaise stopped opposite to the door of entrance, and I immediately sprang from my seat, ran up the walk, and sounded the knocker. After an infinitely longer lapse of time than I could have supposed necessary for replying to the summons for admission, the door opened, and a servant unknown to me appeared.

"Pray inform Mrs. Allingham that Mr. Brown requests permission to see her immediately on business of the first importance," I directed.

"Indeed, sir, I cannot deliver your message," the servant replied. "It is utterly impossible that you can see my mistress."

"Impossible?!" I echoed. "Why so? The communication which I have to make to her admits of no delay." I made an attempt to pass over the threshold, but the servant prevented my entry.

"Sir, I repeat that it is impossible for you to see Mrs. Allingham," his hand grasped my shoulder. "Nor dare I grant you admittance, unless you are one of the physicians who have been summoned from town."

Before I could respond, a voice from the vestibule exclaimed, "Ay, but I'll admit you, in spite of any body, for I'm sure I knows who you are—it's M*u*ster Brown! I'm sure it's M*u*ster Brown or I'm not a live woman in my sober senses!" The speaker advanced and I beheld Mrs. Dickens, the doctor's wife from Oldham, attired in all the tawdry magnificence of fashion. "Oh, M*u*ster Brown, M*u*ster Brown!" she exclaimed. "How glad I be to see thee! How delighted I be thou art comed! I's sure I little expected to see thee just now!"

The surprise seemed mutual. "And I can truly assert, madam, that I as little expected the pleasure of encountering you."

"I dare say not—I dare say not," she replied, "but the ends of the world will meet, as the saying is. But come along with me." She reached out and seized my hand, drawing me forward. "I'll tell thee all about it."

Mrs. Dickens led me to a well-appointed parlour, forced me into a chair and placed herself by my side. "Yes, please," I managed to squeak.

"No, you can't see my s*u*ster just now, that's *u*npossible, as the man-servant said. She's very sadly on, you may depend upon it."

"Your sister, ma'am?!" I repeated with disbelief. "Pray to whom is it that you refer?"

"*Whoy*, M*u*stress Allingham, to be sure," she replied. "Who else do you think I could mean?"

"Mrs. Allingham is your sister, ma'am?" I still found it difficult to accept.

"Or else the one of us was misbegotten," she returned, laughing. "And don't think that, for I believe my poor mother was as honest a woman, Heaven rest her memory!" She raised her glance briefly. "As ever broke bread. My s*u*ster! To be sure she is. *Whoy* did you never know that Betty Burkitt was bred and born, like myself, i' the fens of Cleathorpe, only she had the good for*tin* to get taken up to *Lunnon* by a lady for a s*a*rvant, and afterwards to marry her old master, Treadaway, the pawnbroker. So she got on, step-by-step, to what she is now, did Betty."

"But permit me to inquire what is the occasion of Mrs. Allingham's inability to be seen?"

"Oh, it's a dismal thin*k*–it is indeed," she responded, head shaking slowly from side to side with chin pointed downward. "I do hate murder and manslaughter most abominably, I do indeed, M*u*ster Brown, but I'll tell you the whole truth of the business, just as it happened." She placed both hands upon her lap. "I were here at the unfortunate *cataristope*, M*u*ster Brown, and knows all about it." A nod confirmed her familiarity.

"Pray continued, Mrs. Dickens. You have my full attention."

"*Whoy* you see, M*u*ster Brown,"–a smile of the utmost self-satisfaction over-spread her features as she spoke–"two mighty for*tin*ate chances has happened to me and my goodman since you left our parts. I believe as how you knows as I were always a bit of a dabbler in t'lottery, and at the long last, would you believe it! I have catched a prize of seven hundred–ain't that luck? But that's nought to what M*u*ster Dickens has done. He has had a rich relation die–that he never knowed nothin*k* at all about–as has left him almost twice as many *thousands*–aye, thousands… ten hundreds–M*u*ster Brown. What do you think of that? It is not always misfortunes only as comes single, as I have said many a time since this good for*tin* befell us. Is it sir?"

How extraordinary the ways of fate. "I congratulate you upon your accession of wealth. But please, Mrs. Dickens, relieve my anxiety by proceeding, as quickly as possible, to explain Mrs. Allingham's case."

"Well, *mun, been't* I coming to it as fast as I can?" Her eyes bulged as she spat out the words. "One can't go on to treat great *B* till one's done with little *a*." She brushed the front of her bodice with one hand. "Well, you see, when we'd gotten this money, Dickens and I was both of a mind that we would not stay grubbing on no longer i' the country, where, for all our money, we knowed as how we should not be thought much on, but go up at once to *Lunnon*, and my goodman set up there in his *purfession*, in a genteel way, and live a little like somebody, and have a little pleasure, as it were." She paused for a long breath. "Well, so matters was all settled, and so, as I were determined to give my *suster* a surprise, I never wrote her word nothin*k* about what had happened, but up to *Lunnon* we jigged, and here we arrived this blessed morning." Mrs. Dickens turned her head about then looked back at me. "Lord love you, Betty and I hardly knowed one another. We had never *seed* one another, but only once, since we were quite girls, and I'm sure Betty's hugely altered, if I'm not. But I dare say I'm just the same. Time don't stand still for nobody, M*u*ster Brown." She gave a few bounces of her hair with a hand before continuing. "Ay, she was pleased to see my husband as she were me, and as civil to Miss Clack as if she had knowed her all her life long." Her right eye made an obvious wink to me. "For, what do you think! I've brought Jemima Clack with me for to be a bit of company to me like, when Dickens is out, and to let her see a sight of the world, and the fashions, as she's so fond of, you know. But for all Betty's good temper and kindness and civility, I couldn't help thinking but what she appeared very *melumcholy* and down in the mouth, as it were, about *somat* or another, M*u*ster Brown. Well, I hadn't no opportunity of *ax*ing Betty any questions in private, for we didn't get here till it was going on for the afternoon, and we hadn't been housed above an hour, when there comed a knock at the door, enough to split the very boards. After that, up drives a carriage, and I ran to the window and looked out. Inside the chay I *seed* one gentleman, as pale as a sheet, with marks of blood on his neckcloth and waistcoat, and he were supported in the arms of another gentleman. Before I'd time to make any remarks upon the matter –"

The door of the apartment opened, and the same servant who had endeavoured to oppose my entrance into the house appeared. "Pray, sir, was I mistaken in supposing that you announced yourself to me as Mr. Brown?" he posed.

"By no means. Mr. Brown is my name," I answered.

"Mr. *John* Brown, sir?" came the subsequent inquiry.

"The same."

"Then, sir, Mrs. Ansel presents her compliments and requests to see you immediately in another apartment." He turned and gave a motion for me to quit the room.

I first turned to Mrs. Dickens, "Please accept my apologies, ma'am," and I followed the servant out of the room.

The servant conducted me into another apartment. Near the door sat Mrs. Ansel, who stood up at my appearance. She patted down her smart suit, touched at her neatly-arranged hair, and advanced a few steps to meet me, extending her hand, which I most gratefully accepted.

"Mr. Brown," she began, "whether your affection for August Evelyne, or your sympathy in the calamity under which his family are at this moment suffering, has brought you hither, I rejoice to see you."

I had not expected such a flattering reception, after the recent events and flurry of exchanged correspondence. From the first moment of my introduction to Mrs. Ansel, I both admired and esteemed her. "Believe me, that words are incapable of expressing the satisfaction communicated to my heart by the knowledge that I am still regarded by you as deserving a place in your favour and consequently exculpated by you from the guilt which is by others so unjustly attached to me."

"By others?!" she exclaimed with a half-contemptuous smile. "What others?" Her head cocked slightly. "None deserving the name of human beings or meriting the rank in that class of society in which the carelessness of custom still assigns them a place."

"Oh, madam," I began as colour rose to my face. "Excuse me, but the kindness of your expressions overwhelms and confounds me. Pardon the agitation and incoherency of my mind, but do the Allinghams not believe me to have capriciously abandoned their beloved son, August?"

Mrs. Ansel looked quite surprised. "I am not entirely sure as to the matters you address, Mr. Brown. My dearest friend, Mrs.

Allingham, has every intention of allowing you to continue your association and society with her darling child."

It became my turn to exhibit surprise. "Is August not then upon the point of wardship under Sir Malcolm Brockelsbie?"

Without uttering a sound, Mrs. Ansel replied to my inquiry with an expression of her countenance more eloquent to my heart than a thousand studied sentences. The slight smile and shaking of her head communicated everything I needed to know.

"And I am also then, I doubt not, to conclude that Mrs. Allingham never addressed to me a letter to that effect?"

"Sit down and compose yourself, Mr. Brown." She indicated a nearby chair, and I sat. "For I am almost at a loss to guess from whence your questions and agitation of mind arise. If any anxiety has been created to you by the attempts of Mr. Allingham to procure some sort of aberrant wardship with his friend Sir Malcolm Brockelsbie for August, dismiss from this instant every apprehension to which the idea may have given birth from your mind." She smiled pertly, providing the comfort and satisfaction I had so much desired.

I rose from the seat and walked to the opposite side of the apartment to conceal my excessive joy, which I struggled–in vain–to repress.

Chapter Twenty-Two:
Revelations and Retributions

THE COMFORT OF DISCOVERING Mrs. Allingham did not receive any letter from me, that she herself did not send the false note—along with the knowledge that Sir Malcolm had no plans to make August his legal ward—should have eased my mind and my soul. However, these disclosures only served to heighten my anxiety regarding the puzzling set of circumstances circling about me. If her correspondence had been an invention, and the plot to make Master Evelyne his ward a ploy, I had to wonder what Sir Malcolm's true motives might have been for launching such an elaborate and convoluted charade.

"But where have you been?" Mrs. Ansel's inquiry interrupted my internal colloquy. "What has been the reason that nearly a week has elapsed without us seeing you? We have experienced great anxiety, and even apprehended that you had desisted from visiting on account of some foolish rumour propagated by Mr. Allingham."

I looked directly at her and caught her gaze. "The cause, madam, of my not having made my usual calls for some days past is comprised in a long and intricate narrative, of which, permit me to postpone reciting in this moment. I beg that you will favour me with an explanation of the calamity under which you and Mrs. Dickens just expressed to me that the Allinghams are labouring."

Mrs. Ansel motioned for me to resume my seat. Once I had complied, she began, "Recently, Mr. Allingham took to the gaming-table with his close ally, your Sir Malcolm Brockelsbie. The luck ran all in the favour of the baronet, and Mr. Allingham accumulated a large debt to Sir Malcolm." She paused for an audible breath. "In the early afternoon—perhaps two o'clock or so—Mrs. Allingham's waiting-woman approached me in an agitation, which convinced me that she might be the bearer of some intelligence of an unpleasant nature." Mrs. Ansel turned her head slightly and stretched her neck. "I enjoined the poor woman to speak freely—to relieve the suspense—and she stated that her mistress had commissioned her to inform me that Mr. Allingham had–a couple of hours before–been brought home wounded from a duel in which he had been that morning engaged." She turned to face me once again. "You will not doubt, Mr. Brown, that I hastened, without delay, to administer such relief as I was capable of affording her, to my afflicted friend."

As a small tear formed along the crease of one eye, I began to wonder the true nature of the relationship between these two women. Mrs. Ansel has been nothing if not overly-generous to Mrs. Allingham, providing her with lodgings and wardrobe following the conflagration in Oxford-street, and now, Mrs. Ansel resides at the Allingham house in Turnham-green, providing solace and succour to her friend in an unfortunate and intimate moment.

"I found her in a most violent paroxysm of grief," she went on. "For although her unguarded union with Mr. Allingham has, to my certain knowledge"–again she stretched her neck–"been attended only with chagrin, unhappiness, and regret. You must have perceived that she possesses a heart which is incapable of witnessing the sufferings of a stranger unmoved, much less those of an individual, her intimate connexion with whom, in spite of his unkind treatment, has, in some measure, insinuated him into her heart." She blinked away a few more tears. "The account which was given to me of the transaction of which Mr. Allingham's wound had been the result was that a quarrel had taken place at one of those notorious gambling-houses–which disgrace alike the annals of morality and good sense–between him and a Colonel Percival, the consequence of which had been a challenge, and –"

"Pardon me, madam, for interrupting your narrative,"–I raised a hand–"but I cannot forbear requesting you to inform me whether the Colonel Percival, to whom you are alluding, is the second husband of a lady whose former name was Mandover?"

Mrs. Ansel blinked a few times before responding, "Why, yes, I believe her preceding married name was, indeed, Mandover."

"Again, I beg your pardon for interrupting," I managed to say while stifling a groan of contempt. "Pray proceed."

"The sequel of the tale," Mrs. Ansel continued, "was short but dreadful. They had met; at the first fire Colonel Percival had dropped to the earth a corpse, and Mr. Allingham been wounded.

Their seconds, who had been Sir Ambrose Panther—one of the colonel's most intimate associates—and your Sir Malcolm Brockelsbie had, of course, been compelled either to fly or to secrete themselves from the apprehension of an arrest."

I stood, shook my fist at the sky, and exclaimed, "Partial retribution has then already overtaken thee, thou guilty monster!"

Mrs. Ansel observed my emotional eruption with widened eyes. A silent pause ensued, but she resumed after a few seconds. "There are already a surgeon and physician of the first eminence attending the deathbed of Mr. Allingham. A third has been summoned, for whom I understand that you were, on your arrival, mistaken by the servant, who had received orders to deny admittance to everyone else." She pressed her lips together. "The physician at present in the house has assured me that he believes every exertion to be in vain and that he regards every hour as the last of his patient's existence." Tears began to flow most noticeably. "To poor Mrs. Allingham I contrived, unknown to her, a short time ago to administer a gentle opiate, and she is, at present, tranquil under its influence. As the dissolution of Mr. Allingham appears so near at hand, it is my earnest prayer that she may not awake till the event she dreads is past." She pressed a lace cloth to her face.

I walked across the room to her and placed a comforting hand upon her shoulder. "And August, my beloved August, how does he support his mother's fortitude in this scene of horror?"

She looked up with eyes of red. "August is an utter stranger to all that is past, and it is my wish that he should be for some time continue so—I mean till his mother has in some degree regained her composure of mind—as I consider that it would be equally unfeeling and unnecessary to wound the feelings of the tenderhearted boy by making him a witness of his mother's anguish." Once again, she applied the cloth to her eyes.

"But how can it be retained a secret from him?" I inquired. "The confusion which such an event has necessarily occasioned must have excited his curiosity."

"Our dear August is no longer an inhabitant of this house, Mr. Brown," responded Mrs. Ansel. "He left it yesterday evening."

"Left it?!" I echoed, removing my hand from the lady's shoulder, and I began pacing about. "Whither is he gone? What could be the occasion of him quitting it? Under whose protection is he now existing?"

"Under that of a single gentleman," she answered, "but one of whom I dare venture to affirm that you will not feel yourself inclined to be jealous. In only one word, he has been demanded hence by your friend, Sir Julius Maberly."

"Demanded?!" I halted and exclaimed.

"Even so," came the soft response. "Demanded in the name of his father."

"His father?!" I roared, and my pacing resumed. "Was not his father, Mr. Evelyne, the first husband of Mrs. Allingham, now many years dead?"

Mrs. Ansel smiled, somewhat comfortingly. "I beg you to please sit, grant me your patience, and I shall unravel to you a mystery which I now consider it necessary for you to hear." She indicated the chair I had vacated.

With much anxiety, I returned to the seat and faced Mrs. Ansel. She delivered to me an extensive outline of the circumstances relative to my beloved August, and his first introduction. Rather than quote her lengthy narrative verbatim, I have chosen to summarise and abridge the account, presenting only the relevant facts germane to this chronicle.

Some eighteen years prior, one Saturday morning towards the conclusion of the month of August, about eight o'clock in the evening, a female of the middle age, and apparently of the middle rank in life, whose milky tones and faded red hair denoted her to have crossed the Irish Channel, entered the shop of Mr. Evelyne, a considerable pawnbroker in Tottenham-court-road. She indicated a large bundle carried in her arms, enveloped in a crimson shawl, inquiring whether they took in table-linen upon pledge. The shopman replied in the affirmative, and the woman lay down the bundle upon the counter. She begged him to take care of it for a few minutes while she stepped to a neighbouring public-house where she expected to meet her husband, as she wanted to inquire what was the sum which he wished her to raise upon the articles contained in the parcel.

The Irishwoman's bundle had remained upon the counter some minutes, when the shopman imagined he heard a child cry. As no person at that time in the shop had a child in their arms, he expressed surprise—and almost a doubt—whether he had heard aright. A woman who came to redeem her Sunday gown said that she also had heard the cry and that it proceeded from the crimson bundle.

They opened the parcel and discovered, nestled amidst various articles of infantine apparel, a lovely baby boy, apparently of about two months, upon whose breast a paper had been pinned. The note requested Mr. Evelyne and his wife to receive this pledge and to rely that its redemption will amply requite them for any pains or expense.

At that time, Mrs. Evelyne (first introduced to me as Mrs. Allingham) had seen forty summers; however, Mr. Evelyne, a swarthy, thin, young man had only passed twenty-five. He had served six years as the apprentice of Jacob Treadaway, a pawn-broker, in the same establishment he had unexpectedly become the head. When old Jacob suddenly died, Mrs. Treadaway chose Joey Evelyne to carry on her husband's business, as he had been the most active assistant in all his concerns. To seal the deal, Mr. Evelyne married the widow Abigail, and he placed his own name on the signboard over the shop-door.

As a marriage pledge, she presented him with the handsomest unredeemed gold repeater pocket-watch the shop could produce and informed him that if he did not make a good husband she would run away. He gave her a treble kiss and swore he would love her the longest day he had to live.

Three years glided away, and the couple produced no children. Joey began to visit Vauxhall and the occasional masquerade, frequently not returning home until till breakfast-time the next morning. Abigail continued to subsidise to his pleasures, as her contentment flowed from being valued upon any consideration.

Abigail died a year later, leaving the shop to Mr. Evelyne. Not more than a month after, he met Betty Burkitt and married her in the belief she would be the best person to assist in his pawn-shop work.

Returning to the main story, the child in the crimson shawl soon cried itself to sleep. As the Evelynes had tickets to a Drury-lane theatre that evening, they asked one of the female workers, a woman of about fifty years named Nelly, to take the little stranger into her charge. A few minutes after the owners quit the shop, a gentleman of a most interesting appearance entered. Tall, well-formed, and of a most intelligent and persuasive countenance, slightly tinged with an expression of melancholy, which heightened the interest of his features, he advanced to the counter. As he did so, he unbuttoned his surtout, displaying a watch with several elegant seals and a valuable diamond ring on the little finger of his right hand. From his pocket, he drew a miniature picture of a lady set in gold and requested upon it the loan of ten shillings. He probably could have requested thrice the amount, but they signed a duplicate, and he received just the money he had demanded. In the transaction, Nelly carelessly awakened the child from its slumbers, and everyone in the shop crowded round to catch a view of its features. The gentleman who had pawned the miniature told Nelly he found the infant quite lovely and Heaven bless it. He imprinted a fervent kiss on its cheek and departed.

When the Evelynes returned to their shop following the theatre, Nelly immediately informed them of the strange adventure, the elegant gentleman's call, that had occurred in their absence. Mrs. Evelyne directed the infant be brought to her immediately. Upon beholding it, she exclaimed words of joy and admiration, declaring her pleasure that Heaven had made her the mother of so delightful a babe.

Her husband perused the label affixed to its breast and pronounced the occurrence as a hum, saying that if they maintained the child for twenty years they would never be a halfpenny better for their pains. Mrs. Evelyne kissed the child, whom she had already placed on her knee, and declared her determination that the infant shall neither be cast on the world nor on the parish as long as they had a morsel of bread to give him. Following a bit of back-and-forth, Mrs. Evelyne prevailed. She decided to name the baby August, after the blessed month he had arrived.

As part of an appeasement to Mr. Evelyne's allowing her to keep the child, she suggested he set up the gig he had been talking about for the past two years. He wasted little time obtaining a carriage and horse.

Soon after, a letter arrived for Mrs. Evelyne containing two banknotes for five hundred pounds each. The accompanying letter came from an anonymous writer who expressed gratitude to the couple for adopting the baby and explained the sum enclosed had been meant to provide for proper upbringing. Half the money went to raising the child, but Joey used the other half to buy a second horse, converting his gig into a tandem.

Joseph Evelyne proved not sufficiently adept in the science of the whip, and one evening, during a return from a jovial dinner, the cart overturned, fatally mangling its driver.

About a month after the death of Mr. Evelyne, Mrs. Ansel and her husband sought lodgings in the house, responding to a notice placed by the recently-widowed Mrs. Evelyne. The two women quickly established a mutual fondness (which explained how Mrs. Ansel knew so many details of the child's story).

With time, Mr. Ansel possessed insufficient assets to maintain their lodgings. He sought employment and procured an appointment to sail with the first ships for Jamaica. As Mrs. Ansel's heath had suffered, her physician pronounced her infinitely too weak to encounter the fatigue of a sea-voyage, not to mention the heat and tropical climate at journey's end, and she remained behind. Mrs. Evelyne assured them that Mrs. Ansel could continue her lodging as long as necessary for her complete recovery. As little August grew, his mother realised she needed more support with the rearing, and this unexpected lodger could provide such assistance.

Each day, the two women walked about London in an effort to improve the health of Mrs. Ansel so that she could eventually join her husband in Jamaica. Weeks passed with no news of Mr. Ansel. Eventually, the intelligence returned that the vessel in which he had gone out had perished at sea. Mrs. Ansel's health took a steep decline, and Mrs. Evelyne attended her as best as possible while remaining at her shop work and raising young August.

Following a proper period of grief, Mrs. Evelyne proposed that Mrs. Ansel take on the role of governess for little August, thus freeing the shopkeeper to return to her work more fully. At that time, Mrs. Ansel also removed herself from the rented room and made her home in the Evelynes' apartments upstairs.

About a year hence, a summons came for Mrs. Ansel, requesting her presence at the house of a solicitor in the Court of Lincoln's Inn. At the meeting, the solicitor revealed the godmother of Mrs. Ansel had recently died and bequeathed the entire estate to her. Given this turn of good fortune, Mrs. Ansel believed she could no longer serve as governess and lodger. She purchased a substantial home in her own right and invited the Evelynes to live with her instead. Weary of living above the Tottenham-court-road pawnshop that had supported her livelihood those many years, Mrs. Evelyne quickly accepted the invitation.

August had then been raised to regard both women as parents; however, only Mrs. Allingham called herself his mother. At the age of six years, August had been riding a donkey, and the sudden blast of a soldier's trumpet nearby caused it to kick its heels and run rampant. A gentleman who had witnessed the event approached and darted across the animal's path, caught August in his arms, and returned the child safely to his mother, who stood watching the proceedings with dread. As it turns out, the saviour was none other than my good friend, Sir Julius Maberly. He immediately took a liking to the child and offered to see mother and son safe home.

Over the years, an intimacy grew between Sir Julius and the Evelynes. Sir Julius never visited Bath without bestowing the most flattering marks of predilection on August.

When her son had attained the age of seventeen, Mrs. Evelyne removed him from the seminary he had been attending and allowed Mrs. Ansel to make the necessary introductions to the society she had fostered. The young man became sought after by many young ladies, as both his protectresses maintained impressive fortunes. However, August showed no interest in the many females who fought for his attentions. It did not require what mathematicians call a long head to calculate that the young fellow's fascination lay with other young fellows.

When Mrs. Evelyne realised her son's penchant, she withdrew him from the social circles and kept him separate from other young people his age. She then calculated that a father figure might protect August against the designing and iniquitous part of mankind. At a friend's card party, a dashing fellow named Allingham approached her, and soon after pled his troth to her.

The widow broke two or three sticks of her ivory fan, but answer made she none. The chap's continued attentions and affections at long last wore down her resistance, and August's mother consented to become Mrs. Allingham. Upon hearing the impending good-tidings, her friend Mrs. Ansel became sullen and withdrawn.

Following the nuptials, the new Mrs. Allingham and Master August moved to the Turnham-green residence. Only then did Mrs. Allingham discover the true nature of her husband's affairs. He had an addiction to the gaming-table, and his own finances approached a ruinous state. When she discovered these defects, it became clear to her that his marriage proposal had been more of belongings than longings.

In an effort to avoid the problematic domestic situation, Mrs. Allingham and her son would spend most of their time at the home of Mrs. Ansel, who had moderated her feelings and seemed to enjoy playing the role of champion. It seemed that as long as Mr. Allingham had pocket money for gambling, he did not give the proverbial fig where his wife and son resided.

A while back, on the night of the Oxford-street conflagration, Mr. Ferguson and I effected the rescue of young August, introducing us into the story. The subsequent attentions paid by me assured Mrs. Allingham that I would be the gentleman for her son and she could depend upon me to provide the necessary care when the time came for him to leave her nest.

Recently, Mr. Allingham summoned his wife to the Turnham-green cottage *ornée* to advise her than he had lost fifteen thousand pounds to his friend Sir Malcolm Brockelsbie at the gaming-table. While that amount approached their entire fortune, it appeared Sir Malcolm had no knowledge of the true and correct sum of the Allingham purse. Apparently, Sir Malcolm also found himself contemporaneously in desperate and dire circumstances. Unaware of the Allingham reserves, he proposed a remedy for the fifteen thousand encumbrance, and offered to erase the debt if the Allinghams would allow him wardship of Master August. Upon hearing this, Mrs. Allingham sent her son to stay with Sir Julius Maberly, who had always adored the young man.

Subsequently, Mr. Allingham experienced the aforementioned quarrel with Colonel Percival, resulting in the duel and his grave injury. My small hours arrival left me finding the house in disarray and pandemonium.

Given this intelligence, I wished to fly directly to the home of Sir Julius Maberly to reunite with my beloved August; however, I felt it more important to remain in the house with Mrs. Ansel and Mrs. Allingham until the current situation had sorted out. How curious the story! Such a tale of mystery and fascination.

"The conversation of Mrs. Allingham is at present wild and incoherent," Mrs. Ansel informed me. "Broken sentences alone proceed from her lips. From what I have been able to gather from the words which she has this day addressed to me, Sir Julius Maberly arrived at the cottage yesterday evening and requested an interview with Mr. Allingham. In that interview, Sir Julius explained to him that August was not the child of his wife–a fact which Mrs. Allingham herself was called upon by him to corroborate." She raised a finger. "In point of fact, Sir Julius confessed, and acknowledged, that he himself is the father of our child known as August Evelyne."

"His father?!" The idea seemed so fantastic I repeated myself, "His father?!" I could hardly contain my bliss. "And August is then, at present, under the immediate protection of the excellent Sir Julius Maberly?" I asked of Mrs. Ansel.

"Affirmatived!" she responded.

"Heaven!" I exclaimed. "Heaven be praised! Heaven, in its mercy, eternally bless them both!" I wiped at my eyes with a handkerchief as a servant announced breakfast to be ready.

"Come, come, arouse yourself, my dear sir," Mrs. Ansel proclaimed once the servant had left. She stepped to me and pressed my hand affectionately. "I am sure, both in the case of your dear August and yourself, Fortune has stood your sincere friend."

"Indeed, madam, she has," I returned. "Were it at this moment permitted me to narrate to you the cause of my long absence from your society, you would perceive that I owe her still more extended favours than those with which you are already acquainted."

"We must, however, put a truce to our communications at present," Mrs. Ansel stated. "I hope you will make a point of assisting me to entertain those country relatives of my poor friend, and their affected acquaintance, Miss Clack, to all of whom I understand you are well known." She made a slight tilt of her head. "In Mrs. Allingham's present state, it devolves upon me, at her request, to do the honours of the house. How unfortunate those people should have arrived at this critical time! But I shall exert every endeavour to make them happy, as Mrs. Allingham desired that I would treat them as she herself would do if capable of entertaining them in person. The little surgeon and Miss Clack have taken a few hours rest, but Mrs. Dickens has insisted upon sitting up to keep me company, and, indeed,"—she swallowed hard—"although her manners and mine do not exactly assimilate, I cannot forbear feeling a distant liking for her, there is so much in her unrefined disposition that reminds me of the amiability of her sister's heart."

The Dickens and Miss Clack had already arrived at the breakfast-room when we entered. I greeted Mr. Dickens and Jemima before filling up my plate.

Once we had all taken a seat, Mrs. Dickens began, "Well, M*u*stress Ansel, ma'am, I am sorry to say as how I hears matters is going on very badly upstairs."

"Vexed to understand so—very vexed to understand so, indeed," remarked Mr. Dickens. "I should have been truly happy to have been permitted to visit the invalid. I don't pretend to the eminence of these gentlemen who are in attendance upon him, but sometimes fortune smiles upon humble endeavours. One man may conceive an idea which another overlooks."

"Lord *a*-mighty! Hold your tongue about that, can't you?" exclaimed Mrs. Dickens. "You always want to be thrusting your nose into every chink!" Her countenance turned stern. "Betty knows you are in the house, does she not? If she had wanted your help for the dying gentleman, why she'd *ha* sent for you—so there's an end of that!" She pointed at her husband. "*Whoy*, to be sure, we know you *h*ain't got no eminence yet, and that's the reason as I persuaded you up to *Lunnon*, that you *moight* get to be somebody as well as another. The road to *purferment* is open to all as strives it, ain't it M*u*ster Brown?" Her eyes shifted to me, and I found myself dumb-struck.

Miss Clack broke the uncomfortable silence. "I hope, Mr. Brown, *pardonnez-moi, mounseer*, you don't intend to return a bachelor into the country? Ashbank Hall does look so *uncommon* dull without a lady of the manor."

"There now! Do you hear that?" cried Mr. Dickens between bites of bread and jam. "Because she has come to look out for a husband herself, she thinks everybody that goes to London must be come up to get married."

"Lard, sir!" exclaimed Miss Clack, simpering and attempting to look interesting. "You really make such *uncommon* strange remarks, there's no venturing to speak a word where you are."

Mrs. Dickens clucked her tongue before speaking. "I wonder he ain't *asheamed* of *hissel*. To sit there making *geames* and laughs when there is a gentleman, and a near relation of his own too, manslaughtered, and laying, for aught he knows, at the point of death. I'm sure, for my part, the thoughts of it has put me into such a *twitteration* that I've neither slept, nor eat, nor drank since it happened." She held a cup of chocolate in one hand and half a muffin in the other.

"And so now you are going to make up for lost time, eh, my dear?" returned her husband.

"I declare, Muster Dickens, as I often tells you, our boy Bob could not be more *vulgarer* nor you are sometimes, for all you knows how to demean yourself when you chooses—I will say that of you." Mrs. Dickens turned to me. "You remember our Bob, don't you, Muster Brown?"

"Yes, ma'am," I replied. "The hearth-brushes too."

"Oh, boys must be trimmed sometimes or they are not worth tuppence," she returned, apparently somewhat abashed at the recollection of her castigation methods. "You may talk your tongue out of your head, they don't mind that a whistle. I've brought Bob wi' me, for he's hard-working and puts up wi' little wages." She turned to Mrs. Ansel. "I'm told your *Lunnon* sarvants are both idle and *sacy*, so I'll try him a bit, and if he don't come on *cannily*, I can but send him *whoam* again by t'Lincoln waggon." Her thumb pointed back over her shoulder.

Miss Clack then turned to me. "Pray, Mr. Brown, have you seen the Bonassus? I am told it is a monster of such an *uncommon* size —"

"Oh, ay!" interrupted Mrs. Dickens. "That's the huge, big, foreign beastie as we seed the *neame* of wrote all over the walls, as we comed along. I say, for my part, I think folks *maun* want *somat* to do, to scribble all the nonsense as I sees wrote atop o' th' walls in and about this *Lunnon*. I never read *sich* stuff in my life." She placed one hand on her midsection.

A sidelong glance from her husband checked her from pursuing the subject. One of the servants approached Mrs. Ansel and whispered something in her ear.

"I am afraid I must quit you now," she informed us. "Mrs. Allingham has requested to see me immediately."

Once she had left the room, Mrs. Dickens began again. "I wish I knew whether it would be counted right for me to follow her or not. I'm sure I'd die to serve my poor sister Betty. Heaven above knows I would, only perhaps I might fluster her by going up the stairs to her just now."

"Why, she knows you are here," answered her husband, "as you told me just now, my dear." A tight-lipped smile appeared. "And so, if she wants your help, she'll send for you."

Miss Clack and I exchanged amused expressions.

Mrs. Dickens turned to me, ignoring her husband's last remark. "To be sure, poor Betty and I is almost strangers to one another, seeing how long we have been separated." She pointed to the door. "That lady has been intimate with her year in and year out, I understand, for this long while past, so it is *naturable* for her to lean to them as she knows most of, at a time of trial like this."

I had to wonder if Mrs. Dickens knew exactly how intimate Mrs. Ansel and Mrs. Allingham had become.

"Lord *a*-mighty, M*u*ster Brown!" exclaimed Mrs. Dickens. "I'd almost forgot to tell you the news! Don't you remember Miss Nettle as was catched mending Mr. *Scavendish*—I beg pardon, I should say Mr. Ferguson's—leather breeches and set her wig afire wi' the job? What do you think! She's runned away wi' another player out o' t' Lincoln company and never been heard on since!"

This information brought a welcome smile to my face.

Miss Clack turned to me. "Oh, sir, *milly pardons*, I have been most *uncommon* rude not to inquire after Mr. Ferguson before. I hope *qu'il se portez bien?*"

"Thank you, ma'am," I said as my heart uttered a silent prayer that I might quickly discover him to be so.

The servant appeared again and requested my presence in another room. Perhaps I would be able to meet with Mrs. Allingham once more and express my remorse at both the current situation and my recent actions.

Chapter Twenty-Three:

Further Explanations

THE SERVANT LED ME BACK TO THE ROOM where I had just spoken with Mrs. Ansel. To my extreme satisfaction, I beheld Sir Julius Maberly standing with a stern countenance. "Oh, sir," I exclaimed as I darted forward toward my good friend and extended my hand. "How delighted I am to behold you!"

Contrary to my expectation, Sir Julius did not stretch out his hand to meet mine. His brow contracted, and he assumed a steadier physiognomy than I had encountered. "I pledge my word to you, sir, that I am by no means convinced I can return your courtesy. Where have you hid yourself for so long a time past, bidding defiance to the researches which I have set on foot after you?" His eyes burned. "I, you may say, have no authority to become the inquisitor of your actions. Granted!" A finger pointed upward. "Granted, but the inquiry which I am advancing, I make in the behalf of those whose feelings I think you ought to have displayed more consideration at a period when our minds have been harassed, and our peace interrupted, by impertinent tormentors. I pledge my word to you, I mean what I say."

To me, the explanation rang clear in my mind, but to one who had no notion of my whereabouts or tribulations, recent events could easily have been misinterpreted. "And I, Sir Julius, commend and revere you for the warmth with which you interest yourself in the cause. I am fully convinced that if you will only permit me to give you a full explanation of the scenes in which I have been engaged since I saw you last, you will not only exculpate me from every imaginary error but execrate the unworthy beings whose victim I have been made."

"Astonished!" exclaimed the baronet. "Victim! Victim! What do you mean?" He moved toward me. "Explain yourself—calm your feelings—give me your hand—sit down and tell me what has happened to you. I pledge my word to you, that if you have been insulted or injured, your quarrel is mine, from this very instant." He shook my hand cordially and led us to nearby chairs, and we sat. With a most vivid interest depicted on his features, Sir

Julius demanded, "Give me an immediate explanation of the occurrences at which you have hinted."

I began to recount the events as best as I could recall under the circumstances, beginning with the evening I had been summoned at our lodgings with a pretended tale of Mr. Ferguson having been engaged in a quarrel at the theatre.

Before I could relate more of my tale, Mrs. Ansel suddenly burst into the room. "Excuse my abruptness, but the present is not a time which admits of ceremony. Mr. Allingham has partially recovered his recollection—a symptom, as his medical attendants predict, of his speedily-approaching dissolution." She addressed the baronet directly, "I heard you were here, Sir Julius, and you could not have arrived at a more opportune moment."

"Gratified!" returned the baronet. "However, I have no medical training, and I cannot fathom what value my presence could contain."

"Mr. Allingham is attempting to address those around him. His words are scarcely articulate, and his ideas unconnected, but he has frequently pronounced the name of Mr. Brown, as if some circumstance concerning him pressed on his mind," Mrs. Ansel informed us. "What is your opinion? Shall Mr. Brown present himself before him, or will you, or will both of you, ascend to his chamber?"

Sir Julius and I looked to each other, then he spoke, "I will go alone. If it is possible that there is any circumstance connected with Mr. Brown which he wishes to reveal, the unexpected appearance of the individual himself may utterly derange his thoughts and close his lips for ever upon the subject." He stood and moved toward the door. "I will go alone. Where is his unhappy wife?"

"Heaven be praised, she still sleeps!" replied Mrs. Ansel. "The servant who is watching by her side only believed her to be waking because her sleep was disturbed."

Sir Julius replied by a gentle inclination of his head and left the room.

I turned to Mrs. Ansel. "Is it not extraordinary, madam, that at this awful moment of Mr. Allingham's fate I should be present to his imagination?"

"Indeed, it appears so," she replied. "There are many actions of greater enormity of which the recollection must at this moment press upon his mind with infinitely greater acuteness."

Mrs. Ansel placed herself near the door of the apartment, as if anxious to catch approaching sounds. I paced the room with hasty and uneven steps while the mystery of my name lingering on the lips of the dying man revolved in my mind. Nearly a half-an-hour elapsed in silence, when the door hastily opened.

A female servant stepped in and addressed Mrs. Ansel. "Oh, madam, my master is no more!" She made a few sobbing sounds. "My mistress heard his dying groans and without your assistance we shall not be able to prevent her from entering his chamber."

Mrs. Ansel cast a look of eloquence at me and then darted from the apartment, followed by the servant.

I said a silent prayer for the infuriated man, asking for mercy upon the departed, atonement for his sins, and that his transgressions be blotted out from the book of fate.

A few minutes later, the door opened again, and Sir Julius appeared. "Every bad man," he began, "should see a villain die!" He threw himself into a chair and placed a hand before his eyes.

I positioned myself before him, panting to learn the result of his visit to the dead man's chamber. After a minute of silence, the baronet turned his unshielded eyes toward me.

"It is my opinion that incoherency of mind alone instigated the wretched being who has just breathed his last to pronounce your name." Audible exhales punctuated his speech. "Once only he repeated it after my entering his chamber, and he then spoke as if believing himself addressing you. 'Mr. Brown,' he gasped, 'beware of Sir –' but the remainder of his words were unintelligible. The violent agonies which terminated his existence a few moments after deprived him of the power to articulate."

How queer that a dying man would want to advise me thusly. "Do you suppose it possible, sir, that he meant Sir Malcolm Brockelsbie? Did you hear him breathe any sound which appeared to assimilate with that name?"

Sir Julius lowered his eyebrows in thought then replied, "No, I pledge my word to you that I did not."

"Because, sir, had you heard to its conclusion the narrative which I had just commenced relating to you when we were, a short time ago, interrupted by the entrance of Mrs. Ansel, you would, I am sure, allow my suspicions to be reasonable, if not just. Shall I proceed in my detail?" I asked before continuing.

"Negatived!" returned Sir Julius. "We have no farther business in this house at present. The feelings of Mrs. Allingham must have a time to compose themselves, and she is attended by friends of her own sex, better able to soothe her afflictions than we are." He waved a hand to me. "Come, my chariot is at the door. I'll carry you to town."

"Shall we not, sir, bid farewell to –"

"To no one," he interrupted me. "To no one! This is not a time for idle ceremonies. Come!"

We somehow managed to quit the house without anyone–including Mrs. Dickens or any of her party–seeing us, a circumstance by which no means displeased me. We entered the baronet's carriage, and he gave the driver directions.

Once we had turned out of the short avenue leading from the cottage, he said, "Now then, pursue your story, for I pledge my word to you that I am as impatient to hear an account of your adventures as you can be to impart them to me."

During the course of our travels from Turnham-green back to the crowded city, I continued my narrative, and Sir Julius listened attentively. Upon its conclusion, I inquired, "Now, sir, what is your opinion of this extraordinary transaction? Does it not appear evident to you that the mainspring which set the minor agents employed in the business into motion was Sir Malcolm Brockelsbie?"

"Allowed!" he chimed. "Allowed. *That* I considered to be a fact beyond all doubt."

"And to what motive on his part, sir, can you impute so extraordinary–so unjust–a proceeding?"

He cupped his chin in one hand. "When an obscure case, like the present, offers itself to my consideration, I am never hasty in forming my judgment. Some mystery appears to me to lurk beneath the conduct of the daring baronet. I will deliberate upon it in solitude, and when I have done so, I will impart to you my sentiments." Sir Julius peered out a window. "We are nearing Upper Brook-street. Will you walk home to your lodgings or shall my chariot set you down?"

My first impulse had me desirous to pay a call upon August, from whom I had been separated far longer than I wished. "Will you not indulge me by permitting me to pay my respects at your house?"

"Denied!" he rejoined quickly. "I have—as I perceive by your question you are already acquainted—taken Master Evelyne under my protection. For reasons which are perhaps not quite so obvious to you as they are to me, I assured Mrs. Allingham that he would have no visitors, including you. In a few days no obstacle will exist to his returning to Turnham-green, and when once more nestled under his mother's wing, I pledge my word to you, that no one will be more happy to see you together than I shall. But you must excuse me just now; I am resolute in adhering to what I say."

While such adherence to this commitment would normally be laudable, I felt frustrated in delaying my reunion for yet a few days more. "I am convinced, Sir Julius, that you are the sincere friend of us both, and, therefore, without a murmur, I yield obeisance to the restriction which you impose on me. But, indeed, sir, you know not my feelings at this moment."

"Contradicted!" answered the baronet. "You say so because you imagine that I have never had longings like yourself, but I have, my young friend, deeply, dreadfully so, although nobody gives me credit for it. What is more, I pledge my word to you that I do not wish anyone to imagine such ever was the case. Perhaps, one of these days, I may entrust you with the secret, but no more upon the subject at present. I am going to pull the check-string. We are at the Oxford-street corner."

"Grant me yet one instant, I entreat you, sir," I begged. "Mrs. Ansel has informed me that you yourself are the father of my beloved August. I shall suffer the slings and arrows until you can confirm this."

With an enigmatic smile he opened the door. "Console yourself with the reflection that happiness is greater when it succeeds pain." He pressed my hand in his and added, "God bless you! I suppose you will hardly leave your lodgings to-night, and you shall either see me, or hear from me, in the course of the evening."

I had no alternative but to comply with the baronet's mandate for quitting him. With a reluctant step, I descended from the carriage, and in a few moments lost sight of Sir Julius.

Given the early hour of my return to the Titmus residence, I did not encounter any of the family members on my ascendance to our apartments. On the desk in the sitting-room, I discovered a letter bearing the Edinburgh postmark with handwriting which appeared to be that of Mr. Ferguson. What new wonder would unfold itself to my cognisance? I hastily proceeded to peruse the epistle.

My Dear Friend,

Confident that the spot from which I have dated my letter will affect you with no considerable surprise, the sooner I reveal to you the cause which has transported me hither, the more readily, I imagine, I shall be pardoned by you for the abrupt and apparently mysterious departure from London.

On the evening which I left you seated at your writing-desk, while strolling through Soho-square, with the intention of proceeding to Covent-garden, my attention was attracted by a crowd assembling round a carriage which had just been overturned. A few seconds brought me closer to the vehicle, which I found to be a chariot, lying upon its side. Some of the humane members of the crowd had already raised an elderly lady of a most prepossessing and interesting countenance. She announced she had sustained scarcely any injury herself, but her friend must be considerably hurt, as she had unavoidably been thrown upon her by the fall of the carriage. She spoke through an aperture to her companion still trapped inside. A voice from within replied to her inquiry, but its tones were so faint, I could not distinguish the words.

The elderly woman proclaimed her riding companion was very much hurt. As onlookers began to extend their hands into the carriage for the purpose of lifting the injured lady from it, the older woman warned that they should use the utmost gentleness lest any of her companion's limbs should have been broken or dislocated.

I kept my distance, as a sufficient number of respectable persons had begun the task of releasing the lady still in the carriage. At length, the second woman appeared. A lace veil concealed her features, but the tout-ensemble of her figure and dress bespoke her to be infinitely younger than her companion. Upon questioning by the older woman, a sprained ankle turned out to be the sole injury sustained.

One of the gentleman invited the ladies to his jewellery shop opposite the spot where the accident had taken place to await further conveyance. The older woman began to walk arm-in-arm with her younger companion, who halted after a few steps requesting air, and that her veil be lifted for her.

You can well imagine my surprise when the countenance presented from beneath the lace cloth was none other than that of the lovely, injured, and reported suicide, Mrs Percival! When our good friend, Sir Julius Maberly, reported—erroneously—her self-inflicted death, I thought I might never enjoy life again. But now, I had a second opportunity to acquaint myself with the lovely Jessy.

I watched from a coffeehouse across the way, waiting for the ladies to emerge from the jewellery shop. At the expiration of nearly three hours, a hack-chariot drew up to the door, and I immediately went out into the street. The two ladies entered the carriage, and I followed them about London. Eventually, they stopped opposite the door of a handsome house in Finsbury-square with a label in one window announcing apartments to let.

I engaged the house mother and took the last room available. Leaving the door ajar, I watched for the first sign of egress from the ladies' room. A few hours after sunrise, they proceeded, with many trunks and packages, to the Tower-stairs dock. After determining which vessel they boarded, I purchased fare for myself, without knowing whither the voyage would take us. We anchored off Leith, and it felt good to be back in Edinburgh. I hired a coach to follow the ladies to their lodgings, which was a fashionable hotel at

the corner of Prince's-street. As you might have
surmised, I took a room as well.

I write this as I wait for their next movements.
Please judge me as leniently as the romance of
my case will permit. I promise to send you a
constant account of my proceedings. I remain,

Yours most sincerely,

David Ferguson

So sincerely did I esteem my friend, and sincerely did I wish that circumstances might eventually conspire to reward him for his attachment. However, the fatigue from the exertions I had lately undergone overwhelmed me, and, with my mind at ease, I dropped into a deep, well-deserved, slumber.

Upon my waking, I made my way to the dining-room to ease my growing hunger. There I encountered a servant, to whom I said, "I have not seen either your master or mistress since my return. I hope they are well!"

"Oh, no, sir! They are both very sadly, very sadly indeed, sir, that's what they are," the girl replied.

"Indeed! I am very sorry to hear that. Are they ill?"

"Not ill, sir. They are gone to Newgate prison."

"To Newgate?!" I repeated.

"Yes, sir," she answered, stifling a cry as she spoke. "Both are gone to Newgate, sir, and Miss Charlotte is gone with them, sir. They went away a good while ago, altogether, sir, in a coach."

"Gone to Newgate?!" I repeated once again.

"Yes, sir, and there is a public officer gone with them, sir. Lord help me! How sad I was to see them set off! The sight almost broke my heart, sir, that's what it did!"

"Were they taken to prison?" I asked.

"No, sir, not taken. They are gone to visit a criminal whom they have learnt is in confinement there—the pretended Sir Frederick Latimer, sir, by whom they suspect their daughter to have been carried off. They are gone to see him in the hope of procuring some information from him where she may be found."

At that moment, a rap at the door of the house called the girl downstairs, and I took a few items for a quick meal. To learn that a character like Harry Glara had at last fallen into the toils of the law did not surprise me. I hoped the old couple might be able to collect some intelligence from the hardened seducer to relieve the anxiety which had preyed upon their minds, relative to the obscure fate of their child.

When the servant returned, I asked, "During the period of my absence, did a female negro ever inquire for Mr. Ferguson?"

"Oh, yes, sir," the girl replied. "A few days back. We told her that Mr. Ferguson was not at home and asked her business with him, but she told us she would not speak with any other person."

So, Loora had been faithful to my cause. I had to wonder what became of her after that. I hoped to find her and reward her for her diligence and faith.

As I sat in contemplation and finishing my bare repast, I heard the wheels of a carriage stop immediately outside the door followed by a thundering peal for admittance. The servant went down to the door and returned with a note for me from Sir Julius Maberly:

My Dear Sir,

Contrary to my expectations this morning, I am entirely alone, and you cannot do me a greater favour than to come and pass the evening tête-à-tête with me. I can admit no denial. My chariot attends to convey you to yours, most sincerely,

Julius Maberly

Without hesitation, I went down to the street and boarded the baronet's carriage. Instead of proceeding directly to Upper Brook-street, I asked the coachman to take me to my bank, where I was supposed to meet my liberator and redeem his funds. We waited outside until the manager locked the doors, but the fellow never materialised.

We resumed our journey, and I had to wonder if further calamity befell the poor gentleman with seven children and a sickly wife. I felt confident he knew my particulars and where to find me when he was ready to receive his due compensation. Upon arrival at the Maberly house, I rang the bell, and his man-servant admitted me directly.

"I am heartily glad to see you," said Sir Julius as I entered his apartment. He sat in his favourite chair and did not rise to greet me. "Much obliged to you for accepting my invitation, I pledge my word to you. I feel some ugly twinges of the gout in my left foot, and I was afraid of venturing out in the night-air, or else I would have come to you." I looked about the room but saw only the two of us. "If you have buoyed yourself up with the expectation of seeing our ginger-pated August to-night, there is a disappointment in store for you, I promise you, as he has left my house." I opened my mouth to make an inquiry, but before I could utter a single syllable, he continued, "Mrs. Ansel called upon me a couple of hours ago claiming that the presence of the child was the only solace for the affliction which his mother was at that time labouring. Our dear August then accompanied her back to Turnham-green." A look of sadness upon my countenance must have urged him to remind me, "Dear boy, after this night, you will be at liberty to call upon him when you please."

My frown became a smile as the anticipated happiness overtook my gloom. The wait to be reunited with my dearest August would last but a few hours more.

Sir Julius indicated a chair next to him, and I sat. "A friend of mine," he continued, "has informed me that Sir Malcolm Brockelsbie and Sir Ambrose Panther, as seconds in the fatal duel which took place yesterday morning, have been committed to prison for trial. If you and I should, upon mature deliberation, judge it expedient to put a few questions to Sir Malcolm relative to the illegal restraint under which you have lately been suffering, we shall know where to find him."

"Pray, sir, who is Sir Ambrose Panther, Colonel Percival's second?" I inquired.

"One who will excite the pity of no honest man, whatever may be the penalty or punishment adjudged to him," Sir Julius opined. "He is a being—for I do not deem him worthy of the name of 'man'—who avowedly lives by gambling, betting, and swindling, and one of Sir Malcolm's most intimate friends."

My gaze drew upward to the panelled ceiling. "Sir Malcolm seems to have many 'friends,' though I believe them more to be associates in his devilish ploys."

"I will give you one specimen of his character which will convince you that however dark we may discover the shades to be which cloud that of Sir Malcolm, Panther cannot rank above him either in point of libertinism, insensibility, or avarice." I turned to the baronet as he spoke. "A few years ago, Sir Ambrose married a woman of the town who was noted only as excelling in the single quality of audacity. It became his practice to make himself acquainted with young men who were new to the city, invite them to his house, and load them with his civilities. This done, it became the business of his wife to instil into their unwary minds the idea of regarding her with an eye of partiality, and the climax of the scheme was Sir Ambrose detecting them in a situation to authorise his entering an action against the despoiler of his honour. Twice he succeeded in procuring damages to a considerable amount, but his third attempt proved futile, as the bill was thrown out and his character exposed in court. Even so, he visits every place of public amusement with the same firmness and self-importance by which he has even been characterised, silencing those whom he suspects of whispering a breath derogatory to his good name. He accomplishes this by vaunting his skill in splitting a bullet upon the edge of a penknife." He shuddered. "But let us dismiss the subject, for I pledge my word to you that I sicken over the reflection of these modern Satans in mortal guise who ramble over our metropolis for the exercise of evil and the dissemination of vice."

It heartened me that the baronet also had a strong distaste for the practices of those gaggers and swindlers. However, I had a more pressing issue to discuss with him. "Sir Julius, I wanted to inform you that I received a letter from my friend Mr. Ferguson stating he had found his Mrs. Percival here in London, alive, and has followed her to Scotland."

"Surprised!" he exclaimed. "That gives me the greatest satisfaction to learn the dreadful report of her death was without foundation. It is my sincerest wish that he may win her and wear her, for I consider him a worthy young man, capable of rendering any woman to whom he attaches himself happy." He adjusted himself in the chair. "It may be a fortunate circumstance for them both as Mr. Ferguson probably considered himself impelled to assert the innocence of the woman upon whom his affections were placed before he offered her the title of his wife. Colonel Percival, whose existence has been a scene of warfare with his fellow-beings, and whose aim has already, as I have understood, in many instances, been too certain, might have proved an overmatch for a man unaccustomed to bolt at human beings like rooks."

"My friend's adventure, be its termination what it may, is, however, sufficiently romantic," I asserted.

"It is fate, Mr. Brown, fate, I am incontestably convinced." Sir Julius fetched his pocket-watch and glanced at the hour. "Oh, it is getting on. Shall I order coffee?"

I replied, "It is a refreshment to which I am at all times very indifferent."

"I am as careless of it just now as you can be," answered the baronet. "I think slip-slops only weaken my system and stand auxiliaries to my sworn enemy, the gout." He pointed at his foot. "When I feel it approaching to an attack, as I do just now, I know no weapon with which I can more successfully combat its advances than a good bottle of Madeira. What say you? Shall we crack a flask together?"

"I can have no objection, sir, to join you in a glass," came my response. Only the presence of my dearest August could have helped lightened my mood more than a bumper of Madeira at that point.

"Approved!" exclaimed the baronet. He rang a bell and his servant approached. "Madeira!" he ordered, and the man retired directly.

He began shifting his chair closer to the table, and I moved to assist him.

"Thank you, my boy." His eyes gazed deeply into mine. "From the first week of our acquaintance I have daily felt my esteem and my attachment for you increase. In point of fact, I have detected a closeness with you similar to what I enjoyed with my dear old friend, Oliver Clarington. Whilst Oliver and myself continued together, our breasts were the inviolable and invariable repositories of each other's secrets. Since our separation, mine have been buried in my own heart, for I have known no one whose manners or principles I sufficiently approved to elect him into the confidential situation of him whom I had lost." Moisture appeared in his eyes. "Incredible as you may consider it, there has, for nearly one-and-twenty years, been a secret carefully hidden in my own breast, which I think I may venture to affirm there is not a being in the world to whom it is known. Had Oliver been with me, it would have been shared with him, and I now feel an insuperable inclination to repose it in your confidence."

Chapter Twenty-Four:

Good News

IMAGINE, IF YOU CAN, the surprise and happiness I felt upon hearing the baronet declaim that he felt an insuperable inclination to share his darkest, innermost secret with me, a man whom he had only recently met, the country neighbour of his long-unseen in-laws. "You confer on me an honour, sir, which –"

"Silenced! Silenced and negatived–positively negatived!" Sir Julius interrupted me. "It is a subject on which I very frequently cannot forbear to ponder in solitude, and it will be an actual relief to my feelings to repose it in your keeping." He refilled our glasses. "Come, let us toast to our August's health, and then I'll tell you a story of which you will little imagine that I can have been the hero."

"To August," I toasted. We raised and emptied our glasses.

"I told you this morning that I had been in love, deeply, desperately in love, as I recollect that I then expressed myself to you. Nay, more, I have been married. Yes, I have been a husband, although the majority of the world point their finger at me, as a crabbed old bachelor and a cynic." He stopped to pour more of the Madeira for us. "As I have heretofore mentioned, Mr. Oliver Clarington and I had met in school, and we shared a deep–very deep–relationship for many years with no one else being the wiser. However, as a titled man, it behoved me to take a wife, and when I discussed this topic with dear, old Oliver, he became dour, cursed me, and disappeared entirely from my life, never to be seen by the likes of me ever since." He paused for a quick sip. I observed some sadness in his face on recounting this separation from his beloved friend.

A small smile appeared, and he continued, "Much like Miss Hannah More's Cœleb, I began my intrepid search for the peerless and perfect woman. It would need to be someone who could accept me for who I was and not attempt to make an ordinary goodman of me. Friends attempted to introduce me to persons of their societies, but I only found candidates who fell well short of my ideals. In a nutshell, every foible to which I perceived others inclined, every fault of which I observed others guilty, dissuaded my quest, yet I still persevered to find a woman who was exactly suited to my ideas of matrimonial felicity."

After emptying his glass once more, he poured another draught for himself. "The time at length came, but it was tedious in its approach, for I had completed my thirty-fourth year before the arrival of the happy period. Her name was Anastasia Somerville, and I first saw her at Cheltenham, where I passed the summer months, and she visited with her brother, an officer in the army. She charmed me with her person, as she could play and sing tastefully, and her conversation was sufficiently elegant and edifying for a female. I say a female because I have always been an enemy to the petticoat pedagogue who, when cresting herself upon the knowledge of the opposite sex, in my opinion, never fails to sacrifice, for that advantage, the most exquisite of those charms which bestow fascination on her own."

Sir Julius hoisted his glass. "To Anastasia."

I followed his toast, "To Anastasia."

"Fate had not bestowed great wealth upon their family, but they seemed accustomed to mix with the best of society. At the expiration of a couple of months, and having carefully weighed every circumstance connected with my intended union, and firmly convinced that my plan gave me every promise of happiness—despite her being fifteen years younger than myself—I made her an offer of my hand." A nostalgic smile beamed from his otherwise pale face. "In the course of a few days, her brother informed me that my proposal had been accepted. At the expiration of six weeks more, she became my bride. Immediately after the solemnisation of our nuptials, we quitted Cheltenham and proceeded to the country mansion in Shropshire bequeathed to me by the relation from whom I inherited my title and wealth. Her brother accompanied us and then a few days later left to join his regiment in the North."

He paused as a dark mood passed over the previously smiling countenance. "Rare, I believe, is the instance where the honeymoon does not pass in happiness and amiability, with equal smoothness and satisfaction glided on in the second month. However, towards the end of the third month, I began to make some discoveries which did not exactly vibrate in unison with the chords of my heart. When I requested Anastasia to indulge me by suffering me to witness her in the exercise of the pencil and the chisel, she deferred for a while but reluctantly complied. Her efforts, which had been represented to me as the performance of her own hands, proved so inferior to those I had previously witnessed. She ultimately confessed that those works which had obtained my admiration were considerably indebted to the finishing touches of her masters." He glanced away with a long look in his eyes. "In her music also I found a similar coincidence. What she sang and played she had learned by rote, and she was very inadequate to increase her stock of musical knowledge by an application to notes, of which she was almost entirely ignorant."

Sir Julius reached across the small table and grasped my hand lightly. "Her temper and principles, however, I congratulated myself that I had no cause to doubt, and with these two essential requisites for the preservation of my happiness, I resolved to hold myself content. But as time moved on, I began to apprehend that she appeared to become weary of my society. The expression 'at your age' occasionally fell from her pouting lips and tingled on my ear like the crackling of a burning coal." Again, he turned away. "Even though I believed she repented of her union with me, I thought her honour to be as inviolate as I could wish it."

The bottle between us stood empty, and the baronet rang for his servant. "I shall need another," he ordered. Once the man had left the room, Sir Julius leaned forward and whispered to me, "The subsequent part of my tale requires further fortification, my dear boy."

When the servant returned with a full Madeira, I observed my host and noticed how he seemed to have aged a handful of years since his revelations commenced. Once he had filled and emptied another bumper, he sat back in his chair.

"A few weeks later, we agreed to quit the country for town. Two days before our scheduled departure–upon a wet afternoon, and a bad day's sport–I returned home from shooting much earlier than my accustomed hour. On entering the house, I proceeded towards my chamber to change my wet clothes. As I approached near the dressing-room of my wife, I plainly heard the voice of a man within it. Thunderstruck by what I had heard, I demanded to know the identity of her visitor. She refused to allow me entry into the locked room nor deliver the name of the guest. When I ordered her to enlighten me, she declined and said she would tell me the next day." He paused for another sip. "I approached my servant to inquire about the unknown visitor. He did not know the gentleman's identity, only that he had appeared an hour prior, closely wrapped up in a blue roquelaure and appeared desirous of concealing his countenance. The only conversation he had overheard was Anastasia commenting that her husband would not return these three hours yet. I proceeded to town in a state of mind little removed from distraction."

As he filled his empty glass, I inquired, "And what of Lady Maberly?"

After a long swallow, he continued, "I instructed my banker to send her a cheque for ten thousand pounds with instructions that she must never expect to see me again."

How difficult it must have been for such a kind and loving man as Sir Julius to suffer such humiliation at the hands of a woman he had trusted. "And are you acquainted what has been her fate since the hour of your extraordinary separation?"

"Negatived!" he returned. "She immediately quitted Shropshire, whether in company with her gallant I know not, for I have never heard of her since. Her brother, I have understood, was shortly after ordered abroad with his regiment and speedily fell a victim to the climate."

Rather than feeling hatred toward the fallen Anastasia, I perceived a tear of pity starting into the baronet's eye. To withdraw his reflections from the past, I filled his glass and moved it toward him.

"Approved!" he chimed. "Approved! I have been an old fool to indulge myself in relating the miseries which I experienced as a married bachelor. It has given a little shake to my feelings, I pledge my word to you. It is a folly, say the senseless part of mankind, to grieve for those who do not value our esteem, but the heart of feeling will lament the liability of its fellow-beings to error."

At that point, I believed I could understand the unhappy dilemma Sir Julius had wrestled with all those years. As he had never attained an official separation from Anastasia, he was not free to remarry. His bosom companion, Oliver Clarington, had also been lost to him, with no hope of reclaiming their prior friendship. Loneliness had been his only companion for quite a long time.

Just as I started to reply, the servant returned to the apartment. "There is, sir, a woman below who will take no denial to seeing you. She has, she says, a communication of the most important nature to make to you, and nothing shall prevent her obtaining an interview."

Sir Julius glanced at me. "Imperative indeed!" He then turned back to the servant. "Have you any idea who she is?"

"She refuses to give me her name, sir, but I think, unless I am much mistaken, that I have seen her at Mrs. Allingham's."

"Mrs. Allingham and important business!" exclaimed Sir Julius. "Heaven comfort that poor afflicted woman! Shew her into one of the parlous below and tell her that I will come directly." When the servant had gone, the baronet raised his eyes heavenward. "God grant that no misfortune may have happened to that poor, good creature, whom you and I must ever respect, for having been, for so long a time, the affectionate protectress of our beloved August! I am all impatience, I pledge my word to you, to hear what the person has to communicate and will keep you as short a time as possible in suspense." He rose slowly, grunting in pain. "Feel free to examine any of my volumes." With a wave of his arm, he indicated the various bookshelves, then he slowly crept toward the door, the tenderness of his tortured body evident upon his countenance.

My mind swirled so, thwarting such attempts to concentrate upon any books or reading. Who could the unexpected visitor be? And what could be so important as to demand the immediate attention of my host so late in the evening? All I knew was that she had been seen at the Allingham home.

The minutes crept on slowly at first, then became even slower after the expiration of the first half-hour. I began to have apprehensions that some other dreadful calamity had taken place at Turnham-green.

Nearly an hour had passed since the departure of my host when I heard a hasty step ascending the stairs. The door flew open, Sir Julius rushed into the apartment, threw himself into my arms, and exclaimed, "Oh, my boy! My boy!" He strained himself to my breast. "I can now resolve the mystery that has caused you to suffer these slings and arrows. Yes! Yes, indeed. Master August Evelyne is my son, and I am his father!"

My heart raced and roared within my breast at this unravelling. With Sir Julius Maberly now acknowledged as the father of August, and given Mrs. Allingham's preference of me to be the protector of her son, no obstacle remained between my golden angel and me.

Sir Julius paused a few moments, scarcely able to command his utterance, overpowered by the agitation of his mind. The agony of his gout now secondary to this announcement. "Our August, whom we both adore, is my child–the child of Anastasia Somerville!" He uttered a convulsive groan and sunk, senseless, into my arms.

I called out for the servant, who appeared moments later. "Sir Julius has collapsed from such excitement. Please see him to his bed. Does the woman visitor remain downstairs?"

As the man-servant gently carried my host out the door, he nodded his head in response to my query. I descended to the parlour to find a respectable, elderly lady–grey of hair and with a motherly countenance–sitting in one of the comfortable chairs. "Good evening. I am Mr. John Brown, an associate of Sir Julius," I announced.

She began to stand. "I know who you are, Mr. Brown, and I need no introduction, but I am quite certain you have no idea who I am."

"Quite right, madam. Please remove the mystery at once," I requested.

"My name is Elinor Hyde, Mr. Brown. Please sit with me, as our host has requested I share with you what information I have furnished him." She sat, and I took a chair next to her. "Many years ago–approximately twenty summers or so–I had the good fortune to serve Lady Anastasia Maberly during the time she lived at Shropshire with the baronet." She lowered her eyes. "I happened to be in the lady's dressing-room one day when her husband returned early from hunting, and –"

"Sir Julius has acquainted me with this, Miss Hyde. He had gotten drenched from the heavy rains and went home to dry off only to discover an unknown male visitor entertaining his wife."

"Yes, Mr. Brown, the incident which led to the inopportune departure of Sir Julius. As it happened, the visiting man was Lady Anastasia's brother, Captain Alfred Somerville."

"Her brother?!" I exclaimed. "Why did she not admit Sir Julius and explain the circumstances? Her foolish actions led to the ruin of my good friend."

"Why, Mr. Brown, I believe you have arrived at a conclusion bereft of all the facts in the matter. Please allow me to conclude my tale to your satisfaction." I nodded my head to her. "Yes, Alfred had been wounded in a duel with a brother-officer in which he believed himself to have killed his antagonist. He fled to the home of his sister in Shropshire. There, he sought protection against the arm of the law, and Lady Anastasia solemnly promised to secrete him beneath her roof. When Sir Julius returned unexpectedly, the situation alarmed and agitated my mistress. With her mind almost bewildering her senses, she preserved her faith to her beloved brother and lost her husband."

"You mean to say that Anastasia was innocent of the trespass assigned by Sir Julius?" How the spirit of my dear friend must have broken with this intelligence.

"Yes, but the entanglements become even more complicated subsequently. You see, being a warm and comforting woman, I offered my bed to the captain that night, and he left me with a child. As it so happened, Lady Anastasia was also expecting a baby by her husband, Sir Julius. Alfred returned to his regiment soon after, but news came that he had been killed in battle, and we never saw him again. When the time came for us to deliver our babes, my poor child lacked sufficient strength to survive, and my mistress herself suffered similarly, leaving me a childless mother with a motherless child. As my body could easily function as wet nurse for the Maberly babe, I raised him as my own for the first month. Soon after, I moved to London and took a position in the pawnbroker shop of Mr. Evelyne. It became apparent –"

"Elinor!" I interrupted. "You are the Nelly who worked for the Evelynes when August's mother abandoned him in the shop!"

"Yes, Mr. Brown, my name is Nelly, and I did work for the Evelynes, but, once again, you have reached a false conclusion. Please allow me to continue." I nodded again. "When it became apparent that I could neither raise my son alone, nor could it be known that I had a child without a legal husband, I devised a scheme. I hired the woman who left the babe in the shop knowing the Evelynes would ask me to raise him. That way I could provide proper mothering without any unwarranted embarrassment. The crook in my branch, so to speak, came when Mrs. Evelyne, now Allingham, decided to raise the boy as her own, removing the baby from my care."

"How sad for you to lose your babe, its father, your mistress, and her baby all in such close succession," I murmured.

"Yes, and now I am advanced in age, and I wished to impart this knowledge to Sir Julius while I still had a breath in my body so that he could enjoy the remainder of his days in peace. And if you will now excuse me, Mr. Brown, I should be returning to my lodgings before the hour becomes extremely advanced."

"If you please, before you depart, I must ask, the thousand pounds sent to the Evelynes, from where did it come?"

"Oh, yes," she stood. "That. I had saved money from my mistress, and Captain Alfred had gifted me a large sum for my comfort. I sent the thousand pounds surreptitiously to assure that the Evelynes raised the babe properly." She walked to the door, and I followed her.

"Miss Hyde, thank you for regaling me with your fascinating story. I am happy to have met you. Shall I call a coach for you?"

Her eyes beamed and her smile brightened. "Young man, I am fully capable of walking myself home." She turned and strolled out.

As I stood in thought, attempting to sort out these new revelations, a servant approached and addressed me, "Mr. Brown, sir, Sir Julius requests your presence in the morning at nine o'clock for the purpose of joining him and Miss Hyde for breakfast."

"Yes, of course!" I promised.

"He has also ordered his carriage to return you to your lodgings." We went to the front door, and I stepped up into the waiting box. As I rode along, I enjoyed a disposition of mind which more than compensated me for all the sufferings of the preceding days. Impossible as I had once believed that any event could have arisen to increase my respect, love, and admiration of my dear August, the discovery of his near affinity to the man who had so unaccountably attached himself to me from the first hour of our acquaintance communicated a satisfaction to my heart. In those moments, my feelings raised to the very acme of human gratification.

As we approached the Titmus home, a watchman proclaimed, "Past one o'clock." I had not realised how late the hour.

When I arrived at my lodgings, the girl from the kitchen admitted me and informed me that the family had returned home in the course of the evening, fatigued with the exertions of the day, and retired early to rest.

"Did they mention the success of their visit to Newgate?" I inquired.

"Mr. Titmus and his wife both appeared violently enraged against the fictitious Sir Frederick, whom the mister threatened to hang for bigamy, and the missus denounced unheard-of punishments against him for having stolen an heiress," replied the girl.

"Did they ask for me?"

"Yes, sir they did," the servant answered. "But they appeared more particularly anxious to see Mr. Ferguson. The prisoner having, it appeared, declared that if Mr. Ferguson would interest himself in his favour in the present dilemma, he would, in return, disclose to him a secret of the utmost importance both to himself and those with whom he was connected."

Given what I knew about the specious Sir Frederick, Harry Glara, it would have been wasted moments attempting to decipher his communication. I ascended to my chamber and proceeded to have the most wonderful night of slumber.

Following a restful night, I arose early and made my way to Upper Brook-street. Sir Julius, Miss Hyde, and I ate a hasty breakfast then proceeded in the baronet's carriage to Turnham-green.

Mrs. Allingham joined us in the parlour. Her former bearing and demeanour had almost entirely returned, and I marvelled at her feminine resiliency. She cried out, "Oh, Nelly, Nelly!" as she entered the room and approached Miss Hyde. "Could I have ever believed that you were acquainted with this important secret and never confided it even to me when you knew that no mother alive could have loved the dear child as I did!"

The two women hugged briefly. "Well, Mrs. Allingham, I did what I did for the benefit of the child and out of respect for my Lady Anastasia and her brother, the Captain. Your actions were no less than mine would have been, my lady."

Mrs. Allingham reached out and clasped Nelly's hands in hers. "Your conduct proves you to have been the honest creature I always considered you, and I am sure you would have served the dear child with your life and soul. I am sure you would have done that, either by day or by night." She dropped her hands and looked about at all of us. "Oh! How extraordinary, how mysterious to us weak mortals are the ways of Providence!" Mrs. Allingham turned to the baronet. "And now, Sir Julius, since we are convinced that we are in the midst of friends, and friends only, may I inquire of you who the supposed father was upon whose authority you made the demand to withdraw my son a few evenings before?"

"Negatived!" he responded. "The permission of revealing that secret is at this moment withheld from me, but I pledge my word to you that you are one of the first to whom it shall, in the due course of time, be explained." He produced a pocket-handkerchief and blotted his damp forehead. "Please console yourselves with the reflection that happiness is greater when it succeeds pain."

"Yes, of course, Sir Julius, of course." Mrs. Allingham then turned to me. "Mr. Brown, I do believe there is someone who has been waiting, very patiently I may add, to see you." She grasped a small hand bell from a table and rang it.

My heart had never leapt higher than that moment when Master August Evelyne appeared in the doorway. My first impulse had been to run to him and hug him closely. I could observe a similar inclination in August's beautiful pale blue eyes.

"Perhaps the two of you would like to adjourn to the sitting-room, my dears," Mrs. Allingham suggested.

"Thank you, mother," August replied. He held his hand out to me, and I stiffened in place. I first glanced to Mrs. Allingham, then to Sir Julius. Both nodded their heads with a smile. With the lightest and brightest of steps, I approached my dearest, took his soft hand in mine, and we walked together down the hallway to the sitting-room.

"So much has transpired since our last encounter," I began. "I am certain the mysteries of the past week—as well as the passing of Mr. Allingham—must have weighed heavily upon you." We continued to gaze into each other's eyes.

"Yes, there were times when I pondered if I might not ever see you again, my dearest—John." His voice cooed in the manner of a romantic ballad.

"And I can assure you, my dearest August,"—the pronunciation of his name caused swelling in my breast—"that I never lost sight of you in my heart during this time of many trials."

We sat smiling at each other for a while. "Please tell me about your trials. I wish to know everything," he entreated.

As with Sir Julius, I began with the evening when Mr. Ferguson left for the theatre unaccompanied and continued through the present moment, leaving no detail untold. "And I believe your life during our time apart has been somewhat in turmoil as well," I expressed my own concerns.

"I have felt something of the shuttlecock in a game of battledore." He moved his hands about in a back-and-forth manner. "August, come here. August, go there…"

"All through my days of detention, the words of sweet Miranda inhabited my brain: 'I would not wish any companion in the world but you, Nor can imagination form a shape besides your-self to like of.'"

Colour came to his face, and he turned away slightly. "Not 'what light through yonder window breaks'?"

"During my early days at Ashbank Hall, the Bard's volumes in the library kept me the closest company. When you come to live with me there, you can also enjoy the…" I broke off when his gaze returned to mine.

"I believe I shall enjoy that very, very much."

We spoke for a short while more. I described, in as much detail as I could, my home in Oldham. August listened intently, his eyes never leaving my face.

A knock at the doorframe interrupted us. "I must interject for now," spoke Sir Julius, "as Mrs. Allingham requests to resume her full mourning and she can don her widow's weeds in private. Come, sir, you and I shall retire to my residence. You shall have further time for reacquaintance soon enough."

"And what of Miss Hyde? Will she be joining us?" I asked.

"Negatived!" stated Sir Julius. "Miss Nelly peremptorily refused to quit her respected mistress as she considers her services might be beneficial at the present melancholy crisis of these affairs."

I took August's hands once more, squeezed gently, and we both smiled. "Parting," he whispered, "such sweet sorrow."

Chapter Twenty-Five:
Bad News

IN THE COACH DURING OUR RETURN to Upper Brook-street, Sir Julius inquired of me, "What did you inform me was the name of the young man to whom you were indebted for your liberation from the house of the Frenchman?"

I searched my memory, having only seen it once, written upon the document I had signed. "Roberts, sir. William Roberts."

"Hmmmmm. And do you really suppose him to have been a waiter belonging to that house?" the baronet asked.

I paused in thought, then replied, "He represented himself as such to me, sir."

"But did his appearance strike you as corresponding with the account he gave of himself? Was there nothing in his manners or language which led you to consider him as moving in a station of life superior to that of a servant?"

"I only had the occasion to observe him briefly," I responded. "At each occurrence, my mind caused me to observe him very super-ficially. I only recollect that his countenance appeared lively, and that his dress was good and fashionable—a point in which you know most servants of respectability are not deficient." I studied his stern face for a moment. "But what, may I ask, is your motive for making this inquiry?"

Sir Julius produced a letter. "I discovered this among the de-ceased's belongings today. Mrs. Allingham requested me to make a quick perusal of her late husband's possessions while you and August batted eyelashes at each other in the sitting-room." I smiled without wishing it. "Read that, and when you have done so, we will compare our opinions upon the subject of which it treats."

I took the paper from his outstretched hand and read:

> Dear Allingham,
>
> I should be sorry to suspect, much less to accuse you, unjustly, of dishonourable intentions

towards me, but I have, as I consider, been credibly informed that you have been tampering with our mutual acquaintance, William Roberts, and endeavouring to tempt him to turn traitor to my cause, upon the persuasion that you have resolved to do so yourself. The motive which I understand you assign for your ambiguous conduct is that you have conceived the idea of imparting to Mr Brown the plan which I have laid to inveigle him into my power by throwing yourself upon his mercy, in the character of an informer, in violation of your promise to faithfully adhere to my interests. I expect that you will immediately transmit to me an explanation of those circumstances which at present appear to militate against your honour, and beg you to recollect that if you are not stimulated by the sentiments of friendship to proceed on the path in which you have enlisted, I shall, upon such conviction—without a moment's hesitation—expose you as a nefarious character to public censure and disgrace.

Yours, &c.

Malcolm Brockelsbie

"That epistle,"–the baronet had waited until I had completed my perusal–"contains, at all events, evidence that Sir Malcolm was the rascal who placed the restraint upon your liberty under which you have been suffering. It also furnishes a sufficient proof that he had some infamous scheme in agitation against either your peace or person, which your unwarrantable imprisonment was intended to further."

"And does it not also appear plainly to prove that Mr. Allingham, in his dying moments, wished to see and caution me against the baronet's intended villainy?"

"It does indeed appear to present an unequivocal proof of such having been the case," Sir Julius rejoined, "but tell me, what is not your opinion of their mutual acquaintance—as Sir Malcolm terms him—William Roberts?"

I gathered my thoughts before speaking. "It has appeared to me very extraordinary that he did not appear at my bank on the agreed-upon hour, nor has he made any attempt to call upon me for his promised reward. This circumstance has in some degree rendered me suspicious of the fairness of his character, even before I read this letter, in which his adherence to Sir Malcolm places his guilt beyond a doubt."

"Set your heart perfectly at rest," Sir Julius advised. "Just be satisfied to let time unravel the enigma. This letter has effectually wrested out of the hands of Sir Malcolm the power which he here expresses himself as anticipating to possess over you and places it exclusively in yours."

When we arrived at the baronet's home in Upper Brook-street, he requested food for us and we took up chairs in his dining-room. Over the meal, he informed me of events that had occurred in the world at large since my disappearance. None of them seemed to affect me directly.

The servant poured coffee for us and delivered the newspaper. As I sipped slowly from my cup, Sir Julius read aloud some of the paragraphs he deemed worthy of notice. At length, his eye became rivetted to a passage which appeared to excite his utmost attention. I observed him read it twice over, which excited my curiosity to utmost attention. His countenance appeared agitated and a varied expression of feeling became marked upon it.

He stammered a bit as he spoke, "I have stumbled upon something here which appears to cast some light upon the hitherto mysterious conduct of Sir Malcolm Brockelsbie and the design connected with your imprisonment."

I leaned forward in my chair. "What is it, my good man?"

"Did you give that William Roberts a promissory note for the two hundred pounds at which you contracted with him for your release?"

"No, sir," I replied. "Merely an acknowledgement of my considering myself indebted to him that sum, written upon a plain slip of paper."

He nodded his head a few times in silence before speaking again. "Such an instrument as you mention is undoubtedly not binding in law, but I have just met with a paragraph here which states the matter in a different point of view."

"There, sir?!" I exclaimed in downright astonishment while pointing at the paper. "In the *Morning Chronicle*? Is it possible that the circumstance can have found its way into the public prints?"

"Affirmed!" replied the baronet. "Listen and you shall hear what is said upon the subject." He held the paper up to his face and read: "A while ago we presented our readers with an account of the death of an extraordinary character in Lincolnshire, Mr. Oliver Clarington, who apparently maintained some dislike of his own relatives. He bequeathed his property to the first John Brown who should appear to claim it. Among the conditions for maintaining the bequest, the will stipulated if this John Brown contracted a debt exceeding one hundred pounds before he had attained his twenty-fifth year, he should forfeit every right to the property of the defunct and it should be transferred to his nearest male relative who should appear to demand it."

"Yes, that is correct," I spoke up. "The solicitor made that quite clear."

"Then, pray, let me continue," the baronet snipped. "In a fit of either folly or insanity, as it is reported, the fortunate John Brown has granted a promissory note for two hundred pounds, the circumstance having become known to Sir Malcolm Brockelsbie, the heir-at-law of the late Mr. Clarington."

I stood. "The artful designs of the villainous Sir Malcolm are now then obvious!" I shouted.

"And yet there is more, my boy." He resumed reading while I paced about. "His legal claim to the property of his deceased relative will be made an immediate subject of discussion for the courts of justice. The decision of the case cannot admit of a monetary amount, but it is rumoured that such is the benevolence of the Scotch baronet that he might still be induced to a compromise, if satisfactorily treated with on the subject."

"A compromise?!" I screamed. "That bloody blacklegs! An excess of humanity led me to extricate him from the misery under which he represented himself as suffering from the forgery which he pretended to have committed. By passing my bond for the money that he endeavoured to persuade me to raise for his relief, my ruin has been sealed."

Sir Julius lowered the newspaper. "Are you certain that the paper upon which you gave your acknowledgment for the two hundred pounds to that William Roberts was not stamped?"

"I am positive that it was not, sir," I responded while continuing to pace. "It was a slip torn from a sheet of paper upon the table in the apartment where I had been restrained."

"Then you have nothing to apprehend," the baronet returned. "These very lines, I pledge my word to you, fully convince me that you have nothing to fear. They must have been inserted by the guilty party himself to pay dearly for your non-removal from your present rights. In the first instance, probably to intimidate you; in the second, doubtless, to endeavour to tempt you, by the hint which they convey of a compromise with the merciful baronet not being impossible to be effected."

There could be no explanation other than Sir Malcolm himself having provided this intelligence. Regarding how to proceed, I had no idea. "And what steps, sir, would you advise me to pursue in this unforeseen, this extraordinary dilemma in which I am placed?"

Sir Julius posed in thought then responded, "Not to stir an inch in the business. Let every information of the cause instituted against you come legally from them, if they are rash enough to pursue it. You have nothing to do but be prepared to reply to their accusations, and I tell you once more, that I pledge my word to you, you may defy them."

These arguments added to the developing conviction in my own mind. Upon observing my host and dearly-respected friend more closely, I detected considerable fatigue from the day's events. "I thank you heartily, Sir Julius. It is getting late, and perhaps I should take my leave."

"Affirmatived!" he responded. "I believe the time for slumber is quickly approaching. Please direct my coachman to transport you back to your lodgings."

As I walked toward the door, I smiled back at my highly-respected friend. "A good night to you, sir."

The baronet's coach delivered me to the Titmus residence a few minutes after a watchman we passed announced the ten o'clock hour. Although it would have been my fondest wish to ascend to our rooms and pass the remainder of the evening in reflective solitude alone, the family assailed me and directed me into their parlour with entreaties for the satisfaction of seeing their lodger once more seated amongst them.

Fortunately for me, they received even the most evasive answers unremarked upon in reply to their inquiries concerning my late absence from their lodgings, as their own affairs occupied them so fully. They seemed quite impatient to impart their account of the results of their visit to Newgate the previous day.

"I'll tell you what it is, sir," Mrs. Titmus began, "the thing is this 'ere—me 'usband had read in the papers of a *h*offender being taken into custody, that had been a great swindler, and amongst other names had passed by that of Sir Frederick Latimer. An' when he come an' tol' me of't, we took a coach to Newgate to see 'im. 'For whatever his spirit was afore,' says I, "*e'll* be so down-*arted* at this 'ere misfortune as has befallen '*im*, that '*is* mind will be *h*open, and 'e'll tell us where to find our dear undutiful Betsey.' Well, sir, so as I *h*am a-saying, away we went *h*all in a coach together..."

"Yes, and when we got there,"–Mr. Titmus took up the thread of the narrative–"instead of the broken-hearted gentleman she expected to see, there was the abandoned rascal, as drunk as a lord, surrounded by a set of wenches and profligate fellows like himself, and playing at cards, as I understand, for the very shirt on his back!" Heads shook from side-to-side reproachfully upon hearing the recount. "Oh, damn him! It's a pity but he should be obligated, all the rest of his life, to go as naked as a black-a-moor in a sugar plantation. That's my opinion. I'm a Dutchman if it ain't!"

I felt the need to make an inquiry. "Let me understand, if you please, before you proceed, what is the crime for which he is now imprisoned?"

"Why, sir, at present, it appears that he is only detained for a second examination upon the charge of his having bought a horse of a gentleman, in payment of which he gave him a cheque upon a banker, in whose hands you may readily imagine he had no cash, and immediately selling the animal again to a dealer for eighty guineas," Mr. Titmus reported. "I wish to the Lord the pillory was not out of vogue. I could stare my eyes out with satisfaction to see that rascal exposed in it!"

"Yes!" exclaimed Mrs. Titmus in affirmation. "I'd pelt '*im* meself till there wasn't a rotten *h*egg left in the market, if I dropped down with fatigue the moment he was taken *h*out, that's what I would!"

Miss Charlotte then took her turn. "Oh, indeed, Mr. Brown, he's a much more '*orrider* man than you can have any *h*idear of. For if '*e's* married to our Betsey, and I am sure, bad as '*e* is, I '*ope* in my '*art* '*e's* '*er* '*usband*, for the sake of her being a *h*onest woman, '*e* has two wives. Yes, Mr. Brown, sir, would you believe it? Two wives at once? Could you '*ave* imagined there could '*ave* been such a wicked, unconscionable being in the world?"

From what my dear Mr. Ferguson had imparted to me regarding the disreputable Harry Glara, I considered two wives as a very moderate number of helpmates for the polygamatic fellow. In response to Miss Charlotte's rhetorical query, I merely replied with a silent look of concern.

"The bloody bugger!" cried Mr. Titmus.

"Did he provide you with any clews regarding the whereabouts of your Miss Betsey?" I asked.

"Well, Mr. Brown, I will tell you," answered Mrs. Titmus, "the bloody son-of-a-whore solemnly declared '*e* '*ad* not set '*is* beady, little *h*eyes upon '*er* from the *hour* of '*is* quitting this house on account-a we unhandsomely dunned '*im* for the payment of '*is* lodgings '*ere*!"

"The devil dun him!" exclaimed Mr. Titmus. "But I will dun him no more now. I take out a writ against him for the money he owes me, and if he gets clear of the scrape he is in now, he shall walk to the other end of the bird-cage for debt, I can promise him that!" He pointed in the general direction of Newgate.

I considered there would probably arrive a time much more expedient for explaining to them my knowledge of the falsity of Glara's assertion regarding Miss Titmus, and I forbore to speak upon the subject.

Mr. Titmus continued, "And if that were not strange enough, he told us that if your Mr. Ferguson should favour him, he would disclose a secret of the utmost importance." I remember the kitchen servant having mentioned this to me previously. "No entreaty we could offer proved successful in obtaining from him the slightest hint of his motive for desiring to behold that gentleman."

"But now comes a story that tops the *'ole* of his rascality," testified Mrs. Titmus. "Just as we was a-coming away, I seed a decent-looking *h*old lady sitting crying bitterly in a corner, apart from *h*all the ragamuffin gang that the *h*audacious Sir Frederick, as he calls *'imself*, was sitting in the middle of. And when I turned me *'ead* towards *'er*, I dare say I looked very compassionate, for I was a-thinking of me *h*own poor *darter*. 'Oh, madam,' says she, 'what is my misfortune compared to *yourn*! I am *'is h*own lawful wife, ma'am, and comed of one of the first families in *h*all *H*ingland, and I have neither *'ouse* nor *'ome* to *'ide* me *'ead* in.'"

"The poor woman," I uttered. "How sad."

"One of the reprobate's companions taunted *'er*, 'Well, then you must go a-bunting, Missus. That's *h*all the *h*advice I can give you,' and then they *h*all burst out into an *'orse*-laugh, and the poor creature in the corner fell a-crying again. Me *'art h*ached for *'er* so that I wanted to give *'er* a sixpence to comfort *'er*, but Mr. Titmus would not let me stay no longer in such company." She gave her husband a reproving look. "But, Lord be good to me, Mr. Brown, could you *h*even *'ave* believed that such a drest-up, rakish, wicked feller as *'e* was could ever *'ave 'ad* such a *h*onest, *h*elderly-looking woman for wife? Well, I'll tell you what it is, wonders never ceases, as I say, that's what it is! Oh, Lord *'elp* us, what a world!"

"Poor Betsey!" decried Miss Charlotte.

"Poor Betsey, indeed," echoed her father.

"I do hope the period of her restoration will not be too far distant," I offered. "For now, I bid you all a good-night." They verbalised their own well-wishes, and I retired to my own apartment.

With the uncertainty generated by the commentary in the newspaper regarding my inheritance, as related to the note I signed in order to effect my freedom, my sleep felt less restful than the previous night. I rose early, took a light breakfast and prepared to return to Upper Brook-street. However, shortly before my planned departure time, one of the servants announced the arrival of Mr. Fortescue. Upon his appearance at the top of the stairs, I immediately ushered him into the apartment.

"Mr. Brown," the solicitor uttered in a flat tone.

"Mr. Fortescue, I apologise for declining your most excellent invitation to dine at your house, but a previous engagement compelled me," I responded.

"An invitation to dinner?" he queried. "Ah, yes, when you had first arrived in London, following your first call upon me."

"I trust that you and Mrs. Fortescue are well."

"Well, yes, well. We are well." His bearing indicated a certain uncomfortableness, but I believed I knew the reason for his unexpected visit. "I am extremely sorry, sir," he continued, "to inform you that I appear before you the bearer of unpleasant intelligence."

I had surmised the solicitor's appearance might have dealt with the account Sir Julius had read to me from the newspaper. Therefore, this 'unpleasant intelligence' came as no surprise.

"I cannot forbear imagining that some fraud, still to be unfolded, is attempting to be practised upon you. For, acquainted as you are with the clauses annexed to the late Mr. Clarington's will, I cannot for a moment apprehend that you should have been sufficiently unguarded to have placed your hand to a promissory note for two hundred pounds."

A look of genuine concern showed upon his countenance, and my respect for him increased. I exerted myself to the utmost in concealing the effect produced on my feelings by this inquiry. "My dear Mr. Fortescue, I acknowledge that your concerns for that of your former client, the late Mr. Clarington, and myself are admirable. I beg favour of you to listen to my account of the extraordinary situation which I had lately been placed, as I had already considered soliciting your advice upon it."

"Pray proceed, Mr. Brown. I shall give you my most serious attention. Leave out no detail." He pointed at one of the chairs. "May I take a seat?"

"Of course, of course," I bumbled. "How uncivil of me not to offer you." Once he had seated himself, I once again told the tale of my unwarranted abduction and imprisonment, taking care to describe the acknowledgment which I had given to my liberator, William Roberts. "It had been written upon an invalid slip of paper and could not conceivably mitigate against my future expectations."

Mr. Fortescue turned his head one way and another before speaking. "The acknowledgment to which your signature was affixed—and which had this morning been shewn to me—was drawn upon a regular stamp."

"No, no!" I began to pace about the small apartment. "He took a slip of paper from the writing-desk. He even tore it cross-wise before writing upon it. I give you my word of honour it was not stamped at the time I annexed to it my name."

"But are you not aware, sir," the solicitor responded, "as I have the strongest suspicion has—in the present instance—been the case, that a very slight expense will purchase the affixing of a stamp to a previously invalid paper and render it of legal importance?"

"One can do that?" I asked in astonishment. The conviction shot like a bolt of ice to my benumbed senses, and I cast myself, in despair, upon the sofa, my heart in silent agony. "Must I then forever relinquish my claim to the property and live the life of a beggar?"

A knock at the door announced the arrival of Sir Julius Maberly, whom Mr. Fortescue had never met. I rose to make the proper introductions in scarcely audible accents.

"Ah, Mr. Fortescue! Your name is well-known to me," the baronet offered.

"And I must confess, sir, yours is unknown to me."

"In time, I hope it shall be as common as ribs." The baronet then turned to me. "My dear sir, what has befallen you? If you were groaning under the weight of the national debt you could not present a more complete picture of misery than you do at the present moment! In Heaven's name, tell me what occasions us to behold you with a countenance so unlike your own?"

I moved to a window to conceal the agitation of my feelings. "Mr. Fortescue, could you please relate to Sir Julius the unhappy intelligence you have already imparted to me?"

"Astonished!" exclaimed the baronet. He addressed Mr. Fortescue, "You will not, sir, be surprised at the interest which I take in that gentleman's concerns as I think of him as my own son. Shall I beg of you, sir, to relieve my suspense by unfolding to me the cause of his present emotion?"

"Most readily, sir." The solicitor repeated what he had told me.

I felt the clap of the baronet's hand upon my shoulder. He turned me about and proclaimed, with a smile of the greatest complacency, "And is this all you have to vex you? This foolish promissory note?"

Dryness in my throat caused some difficulty in speaking. "Vilely as my action has been abused, Sir Julius, I shall never repent having placed my signature to that paper. It was done in the anxious hope of preserving one infinitely dearer to me than my own interests from falling a sacrifice to that villain." My resolution remained. "Whatever the issue of the nefarious advantage which has been taken of my unguarded conduct, the motive from which I acted will never fail to console me for the event."

Sir Julius pressed my hand and spoke in a partially faltering voice, "My dear boy, is there a being who can doubt the honourable and benevolent affections of your heart or hesitate to pronounce that you are beset by a gang of villains who, banditti-like, would rob and plunder you in broad day without remorse if they could devise the means of screening themselves from the retribution of their crime beneath a single feather of the law's protecting wing? But I repeat to you, as I have already told you before, fear them not." He squeezed my hand for effect.

"Oh, sir," I returned, "do not, I beseech you, animate me with false hopes. If that instrument is rendered legal, as Mr.

Fortescue informs us that it undoubtedly is, by the stamp that is now affixed to it, I... I don't..."

"Were it for two million, instead of two hundred," Sir Julius rejoined, "it would not benefit Sir Malcolm Brockelsbie two single farthings. I pledge my word to you that I do not advance my opinion without having duly considered the case in question. And I once more repeat that neither Sir Malcolm, nor his host of myrmidons, if he possesses one at his command, either can, or will, affect your rights."

I cast a complaisant but incredulous look at the baronet, as my spirits had not been cheered by the assertions of Sir Julius. They did not appear to carry weight with Mr. Fortescue either.

"You still doubt me, then, do you?" the baronet taunted. "I never was addicted to gambling in my life, but, if you please, Mr. Brown, I will bet you ten thousand pounds sterling to the smallest seal on your watch-chain that Sir Malcolm Brockelsbie—oh, let him bring forward his cause when he will—is nonsuited and that you remain lawful heir to the Oldham estate."

"Oh, Sir Julius! Best of friends! Worthiest of men!" I burbled. I clasped the man's hand and shook enthusiastically.

He turned to Mr. Fortescue. "Will you, sir, have the kindness to bear witness to our contract?"

"Yes, of course," replied the solicitor.

"Mr. Brown," Sir Julius addressed me with a jaunty lilt. "I am very anxious to know how they all do at Turnham-green this morning, and I dare say you would have no objection to make the inquiry for me?"

"No, not at all, Sir Julius," I responded. "Shall I show you two out?"

"Negatived!" he exclaimed. "You will say I am in an extraordinary humour this morning. Granted, I have drawn you into a bet for which I plainly perceive you had no great inclination, and now I am going to put you to a further inconvenience by requesting you to quit your own apartment and permit me the use of it. I wish for some private conversation with Mr. Fortescue." He turned to the solicitor, who bowed slightly in affirmation. "Whilst this gentleman and I are engaged in a conversation, in which there is no necessity for your joining, as I pledge my word to you, that your interests will be as rigidly attended to as if canvassed by yourself, take your horse and ride to the cottage and call at my home to dinner with me at five o'clock."

"To compliance with a wish of yours, Sir —"

"And compliance with an inclination of your own," the baronet interrupted with a smile. "Wish us a cheerful good-morning and take a gallop to dispel the vapours which are filling your brain." He smiled then continued in a serious tone of voice, "Mr. Brown, for Heaven's sake expel all anxiety from your mind. I am not accustomed to jest with feelings which I am not competent to soothe or relieve. So, once more, believe me when I aver that I shall be a true prophet and that your bet is already lost. But one more word—you recollect what you once advanced to me yourself upon the subject of not giving unnecessary pain to the sensitive heart of our dear August; please do not mention this subject to him at all. Now, away, away. I want to be alone with this gentleman." He grabbed the arm of Mr. Fortescue.

I bowed to each of the men in turn then quit the house.

Chapter Twenty-Six:
A Matter of Trust

ON MY WALK TO THE LIVERY-STABLES I reflected upon the possible motive from which Sir Julius had acted. Could he be in possession of any private reason for supposing that we would eventually triumph over the machinations of the perfidious Sir Malcolm? Could he be satisfied with his own wealth that he became indifferent to the issue of the threatened suit, providing the necessary funds for me to have a suitable life with his lately-revealed son, Master August?

Once upon the steed who would propel me to Turnham-green I considered the extraordinary circumstances of the case again, and my ideas grew bewildered and perplexed. I arrived at the cottage with my feelings comparatively wrapt in a waking dream.

Mrs. Allingham and Mrs. Ansel met me in the vestibule, and I greeted them, "I come to satisfy the kind inquiries of Sir Julius, madam, accompanied by apologies which have detained him from paying his respects in person. Business of importance currently occupies him."

August's mother smiled angelically before responding. "In answer to the baronet's query, I find myself infinitely more composed and resigned than I could have anticipated so early a period after the dreadful catastrophe which has attended the fate of one with whom I had been so nearly connected." She reached for my hand. "With the number of true and valuable friends who survive to me, I should display myself ungrateful to Providence not to suffer the greater portion of happiness which remains to me to overbalance the misfortune which I have experienced." She gazed heavenward.

My admiration of the amiability of her character increased considering the delicacy with which she forbore to utter a single hint of the discordant sentiments which had existed in the breasts of herself and him to whom she had voluntarily—although blindly—plighted the vows of obedience and faith.

"Mrs. Allingham and myself," Mrs. Ansel then spoke, "are going to be engaged with some tradespeople, from whom she expects to receive her orders relative to the family mourning. I therefore advise you to visit the arbour at the bottom of the garden, where you will find a companion who, I dare say, will be able to entertain you during our absence." She indicated with an open hand the direction toward the door to the garden.

"Thank you. Thank you both." I smiled and proceeded to the setting that she had named. As expected, I beheld my beloved August seated, and he sat perusing a volume in his hand. Could it, perhaps, be Shakespeare?

At the sound of my approaching steps, he raised his boyish eyes and closed the book. "You could not have arrived at a more lucky moment."

"Then that moment is at least a happy one to me," I replied with a grin. "But why is my arrival at this particular moment so very fortunate?"

"Because I was beginning to be out of humour with my author, and as I consider it even more foolish to quarrel with books than human beings, I was glad of an apology for throwing his work aside without suffering his ideas to irritate me any further." He indifferently tossed the book to one side.

I had to surmise that the work did not contain Shakespeare after all. "What is the subject of the volume which has been engaging your attention?

"You have doubtless heard that Mr. Allingham either purchased or came into possession of this cottage ready furnished. Amongst other articles, it contained a few shelves of insignificant volumes, powerfully descriptive of those trifling minds who had been its former inhabitants. This morning, partly for lack of wit and partly for want of employment, I casually selected this book of which you have just heard me express my sentiments. It is one of the most trivial of French novels."

"If such is its nature, I should have imagined that it could not have possessed the power of exciting either your interest or prejudice."

"The protagonist of the story is torn between two suitors," August summarised for me. "One became weary of the protracted indecision and feigned to have been suddenly reduced to poverty, not doubting his love would succour him in his indigence; however, the sought-after hand went to the more fortunate rival."

"And which of the characters do you fancy yourself?" It seemed a natural question.

August glared at me with raised eyebrows. "I believe, in general, that I am the protagonist. Wouldn't you agree?"

Given his remarkable life story, it seemed fairly reasonable for him to have such perspective. Instead of answering with words, I smiled adoringly, and he returned the expression.

"Then you consider the protagonist's decision ungenerous?" I asked.

"I think I know your sentiments too well—at least I hope I do—to apprehend that your opinion of the subject can be dissimilar to mine." A brightening of his eyes followed. "Your beloved Bard has depicted time and time again that feigning deception carries with it certain risks. As the great Scotsman himself decried, 'False face must hide what the false heart doth know.'"

In that moment, my admiration for dear August elevated even farther, as he could freely quote from Shakespeare. Unfortunately, I could not help but regret the revolution of fortune's unstable wheel with which I was at that moment threatened.

"But a truce to French novels!" he exclaimed. "I fear my chattering has made you either weary or sleepy, the same effect the unceasing prattle of poor Mrs. Dickens and her friend Miss Clack produces on me." With a clever smile, he asked, "And where is my dearest father this morning?"

"He is detained by business of importance, and I appear in his stead, if you please."

Colour rose in his cheeks. "I please very much." He turned his head away then back to me with a serious countenance. "I see Mrs. Ansel approaching. Our conversation must now become general."

"I come to inform Mr. Brown"—Mrs. Ansel spoke as she advanced toward us—"that if he will dine at the cottage to-day, Mrs. Allingham will exert herself to appear at the table." August bristled and smiled at me. "Her relatives and their friend are just returned home from visiting town. They have, it appears, engaged a house and shop in the Borough and are to take possession of it to-morrow. As Mrs. Allingham has, as yet, scarcely passed an hour in their society, her good-nature induces her to attempt presiding at dinner." She looked directly at me. "You will not return to town till this evening, will you, Mr. Brown?"

"Would that I could stay to partake in the festivities you have described, Mrs. Ansel." My speech became unsteady because as much as I wished to remain, I had promised to dine with Sir Julius that evening. "However, I am already committed to dinner with August's father to-day, and I must return to town quite soon in order to be punctual to that appointment." I turned to see August's saddened eyes. "I will wish Mrs. Allingham good-morning."

August and I entered the house together. We approached his mother, and I offered my well wishes.

"It is so good to see you again Mr. Brown, and I anticipate seeing you again soon," she responded.

Dear August accompanied me to the horse, and just as I sprung into the saddle, Mrs. Dickens screamed from an upper window, "Oh, M*u*ster Brown! M*u*ster Brown! Do stop a minute, m*u*n, I beg of you! I have *sich* a thin*k* to tell you as never were! Pray, ye, *doant* go till I come down."

With a grin of delight, August whispered, "Pray ye, have a pleasant *tête-à-tête*, my darling." He made a rolling motion with his eyes and retired into the house.

At the same instant, Mrs. Dickens appeared. "Lord Amighty, sir!" she exclaimed as she approached in her dressing-jacket with her hair in papillots. "I'm quite ash*ea*med of coming down to you in this *ploight*. Do pray, come as near the door as ever you can, for I *maun* stand behind one-half on't, as nobody may see me as goes by."

I dismounted and stepped back to the house as requested.

"I *ha'* met wi' *sommat* to-day i' my travels about *Lunnon* as will so surprise you that I could not let you go without telling you on't for the life o' me. What do you think? If I did not meet poor Miss Nettle as were, as dirty as a sweep–the Lord above help her silly soul!" Her eyes grew to saucer size. "When she seed me, she burst out a-crying at the sight o' me. For my part, I thought she'd ha' fainted in t' street, so I were fain to take her into a house close by. There she told me that the *fo-in* gentleman play-actor what runned away wi' her out *o't* Lincoln company–and called *hissel* a lord's discarded son, the honourable Mr. Dingdashingly, I think his *neame* were–had turned out to be only a common swindler, and that he were now in Newgate, a prisoner, for some unlawful conduct about a horse, and that she were *amost* begging her bread about the streets. There's for you then, M*u*ster Brown! Foolish body as she's been, I'm sure I pity her. Di' not you, sir?"

I answered, "I do indeed," as I considered that Dingdashingly might have been yet another false name given by the dastardly Harry Glara. Could Miss Nettle have been the old wife Mrs. Titmus engaged upon her visit to Newgate?

"Well, sir," resumed Mrs. Dickens, "I *gied* her half-a-crown to get her bread and meat, as the saying is, but I could not help telling on her that I always thought she'd bring her hogs to a fine market at last. So she has, has not she, M*u*ster Brown?" She cocked her head and continued before I could respond. "But the poor body *maunt* starve for all that, and so I promised to try and raise her a bit o' money if I could, *agin* I see her *agin*. So, if you'd be half-a-crown, sir, a little picked up in one place, and a little picked up in another, may serve her i' the time o' need till she can turn herself round like." Her head wagged from side-to-side. "Poor crack-brained old body! Sure, this will bring her to her senses, but I shall never forget her mending your friend's leather breeches, and so I told her to-day."

While it perplexed me as to why this woman, who had recently made good at the lottery and with her husband's inheritance, would seek alms from friends to give to strangers. However, I had been brought up to be a good, charitable Christian, gave it no second thought, produced a sovereign from my pocket, and handed it to her before I stepped back the horse once again. "I commend you on your benevolence, Mrs. Dickens. A good-morning to you."

"Only one word more!" she exclaimed, stopping my upward motion. "Only one word more. I say, sir, I'm sure M*u*ster *Scavendish*, I beg his pardon, M*u*ster Ferguson–I can't think why I make that mistake, but I always does–will give his trifle towards her subscription, Lord help his good-natured soul, if you only put him in mind, for the joke's sake, of her setting fire to her wig over his inexpressibles. Well, good-bye. God bless ye! We are going to the *Burrow*, and be sure you call and be quite at *hoame* wi' us—mind that."

At long last, I leapt up to the mount, saluted Mrs. Dickens with a hand, and rode off.

On my ride toward town, the extraordinary character of Harry Glara occupied my thoughts. Undaunted and most unusually adventurous, he welcomed old, young, and middle-aged equally, it appeared, into his hymeneal seraglio, so long as they could pay for admission into the happy circle. If three wives could defend a man from the interference of law, it appeared by no means improbable that he could, if necessity required it, produce treble that number to vouch for the integrity of his character. It also amused me to consider that Glara might also, in accordance with his naturally cool and unshaken impudence, petition the government to recompence him for the regard which he had shewn to extending the population of the country.

Arriving in Upper Brook-street, my pocket-watch displayed ten minutes past five o'clock. Upon entering the house, a servant ushered me directly into the dining-room, where I found the baronet seated with Mr. Fortescue.

"I am glad you are come, I pledge my word to you, for you know the punctuality of me and my cook," Sir Julius admonished. "If you had been five minutes longer, it's odds but either she or I should have considered that we had a crow to pluck with you." He smiled and indicated a chair for me next to him. "I have much pleasure in acquainting you that Mr. Fortescue favours us with his company *en famille* to-day. After the cloth is removed, I have a very serious matter to discuss with you." An arch smile played upon the lips of the baronet.

"Serious, sir?" I replied.

"Yes. I have already informed this gentleman that I shall solicit his attention for this serious subject." He indicated Mr. Fortescue.

Throughout the dinner, conversation between our host and Mr. Fortescue occupied most of the time. Occasionally Sir Julius made inquiries relative to the friends whom I had that morning visited, which I answered with absent-minded, brief responses. My own breast tormented with the various anticipations which

I could not forbear forming, relative to the baronet's informing me of the discussion succeeding the meal. As I witnessed the unusual cheerfulness and animation of Sir Julius, my own spirits rose unconsciously.

At the conclusion of the meal, the servants removed the cloth, set a few bottles of wine upon the table, then withdrew. Sir Julius addressed me directly, "Now then, my dear young friend, let me request you to answer a question without hesitation or prevarication which I am going to propose to you."

As I never prevaricate, at least willingly, and hesitation is foreign to my being, I made a slight inclination of my head to indicate the acceptance of the baronet's terms.

"Have you not long since confessed to me that you preferred the company of my son, August, to that of all others and that you would constitute the greatest happiness of your life to unite your fate with his?"

The question put me off balance as I had never discussed my inclination toward the male sex with Mr. Fortescue. Also, he oversaw the executor duties of Mr. Clarington's will, and one of the conditions forbade romantic entanglements. However, Sir Julius requested that I neither hesitate nor prevaricate, and I answered, "I own, sir, that it was a felicity to which I once looked forward with hope and exultation."

"And what occasions you not to do so still?" he inquired further.

Many reasons arose in my mind, with potential loss of the Clarington estate the most important. I sat in silence rather than speak my heart only to lose all.

"It surely cannot be possible that you can apprehend any change in mine or my son's sentiments towards you," Sir Julius continued, "arising from the cause in which you are threatened to be involved by Sir Malcolm Brockelsbie?"

"I believe you both, sir, too noble—too generous—to be biased by an impression of the kind," I replied. "But I must not permit your excellence to blind me to the humble situation to which it is probable that I may quickly be reduced and tempt me to convert your benevolence of feeling into shelter for what might justly be deemed the arrogance or avarice of my own heart." I gazed down at the table before me.

Sir Julius smiled a bit. "It is my wish and my intention to place the contingency beyond your power. Mr. Fortescue and I have discussed facts pertinent to the pending legal proceedings. However, we are not at liberty to discuss these facts with you prior to the impending trial."

"The kindness and generosity of your disposition, sir, so far exceed the common limits of human benevolence that I am at a loss for expressions to convey to you the sentiments with which you have inspired me," I returned with a smile of my own.

"Approved!" exclaimed the baronet. "Approved! I am heartily glad that such is the case, as I do not wish any words from you on the subject. You have known me some time in the character of a friend, I and believe respected me as such."

"Of course," I stated without hesitation. Should whatever intelligence these two gentlemen held prove strong enough to overcome the accusations of Sir Malcolm Brockelsbie, I would be able to remove August to Ashbank Hall, and the two of us could live out our lives in pastoral harmony. Perhaps Mrs. Allingham and Mrs. Ansel would consider residing with us in the country. Many rooms went unused in the great house in Oldham.

"In your friendship," I began, "I am satisfactorily convinced that no equivocation can exist, and still, I find myself restrained in this matter and entirely in your capable hands, which —"

"And so," Sir Julius interrupted, "my dear young friend, you must be satisfied that Mr. Fortescue and myself have your best interests in our hearts—as well as those of our dear August. Dare you trust to me?"

"You are, Sir Julius, the father of the one in whom alone my soul exists," I responded. "Those words reply to every doubt."

"Affirmatived!" chimed Sir Julius, fixing his eye upon me.

For a moment I experienced inexplicable bliss, knowing I had allied to myself the most ardent of friends. As to why they had, with such unbounded fervour, attached themselves to my interests and displayed their devotion to my happiness, I could not apprehend. Then, an unhappy question crossed my mind. "When is Sir Malcolm bringing his suit to court?"

"I believe I can respond to that query." Mr. Fortescue coughed into his fist twice before continuing. "There can be no doubt that the point at which he aimed would be pursued with spirit and perseverance. I have received formal information from the agents of Sir Malcolm that a process would be instituted against you in the Court of Chancery within two weeks." He looked directly at me. "I must make an emphatic request that if you encounter any of your adversaries, or their agents, studiously avoid all conversation with them, neither advancing to them a single inquiry, or replying to any question which they might propose to you."

I nodded in accordance. "For my own benefit, sir, I shall indubitably make your counsel the rule of my conduct, although, I must confess it appears to me a most mysterious character which is assigned me to perform in this drama of real life."

Both Sir Julius and Mr. Fortescue smiled, with the former's appearing somewhat grander. Seeing their smiles brought a similar expression to my countenance as well. I had considered suggesting the instigation of a search for the spot where I had been confined, with the hopes of, perhaps, even winning some of Sir Malcolm's agents to my cause and his exposure. Given the conviction of Sir Julius in the matter, and the instructions from Mr. Fortescue, I felt it best to avoid any potential contact with any of that lot. So many uncertainties abounded, and I felt myself at the gate of a perplexing labyrinth, poised to enter.

A few days later, we attended the interment of Mr. Allingham, which the family conducted in a most private manner. The widow and her son then departed from the melancholy scene in the cottage at Turnham-green and took up residence at the mansion of Sir Julius Maberly. This brought great joy to everyone, as we could share each other's society more frequently, sparing us the long ride.

One afternoon, upon my return to our lodgings, Mrs. Titmus drew me aside. "Mr. Brown, am I glad to see you. I just '*ad* to *h*inform you that the dishonourable Sir Frederick got '*isself* discharged from the charges preferred *agin 'im* for the '*orse* business, but '*e* got *h*immediately returned to prison by virtue of the writ *h*issued *agin 'im* by me '*usband*, Mr. Titmus."

Such news would be welcomed by Mr. Ferguson, and I wrote him, sharing the intelligence. I used the address from which he sent me his most-recent missive, hoping it would reach him accordingly or follow him to wherever he might have taken up residence.

The following morning, I strolled across Blackfriars Bridge and accidentally encountered Mrs. Dickens, whose family had recently acquired a home nearby.

"Oh, M*u*ster Brown!" she began, "did you remember to ask your friend for a small bit of relief for the unfortunate Niobe, our Miss Nettle?"

Not wanting to have to explain the events of the last month to her while standing in the street, I reached into my pocket, withdrew a sovereign, and handed it to Mrs. Dickens. "He was only too glad to assist a former associate who stands in need."

"Oh, thank ye, thank ye." She placed the coin into her purse quickly. "The m*u*ster and I ha' granted the poor dear the use of an apartment in our house till her annuity payment, when she can return to the spot which she now so bitterly repented of having quitted. Ah, you see, M*u*ster Brown what a foolish thin*k* love is when it's overstrained! But it's always so wi' old maids and overgrown girls. Folks should just love well enough to be happy, if they come together, and not repine if fate keeps them asunder." She paused and smiled at some memory distant in her heart. "That was just the kind of affection I had for me first husband, and now have for me second, and nobody could live more comfortabler than I've done wi' both on 'em. No, no, be easy *ony*way, and you'll save yerself much trouble was always my maxim, and you may believe me that I have found it a very true one." Her finger wagged at me. "I can't stand by *ony* woman as makes a fool of herself for a man, as I tell Dickens, and I am sure we live as canny together as can be, but if he were to die, I shouldn't be the silly pout to go weeping and wailing for him all over the parish."

What a horrid thought! I hoped it would be many years before such a situation confronted me or August.

"I'll do all as I can for him whilst he's here, M*u*ster Brown, and I can't say no more nor than, you know, and p*u*rvided it pleased Heaven to take him to-morrow, why there's as good fish i' the sea as ever comed out of it, and I'd comfort myself as well as I could."

As soon as she stopped babbling, I bid her a good-day and moved on as quickly as possible. How could someone have such dark thoughts regarding their future?

I later discovered that Mr. Fortescue had employed a few agents for a most diligent search after the house in which I had been trepanned. Despite the number of inquiries made, and the time spent on foot in the neighbourhood of Newgate making attempts to produce the desired information, all seemed in vain. Loora had drawn her conclusion of the house's general location from some words which she had once heard expressed by the Frenchman. The agents hired by Mr. Fortescue also visited several low gambling houses for the reception of reprehensible characters in the vicinity, but none could be discovered that was kept by a Frenchman or that bore the slightest resemblance to my accounts. Advertisements in several of the daily prints offered a handsome reward for a conference with either Dennis O'Dottlety or his mistress, Loora. However, from her own lips I learned she did not possess the art of reading, and from the absence of replies to the advertisements, it appeared the Irishman suffered the same defect.

Each passing day increased my anxiety as I awaited the impending confrontation with Sir Malcolm in the Court of Chancery. Also, a fortnight had elapsed since the receipt of Mr. Ferguson's letter.

Chapter Twenty-Seven:

Packets from Glasgow

A T LENGTH, TO MY GREAT SATISFACTION, a small packet that bore the mark of having been booked at the Glasgow mail office arrived. On opening it, a note superscribed with my name presented itself to my observation first. It read:

Glasgow

My Dear Friend,

From my long silence, you have, I doubt not, considered me as having either departed from this earth for the shades below, or as being wholly inattentive to the claims of friendship. I am alive and well, with every prospect before me, and nothing should so long have withheld me from imparting to you my proceedings, but the expectation of being able, when I did address you, to communicate to you some decisive intelligence respecting my future fate. But oh, my friend, I have met with such an adventure that I can at this moment scarcely persuade myself that the fact which I shall presently unfold to you actually passed before my sight. I can now faithfully assure you that I am in possession of positive proof that neither a delusion nor a misconception deceived my senses. In the packet which accompanies this, you will find a journal of my adventures, and I consider that I could not dispatch it to you at a more interesting or

I perused the packet and discovered half-a-dozen folded sheets of paper with notes scrawled upon them at various times. Although denominated a journal by Mr. Ferguson, I did not find it divided into any distinct portions, as in the form of a diary. The remainder of my day I devoted to reading and re-reading the hastily-written words.

Once again, as with the long narrative provided by Mrs. Ansel with regard to August's origins, I shall summarise the lengthy journal entries provided me by my dear friend, Mr. Ferguson. He began by recounting the last bit of his previous letter, where he had followed Mrs. Percival and her companion to Edinburgh and took a rented room at the very same establishment.

The ladies set out the following morning for Glasgow in a hired chaise. Ferguson procured a horse and travelled in their rear. With all the delays occasioned on the road—changing of horses and the ladies stopping occasionally to refresh themselves—it was nearly seven in the evening when they reached the city.

Their chaise traversed the town and proceeded to a beautifully-romantic spot surrounded by delightful villas amidst the embosoming verdure of an umbrageous shrubbery bordered by vividly-ornamented flowers. Mr. Ferguson took note of the number on the gate through which they passed, and he returned to the city to procure quarters.

Early the next morning, he rode back to the same spot and strolled past the gate. Within, he espied an older gentleman tending the garden. Ferguson commented upon his delight at discovering such a charming place, and the other fellow supplied the information that the estate bore the name of The Wilderness, and it belonged to a Mrs. Faulkner.

He then rode back to his inn and composed an anonymous note requesting an interview with Mrs. Percival, directing the response to the inn. Days rolled on with no answer, but finally a reply arrived declining his offer unless he wished to provide a name. He immediately wrote back informing her of his name.

Mrs. Faulkner wrote that Mrs. Percival had yet to recover from her sea voyage from England and that she would write again when the situation improved. Five days later, he finally received a note indicating Mrs. Percival would see him.

Mrs. Faulkner appeared quite elderly but spry. Her manner of dress denoted a period of some twenty-five years or more prior. She sported a bustle with hoops, and the fringe on her forehead peeked from beneath a bonnet secured at her neck with a blue ribbon.

When the young lady glanced at my friend, she called him by his stage name, Mr. Cavendish. She also exonerated him of any guilt over their last encounter, as they had both been victims of the same abandoned characters.

Mr. Ferguson informed her of his true identity and inquired into the false intelligence that she had ended her life in the Clyde. According to Mrs. Percival, her jealous husband had confined her to a private madhouse. Following her escape, she had planned to put a period to her existence by throwing herself into the river. However, her current host, Mrs. Faulkner, had been sailing a pleasure-boat of her own amusement, and Mrs. Percival landed quite near. Mrs. Faulkner took it as Providence and invited the young lady to reside with her.

Mrs. Faulkner commended Mr. Ferguson for his actions and perseverance. In recounting his own story, he mentioned his long convalescence in Oldham and his association with me. At this, Mrs. Faulkner expressed her familiarity with my name, but before an explanation could be provided, a servant announced gentlemen visitors.

To Mr. Ferguson's great surprise, one of the callers turned out to be the person at whose home he had slept on his long hike across the Northumberland moors, the fellow I have known as the White Man. No longer did he dress in the long white habit with the slouched hat and snow-white beard. He appeared in the modern habit of a private country gentleman. With him, the other occupant of the hut, but instead of his previous sable complexion, his countenance appeared European, but partially tanned by the influence of a foreign sun.

At that point, the journal broke off. A maze of thought inexplicable confronted me. The White Man and his once-sable companion had the society of Mrs. Faulkner, whose history and connexions

I had no acquaintance. Another enigma I found impossible to solve.

With no alternative before me, I folded the papers, put them in my pocket, took up my hat, and proceed to Upper Brook-street. I submitted the journal to Sir Julius, and upon the conclusion of his reading the pages, he returned them to my hands.

"I pledge my word to you that I am extremely happy to find that the prospects of your friend are thus promising," he responded with a smile. "Mrs. Faulkner appears, from his account of her, a most interesting woman, as well as Mrs. Percival, although at an infinitely more advanced period of life."

"Is Mrs. Faulkner at all known to you, Sir Julius?" I inquired.

"Negatived!" he responded. "Why did you suppose she was?"

"My conjecture, sir, arises from the interrupted conversation when she acknowledged familiarity with my name."

"I give you my honour that I never saw her in my life," answered Sir Julius. "However, if I remember correctly, the White Man, as you call him, certainly knows who you are."

"Pardon me, sir, but it would occasion me extreme difficulty to persuade myself that I have never seen him in this house," I stated.

"Seen whom?" exclaimed the baronet.

"The White Man, sir," I replied. "I remember seeing his countenance in your library mirror one evening."

"Well, well, well," tutted Sir Julius. "This is the first time my old-fashioned mansion was ever taken for an enchanted castle. A truce to your chimerical wanderings or you will make me afraid to go to bed in the dark, like a spoiled child." He smiled impishly.

The next morning, I received a note from Upper Brook-street indicating Sir Julius requested an audience with me at my earliest opportunity. As I had no obligations that day, I dressed and proceeded on foot.

"A good-morning to you!" cried the baronet as I entered his dining-room, where he sat eating his breakfast. "Please join me. I shall order some food and chocolate for you."

"Yes, please," I responded as I took the chair opposite him.

He turned to the waiting servant, "Breakfast for Mr. Brown, please." The man bent slightly then quit the room. "You are undoubtedly bursting with anticipation as to the reason for my early summons." I nodded. "To put an immediate dissolution to your anxiety, let me inform you that Mr. Fortescue communicated to me late last night that the Court of Chancery requested his presence two days hence to stand for the accusations put forth by Sir Malcolm Brockelsbie against your estate."

A very heavy sigh escaped my lips. "Ah, the day has arrived at last," I managed to say in a cheerless fashion.

"My boy," the baronet chimed, "I glory in the anticipation of that happy day, I pledge my word to you." He smiled broadly. "Nobody can be more averse than myself to wounding the feelings of the deserving, but I consider it a justice to that community, of which I form a member, to expose villainy and to punish the unworthy being who devises it."

"But, still, you cannot convey to me the information you and Mr. Fortescue harbour from me?" I asked glumly.

"Negatived!" he responded. "The knowledge of the means by which our anticipated purpose will be effected is retained in an inviolable secret, which we dare not discuss with anyone, especially you, to whom it appears most intimately to concern."

A servant announced the arrival of Mr. Fortescue, and he appeared.

"Please join us if you have not already partaken of your morning meal," invited Sir Julius.

The solicitor shook his head gently. "While I appreciate the invitation, sir, I had completed my breakfast before appearing here."

Sir Julius replied, "Then you can, at the very least, sit at the table with us. Yes?"

Mr. Fortescue took the chair next to the baronet and turned to me. "I came to inform you of the forthcoming Chancery proceedings. The counsel retained by both parties shall conduct the presentations; therefore, your appearance in court is not considered necessary."

How frustrating! My life rests on the balance of the judge's decision, yet I am not required to attend. "May I beg of you to inform me, sir, what you candidly suppose will be the event of this cause?"

"I cannot misapprehend your ideas, sir," replied Mr. Fortescue, "nor could I justify myself for encouraging you to nourish a false hope. The verdict must inevitably be in favour of your opponent."

This new information caused me to stand in astonishment. "I have never, sir, considered that a contrary issue could be expected, but, sir, what can possibly be the reason that Sir Julius Maberly should thus sanguinely endeavour to inspire me with expectations—the fallacy of which both you, as well as myself, appear to be so decidedly convinced?"

Mr. Fortescue looked to the baronet before responding. "Pardon me, sir, but I am in the confidence of Sir Julius, and I have pledged my honour not to betray it. All that I am permitted to tell you is that the trial, in all probability, will put a period to your suspense."

"Although our appearance is not formally required in court," Sir Julius affirmed, "it is still my intention that you and I shall both be present at the scene of action, and to that end I shall procure seats in a situation where we shall not be suspected of being parties concerned in the affair."

"I understand that it is the intention of Sir Malcolm to do the same," Mr. Fortescue informed us.

"If we can stick him with sufficient charges for conducting such charades, a voyage to New South Wales is an admirable recipe for such a depraved heart," opined Sir Julius. "I wish, from my soul, that Sir Malcolm may find it give a turn to his ideas, rectify his opinions, and excite in him reflections that may lead to his future preservations. Heaven send it may be the case!" He pointed upward.

Before quitting the home of Sir Julius, I spoke briefly with my dearest August, informing him of the predicaments that had provided me with so much frustration.

"We must believe that my father does truly have your best interests in his considerable heart," he stated with a smile. "And what is good for you"—he reached out to take my hand—"is good for me."

His tender caresses and heartening words helped to remove much of the anxiety upon the subject, and I left with more optimism than I had arrived.

Upon my return to the Titmus residence, a packet from the Glasgow post-office awaited me. This cheered me even more so, as I had written Mr. Ferguson nearly every day to keep him apprised of the developments in my own life.

Unfortunately, the packet contained only my own letters with information in the envelope in which they were wrapped that Mr. Ferguson had left Glasgow some time for England. If indeed he were returned to England, what could be the reason that I had neither seen him nor heard from him? Yet, another mystery to excite my anxieties. However, amidst the secondary cares to which these considerations gave birth in my mind, I possessed one essential, one unparalleled joy and consolation, the blessing of my dearest August's unaffected and undivided attention.

Chapter Twenty-Eight:
The Court at Lincoln's Inn

THE MORNING OF THE TRIAL, I rose, dressed, and made my way the home of Sir Julius. Following a quick breakfast, we rode together in his carriage across London to Lincoln's Inn. The building appeared to be more Gothic cathedral than official courthouse. Corner towers, battlements, and flying buttresses denoted its antiquity.

Inside, we made our way to the crowded courtroom amid a throng of spectators. My palpitating heart thundered in my chest. In the chamber full of lookers-on, Sir Julius led me to two unoccupied seats immediately opposite the judge. They appeared to have been reserved for our accommodation.

At the appointed hour, the judge called the counsel for Sir Malcolm forward, and he presented a damning rhetoric against my case. The words he used I scarcely comprehended, and I could only surmise his ferocity through the sound of his voice and fiery expressions upon his countenance. Curls from his moth-eaten wig flounced about as he proceeded to verbalise the faults I had committed with respect to Mr. Clarington's will.

Following the accusations, Mr. Fortescue stood and spoke in my behalf. His words also proved unfamiliar, but his demeanour demonstrated a calm, confident presentation.

The judge then asked both solicitors to approach his table. He gazed down at them with his wizened eyes and spoke. "The evidence presented clearly and indisputably proves that the accused, Mr. Brown, has clearly broken through the conditions upon which the property of the late Mr. Clarington had bequeathed to him." A loud gasp escaped the lips of the assembled, and the judge rapped a small wooden mallet on the table. "Silence!" He looked about the room through a quizzing glass, squinting at various people. "According to the provisions set forth in said will,"–he then used the quizzing glass to read from a paper on the table afore him–"'if before the attainment of that age,'"–the judge glanced up at the solicitors, "otherwise stated as the twenty-fifth year, which the accused, Mr. Brown, has not yet attained," and then he returned to the same paper–"'he shall contract a debt of more than one hundred pounds, he shall forfeit every claim to the inheritance of my property, and it shall be transferred to the first of my relatives who shall appear to demand it.'" The judge placed his glass on the table before continuing. "As the persons bringing this suit have provided a legally-binding promissory note for two hundred pounds–twice the specified value–signed by Mr. Brown in favour of a Mr. William Roberts, or the bearer, I have to concur that the stated conditions have been violated." He stared directly at Mr. Fortescue as he announced, "Verdict for the plaintiff!"

Shocked looks went all around. A gentleman in a fancy suit with many ruffles and embellishments stood up. As he turned in our direction, I could see that the sneering Sir Malcolm had been sitting behind his counsel, out of my sight. People around him began to give their congratulations and exultations, which he heartily accepted. A shiny smile obscured his countenance. As the nearest relative of the deceased Mr. Clarington, he could declare his interest in the estate and the court would immediately award him the future possession.

"By a superior right I supersede any claim." A loud voice with clear articulation proceeded from the vicinity of Mr. Fortescue. "I am the son of the deceased Mr. Clarington and, consequently, his nearest relative."

All eyes of every person in court turned to the speaker. As the man stood, I beheld the well-known features of the White Man, habited in the same manner in which Mr. Ferguson had described him in Glasgow at the home of Mrs. Faulkner.

Whispering murmurs ran through the room, and the judge rapped his mallet once more. Sir Malcolm's solicitor rose and stated, "This assertion, sir, requires incontrovertible proof to obtain our credit."

"That proof, sir," replied the White Man, "I am prepared instantly to adduce." He turned to my companion. "Sir Julius Maberly, my friend, advance and give the sanction of your voice to my assertion,"–he then faced the solicitor–"and if his words are not accepted as a sufficient test of my veracity, behold." He indicated a venerable and interesting woman sitting next to him. "Behold the mother who gave me birth and who now comes forth to enforce my claim by her evidence of the truth."

Sir Malcolm's countenance depicted consternation instantly. His counsel appeared uncertain and apprehensive.

Leaning on my arm, Sir Julius, pressed forward and rose in compliance with the summons of his friend. He took my hand and we walked to the place beside the fellow requesting validation of his integrity. "Thank God!" he exclaimed, dropping my hand and taking that of the White Man in his. "Thank God! The moment is at length arrived at which I behold the oldest and dearest of friends restored to his relatives and his rank in society!" He beamed at the White Man and placed my hand in the older man's, exchanging mine for his. "My dear Oliver, accept this hand from me. Permit me the happiness of being the first to join them, and may unalloyed felicity attend you both to the end of your days!"

This proclamation set me in the very heart of the labyrinth, and I felt wrapped in a bewildering maze of wonder. The power of utterance had, for the moment, deserted me. Even if I had the consciousness to speak, no words to express my jumble of feelings came to mind.

"The hour is now come,"–proclaimed the White Man, pressing my hand energetically in his with an emotion of countenance which bespoke an exulting, yet labouring, heart–"at which I am permitted, without fear, to unravel to you the mystery of that conduct by which I have hitherto perplexed, and even harassed, your mind. I wish to acquaint you that in appearing to have deprived you of those rights which you have hitherto enjoyed, I have only taken them into trust for your future benefit and possession." He smiled down at me. "I have long watched over you and scrutinised the sentiments of your heart. I am not less proud of the splendid virtues which animate your mind than of the benevolent feelings that sway your soul, and that now I glory to clasp you to my heart by the name of father!"

"Father?!" I gasped in scarcely articulate sounds. "Is it possible that you can be my father?" He held his hands apart, and I sunk into the arms of the being whose inexplicable assertion had overwhelmed my feelings.

Universal agitation and confusion, produced by the unexpected and affecting scene, prevailed in the court, and the judge once again tapped his mallet to silence the room. "You, sir,"–he pointed at the White Man with his glass–"pray, what is your name?"

"Your Worship, I am Oliver Clarington, son of the late Oliver Clarington of Oldham," he answered. Sir Julius nodded in agreement.

The judge turned to Sir Julius, "And you, sir, what is your part in this Byzantine story?"

"Well, Your Worship," the baronet began, "many years ago, Oliver–Mr. Clarington–and I sat law together at Cambridge, and we also shared living quarters. Following university, we had some differences and went our separate ways, as they say, but a fortnight or so back, Mr. Clarington appeared at my doorstep in Upper Brook-street, requesting that I not share his whereabouts or identity with anyone. Until a few moments ago, I maintained that confidence with the strictest determination. I can vouch for his claim that he is, in fact, the male offspring of the late Mr. Oliver Clarington of Ashbank Hall in Oldham."

"Once again,"–the judge turned back to the man I shall hence-forth refer to as my father–"please explain satisfactorily to this court your filial claim upon the estate."

He released me from his grasp and approached the judge. "Your Worship, as a child, my family lived in India, where my father, the deceased, held a lucrative situation under government, which he had constantly represented that it was not his inten-tion to resign until he had seen me prosperously settled in my profession." He exchanged smiles with Sir Julius. "Nearly ten years after I had commenced at Cambridge, my father returned to England and requested me to call upon him at his new resi-dence in Lincolnshire. He appeared to have aged much more than the time afforded, and I approached him with sympathy. When I realised that my mother did not accompany him, I asked if she were dead. He replied that she was not dead to the world, only dead to him because she had betrayed his trust in India, and he had left her."

"Is that woman beside you not the one you have previously indi-cated to be your mother?" the judge queried.

"Yes, Your Worship," my father responded. "As a child, I had loved my mother tenderly and believed her the paragon of her sex. Upon hearing her fallen condition, I grieved, naturally, but more for the state of misery to which her crime had reduced my innocent father. I felt compelled to seek her out and discover the true cause of such upheaval. Upon my arrival in India, I made some inquiries regarding her. It had been an army officer named Glanville who had seduced the poor woman, and they were rumoured to be living at an inconsiderable fort under his command. I then called upon my father's sister, who also resided in India and had married an officer by the name of Robert Brockelsbie."

"Why, that is the name of my grandfather!" exclaimed Sir Malcolm.

Without responding to the interruption, my father continued his story. "My aunt informed me that Brockelsbie had died a few years prior, and that they had raised a son, Angus."

"My father!" Sir Malcolm proclaimed.

"Angus had married Sybella Campbell, the only child of Sir John Campbell, who had bequeathed her his most extensive fortune. Angus and Sybella married at Gretna and returned to London, where a son was born to them."

"That would be me," Sir Malcolm stated with an air of arrogance.

My father turned a glaring eye in the direction of the interrupter. "A son by the name of Angus!"

"But I am their only child, as my mother disappeared soon after I was born!" came the response.

"I shall address that complication later in the narrative," my father stated. "From my sister's residence, I made inquiries into the location of this Glanville. He had achieved the rank of captain, and his fort was located outside a village a half-day's ride away. One of my sister's servants, Picaco by name, had come from that village, and I employed him to accompany me. We set out early in the morning, but as we neared the fort, Picaco suddenly stopped and pointed to an opening amidst some shrubs. Through the gap in the greenery I perceived an officer seated on a bank of turf beneath an overhanging plantain. On his breast reclined a woman whom I instantly recognised to be my mother." He smiled at the elderly lady briefly. "At the sight of her I uttered an involuntary exclamation, which served to draw her attention towards me, and she cried out, 'Oliver! Oh, my son! My son!'

When I observed her companion drawing a pistol from his belt, with a rapidity of action superior to his, I snatched one of mine from my girdle and fired it at him.”

Hubbub erupted from the assembled audience, and the judge tapped his mallet once more while crying out, “Silence! Silence!”

My father continued. “My mother shrieked, and after the smoke evaporated, I saw her bathed in blood and wailing, ‘I am murdered!’” He paused and placed a hand up to his face. “The recollection of that moment is still so forcibly imprinted upon my memory that it awakens feelings not easily turned aside or subdued.”

Sir Julius rose. “Your intention was not against the existence of your parent, and the consciousness of your action having been the event of error, cannot fail to furnish you with a solid consolation derived from that reflection.”

“Sincerely,” returned my father. “I have devoted years to repentance for the inadvertency of which my hand was guilty, and the frenzy of passion by which I was at that unhappy moment guided, and Heaven has mercifully accepted my repentance. However, I must not anticipate those events which still remain to be detailed to you.” Before proceeding, he wiped a few tears from his eyes. “Upon hearing the gun firing, a squad of soldiers surrounded us and took us into custody. They conducted us to the fort and placed us in an apartment that undoubtedly had not been used as a prison. When a serjeant later appeared, I first inquired into the health of my mother. He told me she had died of the gunshot. With a guilt-riddled heart I then asked about our confinement. We were to remain in their custody until proper legal officials from the nearby town could be brought to adjudge us for our crime, which might take three or four days. The soldiers treated us more like guests than prisoners. Later that evening, someone slipped a paper under the door, and the note, which addressed me directly by name, indicated I had a friend in the fort and we would be set free early the next day. The only appellation read, ‘A.M.’ and I could not recollect any acquaintance with those particular initials.”

“Mr. Clarington, if that indeed is your name,” the judge interrupted, “your narration appears to be rambling far from the central facts of your relationship to the deceased.”

"Your worship, I beg your indulgence," my father responded. "While I realise this history may be lengthy and tortuous, I am merely revealing that intelligence necessary to support my claim as requested by the Plaintiff's counsel."

"Do not try my patience, sir," the judge advised. "I have plans for dinner!" A few people in the chamber giggled.

"Certainly, Your Worship. It is not my desire to keep you any longer than shall be necessary," replied my father.

"Pray, proceed."

"The following morning, as described in the note, a shadowy figure in a hooded robe beckoned us to follow. Picaco and I had decided to risk our chances with the stranger than remain to face possible imprisonment. Our liberator led us through the buildings and out the front gate of the fort without incident. Outside, an open carriage awaited us, and the three of us boarded. After a considerable distance existed between us and the fort, our hooded companion revealed herself to be a most beautiful woman. She called me by name and seemed surprised that I did not recognise her. 'A.M.' turned out to be Amelia Melcombe, the sister of one of my closest friends at university, Horace Melcombe. She had seen me transported into the fort and resolved to effect my safe exit. Along the ride back to my sister's home, she explained that the Melcombe family had relocated to India when Horace deployed for military service. He had served as counsel to the fort until his death, and Amelia remained on, as she had no other home." He stopped in reflection before continuing. "Amelia transported me safely back to my sister's house, and I resolved to marry her for her kindness, as well as her beauty. We lived in comfort for a while, but word reached us that the fort commander had learned of my location. A ship bound for England carried us away from India and possible incarceration. On the voyage, Amelia, who was in an advanced stage of pregnancy, suffered severely from sea-sickness. One of the other passengers, the wife of an English serjeant who had left India due to illness, was also with child, and she befriended my wife, comforting her during times of distress. About a week from the lovely shores of England, a tremendous storm overtook us, and even the stoutest onboard feared for their lives. In the midst of this awful contention of the elements, my beloved Amelia was seized with those pangs which pronounced the hour of her becoming a mother to be approaching. Whilst the fury of the winds and waves still raged with unabated violence, she gave birth to a male infant whose existence it was the will of Heaven that she should not live to witness."

Once again, tears moistened his cheeks at reciting painful memories. The judge consulted his pocket-watch and coughed admonishingly.

"But your boy," pronounced Sir Julius in an attempt to prompt his friend. "Your boy was spared you to console you for her loss?"

"Blessed be Heaven for its mercy!" my father exclaimed. "He was spared to me—spared to recompense me for every suffering and anxiety which I had endured. As a tribute to the memory of my departed Amelia, I christened my babe Horace, after her idolised brother. The storm, which had proved fatal to the best-beloved of my soul, had likewise snapped the stem of life in the tender breast of the serjeant's newly-born infant. As I could not raise a baby on my own, and as theirs had been taken away precipitously, I offered the unhappy couple a sum of money to undertake the care of my child till I should reclaim him. The serjeant's name happened to be John Brown."

The faces of the assembled then turned in my direction. I had known that my true parents had given me to a Serjeant Brown and his wife to raise; however, my mother never spoke of the strangers who gave up their baby, nor did she mention the unfortunate death of her own.

"Yes, in an act of remorse," he continued, "I expressed my wish to the protectress of my child and her husband that they should not publish whose infant it was that had been entrusted to their care. They voluntarily bound themselves to me that until I recalled it to my protection, it should pass as their own child. After tenderly kissing my boy—and with an anxious heart—I set out in quest of my own father. Before my departure for India in search of my mother, he and I had concurred that I would contact Mr. Fortescue,"—and he indicated the solicitor—"who had many years been the confidential friend, and agent, for my father. Before I could make such contact, I encountered a rather-dark-skinned fellow on a London street who seemed quite familiar to me. His eyes met mine, and in an instant, I recognised my compatriot,

Angus Brockelsbie, dressed in the Indian style. Upon my interrogatory regarding his state, he informed me that someone else had committed a crime and attributed it to him, and that he would have to live his life in such disguise and trappings until the case resolved. I immediately invited him to join me, and we have been inseparable from that moment." He turned and smiled at his companion. "When I met with Mr. Fortescue, he informed me that my father had heard the intelligence that I had shot my mother, his fallen wife, and that he resolved never to behold me again. Furthermore, the solicitor had learned that the return of Captain Glanville had been announced. He advised that I should make every attempt to avoid contact with the unhappy officer. Father had provided some funds for me—let me see if I can recall his words—'lest necessity should lead you into the perpetration of farther crimes.' Angus and I set out for Manchester, the spot where Serjeant Brown's regiment was quartered."

Before my father could continue, the judge held up his hand and turned to Mr. Fortescue. "Sir, is this man's testimony correct?"

The solicitor stood slowly. "Yes, Your Worship. To the best of my knowledge, the man standing before you today, Mr. Oliver Clarington, whom I have had the acquaintance for most of his life, is the son and sole heir of the deceased Mr. Oliver Clarington, late of Oldham."

"Well then," the magistrate responded, "If you place your depositions on a stamp, we can consider this matter closed. The son of the deceased, being the nearest living relative, can then claim the estate of his deceased father." He stood up and prepared to descend from his table.

"Your Worship!" exploded Sir Malcolm, bright red in contrast to his gaily-coloured suit. "You can't —"

"I can,"—the judge interrupted with a stern countenance—"and I shall!"

Once more the room erupted into chaos.

"Hold!" boomed a loud voice. My father held his hands aloft. "Your Worship, your decree stated that you will close this matter if I choose to claim the estate of my deceased father." He glanced about at the lookers-on. "It is my firmest decision *not* to claim the estate!"

The crowd blossomed into a garden of loud wails, murmured epithets, and exclamations of disbelief. Hastily, the judge returned to his post and began banging his mallet loudly.

"Silence!" he proclaimed as he continued an attempt to bring order. "Silence! I will not tolerate such bedlam in my court."

Sir Malcolm roared forth, "In light of Mr. Clarington's proclamation –"

"Hold!" my father bellowed. "Your Worship, please grant me the time to complete my narrative before reaching your final decision."

With a dubious eye, the judge cautioned, "Mr. Clarington, you have already taxed my patience. I advise you not to take further advantage of such consideration." He resumed his seat.

"But Your Worship..." Sir Malcolm shouted.

"You, sir,"–the judge pointed at the interrupter–"must bide your time. Your interests shall be considered once Mr. Clarington has completed his testimony." He turned to my father. "Pray, continue, sir, but I remind you to abridge your chronicle."

Sir Malcolm collapsed into a chair in the manner of a punctured balloon.

"Thank you, Your Worship. I shall be considerate of your attentions." My father glanced at his companion, the one he referred to as Angus. "In an attempt to disguise my true identity, I purchased a white robe and hat, while I let my beard grow long. On our arrival in Manchester, to my great disappointment, I learned that the regiment had marched to Ireland on their way to the Americas. However, I gained still more distressing information. The serjeant himself was lately dead and his wife had returned home to her relatives, who dwelt in a location unfamiliar to all I had queried. Angus and I resolved to make a pilgrimage, donning our assumed garb, to search for my displaced son. After many unsuccessful years, we fixed our abode in a solitary hut on the Northumberland moor." Once again, he turned and smiled at his companion. "An account of my father's death met my eye. The description given of the youth who had become heir to his property excited my feelings, as it could be no other than my long-lost son. The hand of Providence had conducted him to the inheritance of his grandsire's possessions." My father then turned to me. "John Brown, the fortunate youth had been named, the son of a Serjeant Brown who had died at Cork and a mother who had returned home with her infant to her relatives. It was my fondest wish to behold the offspring of my beloved Amelia, and I proceeded immediately to Oldham, still in my disguise. Information I obtained from villagers satisfied my suspicions, and I approached the youth without informing him of my station. As Launcelot proclaimed in *The Merchant of Venice*, 'It is a wise father that knows his own child.'" He smiled at me once more, and my heart swelled with the knowledge that my father prized Shakespeare as well.

"But by what forbearance could you contrive to impose a sufficient restraint on your feelings to tear yourself from him without making the confession of your affinity?" Sir Julius inquired unbidden.

My father's face sank. "In consideration of the boy's happiness, I felt that revealing to him that he was the son of a matricide might be a cruelty, and I resolved to reflect deliberately on the most eligible manner of thereafter disclosing to him the truth." He pointed to his companion. "Following my sojourn, I returned to the solitary habitation with Angus upon the moors."

"This is all very well," the judge remarked, "happy family reunion, and so forth, but what of the woman whom you claim to be your mother, whom you also claim to have murdered?"

"Oh, yes, thank you, Your Worship, I nearly forgot." My father grinned at his oversight. "On a morning walk, my eye caught a post-chariot proceeding along the high road heading northerly at a rapid pace. The passenger sitting by the window resembled my lost mother quite favourably. I quickly returned home and informed Angus of my encounter. We quit our costumes and walked to the first post-town in the northern direction from our abode. Through inquiries, we discovered the destination of the carriage to be Edinburgh and made our way there. Further inquiries led us to Glasgow, where no one seemed to be acquainted with the woman I described. Knowing my mother to be a religious woman, we attended the English chapel on Sunday, and at the moment the congregation had arisen to receive the blessing of the clergyman, a loud shriek from the pew opposite attracted my attention. A woman with a heavy veil approached begging my forgiveness. When she showed me her face, it proved to be none other than my mother. We stepped outside so as not to further interrupt the proceedings, and she explained how she had not been shot at all and that Glanville circulated a death rumour for his own advantage. Over the course of years, she ended up in Glasgow and had taken the name Faulkner."

"Does his testimony coincide with your understanding of the facts, madam?" the judge asked the woman whom I assumed must have been my grandmother. She nodded solemnly. He turned once again to my father. "I believe I have heard enough of your Gothic romantic ramblings, sir. If you have not the wisdom to claim your father's inheritance, what, pray, is your intended course of action?"

My father, with the gentlest of pressure, lifted me up by the elbow. In a blinding instant, the solution poured forth from my mouth, "I, sir, am John Brown, or Horace Clarington, if you like"–I quickly glanced at my father–"and under the terms of my grandfather's will, I demand the estate." Without looking, I could sense my father smiling at me.

"What?!" exclaimed Sir Malcolm as he leapt up out of his chair. "No! No! I had claimed the Clarington estate before these two began their endless prattlings!" He glared at his solicitor.

"Sir Malcolm," the judge pronounced, "I advise you to return to your seat and keep your peace. For as much strutting about and self-congratulatory antics as you have previous displayed, you never uttered the proper words required by the will."

"Besides," my father added, "you are not even part of our family."

"What?!" Sir Malcolm reddened further, approached his boiling point.

"You see," Mrs. Faulkner rose, "I had a cousin, Hannah McDermott, who confessed to me upon her deathbed that her sister Flora had a child by... an undetermined father. Rather than raise that boy under a cloud of ignominy, she presented it to her friend Sybella Brockelsbie, who longed for companionship following the departure of her husband. They had produced a natural son, Angus, but the couple had sent him to live at the boarding school of a relative in Edinburgh. However, soon after, Sybella ran off as well, leaving the house staff to raise the boy they had christened Malcolm." Mrs. Faulkner produced a sheet of paper from her reticule. "This is a letter written by Hannah herself describing the matters I have just enunciated." She gave the sheet to a bailiff and then turned to address Malcolm directly. "You sir, are a bastard! A bastard who is not a Brockelsbie and most definitely not a Clarington! Be gone at once and never darken the lives of my family again!"

Sir Malcolm, or whatever his name might have been, stood frozen and pale, resembling a pillar of Dover chalk. His countenance displayed the shock and horror upon learning the true nature of his identity.

"Leave now before I approach the judge to request bringing you up on a lengthy list of charges!" my grandmother roared. The hapless fellow dashed out of the room closely followed by his consort of hooligans.

"And now that all of *that* has been settled," the judge bellowed, "clear the court!" He rapped his mallet once and stepped down.

Chapter Twenty-Nine:

Happy Ends

Sir Julius Maberly requested all parties in any way related to me join him at his residence. In the various carriages and coaches, we made our way back to Upper Brook-street, where Mrs. Allingham, Mrs. Ansel, and my dearest, dearest August awaited our arrival. The servants had laid out a feast for our partaking.

I ran to my beloved, stretched out my arms to take his open hands. He surprised me by reaching past me and giving me a tender hug. Then, in another unanticipated move, he kissed me lightly on the side of the cheek.

"Welcome back, my love," August cooed in my ear. The colour rose instantly in my face.

Applause and cheers arose from the assembled. "To Horace and August!" shouted Sir Julius. "Three cheers!"

While the crowd bellowed, August asked, "Horace?"

I nodded. "I'll explain later, but that is apparently my christened name."

"And we have yet another surprise for you, my boy," announced Sir Julius as he directed our attention to the archway.

My dear, long-lost Mr. Ferguson entered with a radiant beauty on his arm. "David!" I called out as I approached, bringing August along with me.

Following a hearty handshake, he said, "May I introduce Jessy," indicating his lovely companion.

I took her hand and kissed it gently. "I have heard so much about you, Mrs. Percival. It gives me great pleasure to finally make your acquaintance."

She smiled gently. "I no longer use that name, sir. I am to be Mrs. Ferguson soon."

"Congratulations to you both!" I turned to Mr. Ferguson and shook his hand again.

"Thank you, and I hope you do me the honour of best man," he requested.

"Absolutely!" I grabbed his hand once more.

"But first!" shouted Sir Julius, "we have some important introductions to make and some family secrets to divulge!" He laughed heartily until he began coughing. "Perhaps we should form a circle so that we can see each other better."

The guests moved to the walls, forming a single ring about the room. I held August in my right hand and Mr. Ferguson in my left.

"As you all well know by now, young Master August Evelyne is my true and natural son by my dearest Anastasia. She died shortly after his birth, and Mrs. Allingham, assisted by Miss Hyde, raised him as their own." He turned and smiled at his son by my side. "And as for the Claringtons,"–he winked at me–"my long-lost friend, Mr. Oliver Clarington, who is the son of the deceased estate holder from Oldham, has since revealed he himself produced an heir by his beloved Amelia, one Horace Clarington!" He aimed a stubby finger at me.

August turned in my direction with saucer eyes, and I nodded silently. I turned to the assembled guests. "Yes, as it turned out, my birth mother died shortly after I arrived in this world, and my father gave me to Serjeant John Brown and his wife to raise until he could return to claim me." I smiled at my father. "From today forward, I shall be known as Horace Clarington, proud son of Oliver Clarington."

Applause rang out and cheers resounded.

"And more importantly, the constraining conditions of my grandsire's will are now removed, and I inherit his entire estate without restriction." A few people cheered. "But most importantly,"–and I turned to glance at August–"my fondest wish has been fulfilled in that I can take my true love back to Ashbank Hall and we can live out our days together." This time, I kissed him, and we met on the lips. Gasps erupted and pale faces blushed, but we did not allow the illiberal sensibilities of others to diminish our happiest of moments.

"Affirmatived!" shouted Sir Julius. "Three cheers for the charming young couple!"

"Hold!" boomed the deep voice of my father. "There is yet one more revelation to be made." He took the hand of his companion, Angus and elevated it. "My Angus–for I believe he is mine,"–a few chuckles rang out–"is also about to be reunited with his own heir. It has been many years since they have last seen each other, but it is my proud honour to make the introduction of Angus Brockelsbie"–and he took the man's hand and led him across the room to stand next to my friend, Mr. Ferguson–"to his rightful son, Angus Brockelsbie!" My father then placed the hand of Mr. Ferguson into that of Mr. Brockelsbie.

More gasps abounded, and none seemed more astonished than my dearest friend.

"Yes, my boy," Angus spoke. "You were a mere babe when Sybella and I gave you up. I did not believe that malevolent woman capable of properly raising a child." He reached out and hugged my friend. "I am truly sorry that my family cannot provide the level of estate and inheritance that –"

My friend held up his hand to interrupt his newly-found father. "Sir, given that I have captured the loveliest woman in all of Britain"–and he took up Jessy's hand–"as well as discovered my previously-unknown heritage,"–and he took up his father's hand–"I believe I find myself sufficiently wealthy beyond all measure."

People cheered and clapped.

I walked over to him, clapped his back, and clasped his hand. "Angus!"

"Horace!" he smiled back.

"I believe that makes us cousins, does it not?" I asked.

"Affirmatived!" shouted Sir Julius. "Second cousins, I believe, and if there are no more hidden relationships to reveal, I suggest we proceed to consume these fine refreshments set out for our enjoyment! Pour the Madeira!"

During the course of the afternoon, Mr. Fortescue approached me and asked, "Mr. Clarington, sir,"–at first I did not realise he had addressed me by my restored name–"would you wish that my office draw up papers for the arraignment of the fellow formerly known as Sir Malcolm Brockelsbie? We would pursue the charge of illegal restraint upon your person."

How right it would have felt to effect the capture and imprisonment of one so heinous, thereby removing the possibility of his future ensnarement of others. However, given the happy ends I enjoyed in that moment, I responded, "Mr. Fortescue, for the meantime, I believe his disappointment and exposure should be permitted to become his punishment for the crimes against me. After all, a creature with an innately depraved heart like that will most assuredly surface again somewhere, and when he does, it is my fondest wish that someone with much more legal authority than myself shall take the poor wretch on and deliver his final accounting."

The solicitor smiled, an expression heretofore unseen upon his countenance. "You are a wise man, Mr. Clarington, for one so young." He seized my hand and shook it vigorously. "I wish you all the health and happiness in life." He turned and walked off.

"Young man!" resounded in my ear. I turned about to discover Mrs. Faulkner standing behind me. "Young man, I have some important intelligence to bestow upon you."

"Yes, of course, Mrs. Faulkner—or shall I call you grandmother?"

"You must call me grandmother, as that is my position in your life." She clasped my hand in her slightly moist and clammy one. "I wish to inform you of the true identity of the one who falsely claimed to be Sir Malcolm Brockelsbie."

I smiled down at her. "I believe there is nothing to be gained by me obtaining such knowledge."

Her hand tightened upon mine. "Oh, but there is! Pray, summon your friend, the Scottish actor one."

Across the room I espied the newly-christened Angus Brockelsbie and waved him to my position.

Once my friend stood by my side, my grandmother began in hushed tones. "I believe you knew a fellow by the name of Harry Glara, who is currently housed in Newgate." Angus nodded and looked at me quizzically. "Harry's father was a wounded soldier by the name of Terence who had married a rich woman named Kathalene. My cousin Flora was in service to the family. While she began the raising of their child Harry, the father Terence became intimate with my cousin, producing the boy Teddy, whom she passed to your mother Sybella to raise as her own.”

Angus and I looked at each other seriously. “Grandmother,” I spoke, “you are saying that Harry Glara and the one known as Sir Malcolm were actually brothers?”

“Yes,” she nodded. “For all the trouble the two have caused in your lives, I thought it best you know all. Hannah’s letter described the circumstances, but I felt it best not to reveal all in public.” She smiled at us both and returned to the throng.

Angus and I stared at each other for a few moments before I paraphrased the Bard, “They ‘came into the world like brother and brother, and now,’ they ‘go hand in hand, not one before another.’”

“Dromio’s concluding remarks in *Comedy of Errors*. However, my dear cousin and friend”–I smiled at hearing him denominate me as such–“I believe those two to play more of a tragedy than of a comedy.”

“Most assuredly,” I concurred. “Now, let us both get to the tables while there is still food and drink to be had!”

The remainder of the afternoon passed in family, friendship, and frivolity. All wrongs had been righted, and all lost souls reunited. In many ways, it felt as though I had appeared in my very own Shakespearean play, a comedy most likely, as the main players came to a happy end, and marriage ensued.

When Angus and I returned to the Titmus residence to gather our belongings and say our farewells, we discovered the family sitting in their parlour with a few unexpected guests.

“Oh, Mr. Brown and Mr. Ferguson! Will ye not join us?” called out Mrs. Titmus.

“Thank you, Mrs. Titmus. I believe we have tidings to share with all of you. But first, I must inform you that my friend and I have discovered our true identities. I shall henceforth be known as Horace Clarington, and this distinguished gentleman”–I indicated my cousin and friend–“is Sir Angus Brockelsbie, by chance, my cousin.”

As the group shouted its praises and well wishes, I noticed Carrotty Jean and Mr. Tunks seated in one corner next to Betsey, Loora alongside Dennis O'Dottlety, and Mr. Dobby, the pawnbroker, holding the hand of Charlotte.

"And we have some explaining of our own as well." Mr. Titmus looked to Mr. Tunks. "Our friend here managed to effect the rescue and return of our dearest Bet. She will be married off soon and moved to his residence." Cheers resounded, but Betsey's face remained plain and unmoved. "And with one daughter to be wed, we removed our restrictions upon Charlotte, and she and her Mr. Dobby will be priest-linked and spliced as well." More cheers.

Angus and I related our tales and we wished the families all the best. Once we had gathered our things, we rode back to Upper Brook-street to rejoin our loved ones.

Following one more night in London, August and I rode off to Oldham. Mrs. Allingham and Mrs. Ansel decided to join us. However, my father, his mother, and his Angus returned to Glasgow. My Angus and his Jessy also returned to their native land, but to Edinburgh instead.

Mr. Radford greeted us with great joy, and we all passed the first night regaling him with our various tales of adventure and luck. August nearly fainted when he first saw the bed we were to share. He had never seen anything so palatial before.

Over time, I introduced him to my old mates in town, and a few nights a week we would descend upon the Black Bull for a few hands of whist, a pint or two, and the local gossip.

Every so often, we would ride up to London and spend a few days with August's father, the most lovely Sir Julius. Of course, we also dropped in on the Titmus home to learn of their latest grandchild. Angus and Jessy visited us once a year or so, each time with yet another babe.

With my beloved August, I continued the tradition of devoted male partnerships that persisted in both our families. My grandfather and Mr. Radford, my father with his Angus, and with August's father, Sir Julius, before that. The addition of Mrs. Allingham and Mrs. Ansel allowed us to transform Ashbank Hall from a large, spacious manor house into a warm-hearted, loving home.

And that concludes this story for now. My twenty-first year
proved to be one of fantastic changes and extraordinary oppor-
tunities. It would be my fondest wish that anyone reading this
chronicle should discover their own penchant for life, love, and—
most importantly—luck. According to the wise Pisanio in
Cymbelline, "Fortune brings in some boats that are not steered."
For without these unsteered boats, none of us would ever receive
our own Fortune's Lot.

WAYNE GOODMAN has lived in the San Francisco Bay Area most of his life (with too many cats). When not writing, he enjoys playing Gilded Age parlor music on the piano, with an emphasis on women, gay, and Black composers.

Other Books by
Wayne Goodman

The Last Great Hope

A retired Secret Service agent, with a secret of his own, is called up for one last mission: find the long-lost child of John and Jacqueline Kennedy, whom he adopted out unknowingly under orders of his power-hungry boss.

Britain's Glory:
Charlotte, the People's Princess

Princess Charlotte was the daughter, and only child, of Princess Caroline of Brunswick and Prince George of Wales, eldest son of King George III. Destined to be Queen of Great Britain, her storybook life ended too soon, leading to a scramble for another, suitable, royal heir to take the throne.

The Seed of Immortality
Mahjong at Changshou Shan

A peasant on his deathbed is given immortality by a less-than-trustworthy Mahjong sharp. They travel around China, learn its secrets, and even meet with the first Emperor of China in his mysterious subterranean palace, complete with rivers of mercury.

Vanya Says, "Go!"
A Retelling of Mikhail Kuzmin's *Wings*

Wings was the first Russian-language novel to deal with same-sex relationships in a positive way. *Vanya Says, "Go!"* presents the story in a modern, more open way with an additional chapter.

Joseph Asten, a handsome, 23-year-old farmer living in the Allegheny River Valley shortly after the Civil War, secretly longed for intimacy and love with other men. He devised a misguided plan to marry a woman who knew of his "dual nature" then his life took some unexpected, fateful turns.

Bayard Taylor's *Joseph and His Friend: A Pennsylvania Story* is considered the first American Gay novel. In *Better Angels*, Goodman retells the tale frankly and candidly, free from antiquated 19th Century cultural restraints.

Praise for *Better Angels*:

"A lovely story, sumptuous in language and ideas with a rich ambience. For people who love a love story, it is thoroughly rewarding."

—**VINCENT MEIS**, author of *Deluge*

"Goodman has turned the pallid prose of travel writer Bayard Taylor into a scintillating trip through 19th Century America. Those who loved James Baldwin's *Another Country* and *Giovanni's Room* will find something of value in Goodman's latest triumph."

—**KEVIN KILLIAN**, author of *Tony Greene Era*

"*Better Angels* is a great read and a wonderful glimpse into a story of the 19th Century that has rarely been told. It writes queerness back into literary history, with an anti-racist spin."

—**DR. AJUAN MANCE**, author of *Before Harlem*

"This adaptation (or re-telling) is written with a masterful command of storytelling and language. Each scene is word painted vividly, the characters are memorable and complex. The dialogue is sharp and authentic. This is a novel that will resonate with readers."

—**D.M. BARNES**, author of *Stronger Than This*

www.ingramcontent.com/pod-product-compliance
Lightning Source LLC
Chambersburg PA
CBHW070759120726
47910CB00001B/231